Praise for THE FIRST DATE
by Kate & Danny Tamberelli

"The characters' eccentricities feel entirely authentic,
while subplots about family drama and friend groups
growing apart add nuance and poignancy to this
sweet romp. Rom-com fans should snap this up."
—*Publishers Weekly*

"This '90s nostalgia-tinged love story will leave
rom-com fans smiling and swooning."
—*Library Journal*, STARRED REVIEW

"A dynamic 'he said, she said' of the current dating scene that will
keep you entertained to the last page." —**Melissa Joan Hart**

"A luminous, hilarious romance that is both equal parts magical
and a heartwarming reminder that when it comes to love,
we make our own fate." —**Ashley Herring Blake**, author of
Delilah Green Doesn't Care

"Vulnerable without being verbose, the authors are skilled at
plumbing the depths of these characters and lend an air of self-
assured authenticity to the courtship proceedings. You can both
read *The First Date Prophecy*, but if you do it together at a bar, that
would be a little . . . on the nose." —**Michael C. Maronna**, actor,
The Adventures of Pete and Pete and *Home Alone*

"A love story as delightful and idiosyncratic as its authors."
—**Mara Wilson**, actress, *Mrs. Doubtfire* and *Matilda*

"*The First Date Prophecy* is a gorgeous, inspiring, and hilarious tale
that also somehow manages to incorporate all of my favorite snacks
and beverages. Perhaps more importantly, it made me believe in love
and Brooklyn again. There—I said it. If Kate and Danny don't write
another book together immediately, I will be completely enraged."
—**Dave Hill**, comedian and author of *Parking the Moose*

THE ROAD TRIP REWIND

Also by Kate & Danny Tamberelli

The First Date Prophecy

THE
ROAD TRIP
REWIND

KATE and DANNY TAMBERELLI

KENSINGTON
PUBLISHING CORP.

www.kensingtonbooks.com

Content Warning: parental death, terminal illness

KENSINGTON BOOKS are published by
Kensington Publishing Corp.
900 Third Avenue
New York, NY 10022

ISBN: 978-1-4967-4287-2 (ebook)

ISBN: 978-1-4967-4286-5

First Kensington Trade Paperback Printing: June 2024

10 9 8 7 6 5 4 3 2 1

Printed in the United States of America

For all our readers who are forever '90s kids at heart,
may this story temporarily transport you
back in time to our golden era

Your future hasn't been written yet. No one's has.
Your future is whatever you make it. So make it a good one.
—Doc Brown, *Back to the Future*

Chapter 1
Beatrix

Wednesday, December 21, 2016

"I'm begging you," Rocco says, voice thick with passion and his electric-blue gaze searing hot, even through the small monitor I'm pinned to behind the director's chair.

God, I *hate* how fucking blue his eyes are.

Hate how outrageously, undeniably talented he is. Hate that he's making me—of all people—believe every single word he's saying on the set that so perfectly mirrors my childhood living room, down to the radioactively bright orange paisley curtains my mom had sewed herself and the highly coveted lumpy brown leather La-Z-Boy recliner we fought over on family movie nights, transporting me back to the most shameful moment of my life.

"You know me, sweetie," he says after a loaded pause, a scratchy, hitched breath, "better than your own mother, probably. Better than anyone. You're my daughter, but you're also my best friend. You get me. I get you. Always have. So you know I couldn't possibly have done this. I'm not a-a . . . *monster.*" His voice cracks as he says it, his whole being breaking, really, and he's looking at her—Maisy Tanner, pop-tart teen

YouTuber extraordinaire turned wannabe indie darling—with an intensity and desperation that has my heart racing and my knees shaking.

Shit.

I might have written the script for *Murder in the Books* myself, spent the last decade of my life obsessively planning and fighting for this very moment—but I am still wholly unprepared.

Because Rocco Riziero has somehow captured the memory, the moment, the feelings, with a clarity that shouldn't be humanly possible for someone who never once met my father. Who didn't stand in that living room with me and Dad the morning the original conversation happened, right before he was taken away.

The last day we'd ever spend at home together.

I know what line is coming next, of course I do. Not just because I wrote the script, but because it's word for word what I said to him that day. Tempting to lie about it, to sugarcoat, make myself seem at least slightly more sympathetic. But no. I made a deal with myself when I started this project—all or nothing.

I decided on all. Truth. Very few details about the story were changed.

Only one very important piece.

One important person.

"I don't know anything about you anymore," Maisy says, her tone flat and empty and exactly as torturous as I'd hoped and dreaded it would be. The camera shifts toward her, closes in on her straight, dead-eyed gaze.

I'll admit I'd had my doubts, many of them, when casting zeroed in on her. For starters, the video that shot her into the stratosphere of internet celebrity showcased her dancing in a pink tutu with a posse of matching pink poodles to that Carly Rae Jepsen song no one ever needs to hear again, capped off by her jumping into an alarmingly neon pink pool. Probably shaving a few years off her life with the chemicals involved to achieve that level of pinkness. But she's surprised me from the first read through with her passion and dedication and genuine talent.

She's surprised me almost as much as Rocco has, damn him. Who knew the chiseled overpaid asshole from *Space Blasters* and *Pirate Kingdom* could actually . . . act?

"I'm starting to think you might be just as fictional as those words you write all day up in your lair," Maisy continues evenly, her calmness more sickening, more cruel than open-faced fury ever could be. I wish I had screamed. Cried. But no. I'd chosen *this*. "Or no," she continues, "I have that all wrong, don't I? Because maybe it's all less fiction than I ever knew."

"I didn't—I could never . . ." Rocco crumples to his knees on cue. "I'm your *father*."

I hold my breath, keep my eyes open, as much as I'm tempted to block the rest out.

"No. I don't have a father anymore."

Rocco lets out an inhuman wail, and there's a knocking sound coming from off set, and I'm sinking, lower and lower, toward my assigned folding chair—my first ever on any set, a grand feat even if it does say "Writer" and not "Beatrix Noel"—then "Cut!" and applause and hoots all a rolling blur of noise threatening to knock me down to my knees, too.

I squeeze my eyes shut, force myself to breathe in and out, remind myself that I asked for exactly this. No complaints. No regrets.

I'm living my dream, aren't I? Watching this movie come to life?

Even if that dream is currently treading into full-blown nightmare territory.

More so than ever, as my bubble of personal space is interrupted by—

"What do you think, Beatrix? Did that feel right?"

My eyes snap open to see Rocco standing over me, a nervous smile hovering on his too-perfect lips, parted just enough to show a small glimpse of his too-perfect teeth, bright against his lightly tanned white skin. Though, huh . . . it actually appears sincere, his need for my approval, his . . . self-doubt? An expression I wouldn't have expected to ever have a home on his glossy A-list face. Though he's paid millions of dollars to play pretend with emotions, so how can anyone know what's real?

There's a small crowd eagerly buzzing around him, as per usual, scrappy little bugs clinging to the brightest spotlight. Waiting to hear me fawn, so they can join in, too. One grand never-ending praise party for Rocco—that seems to be the way of things here on set. The way of his every day, wherever he may go, no doubt.

Which leads me to say, "You did fine, I suppose," even if the honest answer would be, "You were fucking sensational, I'm not sure how you so perfectly captured the entire essence of that excruciating memory of mine without somehow traveling back in time to watch it all play out for yourself with those goddamn brilliant ocean-blue eyes of yours."

Yes, very pleased I didn't opt for the latter.

Though perhaps a middle ground would have been the best path, because Rocco visibly shrinks at my words, that smile now pulling tight across his sharp, stubbled jawline.

"Maybe," he says, "I could ask Lanie to do it again another day? Take a beat to work through it more. Do you have any notes for me?"

There's a pause, both of us openly staring at one another before I realize he's waiting for me to answer. Like I have that kind of power on this set. I'm the writer, sure, and an executive producer, in a vague, performative kind of way, but this is Lanie's show. Everyone knows that. Lanie Lea, the newly minted Academy Award–winning director who took a chance on a tiny indie film written by a tiny Hollywood nobody, and somehow managed to rope in Rocco fucking Riziero along the way. Against my initial wishes, though I didn't put up much of a fight. The message from both the studio and Lanie had been crystal clear: having Rocco attached as the star meant a definite greenlight for *Murder in the Books*. Without him? "Hollywood can be so damn fickle, you know," Lanie had said. So I'd gritted my teeth. Chosen the greenlight. Besides, it was about much more than just being made, in the long game. Because a name like Rocco's—and this unexpected shift from his usual substance-free franchise blockbusters to a role requiring actual emotional heft—meant that beyond simply existing, people would actually *know* about this movie; they'd watch it, talk about it, write and read think pieces on it. That kind of attention—that success, if he continues to knock it out of the park the way he did today—is a fact I have to remind myself of every morning when I'm forced to plaster on a smile in Rocco's direction.

He's watching me still, studying my face with an intensity that only fuels my frustrations more.

I shrug, noncommittal, hoping I look at least marginally cool and breezy. "Maisy was such a star in that scene, it was hard to give anything else my full attention. You were . . . adequate, though, I suppose."

"Adequate?" Rocco asks, his dark, neatly arched and plucked eyebrows furrowing in a dazed sort of surprise. I fight back a satisfied chuckle, as tempting as it is to unleash. A man like Rocco has surely had very few encounters with that word. Which means this jab qualifies as my Rocco victory for the day, an ongoing game he doesn't know we're playing—my passive aggressive pleasure project that keeps me pleasant enough on set. Well, pleasant enough to everyone besides Rocco, that is.

I nod then, slowly, like I'm not understanding his confusion. "As in, good enough. I don't have notes, though it's of course

Lanie's call. She's the judge. So, you know, clap clap clap and all that jazz."

"Clap clap clap?" Those brows furrow even deeper as he rakes a hand over his swoop of dark, tangled curls. Messier than he usually wears it, at least based on the glossy tabloid photos I see. But my dad's hair was permanently wild and untethered, "the sign of any good writer worth their salt," he'd always say in interviews, his hair the subject of frequent off-the-pages discourse.

"Yes, I'm applauding you."

"I see. Wouldn't want to tax those precious hands of yours— I know they're needed for all the notes you're continually scribbling away on the scripts. Mostly on mine, I've noticed. Maisy's lines always seem perfect on the first go." Oh yes, one of my favorite modes of victory so far, keeping him on his toes with last minute rewrites. Subtle ones, but enough to toy with his composure. "No smiley stickers or gold stars to reward me, though?"

"I wouldn't have thought stickers would be a motivator for someone of your grand stature, but I'd be happy to pick some up tonight at the Dollar Tree if you'd like. Whatever it takes to keep the talent happy."

He smiles then, in a slow and uncertain kind of way, a dimple flashing on each cheek.

Fuck those dimples.

A quiet cough interrupts our unpleasant little tête-à-tête, and it's only then I glance up to see Lanie among the crowd of sycophants, wearing her usual uniform of black on black on black, each piece costing as much as my monthly rent, the only color popping from her fresh mermaid waves, teal and purple and pink. She has a less-than-enthused look on her pale white face. Rocco was her win, after all; she won't let any of us forget it. Word had gotten out in the industry earlier this year that Rocco was on the market for a meaty indie role, something transformative, career defining. Lanie was first in line to nab him, or at least the most persuasive and persistent of contenders.

"I just mean," I say, my lips turning up into a sugary sweet smile—I'd briefly been an actress, too, back in the day, though accidentally so—"that my dad was a . . . complicated man. Impossible for anyone to fully capture. You did as well as anyone could have, or at least anyone who never had the chance to meet him."

"Ah," Rocco says, though he appears unconvinced. "Okay then. But if you do think of any notes for that scene . . . let me know? I'm sure we could schedule a do-over if I grovel enough. It's too important of a scene to mess up."

"I won't. Have notes, that is."

"Er. Okay. Well, while we're on topic, before we break for the holidays, I was—"

Lanie steps in between us, her obscenely large grin directed Rocco's way. "You were fabulous up there. Just *fabulous*. Maisy, too, she hit her lines nicely enough, but *you* . . . my heart's in shreds! I mean, when she says she doesn't have a father anymore!" She clutches at her chest with both hands, that grin now a deep U of a frown. "Oh, Rocco, I felt every last ounce of that cruelty along with you. The vicious crushing pain, the thought of hearing those words from your own flesh and blood, your *child* . . ."

Wow, what the hell?

"Uh, hi, remember me," I chime in, fluttering my hand in the air to remind everyone of the fact of my existence. "I wouldn't say it was *cruelty* so much as raw honesty at the time. The story is a bit more nuanced than that, I should hope."

"Mm, sure," she says, barely looking my way, already back to Rocco. She puts a hand on his shoulder, ushers him away from the rest of us plebeians while continuing to gush at full speed, her only speed—there's a reason she won her first little gold man at the age of thirty-three. Rocco turns back to look at me again as he goes, like there's more he wants to discuss.

There's nothing to say, though.

It's not a lie; I don't have any notes. He nails every line, including the hastily re-written ones. His performance is legitimately above all critique and reproach. He somehow embodies my father—every irritatingly complex layer of him: dad, husband, author, *suspected murderer*—with a perfection that is almost eerie, wholly uncanny for someone who only has my script and a handful of old interviews and court videos to inform him on my dad's tone and vibe and mannerisms. Dad's books, too, all ten apparently. Rocco was proud to report those efforts to me, back during the first meeting about the movie, that awful lunch at Nobu when Lanie announced he was *our* star. When she first "introduced" us.

As if I needed any introduction.

But Rocco . . .

"Stay cool, girlfriend," a husky voice says quietly from behind.

I turn to see my best friend Sylvie Rodríguez staring down at me with a cocked brow, her bold purple lips pulled up into a pouty smile. That purple would make me look like an un-fresh corpse, but it's fabulous with her warm-brown skin and freshly dyed hot-pink curls; her color palette changes weekly, but the end result of fabulousness is always the same. As one of the stars' favored hair stylists, she's massively lowering herself to head up hair and makeup on our set, but it's a personal gift. She knows how much this movie means to me.

And how much her presence helps lower my blood pressure. Especially in moments like these, after too much face time with a certain leading man.

"Blurgh," I mumble back and go in for a tight hug. She smells like peaches and cream, and as I breathe her in deep, I'm infinitely grateful all over again that she's here, with me, helping bring my past to life. Because unlike everyone else on this set, Sylvie's met my dad. We'd grown up in the same small town outside of Tucson. Casual friends back then, but everyone there knew William Noel. "I love you big-time, do you know that?"

"You better, for the pay cut I'm taking to do this gig." She laughs, squeezing her arms around my shoulders even more tightly. "You got this, okay? Don't let him ruffle you."

"Mhm. Wanna get a drink tonight?"

"Can't do it, girlfriend. I'm on my way out. Eden's got me roped into a triple date with some work buddies."

She pecks me on the cheek and slips away.

I check my phone. Eight o'clock. Time for me to leave, too. Go home for dinner and a very tall, very stiff drink.

One more day on set, I remind myself, the countdown that's become a soothing mantra. And then aside from a "not mandatory" (but of course totally mandatory) cast and crew party at Lanie's palace in Brentwood next week—ten blissful Rocco-free days for the holidays.

"Thanks for the smooth ride, Delilah," I mumble, tapping the steering wheel lovingly for a few beats after I finally park the car, only—I glance at the clock on the dash—an hour and twenty minutes after pulling out of the studio lot. Because: LA. I've had far worse times.

Delilah is my most loyal companion. My 2000 silver Jetta that's carried me gracefully (more or less, minus a few minor bang ups and a handful of inordinately expensive repairs) through my entire adult life. She was the most luxurious gift I'd ever given myself, a reward for wrapping up my unexpected big acting role in the fall of '99, *Cutie Central*—which scored a whopping eighteen percent on Rotten Tomatoes, thank you very much, but somehow still managed to snag top honors at the Teen Choice Awards. "Big" was perhaps . . . too lofty of a descriptor for the giggling, boy-band obsessed best friend of the lead, clocking in with a grand total of seventeen lines ("As if!" being three of the seventeen, a shameless *Clueless* knock-off), but at the very least it had felt like the *start* of something big. I'd just run off to LA, both desperate to be away from my hometown in Arizona and determined to hurl myself into the film industry. I'd always intended to be a writer—it was in my blood, had never felt like a choice—but needed to separate myself from my father. So I'd be different, a *screenwriter*, not an author. But no one just becomes a screenwriter, and I'd been prepared to pay my dues, so long as it didn't involve skin-on-skin currency. Starting with a part-time job in craft services, courtesy of Sylvie—we'd stayed in touch after her post-graduation move to LA, and when she'd scored a job doing hair and make-up for *Cutie Central*, she'd worked her connections until she got me a spot on set, too.

There I'd been on my first day, little old Trixie Teller—I'd slashed Beatrix to Trixie, and co-opted my mom's maiden name at the time, the more Hollywood and less infamous option—a nobody newbie rolling out a fresh selection of prepackaged desserts, chatting amiably about the merits of Rice Krispies treats vs. Dunkaroos with a congenial older man who just so happened to be the director. And it also just so happened they were down a minor member of the cast that morning, some C-list actress who'd gotten her face scraped up in a Rollerblading accident. The director deemed me the perfect replacement on the spot, and I was ambitious enough to not ask questions. Promoted day one from craft services to cast, prepping to scream out a shrill "AS IF!" on the big screen.

That role was enough for me, for a variety of reasons; acting had never been the goal. But it was a pleasant enough temporary reprieve from being a snack minion, and thanks to the heftier paycheck, I had Delilah to show for my efforts. Still nicely shined up seventeen years later, just a few spots of rust around the front wheel to hint at her age. She takes care of me, and I take care of her. I'll pour whatever money I have into her until there's no hope of resuscitation. And then I'll make sure I can afford a house with a nice garage, so she has somewhere to lounge idly for the rest of our days.

I start the tired trek to my building, up the two flights of outdoor stairs, and heave a sigh of weary relief when I unlock the door to my apartment.

It's modest by anyone's standards, but it's the first place I could afford without a roommate or partner since moving to LA—not an achievement to scoff at in this part of the world, especially for someone who's been scraping by on the outer edges of the film industry for the better part of two decades. Sure, it may only be eight hundred square feet or so, and why yes, maybe I *do* have the plumber's number saved in my favorites because the septic system seems to malfunction on a weekly basis. But it's bright and airy and recently renovated (other than those pipes, that is), and most importantly, it's all mine. I'd take it any day over the comparatively palatial Art Deco home I'd shared with my ex-husband Damon in Silver Lake for several inordinately long years.

I drop my backpack on the floor, make my way to the freezer, rummage around for something, anything to pass off as dinner. I land on a box of store brand mac and cheese that looks like it could barely satisfy a toddler let alone a thirty-six-year-old woman and jam it in the microwave. My phone rings out as I stare at the timer, and I fish it out of my pocket, click to answer before processing who's calling.

My mother. Shoot.

I should have poured some whiskey first, dealt with dinner second.

"I expected voicemail," she says, and I can instantly visualize the exact expression she's making on the other end, the little smirk that seemed so endearing back when I was little but became fully weaponized later in life.

"Hi, Mom," I say, my hip banging against the counter as I strain to grab for the bottle of Jameson from the kitchen shelf. "It's lovely talking to you, too."

"Mm, yes. Lovely. Anyway. Just calling to make sure you're still coming back for Christmas. And to see how long you're planning to stay."

Utilitarian, as always. Ticking boxes on her holiday to-do list. *Bake cookies for book club. Wrap presents for charity drive. Call wayward daughter to confirm schedule. Scrub toilets and shower walls.*

"Still coming. I get in Friday evening, fly out Monday morning." Christmas Eve, Christmas Day, done. Leaving well before New Year's Day, the anniversary of Dad's death; a day that's difficult enough as is without having to put on masks for one another.

"Great."

"Great."

I sneak a sip straight from the bottle, hoping she doesn't catch the swallow. She finds it appalling enough as is that I'm a childless singleton—the worst kind of singleton, really, a *divorcee*—at thirty-six, let alone one who comes home from work and drinks whiskey, solo, in her tiny apartment. Eating prepackaged meals. Oh-so-many strikes.

"We'll go to Aunt Rosie's house for an early dinner before church on Christmas Eve, and then Christmas Day she'll come by the house, along with your cousins and the kids."

Just like every year. "Awesome."

"Okay."

The microwave timer zeroes out. I pull open the door before the final beeps sound off, so she doesn't overhear them.

"Alright, well—"

"Are you still shooting that movie of yours?" she asks, a shocking jolt from our usual conversational routine. *That movie.* So casual, like it's just a fluff side hobby. It's rare for us to cover anything but surface pleasantries. Unpleasantries of any kind are not packed in our mother-daughter bag of tricks. And *that movie* comes built-in with a heaping suitcase full of unpleasantries.

"Uh. Yes?"

"You promise it would make your father proud?" There's an edge to her voice now.

I take a second quiet swig.

"Yes, Mom. I promise. That's my entire reason for writing it, you know. For fighting a ridiculously uphill battle this last decade to see it get made. This is all for him."

She's quiet then, long enough that I have to check the phone screen to make sure the call hasn't ended.

"And that . . . Rocco Riz-however-you-say-it? He's capable of pulling this off? No shirtless scenes, I should hope, and that seems like his claim to fame."

She'd been reluctant to approve of him playing her beloved William. Not that we'd needed her formal yes to move ahead— or that Lanie would have cared one way or another if Mom had rejected him—but I had to at least pretend she had a say. For the actress playing her, too, though that was easier: Darla Dee, a B-list former soap star trying to re-brand. We're connected by such a thin, frayed string as is, my mom and I—Christmas dinner and infrequent perfunctory calls—and not asking would have been going at that thread ruthlessly with a pair of kitchen shears.

"He's surprisingly good," I say, stabbing at a clump of limp macaroni and taking a bite. Too hot, and just as soggy and oversalted as anticipated. "Better than good, really. Even with his shirt on. I think you'll be pleasantly surprised."

"Oh, I'm never going to watch it. That would be too much for me."

"You're not going to . . . ?" I stop myself before my voice breaks. My mom and I would never cry in front of one another.

We didn't even cry together after the funeral, not once during those strange, quiet weeks I stayed home with her before Sylvie rang about another set, a solid reason to run back to LA. Far away from the house that could never feel like home again. That time, I'd stayed away for good. Made a new home.

It shouldn't surprise me so much now, her refusal to watch it. Sure, it may be her one chance to see her only child's work on the big screen. The work that child has poured every last searing-hot drip of grief and regret into for her entire adult life.

Because that child devastated her all those years ago. Ruined our perfect family. It was me, always me. Not the arrest, the false charges. No, that was more just happenstance. My mother can make nice, plop a perfectly crisped and stuffed turkey on the table for Christmas dinner—but she'll never forgive.

"I have to go," I say, grabbing the tray of congealing mac and cheese and starting for the couch. "I have to review tomorrow's scripts. I'll see you soon."

"Call me when you land."

I'm not sure who hangs up first, but neither of us says "goodbye" or "goodnight," and we certainly don't say "I love you."

I'd always been a Daddy's girl growing up. Up until the day I stopped. I guess I wasn't anybody's girl, not after that.

I settle in on the couch, a teal leather vintage gem I scored at an estate sale in Malibu, and shovel in the rest of the clumpy noodles. I'll chase it with a few powdered blueberry donut holes I stealthily wrapped up from the craft services table this morning. A sacred place to me still, the beginning of everything. My ticket out.

On reflex I open up Netflix, and—bloody hell—of course it's *his* face grinning down from the promo at the top, a sleek western that has no right being recommended to me.

There's no escaping him apparently. Not on set or off.

I scowl into those blue eyes, looking even bluer than usual in high-def.

Of course he still manages to be outrageously sexy in his towering hat that looks more twenty-gallon than ten, a hat that would be so totally laughable on any other mere mortal. Rocco can wear anything, do anything, be anything.

Some things, at least, never change. Even in Hollywood.

Or maybe especially in Hollywood.

A text pings from my phone, and I glance down to where I tossed it after hanging up on my mother. An unknown number. Probably spam for a grassroots political donation or petition of some kind—the cause for the majority of incoming texts in 2016, at all odd hours of the day.

I pick it up anyway and click to open my messages.

It's no donation or petition request.

Oh no. It's far more egregious.

Hey Beatrix, it's Rocco. Can we pin down a minute to connect tomorrow? I know it's the last day before break, so things will be chaotic. But I'd love to chat.

I throw my phone at the TV, at that ridiculous dimpled cowboy, and let out a primal scream. Pretty satisfying, I must admit.

Though I do have immediate regrets about tossing the phone. I hurry over to check for damage, relieved to see that both screens are unscathed, and then continue to stare down at Rocco's text in a thick haze of disbelief and rage.

It's too late at night—my sacred off hours—for a text on my personal phone.

How dare he?

I'd like to suggest he go *connect* with a wet outlet, but I temper myself.

Instead, I give his text the evil eye for a solid five minutes. And then, with a heavy sigh of professional duty, I jab in my response:

Fine.

I huff as I throw my phone down on the sofa, then stomp toward the kitchen and those glorious donuts in my bag. Much deserved solace.

Cowboy Rocco, however, continues to trail me with that stupidly soulful gaze. Those wide eyes that seem to be staring straight out at me, like he's really seeing me, here and now, shoveling in two donut holes at once in my modest big-girl living room.

Just like he'd first seen me, seventeen years ago.

1999. The set of *Cutie Central.*

Because Rocco, he'd been the lover-boy lead, fresh off his stint doing kid shows—like the '90s cult classic *Black Hole Sons*, about quirky brother aliens who crash-land into the burbs of Jersey, and the gold-standard teen variety show of the day, *The Whiz of Riz. Cutie Central* was his first major role without his little brother Rudy working as his sidekick, his first big break.

I'd fallen under his spell, on set and then off. Our lead-up to the hotly anticipated new millennium. Y2K, uncharted territory.

There's no fighting the traitorous flashback now—my naïve nineteen-year-old lips tracing their way all along that square jawline up on the screen. A slow, meandering path, teasing him, making him wait for anything more. Even back then, barely a movie star yet—still middling in child-star territory—and patience was most definitely not his strong suit. I was helping him, I would joke. Teaching him better self-control.

Until I couldn't control myself either, and we gave in all the way together.

It had been that first lunch with Lanie when I'd realized, absolutely gobsmacked by Rocco's total lack of recognition—that for all the heavy baggage Rocco gifted me seventeen years earlier, I hadn't left him with a single itsy-bitsy parcel. It was crystal clear I'd been nothing more than a casual, write-off fling. A mere blip on the grand ride of Rocco Riziero's meteoric rise to fame and fuckery.

He didn't remember me. Not at all.

And of course, I wasn't going to be the one to remind him. There was nothing to be gained but embarrassment and added rage. I was just the writer to him, the real-life daughter to his first father role. Some warped kind of muse.

And now I have to see him on set, every day.

Starring in my own movie.

Playing my dad.

Rocco had never met my father back then. He'd never had the chance.

To be fair, I never gave him that chance—not that he would have taken me up on it. And then, suddenly, just like that, it was too late.

Rocco was gone.

And the next day, Dad was gone, too.

But here they are now for this movie, together, a man and a ghost, in a way I could never have imagined. A strange and malicious twist of fate. Past, present, now one baffling blur of Hollywood magic.

I pop the last donut in my mouth. Let the berry sweetness soothe my soul.

Enough. Enough brain space devoted to Rocco, at least during off hours.

I flip the bird at the TV screen and shut it off for the night, watching in delight as Rocco's luminous face flickers instantly into blackness.

Chapter 2

Rocco

Thursday, December 22, 2016

I steel myself, lifting my chin higher as I walk through the studio doors this morning. An act because I'm nervous, and that nervousness is uncharacteristic. Unsettling.

I'm never nervous, not on set, because I'm damn good at what I do. That's not immodesty; it's just the facts.

I've been working on sets since I was a blob of a human. I had a director yell at me during a diaper commercial to not suck my thumb when I was still nonverbal—an anecdote my mom's always loved to share with anyone who will listen, mostly because I apparently had a poop-tacular diaper blowout in retaliation. I'd been dropped from the arms of an A-list celebrity onto a hard stage floor for being "too damn precocious for anyone's good," feeding them lines when I was eight. I'd even withstood a body slam sack from professional football player Warren Sapp. That one's a long story. I've endured it all with thick skin, wiseass remarks, and a natural-born ability to charm everyone, at least eventually, from babies on up to nonagenarians. Enemies included, and I've had more than a few, mostly on their terms. Everyone in this town does—at least if you've had even a modicum of success.

Last night, though, I couldn't sleep. Couldn't shut my brain off. Because I kept hearing Beatrix's words on loop:

Adequate. Good enough.

That condescending *clap clap clap.*

It's not like I haven't had worse insults lobbed at me. Critics have had a field day with some of my movies—usually the blockbusters that gross the most ludicrous amounts of millions. Easier to take with a grain of salt, maybe a shot of tequila for added numbing.

Though it's been less easy as I've gotten older. Harder to tune out. No matter how fine the tequila.

An aging teen heartthrob who made good through his twenties . . .

But what now? What next?

I've cruised through so many years on autopilot for the paycheck, and my bank account is more loaded than any one person deserves in a lifetime. Hell, a few lifetimes. There's got to be more than that to this whole acting life. More to me. And if I really try with this role, really nail it, hopefully I'm closer to finding what that more might be.

So far, with the glaring exception of Beatrix, everyone here has been encouraging. Lanie. Producers. Other members of the cast. Even the crew's been generous with praise.

And I know it, too, I *feel* it. Or I thought I did. That this is without a doubt my best work yet. The deepest, most vulnerable. I fully acknowledge that I've been in some seriously shit movies with seriously shit roles. This is different. As different as it gets.

I want Beatrix to recognize that, too. It's the story of her father, her life. Her approval feels like the ultimate thumbs-up. And the need for that validation, from her . . . it burns me.

The cameras start shooting again, and I hang toward the back, waiting. Maisy's in the middle of a single push-in shot where she's deep in retrospection about William. It's a long piece of dialogue, packed to the brim with loads of messy emotions. I'm watching, but I can't seem to focus on what Maisy's saying. I've read it over in the script so many times and heard her in the wide shot, but I'm too busy studying Beatrix from across the room to catch Maisy's performance this time. The thoughtful frown on her face as she closes her eyes, listens rather than watches.

Lanie calls the scene. I start toward Beatrix's chair, weaving through clumps of cast and crew, losing sight of her as I'm pulled into a few stop-and-chats along the way. She should be expecting me after last night's text; a necessity, since she mostly evades me. At least when she isn't directing not-so-subtle jabs my way. I'm not actually needed on set today, but I figured it would give me the best chance to talk to Beatrix before January. Pick her brain for more intel. She might not be my biggest fan, but we both want the same thing: for William to come across as true as can be.

I extricate myself from an uninspired exchange about the weather and spot Beatrix again, talking to Maisy, the two of them deep in conversation as I approach. The expression on Beatrix's face is so earnest, so passionate, I can't help but pause mid-step for a beat, just to take her in. She's always hard to look away from—a fact that's exceptionally aggravating to me. Steel gray eyes that never cease to pin me down with their cool intensity. Pale skin, a few rogue freckles she never tries to cover up. Long, wavy brown hair that's usually swept into a haphazard knot on her head, most often with a pen or straw or whatever object she finds lying around set. Her wardrobe, at least at work, is a combination of black jeans—tight black jeans, seemingly custom made to mold to her every curve— and plain dark shirts, like she's trying her best to blend in with the crew, to not call attention to herself. It does the opposite, though, at least for me. Makes the rest of her features pop in high-def.

She's got one of those faces, too—a face that makes you feel like you know someone, deep down. Like an itch at the back of my brain I can't scratch, which only adds to this mess I'm in with her jabs and backhanded compliments. Let's be real, I'd take a few literal backhanders over the arrows she slings straight at my ego.

I step up beside her now, as close as I can without risking her wrath. Though it's hard to predict what will rub her the wrong way, as most everything I do seems to cause further disdain. She doesn't notice me; she's all eyes on Maisy. Which is fair, because today feels like Maisy's potential breakout moment as an actress if she gets it right—the scene where she's circling through everything her dear dad's been accused of, what she knows and what she can't know for certain, all the stories and rumors taking her town, the nation, by storm. Maisy's got a unicorn arrangement, having the real-life person she's portraying standing right next to her, filling in backstory and motive for emotions. A once-in-a-career opportunity to wholly embody her role.

"In this moment, my father had become someone I couldn't trust, couldn't recognize, just like that," Beatrix says, snapping her fingers. She glances at me sideways, then immediately looks away. "The one figure in my life I'd never doubted, and suddenly I was forced to question everything." She moves in closer to Maisy, saying something else, too quietly for me to hear. It happens so quickly then that it's hard to discern who initiates, but they embrace, holding each other tight.

"Wow," Maisy says, head pressed against Beatrix's shoulder. "That must have been so intense. I totally get how you felt—well, as much as possible, not being you, of course—and appreciate the pep talk. I swear, I'll do you proud!"

"I know you will," Beatrix replies. Sweetly.

Seriously, though, is this a joke? Why can't I have the same kind of relationship with Beatrix? Not necessarily the hugging bit—or maybe a tiny hug would be nice, sure, though that's beside the point—but that deeper character connection. Why is Maisy afforded unfettered access into her brain, but I can only get a salty "you did fine, I suppose"?

Their pep talk works some kind of miracle, because Maisy's back on set, cameras rolling, and this time I can't take my eyes off her. No one can. The scene is beautiful and wrenching, filled with a depth and commitment to the part I hadn't seen yet from this YouTuber wannabe star. Okay, that's maybe harsh . . . this young aspiring actress.

But still, if Beatrix could give that much boost, I want to hit the next level, too. That's the whole reason I took this job. To show the world—my family, too, my little brother Rudy—I'm more than a twelve-pack of abs and a stubbled jawline.

Beatrix and I have yet to say a word to one another by the time they break for lunch. Food first. Conversation second. I need to refuel. And while Michelin-starred social media reviews may be one of my snobbier hobbies, there's something about on-set catering that's always really done it for me. I've been chasing the *Whiz of Riz* catering breakfast tacos and cheesesteaks since I moved to LA. This set has got particularly great service, and today's pre-holiday meal has been heavily publicized as an arroz con pollo treat—or arroz con tofurkey if you're not into eating birds.

I grab the classic option and spot Beatrix already eating alone and looking as pleasant as she gets. I feel like the new kid at school, working myself up to ask if anyone's sitting at her table, but then opt instead to take the bolder route—or maybe more cowardly—and just plop myself down next to her.

"I have to say," I start right in, "you clearly gave Maisy something special to work with for that scene today. She totally shined. Maybe even turned into a real actress, right before our eyes."

Beatrix doesn't look up from her plate—she went for the tofurkey, I note. She only nods, seemingly immersed in forking up some rice. A theme by now. A stonewaller is always going to stonewall.

"Sorry I texted so late last night. I just had such a great day shooting and getting into the character, really being your dad. Or, no . . . not *being* your dad, but you know what I mean. No one can be him. That came out weird."

Nothing. It's like I'm not even here. I give up, take a few bites of chicken. Wait it out. As she finishes chewing on some squeaky fake meat, she finally turns to look at me.

"I'm intentionally helping you by being standoffish. Just like I was with my dad—the man you're currently trying so hard to embody. It's called method acting. And besides, how could I tell you how my dad felt? I cut him off, remember? So alternatively, I'm using my previous behaviors to try and capture a similar effect for you, that's all."

Yikes. Does that even make sense, or is she just riding me again? I can't process fast enough to decide.

"I'm sorry," I say, putting my fork down. "I'm not trying to push. I just want to make sure I'm getting the role right—that it translates for you. I tried asking yesterday, but . . . wasn't sure I got a full read? Lanie pulled me away before we could talk more. So. Yeah. Here I am."

There's another beat of silence, though Beatrix has a look on her face that makes me think there's some kind of pity statement incoming.

Which is apt because I've possibly never felt more pitiful in my life.

"Well, Rocco," she starts, then lets out a loud exhale. In case I couldn't already sense just how trying this was for her. How trying *I* am. "I understand your inclination to want to impress me or to, I don't know, make me feel like I'm back in the '90s, I do. But this isn't about me. It's about the *story*, and I need you to recognize that. I'm not here to give my approval. I'm here to make sure this story is told properly." With that, she quickly stands, picking up her half-full plate. "If you can't figure out my father by reading the script and his books and by doing your own digging online, then I'm not sure what else I can give you."

My mind instinctually races to figure out some kind of retort. Something snarky that lets her know I don't need to be treated this way. That'd be my typical go-to, hackles raised. Instead, though, in a flash of inspiration—or maybe maturity at thirty-seven years young—my brain tells me to belly up.

"Have coffee with me after Christmas. Please? I just want to talk. Genuinely. Not a psychiatrist-on-the-couch kind of talk, but a deeper dive into what you loved and lost with your father. There are some big scenes coming up post-holidays, and I want to make sure I step up to the plate."

Beatrix looks confused, angry, stoic. Like she's shapeshifting right in front of me. It's hard to predict what kind of reaction might rain down on me next.

"Okay," she says finally, with a nod so affirmative that a few kernels of rice shake off her plate. "Coffee. The twenty-seventh. Is that commitment enough for you to leave me alone today? To maybe even . . . escort yourself home, seeing as you're not on the call sheet?"

Nobody . . . I mean *nobody* . . . has spoken to me like this on set, ever. Well, maybe my mom when I was a punk-ass kid. But since becoming of legal age, not a single person on any set has been so blunt and curt with me.

It's equal parts infuriating and intriguing.

"I'll take that coffee date and leave, just as soon as this food is off my plate. You can stay here and finish. Please. I'll move if I'm keeping you from eating your fake meat."

"Tofurkey is delicious, thank you, and I say that as a non-vegetarian. But to answer your question—yes, if you dine elsewhere, I'll be much more inclined to sit back down." She smiles then, possibly the fakest smile I've ever seen. And I've seen a lot of bad fake smiles in my day, on set and off. "Thanks for the talk, Rocco. Hope you have a merry Christmas."

I stand, though I feel unbalanced by the arctic chill. And that face . . . I'm struck by the feeling again—there's just something so familiar about it. The pout. The judging eyes. The nose crinkle intended to look tough, though the end result has a strange charm to it. Déjà vu? Something from a dream? A nightmare? Whatever it is, it's somehow calming and alarming at the same time.

"Did we work together before?" I ask, because curiosity gets the best of me. "I can't put my finger on it, but I feel like I . . . know you? Shit, you weren't the script supervisor on *Rockets to Russia* were you? Because I was really in a bad place with my publicist at the time. Outside baggage. And it wasn't the script, it was the dialogue!"

She avoids my gaze, speaking instead to her tofurkey. "I was never a script supervisor, but I did read about your unruly performance in some tabloids at the time." She looks up to finally meet my eyes, only to flash me a smug, holier-than-thou grin.

I'm silent for a few seconds too long before blurting out, "Hope your Christmas is, uh . . . merry and bright, too."

Damn. Beatrix Noel. What is her *deal*?

Brushing off that question would certainly be the easier route.

But I chose to be here, chose this movie, for a reason, didn't I? I chose the challenge.

My little brother Rudy and his fiancée Lucy—usually New Yorkers—are in the last weeks of a joint residency in LA for their comedy show, *Spiked Lemonade*. A hit in Brooklyn, celebrating horribly awkward dating stories by turning them into comedy gold, relocated temporarily to the West Coast for a few months. I'd offered up my home for their stay—it's stupidly big for one person—but they'd passed. Because they're newly engaged and eager for some alone time, Rudy had said, letting me down gently. More than that, though, I suspect my brother wanted to prove he could do his own thing. Pay his own way. Which I respect. We'd gone our different directions after a childhood acting together on the screen; I kept on with show biz, rode it to the top. And Rudy, he picked college on the East Coast and his own more creative routes from there: music and comedy and whatever else would pay the bills. *Spiked Lemonade* feels like the payoff he's been working so damn hard for.

So, a rental in Venice for him and Lucy it is.

We're all staying put out here for the holiday, our first California Christmas together—much to my parents' chagrin, since we'll be missing their annual Christmas Eve dinner extravaganza in Jersey. But I'm buying their forgiveness by treating the whole family to a week in Turks and Caicos when the movie wraps. My parents and Rudy and Lucy, some aunts and uncles, a few cousins, even ninety-four-year-old Great Uncle Alfred—with his plus one, a woman thirty years his junior. An icon for bachelors everywhere.

I promised Rudy and Lucy I'd meet up with them post-show tonight to kick off our holiday. It's been great, having my little bro back in town—especially after spending too many of our adult years barely speaking, thanks to a jackass move I made on his first great love back in the day. A life choice and era I try to avoid thinking about as much as possible. But we've both been busy, passing ships since I started shooting *Murder in the Books.*

I pull up to a hipster bar across the street from their comedy venue in Silver Lake. It has all the accoutrements my brother Rudy most enjoys, the kind of rock-and-roll dive bar that's not afraid to sell merch with the bar name—Angelenos Inc., in a spiky punk-rock font—surrounded by totally trademarked and licensed '80s and '90s popstar photos. How did he manage a steady gig across the street from such a dream watering hole?

Rudy and Lucy are posted up when I walk in, laughing and nuzzling shoulders, a couple of empties already on the high-top table. I used to want that kind of connection, too, before it became clear I was better suited for the bachelor life. An Uncle Alfred protégée. But seeing the two of them together, those goofy grins—I could almost be tempted to swing back toward my initial path.

Almost.

"Rocco! You dirty sonofabitch! Willing to hang, but always too busy to come to the actual show." Rudy looks at me with his puppy-dog brown eyes and gives a pointed frown to expel his marked displeasure that I, yet again, missed their show. Rudy and I played twins on *Black Hole Sons*, a funny shtick because we couldn't look more different; I got an extra six inches and the Italian genes from Dad, and he got freckles and red hair, courtesy of our Irish mother. But our facial expressions, the way we show ourselves to the world—that's where I always see the sibling link.

"You know," Lucy chimes in, "you might even find a love match there? We had at least two connections in the audience tonight. Nothing says, 'let's grab a drink' more than hearing about the most comically nightmarish first dates." Lucy's smile makes everyone smile, gives a nice serotonin boost. Works on me every time, no matter how shit the day. Tonight included. It's her whole vibe, really; like a modern-day Lucille Ball, her looks, humor, charisma. Except she's got dark brown hair—my brother's the only redhead in their relationship.

"I know, I know . . . I really wanted to come, but I had a long day on set." Great, Rocco. Open with a half lie. The full truth is that Beatrix had me too flustered to appreciate a comedy show. But I might as well dive right into the work mess—maybe they can help me figure Beatrix out. I'm usually good at reading people; it's an actor's gift. But in this case, I'm failing. Miserably.

"Right, your DAD project!" Rudy chuckles. "Sorry, can't help myself, it's just so wild to picture you as a *dad*. I mean, sure, you're old enough, and you very well might have kids somewhere, but you sure as shit don't know 'em."

My little brother seems prepped to engage in a very Jersey-style ball-busting session. It'd usually bounce right off of me, a big brother superpower, but he's hitting my anxieties right to the core. I'm not a dad—I've always been supremely careful about that. No visible protection, no deal, no matter how tempting. Nothing against dads, of course. I have a great dad of my own, I respect the hell out of dads, but no, I am not dad material by any stretch of anyone's imagination, especially my own. Nor have I tried to step into a pair of dad shoes before this role. There's no going back once you've crossed that age barrier. Once a dad, always a dad, at least in Hollywood's eyes.

Worth that leap, for this movie. The right kind of game-changer.

At least, that's what I thought when I'd signed on. Hopefully still true.

I take a second, collect myself with a few deep breaths—my very Irish and semi-*woo-woo* spiritual mom was always big on teaching us meditative strategies when we were kids on set—and dive in. "Speaking of the dad gig, the writer, Beatrix—it's her life the movie's based on, her dad I'm playing—she's just . . . dogging all my scenes. Crushing my confidence at every turn. It's unreal." Wow. I feel epically whiny just saying it. Petulant. No matter how true it may be. And yet I continue. "Also, it's bizarre—she looks so familiar to me, but . . . I'm pretty sure I've never met her before. I did ask if we'd worked together, and she shot me down. I'm not too classy to admit I may have been a bit of a hit with the ladies on set, particularly in my younger years. But the way she despises me, it's like I've wronged her in ten lifetimes before this one."

"Let's be real, brother," Rudy says, grinning widely. "You've encountered far too many faces in your life to remember every single one. Especially when it comes to women."

Lucy elbows him for me. Though Rudy's not wrong—I've been a serial dater for too many years to keep a pristine mental Rolodex.

My problem has always been projecting other people's feelings without any actual consultation. I just go on instinct. Which, in my late teens and twenties—and sure, thirties, too—has amounted to a long run of four-to-five date stretches. Abrupt endings based on my own insecurities, hyper analyzing what's gone wrong in the past. Instead of working on myself, I choose casual. Jump ship before anyone gets in too deep.

There was only ever one true outlier.

Rudy takes a long swig of beer, then puts the bottle down and rests his hand on my shoulder. "Back to the larger issue here. So you aren't getting the customary awe and rapt applause you so dearly desire? That's the problem?"

I'm considering rubbing my knuckles over his scalp when Lucy steps in, verbally this time, reading the room like she does so well. "Rudy, I think Rocco's looking for some real advice here. The show's over. Save it for later, my love."

Rudy backs off immediately—Lucy has that effect on him. I knew from the first time I met her that Lucy was the one. He needs someone checking him now and again, or else he becomes more of a jaded, self-proclaimed "realist." A slippery slope that can easily lead into asshole territory. That didn't change in our years apart; some things never do, apparently.

"Listen," I continue, "I've tried everything to get her to warm up. That YouTuber . . . excuse me, *actress* . . . who's playing Beatrix in the movie gets all the good notes, though. The feelings. The vibes. The context. And me? I get nothing. Which, yeah, it's her character, her role, she gets it better. But surely she still has some workable insights for me? She lived with the man her whole childhood, and all she could give me is that my biggest scene so far was *adequate*. Who says that?"

Lucy's lightning fast with a response—like she can't tell me how it is quick enough. "Maybe the kind of person who wrote a movie about a deeply traumatic point in her life? Full stop. Of course she's going to mentor the person in her role. I know nothing about the script, but I've got enough information to see you're making this way more about yourself than you should be. You're an amazing actor. Trust in that. Without pushing Beatrix to hand over more than she's ready or willing to about her past. She doesn't owe you that."

True. But also: ouch.

"Yeah, bro," Rudy chimes in, "let's be real. You've never needed anyone else to tell you how great you are—you just took a script and owned it. Whether you were playing a total jock who just so happened to save the planet with spectacular abs, or a bumbling convenience store clerk who accidently locked the serial killer in the walk-in freezer while you were busy making out with a customer. I mean, they weren't complex characters, but you made it work. Always."

I can't help but laugh, even if there's a sting to it, too. "Both of those movies made a lot of money, thank you, and the bumbling clerk had plenty of substance! Remember the scene where I had to comfort the woman pinned by the slushie machine? Deep stuff, if you ask me."

"If you'd let me finish, brosef, I was trying to say that ten times out of ten, you had the right read and proper motivation. Why are you letting her get the best of you?"

"Because . . ." I scramble, desperate to get this right—for them, and for me. "It's her *life*, and I genuinely want her to be happy with my work. It's an audience of one for me right now. Beatrix had such a tough past with her dad, and I want to make damn certain I'm capturing the moments and feelings to her liking. She deserves that, you know?"

Well, huh. That felt . . . honest. Am I growing into a more nurturing father type after all? Or at least a more empathetic actor who's thinking beyond his own performance? The critics, the award nominations.

Yeah, keep telling yourself that, Rocco.

More likely, the truth is somewhere in the middle; my ego is still strong, no matter how hard I try to convince myself otherwise. But there's more than ego. At least in this case.

"Anyway," I continue, "I asked to meet for coffee next week. One more solid try to see if she'll open up more, give notes on how I can improve. Be the best William I can be."

"I think," Rudy starts, slowly, like he's talking to a small child, "that all sounds . . . nice. But you need to leave your baggage at the door. Don't play the ol' Rocco *Me-Me-Me* game. Take a page from our playbook," he says, nodding at Lucy. "In a platonic way, but still. The Lucy-putting-Rudy-in-his-place lesson. Be a listener, not just a talker. We're cut from the same cloth, you and me—I'd be feeling the same way in your spot. I just have this fine lady here who helps me to step outside myself."

Lucy wraps her arms around Rudy's shoulders, hugs him tight. It really is kind of endearing. I don't want to gag, at least.

"He's right, Rocco. I'm sure she's still working everything through, and to see it all play out like this must take a heavy toll. Imagine watching your worst private moments relived in that way?" Lucy shudders, downs the dregs of her whiskey. "Not that it compares, but I wouldn't need to see our first date on the big screen. Or a small screen, for that matter." She and Rudy exchange a long, loaded glance. Their first date in Brooklyn: a reading from an old psychic who ended up dying right there on her stage with them, in the midst of an epic prophecy about their bond. Their potential as a couple. A happy ending in that it kept them together despite the odds, sure, riddling through her prophecy as a team. Discovering their comedy show together. But a bizarre and traumatic start to any relationship.

I can't help but think about Rudy and our past now, too. Much as I like to avoid it.

The way I broke his heart when I stole his (semi, not quite) ex-girlfriend away back in '99. Piper Bell. Our co-star from *Black Hole Sons*. The show that put all three of us on the Hollywood map. We were so young during those love triangle days, but still. Old enough to know what we wanted. Rudy and Piper, they'd been together for years—the *Teen Beat* It Couple of the late '90s. Then Rudy left Hollywood for school, and Piper and I stayed behind in LA to make our stars rise higher, and . . . well, I'd loved her secretly for years, too, and when she gave me an inch, we took the rest of the mile together. Kept on running after that. Imploded everything between me and Rudy for far longer than the flash-and-burn courtship lasted. It was only last year, Rudy finding Lucy, a potential fresh start for his love life and his career, a visit to LA to sort through everything, that we really reunited. Had the hard brother talks that'd been so many years in the making. He'd flown out here for a gig that ultimately wasn't meant to be, work-wise at least; the trip here, the time together, it's what saved him and me. Gave us the good sense and life perspective we both needed. A nice brotherly kick in the ass.

I'd give up my whole bank account to never see any of that past on a screen. I think about the thousands of other ways I've been a jackass since, the things people in my life have put up with, especially those who care about me most.

Family—it's complicated on all sides. Beatrix and I can both speak to that.

We spend the rest of the night recounting embarrassing stories from our childhoods. I'm not trying to audition for their show—though I do vow to catch the grand finale in January—but I am putting my best comedy foot forward in a desperate attempt to cheer myself up for the holidays. It works, thankfully. Lucy's laughing hard at ridiculous stories Rudy's neglected to tell her, probably because he's the butt of almost every joke. He takes it like a champ, though. For a little brother, he certainly knows the right time to give his big brother the spotlight. Even if that big brother gets too much spotlight as it is. I would do the same for him, though, always. He was right.

We are cut from the same cloth.

And if he can learn, do better, maybe I can, too.

Chapter 3

BEATRIX

Tuesday, December 27, 2016

I open my eyes and am instantly blasted by the bright California sunshine filtering through the cheap shades that came with the apartment. Someday, when I make it big, I'll make sure the Craftsman house of my dreams comes complete with motorized blinds. A flick of a switch, and total darkness at all hours of the day. Heaven.

This morning, though, the blinding light is a relief; I'm back home, a plane ride away from my museum-like old bedroom in Arizona. A perfectly preserved exhibit of teenage Beatrix's life that no one, least of all myself, wants to witness.

The holiday weekend was exactly as I'd anticipated: stilted, strained, and mostly free of any genuine cheer. Though my cousins' kids are unreasonably adorable, and it's much easier to play hide and seek for hours on end than to attempt to engage in any real adult discourse with my mother and aunt or my cousins and their spouses. I'd been close to them all, once. I lost much more than a father the day I made my decision to turn away.

But that's fine, I reassure myself now, sitting up to admire my view of Westlake—the art deco buildings fringed by a row of tall palms. A view I ignore most days. I'm a grown woman with an excellent life of her own here in LA—or at least a moderately decent one—finally in a place of enough power to be seeing the movie of her dreams (slash nightmares) turned into a reality. It only took a solid seventeen years of odd jobs to get here: first as a craft services minion for a few years after *Cutie Central*, moving on to assisting with props and then locations, bartending on the side. I'd dabbled as a receptionist at *the* hair salon to the stars, also thanks to Sylvie. There was a brief stint as a temp at a casting agency, too—the unfortunate location where I'd met my ex-husband, Damon, forever B-string character actor and more of a D-list player in the story of my life. And of course, I was writing, always writing—just nothing that mattered (or paid a single bill) before *Murder in the Books*.

The weekend in Arizona had proved productive in one regard, though. I'd been able to use my "research" for Rocco to avoid awkward quiet time sitting around with my mother, instead digging through the office that had once been my father's. It had felt like a king's court then, when I was a kid: his puffy red writing chair, the polished mahogany rolltop desk and Tiffany pearl floor lamp, high walls lined with overflowing stacks of books—every kind of book about every kind of thing, place, person—a lush Persian carpet that muffled any trace of footsteps as he'd pace the room, mulling over a snag in his plot. And of course, the crown jewel: his vintage Royal typewriter. I could still hear the way he tapped away on those keys if I closed my eyes and concentrated hard enough. I'd spent hundreds of hours sprawled on that carpet, reading, listening, daydreaming. Sharing "writer's fuel" we'd sneakily squirrel away in his drawers, sweet treats that were sacred offerings within those office walls.

My mom had tried, at first, to keep the room pristine, waiting for him. But after it became clear he'd never write another word on that typewriter he loved more than he loved most people, Mom and I excluded, she stopped going in at all. She could purge his clothes and shoes, his fishing gear, his comic book and record collections. But the office she couldn't touch.

It was a sad shadow of its former self now, dusty and stale and faded. But I spent hours on Christmas Eve looking through old stacks and drawers, collecting "inspiration pieces" for Rocco—photos and journal pages, scrawled fragments of ideas and doodles. Some of his last written notes, from before he was taken away; scraps that either survived the police's original raid or found their way back to us in the end. I was an archivist, not a daughter, a professional with a plan, not a broken woman looking for any kind of peace she doesn't deserve. My mom didn't ask questions—of course she didn't. Just made me an egg salad sandwich for lunch and left it for me in the fridge to eat after I was done. I'd always loved her egg salad and was surprised she remembered. Or maybe it was coincidence—a surplus of nearly expired eggs.

I'm back now, though, with nearly a week left of uncomplicated holiday time.

Once I make it through this morning's coffee with Rocco.

I lounge in bed, exchange a few delightfully salty texts with Sylvie about my Christmas in Arizona and hers in Colorado with Eden and her rabidly evangelical in-laws—only bolting upright when I realize I'm supposed to meet Rocco in less than an hour. We agreed to meet in West Hollywood, which should be a clear route, relatively speaking by LA standards, during the holiday week, but it leaves very little time to fuss over my appearance. Which is for the best, really, since I absolutely shouldn't give any fucks whatsoever about Rocco's opinion of my looks.

After an efficient birdbath-style rinse—a quick scrub with a wet rag and a spritz of lavender deodorant—I force myself to wear the first thing I put on, no dillydallying. Tight black skinny jeans with lightning-bolt-shaped gold ankle zippers, a loose off-the-shoulder black sweater that always gives me feel-good *Flashdance* vibes, and leopard print booties. I run my fingers through my tangled hair—majorly in need of a trim and fresh highlights to cheer up the muddy brown—and pull it up into a messy knot. Finish off with a few swipes of mascara and a dab of blush, a smear of Aquaphor on my lips. Practical and put together. No different than what I'd wear for a day on set.

It's only a coffee meeting, after all.

Even still, I'm too anxious to have much of an appetite, so I skip past the kitchen, stuff the folder filled with William Noel souvenirs into my backpack and head out. The drive is blessedly smooth, and I get to the tiny hole-in-the-wall coffee shop with two minutes to spare. It was Rocco's pick, a place I'd never heard of, and I'm understanding why. It's bland and nondescript, and no one would choose to come here over the string of cute artisanal coffee shops footsteps away. We'll have our privacy here. No risk of the paparazzi snagging a pic of Rocco and some drab-looking mystery brunette.

I'm expecting to have beaten him—the Rocco I knew never went to sleep before four a.m.—but no, he's leaning against the counter, looking bright-eyed and chipper, chatting amiably with the very tan, very blond white woman behind the register.

Ugh. The way people fawn over him, and with so little effort on his part. Honestly, people would fawn even if he weren't a red-carpet commodity. It's his gorgeous face, sure, but it's more than that, too; it's in the way he leans, the casual yet absurdly elegant tilt of that broad chest, the cut of abs that are slightly visible through the thin white T-shirt he's wearing under a plain blue zippered sweatshirt, sleeves rolled up just enough to tease his muscular forearms.

I've never been drawn to an athletic build, or really anyone with an active gym membership—unless they were using it for the yoga classes. I've loved yoga since my early days here.

Hikers were fine, or swimmers, surfers. People who engaged in outdoor activity for pleasure and just so happened to develop a few lean muscles as a byproduct. Damon was a weightlifting devotee, which should have, in hindsight, been my first sign that we wouldn't work out in the end. Or more than a handful of years. The Rocco I'd known, too intimately for my own good, was much leaner—strong but in a casual, careless kind of way that had made him all the more appealing.

"Uh, Beatrix?" Rocco asks, in a politely amused way that makes me think it's not the first time he's saying it.

Damn. I'd been staring, hadn't I? At his wrists to start, and from there his wide-open hands splayed against the counter, those long fingers that had pressed, burning hot, into every last inch of me.

"Sorry." I shake my head, my cheeks undoubtedly glowing an alarming shade of red. "I haven't caffeinated yet today, so I'm a little hazy."

He nods, biting down on his full lower lip to hold back a smile. "I get that. I had a shot of espresso at five before I went for my morning swim in the ocean."

"In January?"

"Sure, with a wetsuit. It's kind of my thing. Wakes me up better than the espresso. That's just my motivator to get out there."

"Where do you go?" I don't know why I'm asking, other than I need a moment for my pulse to go down and my cheeks to de-flame.

"Oh, just down the hill from my house."

"Yes, of course you'd have a private beach. What was I thinking?"

Rocco laughs, a loud outburst that seems to surprise him as much it does me. I've heard Rocco laugh on set, usually in response to his posse of devoted fans, and this is a different one altogether. I remember this laugh. "I don't own the beach, Beatrix. Just the view down. But if I was going to use the money these studios overpay me for a splurge, it would be for the ocean practically in my backyard. I couldn't care less about the rest of the house. Most of the rooms are empty." He shrugs, looking almost apologetic. "Maybe I should open a B&B."

"Mm, yes, would be a real hotbed for your superfan stalkers."

"Right. Yeah. Maybe no B&B then. I love my fans, I do, but a man needs to take his morning shit in peace."

"Especially when you might be taking that morning shit before your sunrise swim."

"Are we really talking about my bowel routines right now?"

"You started it."

"I suppose I did, didn't I." Rocco grins, and despite my better judgement, or any form of judgement whatsoever, I feel my lips grinning back.

A bell chimes behind us as another customer steps in, an older white man in a sweatsuit who looks like he'd go out of his way to pick the least trendy place in the neighborhood.

Rocco clears his throat, turning to study the menu on the wall with great intensity. If I didn't know better, I'd say there's a flush creeping up his throat—like we were caught red-handed in the middle of something. But there was no moment. Nothing to interrupt.

"So yes, that coffee," I say, stepping up to the counter, my shoulder brushing against Rocco's left arm. He immediately straightens from that artful lean, his spine going rigid. Standing like that, fully upright, he's a good foot taller than me, and I remember then—the way my head felt pressed against his collarbone, how he would crouch down to kiss at my level or, better yet, sweep me up into his arms, my toes swirling off the ground.

It was so fast what we had, so whirlwind and abrupt, I shouldn't be able to remember any of it anymore, at least not so well. So *deeply*. Like my skin and bones and blood still carry a trace of him now, a splinter my body absorbed and nurtured and nourished for these last seventeen years. There have been so many others since. So many men who lasted longer, stuck around for months—or, in Damon's case, a few years. But my body has wholly and gladly ejected every last piece of them for good. Fuzzy faces and forgotten voices, details that long ago left the far reaches of my brain and the tip of my tongue. But Rocco. We had months—weeks, if I parse it down to what really mattered—and somehow it's all still a sharp Technicolor montage.

"I'll have a large almond milk latte," Rocco says. "No sugar."

"Same for me," I mumble, inordinately annoyed that we share our taste in coffee. Though I suppose that was true before, too.

"And a banana chocolate-chip muffin," Rocco adds.

"You still eat muffins?" I can't stop myself from asking. I would have guessed these days he was living on bland lean proteins with a side of steamed veggies for every meal.

"Yes? Does that surprise you?"

"It does actually." I turn to the woman at the counter, who's looking between us with what appears to be a not-so-subtle tinge of jealousy. "I'll have a muffin, too."

"Ah, a fellow appreciator then," Rocco says, and I glance over to see him smiling down at me. I have to tilt my chin up to meet his eyes. "Who would've thought we'd have so much in common, you and me? Based on our on-set interactions, I would have expected our breakfast preferences to be polar opposites. You did go for that tofurkey."

"Ha-ha. Well, I think it takes far more than a shared coffee shop order to make for best friends."

"Oh, I don't know. I've always liked a bit of playful conflict in my relationships. It can get a little dull when there's nothing to challenge you. Nothing to push your buttons."

"Well, I suppose you do surround yourself with a hefty dose of people pleasers. I could see how that would get dull."

"People pleasers?"

"Fans, admirers, sycophants, whatever the preferred terminology is."

"I see." His brow crinkles, and for the first time I notice the little wrinkles that fan out from his eyes. Somehow even laugh lines suit him. "And you think that's who I choose to surround myself with in life?"

"Isn't it? Sure seems that way, at least on set."

He shakes his head, a trace of a frown on his lips. "I don't understand. Have I done something to you, Beatrix? Recently, or . . . not so recently? Not the script supervisor, okay. But something else I'm forgetting?"

The words are an electric jolt to my gut, just like last week's lunch on set. *He's getting closer.* "What do you mean?"

"Just that it seems like you don't . . . like me very much? And I feel, I don't know, silly and egocentric even saying this out loud. Of course you don't have to like me. You barely even know me. But it's more than that. Like you actively *dislike* me. As if I've offended you somehow. Is it something about how I've been capturing your dad? Because if so, I'm sincerely sorry, and I don't want you to think—"

"No," I say, too firmly, based on the way Rocco flinches. The barista jumps, too, just as she's pouring thick foam into our cups. A splatter of almond milk pools on the counter. "No," I repeat, more level this time. "You've done nothing wrong on set. This is all just . . . difficult for me. I'm not proud of my decisions, you know. That's why it's so important, making this movie. To honor him. Even if it's years too late for his forgiveness."

It might not be the whole truth, but it's still a heck of a lot more honesty than I was prepared to unload on Rocco this morning. I'm usually not even that honest with myself.

Rocco's brow has softened at my admission, a look of such genuine concern in his eyes now—eyes that are usually so cool, so untouchable when they're not play-acting emotions for his character—I almost want to . . . cry.

And I do not cry.

"Your order is ready," the barista says unceremoniously, and I turn away from both of them, blinking to push away any stray tears.

"Thank god," the man behind us grumbles. "Thought I'd never get to order. I'd rather get a frap-a-latte-whatever at Starbucks than witness these theatrics to start my day."

"Hey," Rocco says softly, eyes fixed on me, "this way." He brushes against me as he carries both cups and both oversized muffins to a small table in the back corner of the shop.

We settle in, neither of us speaking for a few minutes as we sip from our cups and start on our muffins. Rocco eats his muffin the same way he did when we met; it's one of the first things we talked about, actually—our "meet cute." Or at least what had felt like one at the time. I'd caught him at the craft services table—because it all came back to that table, apparently, at least for me—eating a blueberry muffin, devouring the top first with a look of sheer delight, then slowly working on the bottom, more begrudgingly, that rapture gone. Like it was a chore to eat the rest. "You're like a four-year-old at a birthday party, licking the icing off a cupcake," I'd said, without thinking—this was *Rocco*, and I was criticizing his muffin-eating preferences like I was somebody worth having an opinion about anything he did. I couldn't stop myself, though. "You do realize the top and bottom are made from the same ingredients?" He'd looked at me then, really looked at me, for the first time since we'd all been on set together—a few weeks at that point, long after I'd been handpicked from that table and plopped on camera instead. And then he'd laughed, so heartily he started choking on his muffin bottom. "See?" he shouted after I'd pressed a cup of water into his hands and made him drink. "The bottoms are dangerously dry! But my mom's always been a stickler for not wasting food, so I force myself to persist, choking risk be damned. Thanks, by the way, for saving me."

That was our thing, after that. Small talk around the craft services table. That was the beginning.

He's doing it again now—starting on the muffin top, a blissful expression on his face, eyes closed as he savors a swallow. I remember that expression, too, and not only when it came to eating muffins.

"I guess—" *some things never change*, I stop myself from saying. I almost forgot myself. I shouldn't know anything about the way he eats his muffins. I shouldn't know anything about him at all, outside of this role and whatever intel a casual reader might chance upon in a tabloid. "We should talk about the movie," I finish awkwardly, taking a big bite of my muffin to compensate. The normal way, equal parts bottom and top.

"Right." He nods stiffly, and I can't help but sense an edge of . . . disappointment? As if he were hoping for more than jumping straight into shoptalk. "We're starting the jail scenes in January, and I want to understand your dad as much as possible before then. Everything he was thinking about, locked away like that, everyone in the outside world damning him. How it must have felt, as a creator, to have seen his fiction twisted so grotesquely. His latest story coming to life in the most horrendous way possible." He shakes his head, glancing down at his coffee cup. "Sorry," he says. "Maybe that was too direct. I can't imagine how bizarre it must feel, dissecting something so private with a virtual stranger."

"No point in trying to pretty it up," I say, hoping he doesn't hear the tremor in my voice. He's looking at me again, those eyes no doubt seeing too much. "I can't tell you exactly how he felt, because I had . . . *removed* myself from him at that point, as we've discussed. But I did know him better than anyone . . . before. And I brought you a few things of his to potentially help inform and inspire." I reach down to where I'd dropped my backpack on the floor, grateful to have something tangible to focus on. "I visited my mom for the holiday, and I found a few things in my dad's office." I fan it all out on the table—the folder of photos and typed pages and scribbled Post-it notes. It had felt like something, back there in that office, inhaling old air in a space that had once been wholly his. But now it looks like exactly what it is: a sad, quiet echo of a once-brilliant human. "It's not a lot," I say with a shrug. "But maybe it's better than nothing, and—"

"You saw your mom?" he interrupts, like that's the only part he heard. Brow once again deeply furrowed.

"Yeah?"

"Oh. Huh."

"Why is that so baffling?"

"It's not. It's just . . . things don't end well between the two of you in the script. So I . . ." He's flushed now, clearly floundering for words, and I continue to stare at him straight on. Refusing to assist. "I guess I just assumed things still weren't rosy. Which of course is none of my business, and I know this was all years ago, so . . . yeah. I'm happy for you both if you found a way back to one another."

"You're right." I take an angry swig of coffee.

"I am?" he asks, looking utterly baffled.

"Yes." I take another sip, making him wait. "It's absolutely none of your business, my relationship with my mother. The story you need to know about her begins and ends with that script. Our life beyond that is off limits."

"Of course. Totally understood, and I'm sorry if I overstepped. I just . . ."

"You what?"

He takes a deep breath before starting. "This probably won't sound right. I haven't thought it through, and I'm not good off the cuff. But I just . . . care? It might be a film, I understand that, and I realize there's a separation between my character and actual reality, but I care about this role, deeply. And because of that, I care about your dad, and everything that happened to him. I can't not and still do him any justice. That's not my style, not when I'm taking on a role—at least not for a role that matters. This one, it matters. I care about him, so I care about you, too. Like I've said, it sometimes feels like . . . I know you? It sounds strange, I know—but I can't shake that feeling. And what happened back then, it couldn't have been easy for you to walk away. I respect that. For what it's worth, I might have made the same choice."

"It's not worth anything," I say, anger coursing white-hot through every inch of me. Anger and disbelief and something far more painful that I'm nowhere near ready to address. "Because it didn't happen to you, did it? From what I've seen of your life, it looks like a pretty damn perfect joyride. So don't think for a second you understand me, just because you're pretending to be my dad. That's all it is—pretend."

"My life isn't perfect, for one. And I'm not saying—"

"We're done here." I push my chair back, knocking it against the wall behind me with a loud bang. I don't have to look to feel the sear of the barista's drama-thirsty gaze. "You can keep these scraps of my dad for now, but that's all you're getting. You'll have to make the best of what you have. I'm done being some kind of sick muse for you."

"Beatrix, please. It's not like that."

"Oh, I think it's *exactly* like that. See you tomorrow at Lanie's party. Can't wait," I say, as dryly as possible, wishing I could catch a terrible cold tonight and have no choice but to miss out. I'd even take the flu over making merry with Rocco. I pick up my backpack and turn with a huff to leave, take a step forward—retreat back to snatch my coffee and muffin from the table, Rocco can't ruin those for me, too, goddammit—and start again for the door.

It feels like I know you. His words loop as I let the door slam shut behind me.

Because you did, I want to scream. *And I meant too little for you to remember even a moment of it.*

He doesn't deserve to know anything about me now—not a word beyond what I chose to write in that script.

This time I notice the stupidly expensive looking red Maserati sitting next to Delilah in the lot—the most Rocco-looking car one could imagine—and it takes every professional ounce of me to not pelt it with the rest of my coffee. That, and the latte is too delicious.

I climb into Delilah, let her lovingly worn seat swallow me up, and I do something I haven't done in more months, maybe years, than I can remember. I cry.

Chapter 4

Rocco

Tuesday, December 27, 2016

Well. That didn't quite go as planned.

Rudy and Lucy would surely be underwhelmed.

Other than an odd assortment of William's things that I can't unpack without Beatrix to add context—old photos, and some scraps of paper covered in a nearly illegible scrawl—I'm left alone with a café crew of rubberneckers trying to decipher what I'd just done to that poor woman. Reeks of dejected baby-mama territory, I'm sure.

Time to jet. Quickly.

I shuffle her dad's things into the folder. Leave the muffin, take the coffee. I ate most of the top already anyway.

As I'm scurrying away from this little morning mess I've put myself in, the barista rushes over with a coupon card. She's grinning with a rabid level of enthusiasm.

"I added a few extra punches to get you a free cup next time." She waits a half second and then, "Also, I put my number on the back, if you ever want to go out for an evening coffee. Or drinks, dinner. Whatever you'd like. Maybe mornings aren't your thing. Totally respect that."

I grab the card, thank her with a brisk nod, and continue to the door. She won't get a reply from me. Not about that free coffee or the number. My brain's too frazzled for more flirtation, no matter how cute she might be. Even if I did put in a good ten minutes chatting her up when I got there, the most pleasant part of the café experience.

Right now I need to fix this Beatrix . . . problem. How, I have no clue. But there's no choice. Too much on the line, for both of us.

I walk toward the parking lot, grabbing my remote starter from my back pocket. My Maserati is the only thing I own, other than my oversized house with a view, that fully screams "douchey rich celebrity." It's Italian at least, so my second-gen father doesn't bust my balls too much. Just waxes on about how Italian and German cars are engine focused but electrical nightmares. Which I politely tune out because this car's been one of the most reliable things I've got going in my life.

Not today, though. Of course. Because everything about this day feels doomed.

I keep clicking my starter to no avail. It's my favorite feature, because I can just get in and go in a very chilly sixty-degree cabin. A godsend in LA, especially in the summer months. I might've lived in this city for half my life, but I still have my East Coast ketchup blood. You can take the boy out of Jersey, etc.

As I reach the car, still frantically jabbing at the buttons like I'm expecting a miracle to happen, I notice Beatrix parked next to me. Staring out the front window of her silver Jetta. It looks like she's . . . crying?

Shit. Tears—they instantly put me on edge. Especially when it comes to Beatrix, who doesn't strike me as the crying type.

I panic, turn back to my car—which I can immediately tell is dead from the ominous emptiness of that overpriced screen. No clock, no outside temperature, no compass. Must be the battery.

Maybe this is a sign.

Beatrix is still here. I can suck it up and ask her for a ride, try to work it out on her turf. Listen more. Talk less.

Yep, this feels like a solid plan . . . or at least the only one I can think of off the top of my head.

"Damnit!" I yell, slipping into acting mode to heighten the stakes. "Why?! You're a six-figure ride! Only a year old and the battery drains?" I smack the top of the car in a show of outraged disbelief. Loud enough to pull Beatrix from her trance. Our eyes lock, and she looks more mortified than I could've anticipated, swiping a hand across her cheeks to remove any evidence. I edge in closer, motioning for her to lower the window. Beatrix goes directly to a giant eye roll, not missing a beat. That barbed wire guard of hers slamming straight back down. What was just seconds ago a deeply vulnerable moment alone in her car has morphed into a hostile enemy takeover.

I'm the enemy here, if there was ever any doubt.

She rolls the window down, stopping after a few inches. Wide enough to hear me but narrow enough that if I was thinking about putting a limb through the opening—which I certainly am not—I'd be thwarted.

"Wow, what a place to be in, huh? You and your fancy car, stranded at a hole-in-the-wall coffee shop that's clearly already called the paparazzi to report your blowout." She snickers, probably because her comment just made my left eye twitch with a surge of panic. Brutal.

"I'm sure that didn't happen," I lie. It very well could have. "The barista gave me a free coffee *and* her digits. She actually enjoyed my company this morning, unlike certain others." Shoot. I did it again. The low road. Picking fights and pushing back, even if warranted, won't help my case. "Look, you were right," I say, changing course. "I have no business asking for favors or shortcuts to play your dad. Your script, your words— excellent words, I should say, and not just because I'm trying to suck up—should be enough. I'm sorry. Genuinely. And you're also right now—I don't want to stay here for hours waiting on triple A while the people inside would gladly treat me like a zoo animal."

"Wait, hold up. You mean even fancy A-listers call triple A? Not just us plebeians?"

Beatrix sure knows how to serve up pointed faces that capture exactly what she's feeling, or at least what she's choosing to express. This one is the most bitingly sarcastic sad face I've maybe ever witnessed, on or off set. She might as well be doing the tiny violin gesture. It's hard and heavy and holy shit, does it full on get me.

God, it's impossible to not be fascinated by this woman.

"I guess I'm not as fancy as you might think."

"Hm." She shakes her head. "Not possible. I'm sure you have an army of drivers and assistants at your beck and call. But if I rescue you now, will you promise to leave me alone about my dad? Let me process your portrayal of him on my own terms and not incessantly demand my approval? Because it's fucking exhausting, you know."

"Me?"

She waves a hand aimlessly in the air. "Yes, *you.* All of it. Making this movie is my dream, but that doesn't mean it's not also a nightmare. Some days, at least."

I lean in closer to the window, and she rolls it up even more—there's maybe an inch of air space now.

"Yes, Beatrix. I agree to everything. Now, please, I just want to get out of here. See those nosy Nellies in there?" I nod back toward the front window where there's a small crowd of onlookers: the barista, that grouchy regular, a handful of new customers who have wandered in. "They're way too invested in this. I bet they're taking videos of this very moment, wondering if I'm about to carjack your sweet old VW." I tuck the folder under my arm and press my hands together in prayer, giving my best desperate puppy eyes.

The lock clicks. Victory.

I head over to the passenger side and climb in, sliding the folder carefully into the door's side pocket. Take a deep breath as I settle in. The heady smell of . . . crayon . . . fills my nose. I sniff a few more times to be sure. Yep, it's like I'm sitting in a massive Crayola box.

"That's Delilah's perfume," Beatrix says before I have a chance to ask. "Smelled like fresh crayons since day one. Will your olfactory holes be okay?" She side-eyes me as she turns the car on.

This may have been an epic mistake. I suddenly feel like a child who tumbled into a predator's lair.

"No, no, it's fine. Just . . . unexpected? It's comforting, really. Nostalgic. I loved the smell of crayons as a kid. Rudy and I would always draw in coloring books during auditions to keep us grounded. My mom never wanted us to stress about getting gigs. She always wanted us to"—I air-quote—" 'be kids first and foremost.' "

"I'm thrilled Delilah can bring you back to that special place." More side-eye. Clearly exceptionally uninterested in any behind-the-scenes Riziero brother factoids. "Now, where exactly am I taking you? This is LA—I can't believe I didn't ask before agreeing."

"My house would be great. I'll find someone to give me a ride back later when triple A shows."

I'm not sure what answer she expected, but she looks remarkably displeased. Even by Beatrix standards.

"Look," I say, hands raised in surrender, "no funny stuff. This isn't some trick to take you home to my place." She gives me an even sharper what-the-fuck face. Despite my best efforts—or if not best, at least somewhat decent—this is still going rather poorly. "What I mean," I try again, "is that I just need a ride home from an esteemed writer and colleague. Dogs don't shit where they sleep. At least I never do, not anymore, rest assured. And I—"

"Dear god, make it stop," Beatrix cuts in, slapping a hand

against the wheel to shut me up. "Firstly, that's a terrible analogy. Never use it again. Seriously. Ever. Secondly, we may have our issues, but I'm fairly confident you wouldn't be making a move on me after trying to collect the deepest, darkest, most intimate memories from my mind for the sake of your . . . your *craft*. I suspect even you wouldn't do something so stupid and reckless for the sake of a potential hookup. Which I would of course never allow to happen for a vast multitude of reasons, one of which being that you're playing MY FATHER in a movie about MY LIFE!" She's yelling now, full out, and we haven't even left the parking lot.

In hindsight, it would have been far more pleasant to wait out triple A, zoo animal and all.

I clear my throat, trying to gather something useful from the shambles of my composure, because I'm stuck here now, aren't I? "Duly noted. I'd seen your less-than-positive reaction and thought I needed to clarify my intentions. But I value our working relationship, and I respect that your art and your personal life are separate. I'm sorry for botching this all up. Repeatedly."

Her hardened glare softens, ever so slightly. The furrowed brow smooths. The angsty pout remains, but I seem to have worked her down from the highest ledge.

"Where am I going? Right by the ocean, so . . . must be Malibu. Am I right?" Her lips perk up, more smirk than sunshine, like she knows exactly what a predictable cookie-cutter celebrity I am.

I huff, but I smile back, because I can't seem to stop myself. "Close, but no. The Palisades. Just head west on Sunset, and I'll tell you when to turn."

She nods, cruising forward, and the silence sinks in around us. A few minutes later, when it's shifting into awkward territory, Beatrix flicks on the radio, and some vintage No Doubt starts to play. "Don't Speak," appropriately enough. As the bona fide musician in the family, Rudy used to teach me to listen to the bass lines in their music. He was such a fan of Tony Kanal, he'd buy Adidas tracksuit gear that even my Italian uncles would be proud of, just to jump around on stage like a cool guy slapping his bass. Got me into the tracksuit life, too.

"Did you know," I say, tapping my leg to the beat, "Tony and Gwen were a thing back in the day? I think she wrote this song after their relationship ended. Pretty wild they could overcome a breakup like that to stay in the band. I'm sure their massive success was a good incentive, though."

She ignores me. Or so I assume, after a minute passes. But then: "They weren't famous yet when she wrote this. They stayed in the band because they loved the music, not because they were too scared to ruffle the money feathers."

Cool. I can't win, can I? No topic, no matter how innocuous it may seem, is safe territory with her. Best to be as silent and inconspicuous as possible for the rest of our ride.

As I'm cowering in my seat, I spot a glossy tabloid nestled beneath my left foot. Huh. Wouldn't have pegged Beatrix for the tabloid type. Too lowbrow for her. But it's a pleasant surprise, at least in a moment as desperate at this one. A needed distraction. As I grab it from the floor, I see it's a "Best and Worst of the '90s" edition. Complete with my name listed on the cover, amongst the other "it" boys of the era: Andrew Keegan, Jonathan Taylor Thomas, Devon Sawa, etc.

"So," I say, fanning the magazine, unable to resist breaking my silence rule, "on second thought, you're not going to take a wrong turn and slash me up in the hills are you?"

She's too fixated on driving—and ignoring me, generally speaking—to acknowledge my joke.

"Let's see here, just need to flip around these pages to find me, and . . ."

My jaw drops in shock.

Because there, leading the section about Rocco Riziero,

my dewy youthful face has been penned up and vandalized like some junior high burn book. Complete with devil horns, patched-up eyes, and hoop earrings so large even Cher would be envious.

An unexpected development in this all-around unpredictable day.

"Whoa," I say, because I obviously can't just sweep this one under the rug. "You're a regular Picasso, huh? I look good with hoops, I gotta say. I may have to try it sometime."

Beatrix cuts her gaze my way, finally noticing the magazine in my hands. She starts turning a shade of red I've only ever seen in cartoons—and boy, am I enjoying watching the color change in real time. I wasn't supposed to see her artwork, clearly. And yeah—she *should* be embarrassed. What the hell have I done to deserve something as petty as this?

"Give that to me," she snarls, making a futile attempt to grab the magazine out of my hands, just as I realize what's on the bottom of the page.

My ex—Piper. She's undergone a similar treatment. Doodled on and tagged up. Some witchy devil vibes.

"Wow."

Beatrix swipes again, more assertively this time. She rips the page in question out from beneath my fingertips—one large tear at the seam—and tosses it directly behind her. I watch as it flutters and lands under the rear windshield.

"I wasn't planning to murder you in the hills, although now I'm not so sure!" Her eyes are back on the road, making it difficult to decipher just how serious she might be. I drop the rest of the magazine back on the floor. That stuff is such overpriced, mostly inaccurate drivel. The worst part of being in this industry—people believing my personal life is public. "Not that it's any of your business, but my friend gave the magazine to me as a joke, part of my Christmas gift. Some gift, right? But I had a long flight home, and I was stressing about our impending coffee meetup. The doodling was ... surprisingly cathartic."

"So do you typically like to deface people who are asking for your help? Is it some kind of role reversal thing? A confidence builder, knocking someone who's got more clout than you? I guess that's why I never do anything like that. I'm usually on top."

Oof. *What the fuck, Rocco?* No turning back from that ugly comment now.

But still ... what kind of thirtysomething adult human does something like that?

"You're unbelievable, you know that?!" I thought she'd been yelling before; I was mistaken. "I spent a long time trying to figure out how to work with you without spilling this little secret, but you know what? Fuck it! Since I'm chauffeuring you, and you're a captive audience in my car, I guess the moment of truth has arrived."

I'm thrown for a curve—what could I possibly have to know about this now semi-terrifying woman who defaces my photo in a magazine as a coping mechanism? I sit there silently, gearing up to find out.

"Let's start with some clues, shall we? Remember that Y2K New Year's Eve party you hosted at the Roxy? Or how about the trip you took just a few weeks before? I believe you said it was your most 'tourist-y holiday' in New York City ..."

My heart skips a beat. That was the last time I skated at Rockefeller, which means ...

Holy. Shit.

"Trixie?"

The cutting glare she gives in response tells me I guessed right.

Months too late.

"I can't believe it's you! You look so different." Which sounds ... weak and pathetic. She does look different, as everyone does after a seventeen-year lapse. But when I take in the details now—those dark gray eyes and round, pouted lips, the dusting of light freckles across those sharp cheekbones—it's all so her. So obviously, glaringly her.

Our time together on set. And off. Our holiday . . . fling.

I may be the worst human on the planet.

"Wow." I try to collect myself. "I haven't seen you since—"

She cuts me off. "The Roxy party. Where I discovered you casually making out backstage with Piper Bell. After naively thinking we were, I don't know . . . becoming something real. That I maybe meant something to you." She pauses and I'm scrambling, wondering what in the world I could or should say, when she dives right back in for more. "How could you possibly forget an entire month of dating me? You *flew me* on a private jet to New York to see the Rockefeller tree. We had a romantic date in Little Italy—the only 'real' place on Mulberry, you claimed."

"Da Nico's," I say quietly, my brain twisted up in a deluge of memories with ladies from that particular era of my life.

Trixie, though. I see so much Trixie.

"How fitting," she chuckles, eyes fixed beyond her steering wheel, away from me. "You remember that part. A perfect memory when it comes to fine Italian dining, but you can't even recall the woman who shared your favorite wild boar gnocchi. It was magical, Rocco, that trip to New York. All of it, if I'm being honest. Every minute we had together. The best time in my life, followed directly by the worst."

I'm speechless. Totally, wholly dumfounded.

How? How could I not have connected the dots before now?

It's not that I'd forgotten all about Trixie—I'm not that callous. I just hadn't made the mental leap to Beatrix. Those superficial differences, they tripped me up. She'd traded in her signature '90s look: corduroy pants, Airwalk kicks, a rotation of crop-tops and tight button-ups (I'm vividly recalling a particular one, a gas station attendant shirt a few sizes too small, "Bob" embroidered on the pocket), barrettes clipping back her hair. Black hair, much darker than the brunette she is now. Heavy blue lids and eyeliner that would have made Robert Smith from The Cure applaud. She'd always reminded me of a ska/punk Neve Campbell from *Wild Things*. Part of the draw, of course.

This Beatrix here and now, she's still got traces of that edge, but aged up and classed up. Less overtly angsty. She's always been beautiful, but it looks like she doesn't even have to try these days—doesn't care if she's noticed. Which of course just . . . adds to the appeal.

But it's more than the outward appearance, isn't it?

Trixie, she'd disappeared. Not just from the party. But from LA.

Still . . . the reasons aren't good enough. I should've realized from the first day, our lunch with Lanie. God, what must Beatrix have thought at that lunch?

The guilt returns with such vigor, my stomach turns over. I wish I could pop open the door and roll myself out.

Beatrix turns to me, finally taking her eyes off the road.

"What a joke, right? The way the universe threw us back together now. For this movie that means more to me than anything else in the world. So, you know what? Fuck you, Rocco. You wanted to understand why I've been so cold to you on set? Well, there it is. What do you think? Sufficient rationale?"

I open my mouth, no words coming out, right as a bright light fills the Jetta's cabin. Headlights, maybe.

Screeching.

Boom.

Countless exploding stars, and one giant comedic star wipe. Then nothing.

Chapter 5
Beatrix

Monday, December 27, 1999

It's all darkness first. Thick and dense and all-encompassing.

A faint noise close by, a sharp exhalation, followed by a low rumbling moan.

I gasp loudly, confused and terrified—until I realize my eyes are simply closed. I'm caught in the hazy place between sleeping and waking. I'm not stranded, lost somewhere off the grid in the middle of the night.

Silly Beatrix. Nothing to be alarmed about.

Except . . . my eyelids are impossibly heavy on the first go at lifting them. I pause. Try again. Still futile. On the third push, more frantic now, I manage one slow blink. Two. Three.

The sunlight breaks through in sharp splinters, small fragments of a scene I can't yet piece together.

Clue one: Delilah's steering wheel, my hands—fingernails topped in chipped black paint—white-knuckled at ten and two.

Who paints their fingernails black for Christmas, my mother had asked, bewildered, an hour after my plane had landed. *A surly LA screenwriter with a checkered past*, I'd calmly replied, wishing I'd paid an extra fifty bucks to add a skull-and-crossbones on my thumbs. My mother hadn't responded, just stepped past me into the kitchen to pop some slice-and-bakes into the oven.

Clue two: An unfamiliar forearm braced in front of me like some kind of shield. A forearm that is tan and taut and highly out of place extending from Delilah's passenger seat.

Panic sets in again, stranger danger alarms ringing shrilly in the darkness. I force my eyes open, determined to stay alert this time, when—

"Holy shit, you okay, Trixie?"

That forearm has pulled back, and now there's just a hand, hot and tight as it wraps around my wrist.

It all floods back in then, the dam obliterated with those five words, that forearm that's too muscular for anyone's good:

Rocco, the magazine, those devil horns.

He knows.

If I were anywhere else but inside Delilah, I'd throw up. But I refuse to taint Delilah in that way. She's tainted enough as is, just by the sheer presence of Rocco's offending molecules. I may never eradicate every last one, no matter how viciously I deep clean, every first Saturday of the month. A sacred ritual.

"It's Beatrix," I say through gritted teeth, my lifeforce trickling back in along with the rage. Or thanks to the rage, really. My deep loathing of Rocco Riziero is a preternaturally powerful thing.

"Are we really going to argue about semantics right now? After, you know, *crashing the fucking car?*"

I turn quickly to scan out the windshield, assess Delilah's current state. What *did* happen? I have no clear recollection, I realize with a shock. From what I can see now in front of me, we seem to have come to a stop along Sunset Boulevard—not my finest parallel parking job, but close enough to the curb that the lane of traffic still blurs past my window, albeit with some angry honks along the way. But . . . why did we stop here in the first place? Something had jolted me, hadn't it? Made me swerve to the side, a kneejerk reaction. And then what? I'd had the wherewithal to brake, at least. I crane my neck to peer out the windshield and can't detect any visible damage from here, at least not to the hood.

"That's an impressively large vocabulary word," I say, relief sharpening my snark. Jabbing at Rocco—it's the only thing that makes sense right now.

"What?"

"Semantics," I say, looking over at him for the first time. He seems unscathed by the crash, if it can even be called that, despite the lack of anything visible to crash *into*. His hair perhaps mussed a bit more than before, but in an infuriatingly artful kind of way. And his cheeks are flushed, like he just went on a light jog. Or perhaps had a pleasant encounter in bed. Or no, reflecting back, somewhere outside of the bed, based on his past proclivities: the sleek marble kitchen counter he rarely used for cooking, his narrow glass-walled shower that was definitely not intended for two adult-sized humans (yet still worked perfectly), the flat part of his roof we could climb up onto from his bedroom window, quickly and breathlessly, before any unsuspecting neighbors could catch us in the act. . . .

Damnit, Beatrix.

I shake my head, a mostly fruitless attempt to clear out the traitorous throwback montage. Only Rocco could come out on the other end of a car accident looking sexier for it. "I'm just surprised to hear you use it competently, that's all. Who knew those tutors on set did such a good job? Or was it the New Jersey public education you had for half the school year—the 'Jersey Joe' months as you called it, right?" Shit. Too much past knowledge to drop. I'm proving just how much he mattered. How deeply the memories rooted. "On second thought, I'm not sure semantics does work in this case, Beatrix vs. Trixie . . ."

Rocco kneads both palms roughly into his forehead, like

I've accomplished what the accident could not and inflicted actual physical pain. "Dammit, Trixie—*Beatrix*," he corrects before I can do it for him, "this is not the moment. I realize our past makes our present together more . . . complicated. But can we talk about that later? When we're not stranded on the side of Sunset Boulevard?" He waves his hands frantically at the lanes of traffic beside us, and it's only then I realize exactly where we've stopped.

We're directly in front of the Roxy. The venue for the infamous Y2K New Year's Eve party. Our last night together. I haven't been back since.

Rocco follows my gaze. "Shit."

"The universe has a cruel sense of humor, doesn't she?"

He turns back toward me. Sighs. "I'm really sorry for the reminder. But I meant what I said. This is a bad place to be stranded in this old car, and—"

"Delilah doesn't take well to insults."

"Who the hell is Delilah? That's the second time you mentioned her."

I tap my fingers against the steering wheel pointedly. "My beloved chariot. Who, funnily enough, I bought for myself after we filmed *Cutie Central*. The only good thing to come out of my short-lived stint as an actress." I let out a shrill laugh, more of a cackle, really, and Rocco reels back a few inches. I was already thrown enough—the confrontation with Rocco, the confession, the crash that wasn't really a crash—but the Roxy has sent me hurtling into the stratosphere.

"Ah yes, *Cutie Central*." He has the decency to glance away, rightfully intimidated by my razor-edged gaze. "That was how it all started, isn't it?"

"So nice of you to remember."

"Beatrix, please . . ." He nods again toward the other lanes, throws his hands up in the air. "We can dissect this at length, I promise. I fully acknowledge I owe you an apology. Or more like many assorted apologies. A buffet filled with them. But can we, you know, maybe first acknowledge the pressing situation at hand before we get obliterated by a double-decker tourist wagon looking for the Playboy mansion? If you'd like us to sacrifice ourselves—or me at least, as proper atonement—fine, but let's wait until after the shooting wraps. That way the movie will be even more of a success. Win-win for you, right?"

"Ha," I say, genuinely smiling at him for the first time since, oh, 1999. "That's a genius idea. So noble of you to offer it up. We'd be a critics' darling if you were to perish in the lead-up to release. Fans would go positively wild for the drama of it, too. Watch the movie on loop to numb the terrible heartache."

"You look *way* too delighted at the prospect of my sacrifice. I'm mildly terrified."

I wink at him, slowly, before turning my focus back to Delilah. She's turned off, which I have no memory of doing. Huh. I turn the key, and her engine purrs to life. No warning bells, no strange lights flashing on the dashboard. Everything seems as it should be. One minute we were cruising down Sunset, arguing about that stupid tabloid, lighting a match against the gaping gasoline pit of our past, and then the next . . . ?

"What the hell even happened?" I ask, finally feeling what seems like an appropriate level of shock. A feeling I'd chosen to conveniently ignore in favor of frustrating Rocco as much as possible first. Pushing his buttons kept the panic at bay.

"I don't know?" he says, frowning, deep enough that his dimples show. He's the only person I ever met whose dimples shine equally for smiles and frowns. I frown now, too, so thoroughly nonplussed by the unnecessary attractiveness of his frown. "I was hoping," Rocco continues, "you could fill me in. The last thing I remember is reaching out to you, and then it's all black. Until I woke up and saw you, and I thought . . ." He trails off mid-sentence.

I wait a beat, and when he doesn't offer more, I press, "Thought what?"

His neck—already thick and muscular, on par with the rest of him—swells more as he swallows. "That something terrible happened to you. You were just so still. Too still. And then you opened your eyes and immediately started chastising me and—"

"Ohh, another—"

"Right, yes, another impressive vocabulary word." He groans, his eyes fluttering shut. I count as he inhales for five, exhales for another five, three full sets before he opens his eyes again and continues. "As I was saying, in this case at least, your blunt criticisms came as a welcome relief."

"Mm, yes, I'm most definitely both very alive and very awake," I say, making a show of pinching my left wrist a few times, "as absurdly nightmarish as it may feel to be trapped in Delilah with you, experiencing the same freak blackout. But as far as I can tell, my trusty ol' steed is doing just fine, so I'm prepared to accept the inexplicable blip and move on with our days. Maybe that latte was overcaffeinated. Did something funky to our senses." I shrug, turning away from Rocco to shift the car into drive.

We move smoothly away from the side of the road, nothing catching or crunching under the tires. A look in the rearview mirror confirms there's nothing left in our wake. Hm. I'd been kidding about the lattes, but now I'm less certain. What else could explain why we were both equally affected? Maybe that goggle-eyed barista added in some kind of botched love potion for Rocco, hocus-pocusing it into both of our matching cups just to be certain it made its way into him.

I cruise neatly back into the lane, no issue. Equal parts relieved that Delilah seems fine and bewildered by whatever happened back there before the lights went out. It's not as easy as I'd suggested—accepting the blip and moving along.

"The car at least seems fine," Rocco says. I can feel those cool blue eyes boring into me without turning my gaze from the road. "Which means it's our brains we need to to worry about."

"Ha, I'm not worried," I lie.

"So then you black out behind the wheel all the time? If that's the case, perhaps you should have issued a warning before inviting me into your car."

I snort. Defense mechanisms reactivating. My self-preservation tactic of choice, more necessary now than ever. "As if I actually invited you."

"As if . . ." he mutters. "Why does that feel so familiar coming from you?" He chuckles after a beat, too loudly. I tighten my hands on the wheel, a death vise. Pretend it's a sensitive part of Rocco's anatomy. That annoyingly thick neck of his, or maybe that equally annoyingly thick . . . "Right! Your character from *Cutie Central*. In hindsight, a total *Clueless* rip-off, right? I'm surprised the producers didn't get sued."

"It wasn't a rip off. It was '99. Everyone said it."

"Yeah. Because of *Clueless*."

"I'm so not having this argument with you right now."

"I didn't realize you'd be so defensive over a bit part in a movie called *Cutie Central*."

I turn to serve him a searing glare before focusing back on the road. An irritatingly long red light. "Bit part? That wasn't condescending of you at all."

He groans, again. "I didn't mean it like that. It was still a good role in a movie that was surprisingly decent, considering the name. I just meant—"

"It's fine." I release my right hand from its grip to wave him off. "We weren't all born to be leads. And for the record, I never wanted that life for myself."

He's blissfully quiet for, oh, thirty seconds or so, lulling me into a false sense of security as the light goes green, hoping we can pass the rest of the drive to his Palisades palace in silence, and I can then carry on with the rest of my holiday break as if nothing about this morning ever happened. But no. Instead, "Why did you leave?"

"Leave? What do you mean?"

"I get why you left the party. But why LA? I'd called, you know."

My pulse quickens. "What? When?"

"Sometime after the holiday. You didn't have a cell phone, right?"

This—this I can respond to. This is easy, familiar terrain. "Not all of us had a cell phone in 1999—or a beeper for that matter. My god, you looked ridiculous with that thing hooked on your belt. You wore it *everywhere*. I remember being surprised you didn't find a way to attach it to yourself when we . . . you know."

"Beatrix."

"Yes?"

"I'm trying to say that I did call back then—the old landline at your apartment, that is. A roommate picked up, and while I'm afraid I can't recall the exact words, I believe it was along the lines of, 'fuck off, fuckwad, Trixie left and went back home and you're a motherfucker, go jump off the Hollywood sign.' Pure eloquence."

"Ah, yes. Sounds about right. That group of roommates was a bit feral."

"You didn't bring me around enough for me to know, I suppose."

Too much. This is all too much. I swear I can actually feel my brain overheating. "What did you want to say to me?"

"I guess I'd wanted to . . . break it off properly? I hadn't expected things to play out with Piper when they did, and I was an ass for letting it happen before I could talk to you. I might have dated a lot, but I prided myself on not, er . . . overlapping in my pursuits."

He'd called. To part ways, of course. There was never a world in which we'd have been together if I'd stayed—not in a world where Piper Bell existed. But it feels marginally better to know he hadn't forgotten me altogether.

"So . . . why did you leave? Not because of me, I hope. What else was . . . ?" I glance over and watch in slow motion as the pieces finally click together. The party, Piper, the day my dad died. What he knows of me from real life, what he's gleaned from the script. "Oh, shit. *Shit*, Beatrix. You wrote that you were so consumed with a gig in LA, and yeah, right, you were partying with some dude during the ball drop, but he wasn't anyone important. . . . You're telling me that's why you didn't get to say goodbye? To your dad? Because you—"

"Because I chose you." I spell it out without thinking. The truth that has swallowed me whole these last seventeen years. "You were the *dude*. A more important one than the script may let on."

I chose Rocco.

I chose a stupid fucking party.

And because of that, I never got to have a final conversation with my father before he died on New Year's Day. January 1, 2000. Never got to apologize. To tell him I was horrendously, unforgivably wrong.

"I changed very few details in the script, for the record," I say quietly. "But I wasn't going to publicly out our history. So I refused to give the dude any limelight."

"God, I'm . . . so sorry, Beatrix. For having any role in keeping you away. I didn't know." He looks pained—like he might actually tear up. Which I can't allow, because then I would have to cry, too, and that's unacceptable. He's already seen me cry one time too many today.

I shrug. "You couldn't have."

We both go silent then. I focus on the road, the sea of shiny bumpers ahead of me. We're crawling between the traffic lights— when we're moving at all. More traffic than anticipated during a holiday week, but in this city, traffic is never surprising.

It's not until we hit the second red light, my eyes drifting from the lane in front of me, that I feel the first prickle of unease.

A gigantic billboard for *Girl, Interrupted*, with Winona Ryder's eyeball seeming to stare straight out at me. *In Theaters January 14th.* Pristine condition, not faded and tattered.

Followed in quick succession by Matt Damon and Jude Law mean-mugging for *The Talented Mr. Ripley.* Also fresh and glossy.

From there, it's a sudden flurry of confusing, mismatched images—

Mandy Moore looking like a baby-faced child on a billboard for *So Real.*

A line stretching out behind a phone booth.

A taxi topped in a Delia's ad.

And the people themselves on the sidewalks, dressed in bucket hats and denim on denim—mostly acid-washed—ill-fitting logo tees and undersized miniskirts and clunky platforms. It all feels too uniform. Too . . . unironic.

My heart thrums in my chest, coursing blood hot and fast through my veins, a dizzying rush to the head. Was this the goddamn latte, too? A concussion from the accident? I have questions—oh so many of them. But I can't seem to form basic words.

I see it then, right alongside of us, the most jarring discovery yet. Like a giant yellow-and-red phantom rising up from the sidewalk.

Tower Records.

Doors open, lights on, customers milling around the entrance. Windows plastered in Red Hot Chili Peppers and Destiny's Child, Moby and TLC.

"What the actual fuck is going on here?" Rocco asks first.

I turn, open mouthed, to face him, but he's not looking at the storefront. His eyes are on the rows of cars ahead of us. "I've known something was off and couldn't put my finger on it. But it just hit me—I haven't seen a single car that was built after . . . 2000 or so? I mean, look at that." He points animatedly at the red sporty-looking car just ahead of us, a make and model I don't recognize. Which doesn't say much, because I could pinpoint very few vehicles out of a lineup, aside from Jettas. "Brand new '99 Mustang."

"Rocco." I lift my right hand off the wheel and forcefully take his stubbled chin in my palm, tilting his face toward Tower Records. His skin feels as prickly hot as mine. "Look."

"What's . . . ?" He stiffens under my hand. "This place has been closed for what, a decade now?"

"2006. I loved it here so much." An understatement, really. It had always felt to me like cheap therapy—the best kind of therapy, on the nonexistent budget I had at the time, zero health insurance to my name in my early years here. Strolling through the aisles for hours, losing myself in the racks of nicely priced CDs, scouting out the Ramones, The Clash, The Jam— a nice contrast to all the '90s fluff I pretended not to love but of course secretly did. "This can't be some kind of elaborate set, right? We didn't accidentally stumble into some '90s block-buster shoot?"

"Beatrix," Rocco says, slowly shaking his head, eyes still pinned on Tower Records. "No. This isn't a set. It can't be. For one, we couldn't just stumble into the filming. There would be checkpoints. And two, I passed by here this morning and can assure you that Tower Records was no more."

A volley of horns blares from behind us, and I glance up to realize the light's turned green. I make a split-second decision, veer off to the side of Sunset, again. Slam the brakes.

"What the hell are you doing?" Rocco asks, arms braced against the dashboard.

"I've got to ask someone what's happening."

"You're just going to, what, walk right up to—" Before he can finish his question, I'm out of the car, one foot in front of the other, pounding up onto the sidewalk.

I push my way through the glass doors of Tower Records

to be greeted by that achingly familiar red-and-yellow interior, rows of albums stretching out ahead. All the old sensations flood me at once: the heady scent of fresh plastic meets old cardboard, gritty rock blaring overhead, every kind of person milling around the floor.

Customers jostle against me from behind as I stand frozen in front of the door. A guy with a gravity-defying jet-black mohawk, wearing flame-covered pipe jeans that could only be JNCOs, swears under his breath as he passes by me. Two teen girls in mesh tops and neon swoosh pants look me up and down under their bedazzled blue sparkly eyelids.

"Can I help you?" A too-chipper sounding clerk steps up beside me, squinting behind his thick Rivers Cuomo-style glasses. There's a large pin on his shirt for Bad Religion, a bright red slash over a cross.

"Uh, yes? I hope so at least."

"Okay, what kind of music are you looking for?"

"I'm not. Looking for music, that is."

"Hm." His eyes widen—pupils looking unusually large— then roll for a flicker of a second before he seems to catch himself. "You do realize what kind of store this is?"

"What day is today?" I ask. No frills, no lead up.

"Uh." Another flicker of a roll, longer this time. "December. Twenty-seventh."

That part syncs. "Okay. But . . ." I take a deep breath, willing myself to ask the most absurd question I've ever voiced out loud. "What year?"

He takes a step back, craning his neck as he scans the room around us. "Is this like a bad *Candid Camera* bit? That show with the dude from *Full House*?"

"No. Please. I just . . ." My voice cracks, and I press my lips together. I start to turn away, preparing myself to run as fast as I can out of here, to where—and to *when*—I'm not sure. Any place that's not here, a store that was once such a happy haven, reduced now to some kind of neon-lit nightmare funhouse mirror, where the only other person I can commiserate with, of all the millions of humans on planet Earth, is Rocco Riziero.

The clerk sighs behind me. "Fine. I'll play along."

I pause mid-step, my entire body stiffening.

"But seriously, who could forget the year on the brink of the *millennium*?" He does a poorly executed spin and hand clap that I take to be his attempt at a Backstreet Boys move.

"The millennium," I repeat flatly, spinning back to face him.

"Yep." He points above us now, to a bright sign I didn't see before, advertising a New Year's Eve show at the store. "Enjoy your last few days of 1999, lady."

Chapter 6
Rocco

Monday, December 27, 1999

I sit in the car for a few minutes after Trix . . . *Beatrix* leaves, gaping at all the bizarre and inexplicable shit outside the passenger seat window—the people, signs, stores that don't belong here on Sunset, not anymore—and then stumble out to follow Beatrix's path toward Tower Records. I should have left as soon as she did, but I'm too numb to process any of this at a normal speed.

Why does everything look like we're . . . back in the '90s?

Are we dead? Is this purgatory?

I remember that big flash, then . . . nothing. Clearly, it'd been a car crash, despite the lack of visible evidence. What other options are there? We crashed, and now I'm dreaming or hallucinating or some trippy shit like that. Or are we . . . somehow dreaming and hallucinating together? Is this some kind of shared episode? Surely that's impossible, right?

Though every option feels impossible.

There's nothing possible about this.

I trip on my way up the curb, save myself just in time from face-planting. No one in the crowd outside the store seems to notice my near miss. Which makes me wonder . . . can people even see me here?

Am I a ghost now? An invisible voyeur?

Too many questions to process.

Especially right now, when all that matters is finding Beatrix.

As I try to snap back into reality, or purgatory, or whatever kind of fresh hell this place is—because let's be honest, that's probably where I'm headed when my timecard's up—I push through the doors to see Beatrix staring blankly at some cashier, a guy who looks like his sole life aspiration is to land a gig in a Weezer cover band. If something was already said, I missed it. But the strange tension between them is palpable.

I edge in closer, give Beatrix a light elbow bump. "C'mon, let's get back to Delilah."

She doesn't acknowledge me, but the cashier does a double take. So he *does* see me. One question answered, at least. Only about a thousand more to go.

"Wait. Shitballs." He beams at me in a way that makes my skin crawl. "Are you . . . a Riziero? Like a much older brother? I'm loving the last season of *The Whiz of Riz!* Just catching up on the VHS. Also, between us," he's stage whispering now, loudly and not at all discreetly, "I took a very large ganja butter on sourdough toast, and everything is a bit wonky. Shhh. Our little secret, okay? I didn't believe my roommate because he's usually a lightweight but boy, was this batch strong." He looks at his hand, waves it in front of his infrared scanning gun. Giggles.

Beatrix, meanwhile, has backed away from us both, and is pacing the New Releases aisle, mumbling to herself about where she was and who gave her what album and when.

I feel unequipped to deal with any of this.

High Cashier Boy clears his throat, and I pretend not to notice. He talks anyway. "No offense, dude, about you being the older brother. I didn't even know there was a third Riziero! Or are you an uncle or something? Their pop?" No pause for me to answer, not that I would; he takes a quick gulp of air and steamrolls on. "You manage them or anything? Produce any of their stuff? It's got to give you hella more options for work in this town. Who needs a young, pretty face when you get to pull the strings, am I right?"

This guy has zero filter. I can't imagine the weed food is helping matters, but I get the sense he'd always be grating.

"Ha, well—"

"That's rad," he cuts me off, "keep your identity and get all the money. Smart. And hey, if you ever need a punky looking young guy for anything, I'm also an actor." He preens with this, grows at least an inch. Making him all of, oh, five-five, if he's got on thick soles.

"Of course. I'll be sure to circle back on that."

Never happening. Hopefully, first and foremost, because this Tower Records time vortex deal is for a very limited time only. Much as I loved this place, I loved it when it was actually meant to exist. But also because he called me old, obviously. I bet he's even older than me now, in the real world and time, probably balding, wearing a polo shirt and khakis, selling Encyclopedia Brittanicas.

He leans in, way too damn close, whispering again, "Don't worry, I won't tell anyone about this meeting. Be that elusive Riziero, hell yeah." His breath smells like a heady blend of Mountain Dew and Fun Dip. "And FYI, I like to get psychedelic, too. Seems your friend here is tripping pretty dang hard. You have a good connect? I can always use more."

I shrug my shoulders, like I don't have a clue what he's talking about. As I glance around, plotting my escape, my eyes pass over a sign by the register. A corporate sign about unplugging all registers for Y2K.

Y2K.

My brain compresses and squeezes out an order, the system clearly malfunctioning: *Tonight we gonna party like it's 1999.*

I laugh quietly. It bubbles up, and I can't seem to stop.

High Cashier Boy follows my gaze to the sign. "You're whacked out about this whole '99 business, too?"

I laugh, more loudly now, as I back away.

Because Y2K happened seventeen years ago.

This can't be happening.

I move quickly toward the aisle and grab the now almost catatonic Beatrix by the hand, steering her back out the door.

We return to Delilah—which thankfully hasn't been towed—and as I slide Beatrix into the driver's seat, she seems to instantly snap out of her trance. Huh. This car really is her everything. Her center.

I'm envious of that. I'm fairly certain that even if my Maserati were here with us, I'd still be feeling equally out of my mind right now.

"My dad's folder," she says. "You have it?"

I focus—one thing at a time. Check the side door. Still there, thank god. It might not be much, but I know Beatrix well enough to understand that every tiny bit matters. Even these scraps.

She nods at me, relieved. "Put it in the glove box, will you?"

"Sure." I tug it open and find that it's of course pristine. Relic driver's manual, a few napkins, a pack of plastic silverware. I carefully fit the folder in, making sure not to jam any edges, then snap the door shut. "So . . . why don't we try to get back to my house? We can regroup there." I'm desperate to grab at some sense of normalcy, even if odds seem slim that any regrouping will be possible. I mean, we're either time travelers or we're dead. No safe, easy option.

She looks at me with those steely gray eyes, a deep stare that I can only describe as soul searching—deeply fucking penetrating, really, and in a mildly torturous kind of way. Like she's trying to look straight into my body, stripping back each layer one by one, with no remorse, until she unearths my mostly hollow core.

"Right. Your house. Because you somehow think you'll be able to get to your gaudy rich-boy mansion from 2016 in . . . 19-freaking-99? HA!"

I'm shocked that laugh didn't shatter Delilah's windshield. My eardrums may never recover.

"And here I thought *I* had lost it! Don't you get it, Rocco? One or both of us is obviously dead—or dying at least. Hallucinating in some kind of hellish in-between state. And since I know *I'm* here and present, I must be imagining you. Which makes my brain super vindictive, if this is how it's making me spend my last sentient hours. Or . . . we're both caught up in some absurd time-travel scenario, which I'm pretty sure you don't buy into either, because why would you suggest something so outrageously, outlandishly, utterly stupid?"

I take a deep breath. Wish she would do the same. Don't dare suggest it. "As a matter of fact, I was thinking the same thing. Dead or Dr. Who. I'm trying my best to be rational about the most irrational thing that's ever happened to me. Is Delilah related to the TARDIS?"

"Ha. Very funny. And so rational. Why, may I ask, are you even acting and not off winning the Nobel Prize in physics or something like that?"

Yikes. There's the bully I know and used to . . . well . . . *like*, let's say. Though to be fair, she's not wrong right now. This is a stupid idea. Nonsensical, given the circumstances. But I can't think of anything else to do. And everything about this is nonsensical.

"I don't have any other ideas," I admit. "Might as well see if there's a glitch in the matrix. Let's just . . . take it step by step? At the very least, we know we can drive to the ocean. That hasn't moved in millions of years. Guaranteed it will be there."

My attempt at levity seems lost on her, based on the severe frown she dishes up.

"So, you're saying we drive off into the ocean if all else fails? I suppose if we're dead already, we can't die again. Hm. You know what? I like this contingency plan of yours. Because if I have to serve purgatory time with you, I might as well try to move along into the next phase of my afterlife. Alone, hopefully."

"That is . . . so dark. And also rather mean, don't you think?" I sound like a sulky child, but I can't seem to help it. Not with her.

"Well," she says, shrugging, "it's true." Somehow that earnest shrug makes it even worse. "What did I do to deserve being in this place now? With *you*?" She tosses her hands up, smacking them against Delilah's ceiling. Then, without another word, she puts the car in gear and veers back onto Sunset.

Other than a few direction notes, we ride in silence. No signs of present-day 2016 life, even as I desperately scour the view for any scrap of evidence proving otherwise. No one texting while driving, just some good old-fashioned CD changing. A lateral move, still dangerous and distracting. Damn, I was good at it, though. I used to keep a spindle of CDs in my cup holder to flip through while I was pounding In-N-Out burgers into my mouth—simultaneously checking the mirrors for my next lane change, thumbing through my *Thomas Guide* to get to an audition. Those were the days, weren't they?

And, apparently, they're back. Only I'm an old guy this time around. A supremely confused old guy.

The turn onto my road is quite different from when I left this morning. Unpaved. Overgrown. Beatrix fidgets in her seat at every pop from a rock on Delilah.

"This is terrible for her suspension," she says finally, breaking the silence. "And her paint job."

"Don't worry, your girl seems to take a licking and keep on

ticking . . . you know, like the old Timex commercials? Were they from the '90s?"

No smile, but no frown either. I'll accept that.

When we make it to the end of the road, my "gaudy rich-boy mansion" is nowhere to be found, just as Beatrix suspected. The hill overlooking the Pacific is still there, of course, but an old Airstream and a handful of ramshackle sheds and fenced-in pens are littered across the property. No vehicles in sight.

I climb out and decide to brave a perimeter walk, Beatrix tagging along behind me, just to see if there's anyone here, or if there are any memorable pieces of rock or terrain that could be of use. Maybe I could leave a message for our future selves . . . a thought that's so absurd I can't quite believe it's my own. But just in case we aren't already dead or sharing a timeline in purgatory—another absurd thought, absurd on top of absurd, a tower of it that surely has to give at some point, soon—it feels like I have to at least try *something*.

"I don't have a good feeling, trespassing like this," Beatrix says as we're nearing the edge of the overlook.

There should be a protruding rock I've always called The Surveyor, because I'd sit on it and lose myself whenever I needed a good brain cleanse. One would assume, at least, that a giant rock sticking out of the ground would still be here, if this is an accurate re-creation of '99.

And yep, there it is. My good ol' trusty thinking bench.

Beatrix starts back toward Delilah before I can attempt any reassurances. Not that I really have any. How the hell should I know what might happen? Instead I just watch her walk away, that supremely pissed off, purposeful stomp of hers. I try to roll my memories back to '99, everything I knew about her then. Was she always so goddamn terrifying?

When she's nearly at the car, she turns around to face me. "I'm serious, Rocco!" she yells out, surely alerting anyone who might be on the premises of our existence. But there's no movement in response, no sound. Maybe we really are alone. The Airstream does look rather haggard. "I know we might be dead," she continues at the same volume, "and this is somehow almost two decades in the past, and nothing about any of this makes an iota of sense, so who knows what consequences there might be. But this doesn't feel right. I want to leave."

I *don't* want to leave, but that feeling pales in comparison to not wanting to further piss off Beatrix. She's all I have right now. My only connection to 2016. And to my sanity—at least what's left of it. "Fine!" I shout back. "There's a liquor store down the hill, right across from the beach. Let's reconvene there. Make a plan. Just give me a second." I squat down, grab the pointiest pebble in eyeshot, and get to work scratching *TS*, for The Surveyor, as deep as I can on the bottom edge of my rock. If we're time traveling—impossible, but still, might as well play the game—it'll be a nice Easter egg to know we came through to the other side. And if we *are* dead, well, then add vandalism to my list. Further evidence to send me straight down.

As we're settled back in Delilah, Beatrix seeming temporarily mollified, and pulling down the . . . street is too generous a word . . . the vehicle path, we pass a guy in a beat-up red '57 Chevy pickup. I recognize the ride but can't instantly put my finger on it. The driver—a sun-wrinkled white guy with big shades and a graying ponytail—and we do the slow stare at one another as we drive by, and then it clicks. The pickup, the location. I can't believe I didn't connect the dots straightaway. My brain's working on a steep delay.

"It's my neighbor! Tony Vasco, an old hippie who's been hopping around these hills since the great '60s and '70s Laurel Canyon days. Holy shit, Bea, this is so weird. I mean, even weirder than everything's already been."

Beatrix turns to me, gray eyes as wide as I've seen them. "That's your *neighbor*? From 2016? Alright, I need that drink immediately, please. And also, no one calls me Bea."

I keep rolling on, mind buzzing from this development. "He rubbed elbows with Joni Mitchell, CSN, the Byrds, Tom Petty, just about every other musician who made their way around these parts. He cowrote, produced, did whatever it took to be included in the fun. I totally forgot he'd mentioned owning more of the hill once, before parceling it out. He tells a lot of stories—they can blur a bit. But this is great news, since I know him! Well, I didn't in '99. But he's a sweetheart. We should come back later."

Beatrix looks puzzled, brows pinching together as she navigates through to the end of the path. "Later? What do you mean?"

"He's an old hippie, we could totally crash with him tonight. He's not going to slit our throats or anything, I assure you. He likes to drink and tell stories, so we'll just bring some booze and pretend to be curious fans. Or at least I will. You can leave the acting to me. But this way we'll get some sleep, and hopefully have more clarity when we wake up. If we wake up, anyway. Here or anywhere. Whatever comes next after this day."

Beatrix bites her lip—a full, soft-looking lip, a lip that suddenly looks so familiar I can't believe I didn't recognize her the second I saw her again, that first lunch with Lanie—seemingly pondering my idea. Which is a start, considering she has an intense dislike for most things I say. Understandable, considering our past. And present.

I press further, determined to win this particular battle. "If we try to sleep on the beach or some random parking lot, we'll get picked up by the cops. This way, we can have some protection and privacy while we figure out our next move."

"Fine," she says, not looking at me. "I hope you're right about Tony. I don't want to double die yet."

"Agreed," I say, grinning at her. "For once."

We arrive at the tried-and-true local liquor store that's been around for over forty years. Even with my limited New Jersey public school education, I could confidently do the math to know it'd be open now.

"What's your poison these days?" I ask Beatrix as we climb out of the car.

"I'm partial to bourbon. They had Maker's in '99, right? I drank mostly cheap vodka then. Unless you were paying." She wrinkles her nose as she says this, that stink face of hers that is somehow more endearing than should be possible.

"Pretty sure they had that back in the '90s. Jim Beam for sure. Tony subscribes to bourbon, too. Probably has a more sophisticated palate in 2016, but I think he's an equal-opportunity whiskey guy."

As we head inside, I'm realizing the wad of money stuffed in my wallet is, well, new money. I pull it out discreetly to confirm: a couple crisp hundreds and some fresh twenty-dollar bills. Shoot.

"You have any older bills on you?" I ask quietly as we peruse the whiskey aisle.

"Whoa, these prices are wild, so cheap! What a nice perk to this time-travel shitshow!" She laughs to herself, loudly. Causing the elderly Black woman at the counter to look up from her *Entertainment Weekly*. The woman must want to keep her finger on the pulse of anything at all, seeing as she looks every bit of ninety or above. Beatrix combs through her backpack, coming up with a crumpled old five and two equally dingy singles. Good enough. Hopefully the woman won't be able to read the fine print.

"Okay," I say, pulling us farther down the aisle, "so I have a plan that involves just a tad bit of stealing. I'll ask for some nips of Jack Daniels while you stash a bottle of the good stuff in your bag. I bet this woman can barely see a foot in front of her. We'll pay for the nips and 'borrow' the Maker's."

Beatrix smirks. A pouty pinch of her lips that would admittedly be very attractive in any other situation. With any other two people, that is.

"We're really leaning into the nostalgia now," she says, that smirk twisting up to somehow look even smirkier. And, damnit, even sexier. "It feels very '90s of me to be stealing a bottle of booze. I swiped a few cigars from my dad back in the day. And one time, on a dare, I walked out of an Abercrombie with a set of puka shell bracelets. I got caught, of course. Put on a list so I was never allowed back in again. Good thing I despised that place and their heinous short shorts. No loss."

I'm speechless for a moment. What a badass . . . kind of? "Well," I say, clearing my throat, "harness that feeling, and let's try to not get caught this time. Once you grab the bottle, come right up behind me, and we'll walk out together, okay?"

Beatrix nods and gives my hand a quick little slap, unexpected but far better than most exchanges we've had, at least in 2016. As for 1999, the original time around, I recall touching much more than just hands. . . .

"Okay, let's do it," Beatrix says.

I nod and make my way to the counter, calm-and-cool-guy mode fully on. Definitely not thinking about where Beatrix and I touched back in the day. "Hello there, ma'am, I'd like to get seven nips of Jack Daniels, please."

The old woman, who can apparently hear well enough, as she gets it on the first go, reaches into her fishbowl of alcoholic fun and counts out seven nips. "Seven Jacks, seven dollars," she says tersely, glancing up from the register. Her eyes narrow at me. She's perhaps not as unaware and unassuming as I'd hoped.

Just then, Beatrix waltzes up and loops her arm around mine. Her backpack, now loaded with a bottle, swings into my side. "Thanks for the Jack, sweetie pie. Seven should do us just right for a rowdy evening together."

I must look uncomfortable; the unexpected PDA has me

on edge. *Sweetie pie.* The old woman's eyes narrow further. "Ha-ha, you're funny, *dear*," I say, slapping the money down so we can get the heck out of here. "Thanks so much, and lovely establishment you got here. Best of luck on another forty years."

The woman looks peeved at that remark, or maybe it's just her go-to resting face. "I may be older than dirt, but we've only had this place for twenty-four years. And I'll be lucky to make it to twenty-five." She scoops the bills off the counter, deposits them in the register, and reopens her magazine. A clear end to this transaction.

With that we're out the door and back in Delilah, giddy with the rush of juvenile theft as we head across the street to stare at the waves and drink some nips. Liquid courage for whatever's to come. The Pacific looks angry today, especially fierce. Big waves, bigger riptide. I let it all sink in as we sit in silence: the rhythmic crash of waves, the salt-steeped air. This place feels like the only constant I still have. Other than Beatrix, that is. But I'm still not sure how she factors into this equation.

We linger for a while, not talking much. When the sun lowers and the air starts to cool, I nod to Beatrix, and we start back toward the car.

"You're sure this is the right move?" she asks, glancing over at me with an almost smile. Tipsy, obviously. She would never look at me so pleasantly otherwise. We only had two nips of Jack, but it must have gone right to her head on an empty stomach. Those muffins were a lifetime ago now. Seventeen years, to be precise.

"I'm sure!" I say, at least mostly convinced, in my most confident of voices. "He's super friendly. I'm sure he hosted all sorts of strangers during the old party-time days."

I insist on driving this time, and Beatrix doesn't fight me. We wind back up the car path slowly, little stones plinking and

popping at us. As we arrive at the base of my, well, *Tony's* driveway, we're struck by giant floodlights that force me to slam on
the brakes. A familiar voice yells out, though I can't make out
the words.

I'm relieved—until he steps up alongside my door holding
a shotgun. Perhaps not quite as "chill hippie" as anticipated, at
least not back in the day.

"Who the hell are you and why the hell are you on my
property?" Tony grumbles, just as I'm rolling down my window.

Beatrix doesn't move. Her hands clutch her seat belt, white
knuckled, as if that could do anything to save her.

Not that I'm worried we need saving. At least not from
Tony. From this whirlpool of time? Now that's an altogether
different story.

"I sincerely apologize for the intrusion," I start, forcing a
smile, "but I'm a bit of a music junkie, and I heard about a spot
in these hills where all the great Laurel Canyon bands would
come and hang out." Tony's face softens, his gun arm lowering a few inches. "We were hoping to get a glimpse, that's all.
We didn't know it was private property. Just found the general
vicinity from an AOL chat. I'm . . . Rudy, by the way, and this
is Trixie."

"Well, okay then!" He grins, gun now at his side, seemingly forgotten, thank goodness. "Nice to meet you! I'm Tony.
Didn't I see you coming down my driveway a couple of hours
ago? I remember the VW. Anyway, you hip seekers are in luck!
This hill is where a lot of the magic happened. Musically, that
is, though plenty of other stuff, too."

I laugh, probably a little too hard. I'm not winning any
Academy Awards for this acting job. But still, I know what
strings to pull. "If you have any time for us, we have a bottle of
Maker's to share for some stories?"

Tony's grin spreads wider, a five-mile smile that's deeply

contagious. So earnest and genuine. He loves the good old days, loves telling stories about them even more. The Maker's was just the cherry on top to secure the deal.

"Come on, park up top. Over by my truck."

I glance at Beatrix, who still looks mildly terrified—probably related to any number of horror flicks where this inevitably ends in a gory hack-job. Then I nod at Tony anyway, because we're in it now, one way or another, and roll up my window as I pull over to where he's parked.

This will be fine. It's got to be.

"I'm scared," she says as soon as we park, reaching her hand across the center console to grab mine. Her grip is cool and clammy and excessively tight, but I don't pull away. "I know he's your neighbor and all, but he had a *gun*." Her voice ratchets up louder with each word, that "gun" really ringing out. I have to keep her calm—I don't want Tony to get the same idea about a possible slasher flick materializing on his property. Frankly, even considering that gun, Beatrix is still the most frightening person here. At least in my humble opinion.

"Trust me," I say, squeezing her hand in what I hope is a reassuring way. "I'm sure it's to scare off animals. If there were shallow graves, I'd have found them on my lot by now." She doesn't crack a smile, so I give another squeeze for good measure. "We need to sleep and eat, Bea, if we have any chance of figuring out what the hell is going on with us. And I can guarantee you, he'll ask to feed us. All he does is cook. In his big house . . . that doesn't exist yet. Shit. Well, maybe we'll just eat the Lärabars I've got stashed in my bag. Nope, never mind, left that in my car. And before you can make a wiseass cut at me, no, I'm not a Paleo bot. I just like nuts and dates, thank you." Her lips edge up this time, very nearly a smile, but she immediately clamps it down.

"Fine," she says. She turns to look away from me, off toward the horizon—that sharp edge where land meets water meets sky. "It's been a long time for me, lingering over your infidelity or whatever, so . . . trusting you is still hard. But I guess I have no choice, do I?"

"Bea." I sigh.

"Rocco." She sighs back, louder.

"I recognize I was a little shit, and kissing Piper was wrong, but we hadn't ever defined things, had we? Like I told you, I never liked to mess around on people. Wasn't my thing. But we hadn't talked about what we were doing, you and me. There wasn't a label."

"I wouldn't have kissed someone else. Wouldn't have even considered it. What we had was too real to me. But . . . you're right. You couldn't break something that didn't exist in the first place."

With that she drops my hand and throws open her door, steps out of the car.

I get out, too, and we walk silently over to Tony, who's been leaning against the hood of his truck, waiting. Eying us curiously, but wise enough not to poke at whatever's happening between us.

With a nod, he leads us down to the end of the property, where there's already a bright fire going and, lo and behold, a giant rack of ribs, a trough of roasting vegetables, and a pot of refried beans. Classic Tony. More food than he could ever imagine eating by himself, even if we seem to be his only guests. Beatrix and I settle in on what appears to be old minivan seats that circle the firepit.

"This," Tony starts up, "was the campout spot in the hills for all those cats! Jackson Browne, CSN, Joni, and, of course, the Monkees." You can practically see the memories flooding through Tony's brain as his eyes glaze over; he's gone for the next minute or so, lost in another time. A feeling I know too well.

"I've heard about the epic bonfires up here," I say when his eyes regain their focus. "Mama Cass herself bringing an ice chest for the deli meats she shared with Cros."

Tony nods appreciatively as I hand over the bourbon, taking a long swig straight from the bottle before launching into the story of his life—the long version, no cuts. Beatrix seems to warm up after a couple of swigs herself. Whatever happened between us in the car has thawed, at least temporarily.

The night rolls on with Tony and his stories of the good old days. He serves us food and is unfailingly the kind, cool guy I know him to be. I'm glad I did something right—today, at least. Though I feel a small pang of guilt about lying to him, as he's so trusting himself. Options were limited, though. And damn, these ribs are good. . . .

"And that's when I get a call from a drunk John Lennon," Tony says, beaming over the nearly empty bottle, "asking if he and Nilsson could come over to sober up. When I tell you they were drunk, it's an epic understatement. Speaking of, I'm pretty loaded myself. But this was fun. Thanks for finding me here and for being hip cats. Dig? You can just pass out here, of course. I'll probably be gone by the time you get up. Hunkering down by Big Bear in the woods for that Y2K millennium shit. But you're welcome to camp while I'm gone, whatever you need. Just don't fuck with my shit. Peace!"

And with that, he's disappearing in the darkness off by the Airstream, and we're alone again.

"Rocco," Beatrix says then, quietly.

"Yeah?"

"I'm just . . . so confused. With and without the bourbon. Why are we here? In the past? This specific past? The old days with you? I don't understand." She lays her forehead on my shoulder. I'm momentarily stunned by the contact, especially after the way we'd left things earlier. But I collect myself after a beat, wrap my arm around her shoulders. She's shaking. "My dad . . ."

I tighten my grip.

"He'd still be alive, you know. If this is all exactly as it was. These last days of '99."

Shit. The thought hadn't occurred to me. It should have, of course. What happened between Beatrix and me wasn't the worst of what she'd dealt with that week.

"Do you want to . . ." I start without really thinking it through. Go to him in Arizona? And then what?

"I don't know. It feels like . . . we should be here in LA? What if it's only this place that's connecting us to our real life, our real time? It all feels too fragile. I'm scared to mess things up more than they already are."

I nod. It makes sense, as much as anything can right now. This place, right here. Our city. Our past together. "I wish I had answers for you, Bea. Which, sorry—I know you said no one else calls you that. I'll stop."

"No. It's fine," she says, the words muffled against my shoulder. "My dad used to call me Bea. It's kind of nice. Hearing it again."

"Okay," I say. "So Bea it is." And then, because the bourbon left me without enough filter, "Your hair smells just the way I remember it. Same shampoo? Coconut, is it?"

She lifts her head, stares into my eyes for a long moment. Looks away toward the dwindling flames. "I'm going to sleep in Delilah. Maybe we wake up in the morning in a hospital, hooked up to machines. Maybe we wake up here in the past. I don't know. But either way, I need a break from whatever this is." She shrugs out of my embrace and stands, flashing a peace sign at me—Tony rubbed off on her—before walking off toward the car.

I watch as she settles in, the interior lights flicking on for a moment then off, before turning back to stare out over the blackness of the ocean. My view from 2016, too. One and the same. My eyes are heavy.

Everything is heavy.

One last nightcap, and then I sprawl out on my minivan seat bed, close my eyes. Listen for a while to the lapping waves below, the same sound that lulls me every night.

The peace from that—my one anchor—helps me to finally drift off.

Chapter 7

Beatrix

Tuesday, December 28, 1999

Loud knocks against the window wake me.

It's entirely different from the last time I woke up in the driver's seat—this time is instant, my entire body snapping to life as my eyes open. A dream slips away, some nonsensical dramedy involving my mother, decades younger than she is now, and a traveling circus, a wayward band of handsome magicians.

The dream, strange as it was, feels much more rational than the reality that awaits me now—Rocco, standing just outside the car, peering in at me. He pulls his knuckles away from the window, releases his fingers to give an uncertain wave.

Several mostly unpleasant truths hit me, one after another in rapid succession:

One, sunlight is flooding into my car, so we've made it to a new day.

Two, I'm still here, with Rocco, on this mansion-free hilltop overlooking the Pacific, which means we're still trapped in our '99 nightmare. Death, purgatory, a coma, dot dot dot. I can't reflect more on that dot dot dot without proper caffeination.

Three, my head feels as if it's being spliced down the middle courtesy of a dull axe, and my mouth tastes like a decomposing rodent, either because of the side effects of death/purgatory/a coma/dot dot dot or the, oh, six or seven shots of whiskey I drenched my liver in last night during our cozy little BBQ with Tony. Which leads to—

Four, if I'm able to feel a hangover, especially one this brutal, I'm surely living in my corporal body, not existing in some more metaphorical, metaphysical state. Which would imply this is somehow, impossibly and against the course of all nature as I know it . . . real?

Nope.

Refer back to one—somebody get me a damn coffee first.

And five, the last and most irritating truth: Despite the fact that there's not a drop of rain to be seen on the car windows, Rocco's hair is slicked back and dripping onto yesterday's now very wet shirt, a look that screams "I just took a pleasant, invigorating dip in the Pacific to start my day," which, upon zero seconds of further reflection, seems exactly on par for him. Even in this bizarre hellscape we've found ourselves in, Rocco would absolutely start his day with a refreshing jaunt in the sea. And look like a goddamn *GQ* pinup while doing so.

I throw open the car door with a satisfying thwack to his abs. "Sorry," I say, making no effort to sound convincing.

Rocco winces, rubbing his hand over the twelve-pack that's all too clear under his wet shirt. "I'm sure you are."

"Enjoy your swim?"

"How kind of you to ask." He leans against Delilah's hood, looking far too at ease. With me. With this place, this situation. It must be nice to go through life like that. No self-doubt, no uncertainties. Because there's a Rocco Riziero-shaped hole waiting for him everywhere he may deign to go, on every conceivable (and, apparently, inconceivable) timeline. "Yes and no. I love that frigid morning jolt, always kicks my brain into high gear. Bit of a hike downhill without a car this morning, but I do my best thinking after a swim. I was hoping it would somehow unlock the mysteries of this . . . perplexing situation we've found ourselves in. But no such luck. Maybe you should try it?"

I laugh out loud. "Hell no. You couldn't pay me to jump in that water right now. Only when it's at least ninety degrees outside."

"You forget you're talking to a millionaire. I could pay you a lot of money to make it happen."

"No, not even with your dirty blockbuster heartthrob money. Or should I say, *especially* with that money."

"Whoa. Hold on there, Bea. Did you just call me a heartthrob?" He grins, the brightness of it even more staggeringly offensive to my hangover than the rays of Los Angeles sun beating down into my bloodshot eyes.

"It was an accident. My brain is suffering from acute caffeine withdrawal."

"Ah, you're in luck then. I ran into Tony on his way out this morning, and he hooked me up with some instant coffee and a hot plate. The best-by date on the coffee is '98, so I imagine it won't kill us." He pushes off the hood and reaches up and over me to the roof of the car, his bicep—somehow warm despite the cool morning and much cooler dip—grazing my cheek along the way. When he pulls back, he's holding out a steaming paper cup.

"Expired instant coffee," I say, forcing my gaze away from the offending bicep. "Sounds utterly delightful."

"Better than nothing for that acute withdrawal of yours. We'll get you something more luxurious as soon as we can scrape up some vintage bills. Almond milk might be harder to come by in this decade, though. I hope your bowels can handle some good old-fashioned udder byproduct."

"Please refrain from ever commenting on my bowels again," I say, grabbing the cup from his hands, taking care to avoid any slip of skin contact. I may be proud and stubborn, but not nearly enough of either to resist coffee right now, even when factoring in the cheap grounds and annoying benefactor.

"Bit hypocritical, no? Didn't you want to talk about my morning routine?"

"My body, my rules."

His sigh is so exasperated and long suffering, it sounds physically painful.

I grin.

"Listen." He sighs again as he reaches for a second cup, thankfully with a few more inches of distance between us this time. "I know I've been an ass, I do. Fully cognizant of that fact. But could we perhaps, just for now, be on the same team? A temporary truce. I promise, as soon as we're back to normal, you can absolutely rip me a new one. I deserve your worst. And I imagine you've probably spent ample time these last seventeen years daydreaming about a suitable punishment."

"How predictably egocentric to think I've dreamt about torturing you for nearly two decades. I assure you, I've had no shortage of other asinine men vying for top spot on my shit list. Including an ex-husband who had several *years* to irritate and infuriate me in a myriad of wondrous ways, which makes the weeks you gifted me paltry in comparison. The difference with you—the only one that matters now, anyway—is that none of my other exes have been cast to play, oh you know, my fucking *father* in a movie." I take a large sip of coffee to punctuate that last bit, only to quite possibly singe all the tastebuds off my tongue. "Shit, that's hot!" I spit it out, narrowly missing Rocco's fresh white Sambas. "You should have warned me."

"Er, yes, you're right. Sorry? For not explicitly stating that your steaming coffee was hot." He takes a more delicate sip, closes his eyes for a second like he's somehow savoring instant coffee. Goddamn him. "And for, ah, assuming you spent any time at all thinking about me since Y2K. I suppose your dislike of me just seems so . . . fiery and intense . . . I thought perhaps the memories were something you'd stewed on from time to time. My mistake."

I start to turn away, to go where, I'm not sure. Anyplace that I can drink this scalding hot cup of bitter brown water in peace. Collect my thoughts. Come up with anything that remotely resembles a plan for how to get the hell out of here.

"For what it's worth," Rocco continues, and something about his voice stops me mid-step. "Which I realize is little to nothing with you. But. I am sorry to hear you had an ex-husband who sucked. Genuinely. I didn't know. That's why I've steered clear of the whole marriage thing. Or, if I'm being honest, most romantic entanglements that threatened to make it past a few dates. I knew I'd inevitably be the shitty ex, so why take up a few of their years rather than just a few of their nights?"

I stare at him straight on, collecting myself. "Thank you? And for the record, Damon—my ex—wasn't an awful human, he was just . . . awful for me, it turned out, once the honeymoon blinders came off. But I'm genuinely stunned that your words could somehow be so sincere and yet . . . so gross at the same time. Or maybe I should feel blessed? That I was given more than just a few precious nights with you?"

"Beatrix," he says, sighing, and there's a tiny, regrettable piece of myself that's almost disappointed to not hear my nickname. "I just cannot win with you, can I?"

I take another sip, more conservatively sized this time, and while it still tastes like coffee that burned on the bottom of a Mr. Coffee a few days ago and sat around stagnating ever since, I at least don't scald my esophagus as I swallow. "What can I say? I'm not big on second chances, I guess? I screwed my own up royally when it came to my family, so maybe I hate to hand them out to anyone else." The words tumbled out, brain to lips, too fast for me to sort properly. They were intended as a joke, but now, hearing them out loud in the cool morning air, replaying them over in my mind, they feel uncomfortably true.

Rocco seems to recognize this, too, looking perhaps as uncomfortable as I've ever seen him, suddenly far too interested in something lurking at the bottom of his cup—like he's reading our futures somewhere in the dark water. "I'm not idiotic enough to ask for a second chance, at least when it comes to anything beyond coexisting amiably on set, for the sake of your movie's success. You deserve far more than I'd be able to give you otherwise. I'm just asking if we could . . . ease up on the feud until we figure this mess out. If there's even a way to figure it out at all, that is. But we can't know if we don't try."

I take a few sips as I consider. I'm all too aware of my penchant for stubbornness. And how wildly ineffective it can be when it comes to achieving anything positive. "What does trying look like?"

He shrugs. "Hell if I know. Like I said, my arctic swim failed me this morning, for the first time ever. I figured you'd be the brains of the operation after your delicious cup of joe, and I'd be the muscle if needed."

"Okay," I say.

"Okay?"

"Yes, a truce. And yes, agreed that I'll obviously be the brains." I take the last sip of coffee, feeling only slightly fortified, and rest my empty cup on Delilah's hood.

"Thank you."

"I'll be needing this," I say, grabbing his still mostly full coffee cup from his hands, "and that big rock out on the overlook—the one I saw you ogling yesterday. Let's go do a little thinking. Or I'll think, at least. You can, I don't know, pop some squats or do push-ups next to me while you wait."

If I'm being honest with myself, I know Rocco is genuinely rather bright—I remember being pleasantly surprised the first time around, that there was much more going for him than just his A-list exterior. He was self-deprecating, though, cracking jokes about his Jersey public education and the teachers on set who did more coddling than grading. Telling anyone who would listen that Rudy got the brains and the heart and he, Rocco, was just the sexy Tin Man—or the Scarecrow, depending on the day and the role. He was wrong about that. He had depth and dimension, but he kept it closely guarded, subconsciously or not. It hadn't felt like a "blessing" to spend that time with him—I have more self-worth than that—but it had been nice, feeling like I was handed a golden ticket to a private Rocco showing, one the vast majority of the public would never see.

"I served that insult up on a bejeweled platter, didn't I," Rocco says, rolling his eyes, though he looks more amused than insulted as he follows me to the overlook.

We sit side by side on the rock, carefully arranged so as not to brush knees or elbows. The coffee grows on me, tasting slightly more acceptable with each sip. Caffeine is a beautiful drug. And I can see why, when he could afford to live anywhere in this city—anywhere in the world—Rocco chose this spot. It's like we're the only two people who exist. The rest of the city, the noise and the chaos, the stench of desperate ambition that's bandied about with the palm trees in the breeze, all of it gone. It's just us, Rocco and me, in this place, no matter the year.

My mind wanders, and I think about Dad again. How there's a chance that he's out there somewhere in this impossible new—old?—reality, still taking breaths in a hospital room in Tucson. But going to Arizona feels like the wrong answer. Right for my heart, maybe, but wrong for this twisted puzzle we've found ourselves in. Because why be here, with Rocco, if the way out of this loop isn't in LA—rooted somehow to our past together?

"So today is presumably December twenty-eighth," I say, rolling my empty paper cup around in my hands, "if yesterday was the twenty-seventh, both in 2016 and 1999."

"Unless this is like *Groundhog Day*."

"Shoot. Good point."

Rocco's eyes go wide. "Whoa. Thank you."

"A good leader knows the value of positive reinforcement."

"In that case," he says, a slow grin spreading, "you're about to be doling out a second dose of praise."

"Oh?"

"Yep. I already covered that question when I got the coffee from Tony. You're right—it is the twenty-eighth. I just put the *Groundhog Day* idea out there to recognize the fact that there could still be other options we haven't considered."

"Well done," I say, pretending to grit my teeth.

"This might be my new favorite high. Scoring praise from you. Even lukewarm will do. I won't be picky."

I laugh at that. I can't help myself. "Well, hopefully we make it out of here fast, before you get too addled by the high. I wouldn't want you becoming addicted to me."

"There are worse things," he says with a shrug. "Besides, I'm the toxic one between us. You're more like a pleasant buzz."

"Thank you for the unusual compliment. Moving along, maybe we should try to remember what we were doing that day? Apart or together. I stayed put in LA for Christmas." A pathetically sad day that I mostly don't remember, spent gulping down too much cheap booze with roommates who were too broke to leave for the holiday. I'd had a ticket to fly home, my mom's last-ditch effort, but I'd shoved it down the trash compactor on Christmas Eve. Out of sight, out of mind. Naively thinking I'd have more than a week to pull myself together. More than a week to make things right with Dad. "You spent Christmas in Jersey, but you came back soon after. . . ."

Rocco closes his eyes, nods. "You and I spent that whole week together, didn't we? Besides a few meetings and run-throughs for the New Year's Eve party. I'm pretty sure I came back the day after Christmas to start prepping. And . . . to be with you. Shit." He turns back to face me, blue eyes open wide again. "I remember being excited on the plane ride back. To see you again. Christmas with my family had been weird that year, Rudy being all moody. His first semester was over, and he was missing . . . well, you know. I'd never wanted to get away from him before, but I did then. It was too much. And seeing you again had felt like the bright light at the end of the Riziero family holiday tunnel."

I hesitate for a second, not sure what to do, or not do, with that admission. "I remember feeling the same way," I say, quietly, opting for the simple truth.

Because while I have no clue what will get us out of here—if getting out is even a possibility—it seems like honesty might be the best way to start.

Maybe honesty would have helped us the first time around, too.

Rocco clears his throat. Starts. Stops. Starts again. "We were probably still at my place, at least at this time in the morning. I wasn't much of an early riser those days. Hadn't discovered the joy of freezing my ass off in the ocean to kickstart the day. And, if memory serves, we, uh, spent a lot of time . . . *laying* around. Especially in the morning."

Heat floods me from all directions—every appendage suddenly a lit torch, each one pointed in toward my lower core. Rocco's wrong; he *was* an early riser. Up with the sun and always ready. For me.

I hadn't had sex much before him. A few clumsy encounters with a high school boyfriend, a smattering of casual hookups when I moved to LA. Sex with Rocco was the first time it had lived up to the hype, the first time I didn't have to use my mediocre acting skills when I was ready to be done. My first morning sex, too. Slow and lazy and lingering, like neither of us had anywhere else in the world to be. Sex with Rocco was like the double-scoop chocolate gelato cone I'd shared with him that

December, when he flew me to New York City, outside on the streets as snowflakes dusted it like sprinkles. There was no rush to suck it down fast, no risk of dripping precious gelato onto the sidewalk. It was there for as long as I wanted it to be, while I savored it in tiny licks. The polar opposite of most of the sex I'd encountered in life, before and after—soft-serve ice cream on a blistering LA day, melting in on itself as soon as the cone was put in my hands. The mad frenzy to swallow as much as you could before it was reduced to nothing but a messy splatter on hot cement. Or then, as it had become with Damon, learning it was far easier to just skip the ice cream, avoid the splatter altogether.

"Bea?" Rocco says, and I shake off all thoughts of savoring any *gelato* with Rocco, past or present. I give him a quick sidelong glance. He at least has the decency to look a bit flushed, too.

"Yep. That memory seems accurate. And sleepovers were always at your place. Never mine."

"The feral roommates," he says, laughing. "You had a herd of them, right?"

"Four, sometimes five. We weren't all glamorous child stars. I had a few years' worth of pizza shop tips to get me started here, and most of the movie money went to Delilah. But then I left LA, gave up my spot. I found a new sublet when I got back." I shrug, turning back to the Pacific—a much easier blue to face than the icy blue of his eyes, a blue that seems to somehow cut straight through me. Then and now.

"So, my place. I was living by Runyon Canyon then, right? I'd just moved there."

I nod. I still never drive by that stretch if I can help it.

"Why don't we head over there, scout it out? Wait for . . . them? Us? Hell, you know what I mean. Our '99 selves. To come outside."

"What then?"

"Haven't made it that far. That's where your brains come in. I don't know about you, but I think I need to see us for any of this to start making sense. Actually be confronted with our flesh and blood former selves, walking around these streets, talking and partying and living their damn lives. Exactly like we did the first time around."

"But couldn't they be just part of whatever"—I twirl my hands around vaguely in the ocean breeze—"this is? A dream or purgatory, something my sick, twisted mind invented for its own amusement? A final hurrah before I disappear into the ether."

"*My* mind. I'm here, too."

"How do I really know that?"

"How do I know that *you're* really here, and I'm not just imagining your existence right now? Writing the dialogue subconsciously?"

I turn to face him. "Because I'm telling you I'm here."

"Again, hard for either of us to prove, isn't it?" He smiles at me, like he's somehow enjoying this conversation.

"I'm. Fucking. Here," I say, slowly, like Rocco is a toddler who doesn't yet have a grip on basic vocabulary. "Just believe me and move on."

"Great. Well—I'm here, too. So, we've established that much then. We both are equally convinced we exist, so whatever this is, we're in it together."

"Okay. Just pretending for one second I'm going to follow your logic . . . what does seeing our former selves do to help us get back to the real world?"

"I don't know, Bea." He sighs, in an annoyingly pleasant way, though, like he's now the kindly old teacher to my clueless toddler. "But I do know I've got no other ideas, and we have to start somewhere. Unless we want to just sit on this rock and drink instant coffee all day, have another rager here tonight, sans Tony. How about you? Any ideas?"

I close my eyes, frantically scour through my mental database for any suggestion that might outdo his. Problem solving is usually my strength; it's had to be, for the many varied jobs I've worked, most of which involved thinking on my feet under at least semi-hostile conditions. I prided myself on that. I hadn't gone to college, didn't have a degree, but I'd learned everything I needed through experience, carved out a path on my own terms. It's something Damon had never understood—something he'd never failed to be a complete ass about, reminding me at every opportunity he'd gone to Columbia University and I'd gone to "Hard Knocks U," laughing like that was even marginally original. Fucker.

Right now, though, all that real-world training feels useless. I'm coming up blank. I have nothing. Not a single better suggestion.

"Fine," I grumble under my breath.

"What was that?"

"FINE," I repeat, pushing myself up from the rock to stand. "But I'm in the driver's seat again. And we need disguises if we're going to do this right."

"Tell me again," Rocco says, frowning down at me from his post behind a gigantic palm tree, "why I'm wearing a cowboy hat and this godforsaken Kid Rock wig—which, by the way, I'm fairly certain has already infested every hair on my body with lice."

I sigh, attempting to smooth out my own wig, a curly brown monstrosity that surely was a Sexy Little Bo Peep castaway from a long-ago Halloween. "Because the pickings were slim at the thrift shop you chose—the one that had just replaced your favorite surf shop, so you were, quote, 'cool with dropping futuristic Monopoly money on them and ditching.' And anyone who's ever seen or read any story involving time travel knows the cardinal rule is that past you can't see present you.

No one from '99 who knows you can see forty-year-old Rocco, because—"

"Thirty-seven, how dare you," he says, clutching the ancient fringed leather jacket covering the space in his chest where his heart presumably resides.

"Close enough. Point is, it throws off the whole time-space continuum"—shit, is that the right term? I wish I'd re-watched *Back to the Future* at any point over the last two decades. It sounds relatively impressive at least, so I run with it—"if anyone from the past, yourself included, sees this present version of you, it could unravel the natural order of things as we know it. Screw everything up for our future selves, create drastic changes that would make our 2016 lives unrecognizable."

"Let's hope our visit to Tony was forgettable enough that he won't have flashbacks when I move in next door a decade and a half from now."

"Right, well—hopefully this period of life is . . . hazy for him. He did throw back a lot of that bottle. And besides, he'll have no proof. No photos. I think we're okay."

"Maybe we already saw our future selves in '99, too, and just . . . forgot about it."

"Yep, seems quite forgettable. Seeing your middle-aged clone."

"You're right, I wouldn't be able to forget seeing you. . . ." He grins widely. "Not in that rainbow tie-dye Earth Goddess number you're wearing."

"Piss off, the selection was limited."

"It reminds me of those Lick-A-Color popsicles growing up. They were my favorite."

"Great, thank you. Let's stay focused. It's—" I reach for my phone in my pocket to check the time, only to remember it was dead on arrival yesterday. Rocco's, too. Our iPhones are apparently not compatible with this prehistoric '90s world.

"Eleven-oh-five," Rocco says, looking smug as he taps the

screen of his ungodly complex-looking sporty wristwatch. The only device still standing. "Guess I'm good for something, eh?"

I'm sifting between several cutting reply options when the door to Rocco's old bungalow-style house opens.

"Shh!" I lunge from where I'm standing—far too exposed, directly in their line of sight—to hide behind Rocco, clutching his biceps to brace myself.

We both go rigid, waiting, as the door seems to take forever to swing all the way open, a pair of fresh white Nikes appearing first, then black-and-white–striped Adidas track pants, and . . . *holy shit.*

There he is, Rocco—*my* Rocco—in all his glory, nearly fluorescent with pure radiance, looking like he rules the world in the unique way that only a baby twentysomething can. The perfect embodiment of youth.

I was utterly helpless against it then. A petal twirling aimlessly in his windstorm.

Thank god I've grown the hell up.

Rocco, that Rocco, is looking back toward the open door when he lets out a loud, rolling laugh. Another softer peal of laughter follows.

My laugh. The way I used to laugh, anyway.

And there I am—grabbing onto Rocco's outstretched hand as the bungalow door swings shut behind me. Wearing washed-out high-waisted black jeans and a baggy technicolor sweater, chunky black boots.

He pulls me in closer, swings his arm over my shoulder as we continue to laugh. Harder now, higher pitched, like we're both ravenously feeding off the other's joy. I can't imagine what either of us said to possibly warrant such extreme amusement, but I'm stunned to see it. To see myself back then, floating so perilously high, no way of knowing how soon it would all crash to the ground.

"Wow," Rocco whispers, this Rocco here and now, the one,

I realize, I'm clutching too tightly. I release my grip, though I stay put behind him. Not that our former selves would see us, anyway. They only have eyes for one another. "We look . . . really happy."

"We were," I whisper back. My eyes burn at the edges. I blink hard, willing off any tears. "At least, I thought so."

Neither of us says anything more as young Rocco abruptly stops laughing, whirling young me around in a messy pirouette until our faces are inches apart. She instinctively rises on her tiptoes as Rocco leans his head down, their bodies pressing tightly together, no air left between them.

I watch the two of them—holding one another up, kissing like it's their oxygen, their lifeblood. I wonder how that could be bone-deep truth for one of them and nothing at all to the other. Just a casual, temporary high.

I watch them, swallowed up whole in the memory. Until it suddenly goes dark, and I'm falling away.

Chapter 8

Rocco

Tuesday, December 28, 1999

"Bea? Wake up. You just fainted. Hello? You with me?" I shift on my knees closer to where she dropped, reaching my hand out to gently tap her cheek. When that doesn't elicit any reaction, I turn it up: "If you'd done more of this expert acting sooner in life, I bet you would have gotten more work over the years."

Her eyes flip open, and she promptly gives me a good right hook to the upper arm.

"Very funny. I was never here to be an actor. And I don't think I would have been able to conjure so much feeling in my past life. *Her* life." She glances toward where we—they?—had been so intimately present just a few minutes ago, the space empty now. That kiss—holy shit, that kiss—finally over, the two of them jetting off in my old black Tahoe. "Replaying personal history wasn't a thing for me. Still isn't, I suppose. Only for the movie."

Bea reaches for my hand, and I push myself up to stand, slowly pulling her up with me. Her hands are clammy, cold. She seems truly shaken. Should I be, too? Am I? I don't know.

I don't know what I'm feeling right now. While it was certainly wild to see myself like *that*, I've watched enough old screen reruns in my day that perhaps I'm desensitized?

Except . . . the affection toward each other, wow.

That was tough to watch. Was I like that with every fling? Playing the Rocco Riziero card, knowing all the right words to say, spots to kiss, to elicit that kind of happiness? Because I'd said it all, done it all, so many times before, with so many girls just like her?

How could I have kissed like that and forgotten?

Or . . . not forgotten necessarily, because I *do* remember Trixie, of course. Our time together wasn't a total blip. It just . . . wasn't long enough, serious enough for me to connect the dots from Trixie Teller to Beatrix Noel. At least not without a little nudge in the form of Bea's—justified—rage.

But no. Can't dwell. Not now, at least.

We need to get inside, quickly, because I'm realizing that now is the ideal opportunity to grab some of my secret cash stash, while no one's home. That way we can move around more freely in this world. No more playing at petty theft.

"You remember those ads for the rock that hides keys?" I ask, dropping her hand. Or she pulls it away first. It's hard to say, we're both so eager to detach.

"'The rock to get you unlocked,'" she says, her voice going all high and chipper.

"Yep, the cheesy hook. And it worked. Hooked me good. That rock was always moving around, because I had—still have, really—a penchant for losing my keys. Thank god for keypads in our futuristic Jetsons world." I start toward the front steps, and Bea follows in what I can only describe as the Pink Panther slow walk. Conspicuous would be an understatement. We both squat down to scour through the front bushes, eyes scanning for a rock that looks out of place amongst the thousands of gray pebbles.

"Got it!" Bea whisper-screams, like she's won the lottery while also in a library.

"Nice work, super sleuth! Now let's get in there and commit some more offenses. This time breaking and entering!"

Bea winces at the words, shutting her eyes as she's clearly running through the possible implications of cops finding us here.

Which, admittedly, aren't great. Two amateur criminals . . . from seventeen years in the future, based on our IDs. Genetic clones of two other preexisting people. We'd all be carted off to a government lab. The glossies would have a field day.

There's no real choice, though, is there? If we don't break in now, we'll have to keep stealing for however long we're trapped here. My old place feels like the best bet, the most reward for the least amount of risk.

Decision made, I crack open the door—and am instantly blown back in time to my late '90s life. All the way this time, propelled deep beneath the surface.

It's the little things, it turns out.

The little things that make clear exactly how goddamn real this is.

The coat rack, for example, which is actually just a life-sized cutout of Kevin Smith and Jason Mewes, as Jay and Silent Bob, standing in the hallway. The hallway itself, too, canvassed on one side with Jay and Silent Bob movie posters, including for the "newest" one, *Dogma*, a poster I could only take home after sleeping with the manager of the ten plex. Not my finest moment. But hey, I was from New Jersey, so of course a local filmmaker who made good would be my idol. There's very little I *wouldn't* have done for that poster as my reward. And come to think of it, must have been right before the Trixie era. Not during; I really was mostly monogamous, even with flings. Piper . . . she was the one exception. She was always the exception. For better and certainly for worse.

Regardless, nope—won't mention that poster anecdote to Bea.

She laughs now, stepping closer to my shrine. "I remember this sweet obsession of yours. You were *so* into Kevin Smith. My god, I remember you quoting *Mallrats* from start to finish over the course of one of our dates. Some wildly overpriced French bistro, if I recall correctly. The Kevin Smith and coq au vin pairing stands out."

I squint at the posters in an inquisitive way, as if I'm not so sure. I am sure, though. It was a party trick of mine. Anyone could ask me to recite any scene from the first three movies, and I would oblige. Very happily. A lifetime in the biz, and I'm still waiting on a cameo request. They wouldn't even have to pay me. Hell, I would pay *them*.

I'll have to talk to my manager if we get back.

When.

When we get back.

As we continue down the hall and into the living room, we come upon my extensive video game collection. Complete with all the consoles a pro gamer could ever want. Far too many consoles, in hindsight. It looks like the den of some *Final Fantasy* recluse. Just one of the many ridiculous perks of being an overpaid young actor.

"Right, yes, the video games, too. ALL the video games." Her voice cracks as she tries—and fails—to hold in more laughter. Another perk of being a working actor: You can be a total nerd and get away with it. My setup didn't scare off any of the ladies over the years. Probably would have been better if it had; I could have benefited from a filter.

"You made me play *Resident Evil* once, and I had nightmares for weeks. *Weeks*, Rocco." Bea punches me in the arm. She's been holding on to that one, I suppose. Another item on the long list of crimes I've committed against her.

"Sounds accurate. That was my favorite game for a long

time." I do a slow spin, trying to take it all in. "It's wild, being here. Every little detail is spot-on. I forgot what a college dorm vibe I had going on. And I never even went to college!" I shrug, giving her some kind of goofy grimace. I'm not sure what to do, besides make light of the situation. I don't feel capable of processing on any deeper level.

"I know. Neither did I. We bonded over it." She turns away and starts off down the hall, and I follow her, as if it's her place. "Let's head to your bedroom so I can continue to shame you, Mr. One Pillow Only."

"What the hell?"

"You don't remember? You only had one pillow on your bed, and I had to sleep with my head on a crusty throw pillow from your couch the first time I stayed over. And it was covered in old nacho cheese from one of your Madden parties. Not quite the glam experience a lady would have expected from a night with Rocco the Great."

"First, no one's ever called me that. And second, that's so not true! Maybe the second pillow was in the wash. Because I assure you, I didn't only have . . ."

We enter my old bedroom and, sure enough—one bed pillow and one throw pillow on my bed.

Damn.

"Well," I say, clearing my throat, "at least I still had an ounce of chivalry, because that couch pillow is on my side of the bed. So it was my head cushioned by the crusty cheese."

"Mm, what a gentleman you were. Except this wasn't our first night. You'd think you would have splurged on a new one by now. But I guess you didn't want to give me any rations here. Didn't want it to feel too permanent. How utterly terrifying that would have been for you," she says, deadpan, as she leans over the side of the bed '99 Trixie had been sleeping on.

Before I can make any further pathetic excuses—because she's one-hundred-percent accurate, buying a pillow for her would have *absolutely* felt terrifying—she takes a long whiff of the pillow. Sighs.

"I forgot about this Bath and Body Works scent! White Tea and Ginger, my staple. I doused myself in it multiple times a day." She leans in again, even closer, really savoring the smell. While she gets all heady on that Bath and Body Works nostalgia, I use the time to start rummaging under the bed, searching out my Nike box of cash. The old-school Italian in me had to keep savings under the bed, just in case. I still do it to this day. Passed down from my pop, may he rest in peace, who learned it from his pop back in Calabria.

"Well," I call out from under the bed, snorting some dust— my pre-housekeeper days—"once I find this box we can head to the mall, and you can spend the rest of your time in this dimension smelling like Trixie of the turn of the millennium." I pop my head out to glance up at Bea and am met with another funny face scrunch. A potent mix of distaste and amusement, her signature style, at least when it comes to me. As always, it's unnervingly endearing, I have to say—in my head, never aloud.

I prop myself up on the side of the bed and catch a whiff of that White Tea and Ginger, clean and spicy, and I'm reminded of how much I loved the scent, too. And Trixie. Well, maybe not *love*, per say, but a very genuine like. What we had wasn't nothing, and very few, if any, relationships beyond Piper were ever an actual something for me. And now, the smell of her perfume, this bedroom with its one pillow and freshly crumpled sheets, the real Bea, this flesh-and-blood version from our future, it's bringing back . . . everything. All kinds of memories. Many of them X-rated, given our proximity to the bed. But there were plenty of sweet ones, too. Nice and PG.

We were so young, though. So incapable of grasping the true emotions at stake. There was no long term, only that moment. The kind of reckless abandon we lose—hopefully—as we begin to understand that there are some basic rules to life and love.

Or maybe I was the only one who was incapable, reckless.

Though I hadn't been either of those things when it came to Piper. But she was *Piper Bell*. I'd loved her since the first day we met.

She just happened to love my brother first.

"Hello? Rocco?" Bea says, cutting through the buzz of static in my mind. At some point I must have moved from the floor to the bed, where I'm sitting now. "Are you going to just lounge there contemplating the myriad naughty things you did in this room with the countless number of women who also secretly judged your Jay and Silent Bob décor and your lack of bedware? Or could you perhaps snap out of it long enough to find that honeypot so we can move along? I don't want to overstay our welcome. Knowing how things were between us back then, I'm sure we'll be back to your bedroom soon enough."

"Er, yes, sorry." I cough, let go of the throw pillow that somehow ended up squeezed against my chest. "Though for the record, I'm not just contemplating previous conquests, more life in general. Like, if I'd only held onto my collection of Air Jordans, I would have been able to buy five Delilahs."

"Don't you dare talk about her that way! There is, and will always be, only one Delilah. Get that straight." She glares at me and then points her finger to my closet, its door half open.

There are at least fifteen Nike boxes stacked haphazardly on the top shelf.

"Ahh, right. I'd moved it from below the bed to the closet. I thought I was very smart at the time, hiding a shoebox full of money in between shoeboxes full of actual sneakers. Genius, really." I stand up and walk to the closet, run my fingers down the labeled boxes until I get to the "Last Shot" box.

It had been purposeful, picking that box. This money was my emergency stash, a last shot if everything went to shit. It was still early days then, careerwise; the phase where it could all go away overnight. Fame was fickle. Hell, it still is. I've just stashed enough away at this point to get me through a hundred emergencies. Maybe a thousand.

I pull the box out and, not surprisingly, there's a decent load of cash. Time-appropriate money, not our Monopoly bills of the future. I remember buying a few used four-wheelers with this stash in the early aughts, so hopefully it won't mess up the space-time continuum too much. I left them out in the Mojave Desert after a boys' trip not long after I bought them, but . . . that's a different story. Not my best use of "emergency" cash.

This, however, is. For now, I take ten crisp hundreds, put the box back on the stack, and fan the bills out. Wave them across Bea's face.

"Excuse me!" She goes to slap my hand away, but her fingers land on my wrist. Warm and soft. They stay there, pressing lightly into me. "Who knows where those dirty old bills have been?"

"Sorry, just got excited." I lower the money, and her hand lifts from my wrist. I reach out for it before it drops, press the bills against her palm.

"Hold on to this for safekeeping. I'm going to grab a bag and toss some old clothes in—only clothes I don't remember wearing much, ones the other me hopefully won't miss. Luckily I always had a lot of unworn swag."

She nods and pulls her hand away, and I turn to my task. As I'm sorting through the options, picking out a few shirts and some pants I don't recognize, I come across a doodled-over note on my nightstand:

Your ticket for Notting Hill . . . our own private viewing party. I promise you'll love it, superstar! xoxo TT

Dated for January 3, 2000, at my address.
But of course . . . we never made it that far, did we?
I still have never seen the movie, funnily enough.

I reread the note a few times, take in the heart swirls around her letters, then slip it into my pocket. I don't know why. A memento, maybe. Something to take with me.

If Bea notices, she doesn't ask. She's too busy rustling around in my collection of VHS tapes, most notably recordings of my favorite TGIF shows, making occasional jabs at me as she goes.

I take my time leaving my old room, even after Bea goes to monitor the front windows, watching for us. Them.

It's hard to describe, but being able to actually see and smell and feel your past . . . it does something wild to you. Like your brain, your body, your heart, automatically want to revert back to that place. That time. Those feelings. It's in total conflict with any more solid rationale. The need to get home. To go back to normal. That's what needs to matter. Because that's what's *real*—not this. And because my life now is much better. Isn't it? More maturity. More fame. A hell of a lot more money.

More happiness, though?

Focus, Rocco.

Bea isn't wrong—we should get out of here fast, because meeting our old selves would be bad no matter how you shake it. Swiping an old note is one thing. But if we are indeed time traveling, then there must be ripple effects, and who the hell knows what will happen if we come face-to-face with ourselves? I don't want to learn the hard way.

Bag of supplies secured, I head out. Leave the bedroom door open, everything reasonably close to how we found it. I hope.

We shut and lock the front door, and as I go to put the rock key box back in its place, a delivery man approaches the porch. Tall, light brown skin, dark locs tucked under his blue cap. He looks familiar. Too familiar.

"Rocco! What's happening, my man? Looks like you got a whole new stack of games coming in! Any old ones you'd want to share?"

Damn. I totally forgot about this guy. I'd let him borrow

games sometimes after I was finished. Super nice, a solid gamer. He'd sometimes come in and play NCAA Football with me if he was hitting my house at the end of his day.

But seeing him now, here, am I screwing with the space-time continuum?

I glance over at Bea, who looks nervous—supremely so, like she's been caught red-handed stealing much more than puka shells from the mall. There's not a worse poker player around, guaranteed.

I rearrange my face, hopefully a smoother mask than hers. "Hey dude, thanks for thinking I'm the great Rocco Rizicro, but alas, I'm just a lowly relative. His cousin, uh, Vinny. Rocco's out of town for the holidays, so I've been watching his place." I take the package from him, drop it in front of the door. Delivery guy looks at me a little funny, nodding his head slowly. Matt? Max? Martin? He's noticing the wrinkles, presumably.

"Gotcha. Aren't you going to bring those in, though?" He points to the package. "Don't want your cousin's games getting nabbed."

"Yeah, I'm just . . ." I tilt my head toward Bea, flash a devilish little smile, like the two of us have some . . . business to attend to first. "Seeing my lady off."

He grins and flashes a thumbs up, then turns to walk merrily back down the path.

Dammit. An unplanned interaction with someone I knew. Someone I spoke to countless times. I hope to god he never mentions good ol' Vinny to Rocco, because who knows what consequences that could have.

Should I look in the mirror? Has my face changed? More wrinkles, a scar I don't recognize, because of this impromptu rip in the continuum? Did we create a ripple significant enough to re-write time and space for us?

For now, it's easier not to know.

We get back in Delilah. Drive away. Richer in cash, richer still in anxieties.

Because the risks of this impossible place . . . they've never felt so real.

And so absolutely terrifying.

Chapter 9

Beatrix

Wednesday, December 29, 1999

"I haven't been this stiff since I took approximately one Cross-Fit class last year. Paid for the whole year up front, too. Such a shame." Rocco sighs from where he stands next to Delilah's hood, stretching his arms overhead in a graceful arc, biceps flexing as he bends and works the right shoulder, then the left.

"Well," I say, watching from the other side of the hood, pretending not to be. "I don't think almost-forty-year-olds are designed to sleep in the back seat of a Jetta."

"Ha." He stops mid-stretch, working his calves now, one leg propped up against Delilah's bumper. "And what are you? Maybe a whole year younger, if I recall?"

Surprising that he even remembers that detail. I'm about to quip that it still makes me a good decade older than his usual type these days, but I stop myself. Because I don't know anything about his type, not anymore. I didn't know it back then, either. Aside from the fact that it ultimately wasn't me.

"I feel perfectly fine," I lie as I lean back against the hood, ignoring the swift pang of discomfort that radiates up my back.

It had seemed like the best idea yesterday, at least when

ranked next to runner-up options, taking Tony up on his offer
of camping on his property again. Avoiding potential run-ins
with fans, acquaintances, the legion of Rocco's previous one-
night stands trolling the city streets. We'd had some narrow
misses yesterday after leaving Rocco's house, too many lingering side-eyes on our mall run to Aeropostale—still safer than
executing a break-in at my place, with that herd of roommates
and their frequent party line of guests. Rocco said Aeropostale
was too gauche for his people—which I'm pretty sure isn't true,
his fans and hookups alike were surely gauche—but it was easier to just go along with the plan. I knew we wouldn't run into
our '99 doppelgangers, at least, because I'd quite proudly never
been one for logo tees.

Now, though, I have more logo tees than I would've liked
to acquire in a lifetime, all with varying typographies of *Aeropostale* and *Aero* and, most heinously of all, *Aero Girl*. Some
new flared jeans, too, which I'd made a sacred vow to myself to
never wear again. But . . . when in '99.

We did at least make a quick pit stop at the neighboring Bath
and Body Works afterward. Hell yeah, White Tea and Ginger!
Just as good as I remembered. Then we loaded up on buns from
Cinnabon as we left the mall, because of course.

So yes, no overt run-ins, but a general sense of unease that
made another night of me in Delilah, Rocco sleeping wherever
the heck he wanted on the van seats or the grass or a pile of
rocks, anywhere that wasn't near me, seem appealing.

We hadn't accounted for the rain.

It's perhaps one of the hardest adjustments of all so far, beyond, you know, the constant presence of Rocco in my line
of sight: no working smartphone at my fingertips, none of my
three daily go-to weather apps to give my day direction.

Had I known the sky would open up and unleash gusting
curtains of rain all night, I would have voted for a hotel. A motel. A motor inn, a by-the-hour establishment—wouldn't matter, anything with walls and a roof. Bloodstains on the sheets,

roaches in the shower, fine, all fine. I'd take anywhere else, if it meant having more than a foot of space separating me from Rocco for an entire night. Too close for any comfort. I couldn't sleep, not while I was listening to his soft breaths in and out, watching the familiar puff of his lips, a small smile tugging at them every once in a while. Listening, watching, wondering what he was dreaming about. Who.

Wondering what and who I would dream about if I were to let myself sleep.

It had been tempting, the thought of making him set up camp outside. He'd even offered, to his credit. Said he could find a tree for cover if I preferred some privacy. But even my calloused heart wasn't hard enough for that.

"Well," Rocco says, "I was hoping we could spring for a hotel tonight. My treat, of course. But if you're more comfortable here . . ." He shrugs, looking around the lot. "Maybe we could hit up a Walmart or something for camp supplies. Though . . . did Walmart exist in '99? Huh. Weird, isn't it, how hard it is to remember these things. Like when I traded in my beeper for my first brick phone, or when I moved on up to have the internet at my constant disposal. History is hazy like that."

"Truly, again, you and that beeper—that was the real love affair. I'd never seen anyone so moony-eyed over tech."

"How is it even possible," he asks, turning back to me, "that you somehow manage to grab on to whatever possible dig there is, no matter the topic of conversation?"

"A well-honed stockpile of digs, after nearly two decades of stewing."

Shoot. I'd tried to deny that stewing earlier. Now I sound like I cared way too much, which . . . I did. Obviously.

But Rocco doesn't need to be privy to the great depths of my resentment.

"I know. We're overdue for more apology talks." He takes a few steps closer to me, stopping just in front of the hood. "How about this? We find a place to stay, somewhere discreet, and we take a long, hot shower." His face immediately reddens, a brilliant shade of crimson, like he's perhaps choked on a large bite of the Cinnabon stash we'd saved for this morning's breakfast. "Separate showers, that is. Obviously. You can go first. Then me."

Watching him squirm is an utter delight. So I say nothing. Let him keep babbling.

"I just meant it could help to clear our heads, those showers. That we would be taking fully individually. We could even get two rooms if you'd like."

"I would like that very much, yes. My own room. Not the team shower."

A shower with Rocco.

The thought unleashes a very undesirable—undesirable because of how desirable it was, had been, past tense exclusively—torrent of memories. Rocco's glass-walled shower in the house we'd visited just yesterday, the marble claw-foot tub in our hotel in New York, the mildewed plastic stall in my apartment, the one time he'd stopped by to see me there, that glorious hour we'd had the place all to ourselves, mold be damned.

Slick with hot water and lathered in suds, arms and legs and hips sliding against one another, me on tiptoes, hands bracing the sides of the stall, then me lifted into the air, legs hitched around his back, mouth filling with him, with water, with more of him, all of him . . .

"Bea?"

"Huh? What?" Fuck.

"I was just asking if you had a preference. About where we stay."

"Nope. No. We can stay anywhere."

"Got it."

"As long as there are two rooms, that is." And then, as if that's not clear enough, I hear myself doubling down: "Two showers. Two doors. Two beds. Two TVs."

"Two of everything. Got it. Loud and clear."

He nods at me before turning to give one last lingering glance over his future property, then he heads for the passenger side of the car. Opens the door and slides in.

His face through the window is more unreadable than usual, more closed off. He might be an actor with a neatly curated range of expressions, but I'd always found his true emotions easy to read. It had been one of the things I'd found refreshing about him back when we'd first met. Different from the rest of Hollywood.

And right now, if I didn't know better, I would say he's . . . disappointed?

Though maybe I shouldn't be surprised.

Surely Rocco Riziero isn't used to sleeping in separate beds. He's not used to being unwanted.

Rocco made good on his promise, a budget-friendly inn in Burbank with two rooms, two doors, two showers, etc. He'd never been here, before or after, so as low risk as it could be for someone with such a recognizable face. I would never admit it to him out loud, but he really has aged disturbingly well. He looks like someone who can afford to take care of himself, which . . . he can, a cool million times over. Plenty of rest in his plush Palisades pad; a fridge stocked with an organic, artisanal rainbow; the time and space and money to pursue whatever fitness interest tickles his fancy. Like the single CrossFit visit for a year's membership. Aside from a few regrettably endearing laugh lines and a smattering of grays you need to squint to see, he looks remarkably like the Rocco I knew.

Which isn't ideal when it comes to flitting around LA, even if his star was still on the rise in '99. He was extremely recognizable, at least to anyone under the age of twenty-five. And their parents. Aunts, uncles, grandparents, teachers.

It's his eyes, more than anything, that give him away.

I would personally recognize those eyes anywhere. In any decade.

The solo shower is the longest, steamiest, most rewarding of my life, scrubbing off the last two days, a potent '90s grunge. Though it's unsettling to think I'm also losing more of my 2016 self in the purge—the last traces of soap, dirt, sweat that clung to me in the Before, evidence of another time besides the one we're in now.

It's a surface wash, though. Because even after an hour under the hot stream of water, too many lathers to count, my mind is just as muddled.

I tug on a terry cloth robe and step out onto the small balcony overlooking the second wing. No fancy waterfront hotel, not for us; we don't know how long we'll need to stretch Rocco's funds. I'm immediately drawn into observing a man and presumably his daughter, thirteen or so, on a patio a flight below, one unit to the right. They're in loungers reading but looking up from their respective books every page or so to talk, running commentary on something they've read or the perfect December day, their tally of the best tacos they've eaten on this trip, the new Fiona Apple album that's playing quietly from a small boom box propped on their table, next to some Cheetos and Mountain Dew.

It's not one specific thing they say. It's everything. Or more importantly, it's the way they say it to one another, their comfortable back and forth, a conversational volley that feels so completely, perfectly natural; like they could talk to one another about anything, anywhere, anytime. Like they're family, yes, but much more than that, too. They're friends. Best friends, even.

My dad had been my best friend for as far back as I can remember.

Other friends my age came and went, pleasant and cordial attachments, but loose, undefined; I was never a loner, but before Sylvie in my twenties, I was never the one who had a group or a person I wholly attached to, the type of friends who were inseparable, almost indistinguishable beyond their different names. (Or in some cases, not even that; my graduating class had the Melissas Squared, the Trio of Jennifer, the Tiffany Triad.)

My dad was *the* person for me. My mom was my mom, and I loved her for that. But my dad, he was my dad, and then he was also so much more.

I realized that—*really* realized the weight of it, his place in my life—when I was seven. I'd been at a birthday party for a friend I sat with at lunch sometimes, Stacey, one of the Horse Girls—the ones who mostly spent their free time talking about horses, drawing horses, reading books with horses, collecting toy horses, and perhaps, if they were lucky or well-off enough, actually riding horses on occasion. They were some of the friendliest girls, though, the most unassuming, and they didn't seem to care much one way or another if I loved horses as much as they did, as long as I was content to soak in their horse discourse for thirty minutes while we ate our cafeteria sloppy joes and potato sticks. I'd gone to her party—at a stable, obviously—because it had felt like the nice thing to do, and because I knew even then that my mom worried about why I wasn't on a more consistent birthday circuit, like all of her friends' kids, moms who would complain to her about the laundry list of their kids' social events on any given weekend, the constant running around. I didn't want to ride a horse; heights had never been my thing, and horses' legs were way too long. But I'd sucked it up for a few circles on the only pony at the party, ate a slice of Rainbow Brite cake, played a round of pin the tail on the horse. It was fine enough until gift time, always my least favorite part of any party. Sitting in a circle, watching as the birthday kid would unwrap each present, exclaiming over the best ones, feigning delight over the worst—or not even bothering in some cases, straight-faced and moving to the next. Gift time felt like a test: How well do *you* know the birthday kid? It was a test I rarely seemed to pass. For Stacey I'd picked out—carefully, agonizingly, spending an hour combing the aisles at Toys "R" Us—some neon-pink–striped unicorn I'd loved, who came with a brush and barrettes for her mane, crystal stickers to bedazzle her. Stacey took one look at it and declared for the rest of the partygoers to hear: "I love horses, not unicorns. Unicorns aren't real. And even if they were, horses would still be better."

It was stupid and mean and wow, did it flay me open, and when my dad came to pick me up, I ran straight into his arms and hugged him as hard as I could. And just like that, one good hug, and Stacey didn't matter. I wasn't sad anymore. Because I had him, and he was infinitely cooler than Stacey, writing books that had never once featured a single horse—and never would after that day—and that was enough for me.

He was enough.

He was always, always enough. Until he wasn't. Until he couldn't be. Because I let myself believe he was capable of the worst atrocity possible. I *chose* that.

Why?

Why couldn't I have chosen him?

Why couldn't I have fought the media narrative? Pushed back on the local hearsay, the ugly rumors that tore through our town? My neighbors and my classmates—their voices, they'd been so loud.

But his voice should have been the only one that mattered.

We'd always trusted one another implicitly. Always been honest. Until one day, he lied to me. And I let that one lie have the power to topple a lifetime's worth of truths.

A knock at the door to my room startles me, and I realize I'm crying. My messy tears dripping onto the balcony railing.

"Bea?" Rocco's muffled voice calls from out in the hallway.

I swipe at my tears, unwind the towel from my head as I turn and cross through the room to open the door.

A fresh Rocco stands on the other side, hair wet and uncombed, the edges curling up. He's wearing a black Adidas tracksuit, the jacket unzipped, a Reebok shirt underneath.

"Mixing brands, eh? Can't decide who to endorse?" My voice cracks as I say it, giving me away.

Rocco frowns. "You're crying."

"I'm fine."

"Can I come in?"

I step back, motion him inside. It's only now that I realize I'm still wearing nothing but an ill-fitting hotel robe. I cinch the sash around my waist more tightly, though it doesn't magically make the robe cover more than the tippy top of my thighs. There's also an unfortunate lack of coverage on the top, the lapels refusing to meet in the middle, my cleavage left mostly exposed.

"What's wrong?" he asks, his eyes on mine, direct contact. No wandering gaze.

"Nothing."

"Please. You couldn't even make it through one of your usual jabs without breaking up. I know you're upset."

"It's silly."

"I bet it's not."

"How can you know that?"

He shrugs, dropping down onto the edge of my bed to sit. "You never struck me as the type to cry over silly things. Or even not silly things. Didn't we watch *Titanic* together? We were both embarrassed to have never seen it. I bawled like a baby, and you . . . you just laughed at me for bawling. Like a total monster. The only tears on your cheeks were induced from your hysterical laughter over me crying."

"Hm. That does ring a tiny bell." I'm impressed, to be honest, that he remembers. It was a small moment, all things considered.

"I might have missed some time from then until now, but I get the sense you only cry about the really important stuff."

I'm about to deny it, to argue for the sake of arguing, when I stop myself. I'll give him this win. I don't have the emotional energy supply to play pretend. "You're right."

"Whoa. Unexpected confession."

"Time traveling has worn me down." I perch on the edge of the bed next to him, careful to leave a few inches between us.

He waits, leaving the air empty so I can choose if and when to fill it.

"I was watching a dad and daughter on the balcony below mine. They seemed to be having a jolly good time. Not some forced family vacation, togetherness by proximity. It's like they're so much more than blood, you know?"

He nods, his eyes still never leaving mine.

"That's what I had," I continue, "with my dad. For my whole life." I swallow, take a shallow breath. "Up until . . . the murder. The arrest."

It'd been the shock of the town, even before my dad—consummate local darling, born and raised, who'd put them on the map with his bestselling mysteries—became the prime suspect. The shock of the century, really. The ugliest crime in the town's history.

Our next-door neighbor, a single mother, beloved oncology nurse and Girl Scout leader. *Marjorie.* Stabbed in the basement stacks of the local library with scissors swiped from the help desk. Her twin daughters were at soccer practice when it happened. She'd been dating someone at the time, someone new, no one her friends or family knew by name. But she was by all accounts enamored of him, totally in his thrall, always talking about how smart he was, how accomplished. She had reasons, she'd told them, good ones, for why she couldn't name him. Not yet anyway; she would, when the time was right.

That time never came, though, because Marjorie was gone before she could reveal him or explain those reasons. She was gone, and my dad had been at the library that day, too, as he often was, wandering the aisles aimlessly, hoping for ideas to strike when he'd come against a mental block. My mom and I had been in the next town over, on a mother-daughter date to the movie theater and Ruby Tuesday.

Not an alibi in sight.

I was horrified when I heard Marjorie was gone. I'd known her my whole life, in a vague but pleasant kind of way. Her daughters were a year younger than me, and we'd played outside when we were little, traipsing in and out of one another's backyards. We'd grown up since then, grown apart, but we still smiled at one another in passing at school.

I'd never really seen my dad talking to Marjorie. At least not outside of a casual hello at the bus stop or grocery store or school function. No one had. But that didn't matter—not as the evidence began to mount.

The eyewitnesses were the first to turn everyone's eyes on Dad—library patrons who'd seen him enter the stacks, leave shortly after. Alone, both times. Visibly agitated.

Then the real bombshell landed, courtesy of my dad's long-time editor in New York: leaked early pages of his latest project, a manuscript that included a suspicious amount of shared plot points with Marjorie's case. A single mom next door, paragon of the town, with an unraveling secret dating life. Killed with kitchen shears. Not at the library, but amongst old books in the town historical society offices.

He'd always talked to me about his project ideas, usually before making a single keystroke on his typewriter. But he hadn't told me about this one. And when I'd asked why, he didn't have a satisfying answer. "It came in a flash," he'd said; he'd sent the pages off in a fever-dream rush to appease a deadline.

But that wasn't the question and answer that undid us.

I'd spent days combing through everything I knew, everything I didn't know, until I finally approached him in his office late one night as he stared at a blank page, empty tumbler in hand. And I asked him, straight out: "Did you have any connection to Marjorie?"

He looked at me with sunken, red-rimmed eyes and said no. "Nothing, sweet Bea."

I'd known it was a lie, even before the police revealed their call logs a day later. Felt it in deep in my bones, a sickening ache, that he was keeping something bad from me. And if I was being honest with myself, he had been off recently. Distracted, moodier. I'd chalked it up to that deadline, writer's block, the sky-high sales expectations.

As it turned out, Marjorie had called our house a handful of times in the weeks leading up to her death—all during work and school hours, when only Dad was home. There were returned calls, too. When pressed about it by the police, Dad said she'd been interested in writing advice, picking his brain for how-to tips. But no one else in her life had heard about her new hobby. There were no pages, no files to be found anywhere.

By then the local—and national, global even—opinion was unanimous, even with no DNA found at the scene, nothing linking my dad biologically. It was the '90s; forensics weren't what they are now. Because who else was more likely to kill Marjorie than the eccentric writer next door who spent his whole life dwelling in murders and mysteries? A man who so perfectly fit the bill of her secret lover?

Between the eyewitnesses and the manuscript and those call logs, there was enough evidence for the police to make an arrest.

And so I made my decision, too.

Because he'd lied. *To me.*

And if he could tell one lie, who knew what else he was capable of?

Rocco—he knows all this from the script. But it's clear right now, the way he's looking at me, it's not about research for him. It's about me.

"Most days," I say, because now that I've started, I'm not ready to stop, "I'm okay, or okay enough to fight through it. To not cry because, as you so acutely pointed out, I pride myself on keeping it together."

In a normal world, I'd never unload like this, especially to Rocco. But nothing about this—him and me in a hotel room together, my most treasured bits nearly exposed by my robe, *living in another fucking decade*—is normal. I'm not sure what, if any, rules still apply. Maybe nothing matters anymore; maybe none of it's real.

Or maybe it somehow, inexplicably, is all very real.

And the only way to ever get out, to return to our modern world where Rocco is nothing but a temporary on-set itch, is to be open and honest, to break the pattern and the system in some way. To alter our path, whatever mistakes might have been made.

Rocco nudges me, elbow on elbow. Just for a second, though the warmth of him cuts through the thin robe. "It doesn't have to be a badge of honor, you know. It's okay. To cry. To let those emotions of yours hang loose."

"It's been so long, though."

"I don't think grief works like that. I'm no expert, but I would say there's no built-in stopwatch, ticking down to a time where it all disappears."

I laugh, just as a fresh wave of tears pricks at the corners of my eyes. "I wish it was just grief. Grief feels so simple, at least in comparison. No, this feeling? Pure guilt. I couldn't have saved him from the arrest or the time in jail; I was a teenager, not a defense attorney. But I could've made his life better with my support. They say his cancer might've spread so quickly because of the stress."

My dad had suspected his illness early on—it was the reason he'd started calling Marjorie. Asking for her professional take on symptoms he'd been having. Too afraid to go to the doctor and have it confirmed. And more than that, too afraid to tell me anything was wrong.

So he lied.

The first and only lie he ever told me.

Rocco knows this, too; it's all there, in *Murder in the Books*.

But even still, I can see how hard it's hitting now. How real it's become for him.

I watch as he shakes his head, his eyes looking so deeply sad, a bottomless well of concern. If he were any other actor, I'd think it was for effect. A dazzling display of empathy. But somehow, with Rocco, I feel certain it's genuine.

"Bea," he breathes. "You must realize you weren't the sole cause of that stress. There was the highly public arrest for murder; the time he spent behind bars awaiting trial, before they landed on the real killer. That all must have taken a heavy toll."

"The arrest crushed him, sure, and his time trapped in a cell. The way the whole town turned on him. His publisher. Readers all across the world. But none of that's what really broke him." My heart's racing, and I taste bile at the back of my throat. I pause, take a moment to collect myself. Because I want to continue. Against all odds, I want to tell him.

Rocco's hand edges slowly across the comforter, stopping when his pinky brushes up against mine. I don't move away. Instead, I slip my hand under his palm, twine my fingers through his. He squeezes. I squeeze back.

And then I continue: "I cried at the time. For Marjorie, when I heard the news. My god, I couldn't stop crying, even though I barely knew her. She left a tin of gingerbread cookies on our porch every December, and she liked to wear neon tracksuits to the grocery store; that was pretty much the extent of what I knew. It was just so awful, so sad, to think it could happen like that, to a mom, in our own peaceful little suburban town. But when my father was arrested? Taken away from us? Nothing. He'd been my best friend, and I let the public opinion—and that lie, that one fucking lie—make my decision for me. He wrote me so many letters from jail, even after I moved to LA, tried calling so many times. I never wrote back, never picked up. And then it all happened so fast—the official diagnosis, the new lead, the actual boyfriend tracked down, good old Mr. H. My married eighth-grade lit teacher." I shudder, recalling how he used to be so buddy-buddy with me in class, tossing out A-pluses I didn't deserve, trying to get in my dad's good graces. "I knew things were very bad, stage four, aggressive. He'd put it on the back burner for too long, and medical attention in the jail had been a joke. My mom was barely talking to me by then, but she kept me updated on his condition. The day he was officially cleared, it should have been a celebration— the whole town should have thrown him a weeklong apology parade. But he was too sick. Went straight to the hospital in Tucson, just my mom at his side. I should have been there, too. But I wasn't."

I don't need to remind Rocco where I was instead.

What and who was keeping me so busy at the time.

He opens his mouth, probably preparing for another round of apologies, but I cut him off. "It's on me, Rocco—I chose to stay in LA with you, to go to clubs and parties and have sex in that damn glass-tunnel shower of yours. I picked that because it was easy. Safe. Going home to see my dad, finding the right words to apologize? To say *goodbye*?" I shake my head. "No way was I that brave."

"I'm sorry, Bea," he says softly. A softness that makes my chest ache, the full weight of his empathy pressing against me. "Sorry you had to make those tough choices. I get it, why you did what you did. I've never been great with conflict either. To put it mildly."

We sit there in silence for a little while. Still holding hands.

I'm not sure what else to say, if there's anything left.

My truth might not have set us free—because we're still *here*, the splotch of neon orange comforter between us a reminder that we are squarely in the wrong decade.

But maybe we're closer, at least in some minute, ineffable way.

Or maybe not. Maybe there's nothing to be done. This world, this place, it's it for us. Whyever that is, whatever it may mean.

Rocco speaks again first. "Do you think we're . . . here to change something about our past together? To make sure we—they—do something differently this time around?"

I laugh, leaning into him instead of away, my shoulder pushed up against his.

"What? Was that funny?" He doesn't shift to shake me off. Instead, he doubles down, hitching a leg over so the only thing separating us is our hands, tightly held in the middle.

"No. I was just wondering the same thing. It's maybe the first time we've been on the same page."

"Really?" He furrows his brows, tilting his head so we're looking at one another straight on, just a few inches apart. So few. "I'm not so sure about that. I don't think we're nearly as different as you might like to believe. I know you've enjoyed the mortal enemies fantasy, though, so don't let me intrude on that."

"Mm." Not giving him that win, correct or not. Though maybe there *is* something to that fantasy.

"So what do you think? Are we supposed to unlock some kind of puzzle in the time-space continuum? Rewrite world history? Just ours? Nothing at all? Enjoy our shared fever dream, shared afterlife, whatever this is, break all the laws, drink all the booze, eat cake for dinner, have lots of sex?"

I can feel my cheeks flush, against my will.

He coughs. "I wasn't implying with one another."

"Oh?"

"Not that I'd necessarily be opposed to it either."

My breath hitches. It shouldn't; I would be opposed. Should be. Maybe.

Damn.

"I just wasn't er . . . propositioning you," he says, those cool blue eyes drilling straight into mine. "Especially not right now. We just had a serious breakthrough conversation, and I'm trying to be a respectable human being."

"Okay." I nod, trying frantically to think about anything other than his palm against mine, that sturdy shoulder, those stupidly beautiful eyes, the fact that he *wouldn't be opposed.* "So . . . cake for dinner? That's what you would do if nothing mattered? That's the big dream?"

He grins widely, the smile that won me over so completely back then. So boyish and charming, wild and free. It knocks down all the years between us. Like it really is us, back then; not two doppelgangers from the future, loaded down with more wrinkles, more regrets. "Okay then. You choose. What would you do? A night back in the '90s, no limits, no consequences. Well, within reason, given our situation."

I close my eyes. His face makes it too hard to think. But even still, eyes shut, I feel him there. Feel the heat radiating between our bodies, an annoying tug below my belly button. I open my eyes to find him studying me. "Honestly?" I sigh. "I have no clue."

He nods, drops my hand as he pulls away to stand. The room immediately feels ten degrees cooler. "You get dressed. Put on your Aero Girl best. And then come meet me next door. We'll splurge on the 'complimentary' tiny bottles of vanilla vodka in my room, and then? We're going out."

"Out where?"

"No idea." He smiles, the very good one again. "But one way or another, we're going to have ourselves one epic '90s night."

Chapter 10

Rocco

Wednesday, December 29, 1999

A night out in 1999 LA. So many possibilities.

We need to blow off steam—in a controlled way that won't implode our futures, of course, no big deal. But maybe a night of letting loose will clear our heads by fogging them first. Help us figure out what the hell is going on.

Bea is lying stomach down on my bed, Aero gear on and one vanilla vodka deep, her arms propping up her head like a kid in a commercial. Legs in the air, ankles swinging back and forth. It's cute. Makes me want to flop down next to her. Whisper all my secrets.

The vodka must be getting to me.

And the Bath and Body Works goods. The smell of that place always did feel like a special kind of drug.

"So," I start, taking a step back from whiffing range, "there were a lot of music scenes birthed from Los Angeles, but in 1999, swing was king of the small clubs. Maybe we grab dinner, then drinks at this cool place called the Mint, let some zoot-suited musicians time travel us back to 1940s LA—seems in theme, right? Maybe some Big Bad Voodoo Daddy?"

Bea gives me a bewildered squint. "That's the person living or dead you'd invite to our bizarre '90s-themed dinner party? Eh. I'm more Miles Davis Quintet than Glenn Miller." She pauses for a beat, tugging at a stray orange thread from the comforter, then continues, more softly this time. "My dad was such a Miles fan. If I'd been a boy, that would've been my name." A new Dad fact, unasked for. Major headway. A win that has nothing to do with the movie and my role, and everything to do with Bea. "I'm not so sure about wasting my epic '90s Night Out on Big Bad Crash-Test Voodoo Dummies or whatever."

Or . . . maybe not so much headway then.

Fortunately, another idea strikes: "Let's call a cab and head over to Saddle Up Bar on Sunset. It's a gem I discovered while watching the New York Giants get shellacked in the Super Bowl. Bad memory, awesome place, a real Western rock-and-roll bar. They've got surprisingly decent cowboy munchies, and most importantly, a mechanical bull—provides loads of entertainment, trust me. We start there and evaluate. That is, unless you have any better suggestions." Bea rolls her eyes, but it feels more playful than angsty. Or equal parts both, which is still a win with her. "Besides, my Kid Rock wig will fit right in there, a perfect disguise."

She cracks a small smile, just briefly, before it flatlines. "Oh, I'm familiar with the place. An old roommate was hired there, then got fired her first night for telling off a very drunk man at the bar who just so happened to be the owner. I never went because of it, roommate loyalty and all that. But since you're paying, I have always wanted to be a voyeur there. Watching the high hopes and whiskey courage crash and burn headfirst off that bull." She smiles again, a wider, lingering one this time. She looks awfully gleeful at the prospect of seeing people fail at the bull. Downright giddy.

It's kind of sexy, if I'm being honest. Trixie—I remember her being pretty tough. But Bea? She's made of even tougher stuff, and is a constant surprise. More of a good surprise than I could ever have anticipated.

"Done!" I say. "Ribeye, cocky bullshit bull riders, and maybe a swing nightcap if I get my way. Excellent night!"

"We'll see." Bea's smirking, but it's a more pleasant one than usual. Like a Smirk Lite.

"If nothing else," I say, reaching out to help her stand up from the bed, "the best drink deals we've had in seventeen years. That I can promise you."

This place does not disappoint.

The whole bar centers on the bull pit, a large fenced-in circle carved out into the ground, tables set around it for spectators to have a close-up view of the action. I was only here once—part of why I felt comfortable enough choosing the spot for tonight—and the kitsch was too much, in the best way. Extra heavy on the Western vibes, with a side of '90s grunge.

Tonight, me sipping a can of Red Dog beer while Bea drinks a Zima, we're fully embracing 1999. I don't think we're ready to try the Alize, though the ads are tempting.

A yell cuts through the bar—a loud, drunk cheer to mark someone's fall. I turn to see it, glancing down from our ringside table: SLAP! A man goes face first into the mats, and *2.7 seconds* lights up in red on the scoreboard. Bea and I clap as the man slowly stands on wobbly legs, and then we return to hashing out, yet again, the pressing question of every hour: How the hell are we sitting in 1999 Saddle Up?

"If we were dead," I say, "I think we'd have some signs by now. I mean, '99 LA as our purgatory? There's enough good and bad energy alike that I suspect purgatory wouldn't have. Too much for the in-between, if that makes sense. And shouldn't purgatory be something unique, not actual real life down to every last detail? It just doesn't add up for me. I vote . . . time travel."

Wow. I really just said that. And meant it.

Bea sips her Zima. Sighs. Sips again. "As totally batshit kooky as it feels to admit aloud, yes—I think we're back in time. I . . . agree with you. Besides, if I was dead, why would I be spending eternity with *you*? Let's be real, if I could've had my pick of '90s crushes, I would absolutely be pounding Zimas with Joseph Gordon-Levitt right now."

She laughs so I laugh, too, because it was, admittedly, a pretty good dig. I think—hope—it was a joke.

"Damn, Bea, even for you that jab was freezing cold." I reach out and touch the underside of her wrist, like I'm feeling for that cold spell she just delivered. It's the opposite, though. Warm and soft. I consider trailing my fingers farther up, but she pulls away and goes for my hand, and a good old-fashioned round of swat-and-grab ensues. Our palms continue to brush as we slowly lower our arms back to the table.

"Well, it's settled then." I rest my hand next to hers, not touching, but our pinkies only a hairline away. "We're operating under the pretense that this is officially a time travel inci dent. I'll curb the afterlife talk and go right to Michael J. Fox."

"Of course, yes, bring the time travel talk back to the biggest franchise there is. Seems par for the course with you, Mr. Franchise King. Personally, though, I'd be happy with the Bill and Ted time travel. Carlin and a phone booth? Sign me up."

I laugh. She's right—it would be much cooler to see the space-time continuum flashing by while traveling in a phone booth. All we get is a breakthrough frame jump cut in *Back to the Future*. But we didn't exactly get to choose our mode of the impossible.

"Can we talk about something else now?" she asks, taking the last sip of that Zima. Her right eyebrow does a full inch-worm move. High and tight. "Wasn't the point of tonight to lose ourselves in '99? Let's just . . . enjoy the evening together." She crosses over that fraction of space between us, grabbing for my hand.

"So, you're telling me that going to a Western dive bar and seeing some fine swing music is your time travel wish after all? I nailed it?" I try to raise an eyebrow, too, give a playful wiggle, but the effect is likely more earthworm dying in the sun. I am, unfortunately, not a brow raiser, just a furrower. Unlike Bea, a Brow Queen. Part of her smirk appeal.

Bea raises her free hand, extending her pointer finger to try and push my left brow up. To no avail.

"Congrats. You've now discovered my rather unfortunate Achilles' heel. Do you know how many directors have been bummed that I couldn't produce the eyebrow raise?"

Bea laughs and pulls her hand back, her finger still pointing at me. "No superhero movies for you then! Damn, a whole genre of franchise movies lost. And such a perfect *Celebrity Jeopardy!* fun fact."

"I'll take that as a compliment, since you think I'm special enough to make it onto *Jeopardy!*. The celebrity edition, anyway."

The waiter comes over, and I motion for another round.

The conversation and the newly amped-up flirting—or whatever this is because it's confusing as hell and impossible to neatly label—continues.

Perhaps a second round before food was a bad choice.

Or maybe . . . not so bad. Because to be honest, I like this. Our energy, Bea and me. Like the old times, but also not at all. Something completely new. It's interesting, and I'm not often interested. Very rarely so, in fact.

So, is this the grand reason? Are we back here to be the love story?

Except . . . my life is great as is, right? So why would the universe scoop me up and deposit me *here*, just to fall in love with someone? Why Bea, why now? And have I been saying this all inside my head while she's just sitting there, staring me down?

"Earth to Rocco, where the hell did you go?" She makes an amazing polyphonic spaceship sound with her mouth.

"Whoa. Cool sound effect."

"Thanks. I did voice-over once for an alien video game, a favor for a friend, that was really just *Grand Theft Auto* with aliens. That was the whistle to command their flying saucers. I don't think the game saw the light of day because, well, it sucked, quite frankly."

I try to hold in my snort, not wanting to seem insensitive, but it slips out. Loud and honking. We both laugh. We can't *stop* laughing. Crying, shaking, grabbing at one another to stay upright. Like nothing in the world has ever been funnier than this right here. The drinks, the night, the . . . extenuating bizarre circumstances. Whatever the reason, it just hits. And it feels good. Really damn good.

"I know, I know!" she starts, gasping for air. "I'm meant to work behind the scenes. But I couldn't afford to be picky back then! It's . . . different now. Which is why it's frustrating we were pushed back into each other's orbit just as my life felt so good. So stable. Like everything was finally coming around for me."

Her eyes start watering again, though not for hysterically happy reasons this time. It's a rapid-fire switch. Alcohol is one hell of a drug.

"I had my dream movie fall into place," she continues, "after years of fighting for it. And then *you* became attached, of all the father-aged men in Hollywood. Your presence on set every day chipped away at everything I'd worked so hard to build, to create for myself. Brought me back to this place. Here. Now, quite literally. And it's infuriating."

She pauses, and I'm not sure what I should say, if there are any right words. Because I'd seen us, the way it had been. Carefree. Hopeful. That world-at-your-fingertips kind of feeling, and I messed it up. For what? To screw up both of our families?

Hers permanently, her dad gone; and mine, Rudy and me, for too many years. Because I couldn't help myself, couldn't resist Piper. Chose her over everything and everyone else. Maybe this is my ultimate punishment—the powers that be, making me watch my biggest mistake play out all over again. It's exactly what I deserve, isn't it?

I put my hand out for her, initiating this time. Actions over words to start. But if she notices the gesture, she chooses to ignore it. I pull back, busy myself by spinning the soggy paper coaster under my empty glass.

"Clearly, you picked up on my vibe on set, even if you couldn't understand the why." She nudges her knee against mine. It feels like a peace offering. "I wanted nothing to do with fluffing your ego, didn't want to give you another ounce of my time. But now, having to reflect back . . . we were both acting like dumb kids. How could I blame you? You did what you wanted to do, and I did, too. I wanted to be with you, soaking up the good and happy, so I could distract myself from the avalanche of guilt and grief that came along with facing my dad. You didn't even know about him—didn't know the decisions I was making. I chose to stay with you, Rocco. And you chose to be with Piper. We need to own those choices and move on. Stop letting what happened in '99 the first time around dictate who we want to be now."

Hearing those words, I feel a rush of something like . . . hope. Determination to do better. Be better, for this version of Beatrix—Bea. Lean into this redo the universe is granting us, the fairy tale of it all, at least while we're here.

I drop the coaster and reach for her again.

This time, she reaches back. Holds on tight.

"Look, Bea, I really am sorry. What I did back then—it was a shallow, selfish move. I hurt you. I hurt my brother. Everyone got burned in the end, really. It's difficult to explain why I did it exactly, other than that Piper . . . well, I'd believed she was the one for me for so long, like I was just biding my time for her to realize that, too. So that New Year's Eve party, when Rudy was on another coast, and she gave me a window, alone together backstage . . . I jumped. Headfirst, eyes closed. Was too deep in the dream of it all to properly think through the reality. But that person, the guy who didn't stop for a beat to consider anyone else's feelings—it's not who I am anymore, I promise."

Just then, in the midst of my earnest little soliloquy, we hear yet another cocky patron trying to defy physics. SLAP! It both kills and lightens the mood all at once.

I take a beat to appreciate the drama of the fall and then resume my groveling. "I'm also sorry about pushing for more of a positive reaction to how I've been portraying your dad, especially knowing what I do now. I don't think I could've put myself out there the way you do every day on set. You're so much stronger than me."

Bea smirks. As she does. Though this smirk, her red lips parted slightly as they twist up . . . it's incredibly hot.

"Hell yeah, I'm stronger than you. You might have a freakish"—she glances down pointedly, squinting at my midsection—"twelve pack or whatever ridiculous number it is hiding under that shirt, but I'm deceptively wiry. Let's settle this right now, why don't we?"

I can see where this is going, and I don't like it. Not one bit. I am not getting on that bull.

"Do it," she says, or more accurately, *commands*. "Get on that bull. It's dim enough in this place, and your hat brim is low. I know you've been itching to hop on since we got here. Now's your chance, cowboy."

My stomach hurts, and I haven't even eaten my way through the grease-saturated cowboy menu yet. Sure, I like surfing, but otherwise I'm not big on bodily risk. Plus there's the fact that a whole host of strangers will be staring at me. Strangers from another decade, but strangers, nonetheless.

What did I say before about leaning into the fairy tale? Too rash, perhaps.

"Definitely no itching. You have to be a special kind of stupid to want to do that."

Bea takes a swipe at my shoulder. "Talk all you want, Rocco, but if you really want to apologize like the big, reformed grown-up you are, you'll have to show me. Prove yourself. With a final slap on the mat." She smacks her hands together. Hard.

She means business, clearly.

Dammit. I'm doing this aren't I?

I look at Bea. The bull. Back to Bea.

Yep. I am. "You know, I had to train to be a cowboy a few years ago for a movie . . . so I might not be the easy target you're hoping for." It's both true and not true; I had a body double for the difficult bits, of course.

Bea laughs out loud and yells "Newbie!" at the top of her lungs. People at the bar turn their heads our way. My way, specifically.

"Damn, that was dirty, Bea!" I mutter a continuous string of profanities as I stand up and walk toward the sign-up sheet on the bar. I don't have to turn back to feel the high-wattage glow of her victory grin. All names have been crossed out, so— no stalling.

The guy working the bull pit—a mulleted silver-haired dude in black leather everything, wearing massive Pit Viper shades, a total iconoclast—points me in the direction of the bull, as if anyone could miss the hulking mechanical beast set before us. I pull my hat down even farther, though the stares seem to have dwindled, temporarily at least. I'm sure that will change once the buzzer goes off.

I walk down into the pit and climb aboard my untrusty steed. Residual sweat, pride, and fear all palpable on the old leather strap.

If I were the praying type, this would be the moment to beg. Can I even get hurt here, though? What do the laws of time travel and physics allow?

BUZZZ!

The alarm blares, and we're starting to slow turn. Easing in. For one second. Then the motor of the bull revs up, straight from zero to ten, and I'm tossed to the right so hard I lose the reins and flip over sideways, somehow doing a full body roll midair. After what feels like five minutes but is probably more like a half second suspended in the dank bar air, my feet miraculously land first, at the same time, level on the ground, like I'm some pro Olympian freaking medalist. Whoo! The landing doesn't stick, however, my grand moment fleeting, and I end up tipping over, straight down on my face. Right along the edge of the bull cage next to our table. Bea, gazing down at me through the metal bars, laughs as hard as I've ever heard her.

"That was *glorious*! Not even two seconds!" She's applauding with great vigor.

I start to stand—slowly, because this aching body of mine is still very much the 2016 model, closer to four decades old than seems possible—using the metal cage bars for support. "Okay, I see how it is. I assure you, I will not be such a boisterous blowhard when you go flying off. I have respect. For you, and for the nature of this beast."

"A blowhard? I hope that only came out for the sake of alliteration. And you know what? I don't really need to show you I'm stronger by making an ass of myself up there. Convincing you to ride that bull proves it already."

Shit. I can't believe it. I mean—she's right, I did just do exactly what she asked me to do. No matter how much I despised the idea.

Impressive work, really.

I latch my hands around the bars to start climbing up and over the rails between us—to confront her maybe, persuade her to get up on that bull. Or to show her I'm not as inept as I just looked here in the bull pen.

As I grab for the top rail, Bea puts her face right up to mine.

I don't know what she's doing or why, I just know there's suddenly no space between us, not an inch, and her lips—those lips that are both achingly familiar and wholly brand new—are practically grazing against mine. I can smell the Zima on her breath, the White Tea and Ginger and our generic motel bar soap, and beneath that, something else, something powerful, too much so—the kind of familiar scent you come to recognize only in the people you're closest to, the ones you know most intimately. A scent that's somehow both totally nondescript and yet as unique as a fingerprint.

It's a smell that makes me want *her*.

Just her.

Right now.

I hold myself for a beat. Waiting.

But when nothing comes, just those sharp gray eyes of hers drilling straight into mine, filled with more questions than answers, I gently tug a strand of her hair. She goes to reciprocate, reaching a hand up along the brim of my hat that somehow managed to stay put during my epic tumble. Remembering, only as her finger catches, that it's not my actual hair underneath—but a gnarled Kid Rock wig.

She lets out a low, throaty laugh and pulls back, grabbing my shirt collar as she forces me up and over the gate. Rougher than she needs to be, but a good kind of rough.

My feet hit the ground; the moment ends. I shake my head to clear the fog.

What the hell was that?

And . . . why didn't she kiss me?

There's light applause for our off-the-cuff wrestling match— definitely not for my performance on the bull. It feels like the right time to leave, before we get even more deeply on people's radars. If we're not too deep already. The food here isn't delicious enough to risk a time travel infraction. Bea, though, seems oblivious to the attention. She has this happily deranged smile on her lips—those red pouty lips, which I'm clearly staring at again, because I'm suddenly incapable of looking anywhere else—as she sips the dregs of her can. Like she really got one over on me.

"Doubly strong, it would seem." She laughs and then drops her drink to come in for a hug. A good one, every inch of her body pressed up tight against mine. Her head catches me just between my collarbones, resting there for a moment.

My heart beats faster, and I wonder if she notices.

Wonder if hers is speeding up, too.

"We should go," I say, my lips brushing against her temple. "Fly under the radar."

"Good idea." Her breath is hot against my neck. She lets go of me then, too quickly. I immediately miss the feel of her in my arms. "I think you've earned a little swing. Let's go to the Blimp or whatever."

"The *Mint*, thank you very much." I laugh, collecting myself. "And it's the best decision you've made tonight. Well, that and your conniving ways with the bull ride. Good for you, bad for me." Or not so bad at all, considering where it got us.

Bea curls her arm around mine then, like a classy lady in an old Hollywood flick, escorting her cowboy home.

As we exit the saloon doors onto Sunset, a steady stream of people still meandering down the sidewalk, my eyes are hit with a giant billboard for *The Sixth Sense*.

I stop mid-step, Bea's arm dropping from mine. "Hold up. I know what we have to do, Bea." I point to the ad.

"You . . . want to see a movie? Rather than go to your precious minty swing thing?"

"What can I say? I'm a movie buff through and through. I bet Cinerama has it playing. We could catch the late-night showing! And I could totally go for pretzel bites and fake cheese for dinner, since I got robbed on the cowboy munchies." I turn to her and press my hands together, pleading. "Pretty please? We know the ending, sure, but to watch it on the big screen one more time? The bigger the screen, the bigger the apparition!"

She laughs. "I do love that movie—and the neon-orange cheese sauce. I also find it appealingly meta to watch it in our current purgatory state—purgatory-*like*, since we've definitively decided this is no afterlife. Speaking of seeing dead people—see that big van of nuns passing us?" She points to an old Ford fifteen-passenger ride filled with devout elderly women, windows down, peering down their noses at the debauchery of the street. "They're definitely dead in our timeline. So . . . we're basically Haley Joel Osment's character, right?"

I'm not sure the time travel math adds up, but still. I laugh. Hard.

"So, shall we walk then?" I reach for her hand, and she takes it. Twines her fingers around mine.

We begin the long journey down Sunset, taking in the familiar towering palms, the bright lights, the cathartic sense of organized chaos.

It hits me in a fresh wave—that I'm here, in 1999.

With Trixie.

No . . .

This time, I'm with *Bea*.

Chapter 11

Beatrix

Thursday, December 30, 1999

It feels like a dream when I wake in the morning, too early still to be up, and remember I'm not alone in the bed.

That Rocco and I had, by some wordless agreement, both needed the comfort of another warm body last night. A little cuddle before sleep, buzzed from the drinks and the surreal high of a night out in '99.

If either of us had wanted more than that, we made no acknowledgement.

Now, stirring from sleep, I feel him first, before I open my eyes.

Every inch of him.

His firm chest is pressed up against my back, a thin Aero Girl cotton tee the only thing between us. He's got his warm thighs curved around the bottom of my ass, one large bicep tucked around my shoulders, the other nestled under my head. His left hand is draped on my wrist, gently clasping.

Spooning me, just like he did when we'd dated. Lying like this together, so close, so tender—it's somehow the most intimate I've been with anyone in a long time. And yet, we haven't even kissed. Not in seventeen years.

I'd been so surprised, back then—Rocco was an *exceptionally* good cuddler. Attentive, playful, sensitive. Before and after sex, and sometimes just for the sake of it, too, no ulterior motives attached. Most twentysomething Hollywood boys were repelled by anything that could suggest there was meaning attached. Actual *feelings*. But with Rocco, the cuddling was just as good as the sex.

And the sex had been very, *very* good.

Rocco might have had an ego sometimes, but never in the bedroom. Or in the bathroom, kitchen, car—wherever we happened to be when the fancy struck, as it so often did. He checked it the second our clothes came off, even if it was just for some naked spooning under the blankets while we chatted about nothing and everything. We'd stayed up talking until sunrise once, cuddled under a blanket on his roof.

"Hey," Rocco says in a husky voice, his lips brushing against my ear.

I startle, wondering how long he's been awake. If he's been as acutely aware of every inch of my body as I am of his.

As I think this, I become even more aware of him—of his morning excitement. I don't shift my hips away. Neither does he.

What the hell am I doing?

"Last night was . . ." he starts, then waits for me to finish.

"A nice homage to '99," I say, because I'm nowhere near capable of examining it more closely. Why we chose one bed when we're paying for two. Why I felt so secure being back in his arms. He's my steady anchor in this outrageous fever dream, the one real thing I have. But it's more than that, too.

"It didn't feel like '99 to me. Maybe there were nice callbacks, sure, in the way we . . . banter. Some history. But you're not Trixie anymore. And I hope I'm not the same Rocco."

He's right; I'm certainly not. He isn't either, much as I treated him that way for the last few months.

"Maybe," I admit, partial recognition.

"Maybe," he repeats. "That's not a great answer."

I shrug, and his bicep slides from my shoulder to my elbow, though the grip doesn't loosen. "It's too much to contemplate before coffee," I say.

"Were you going to kiss me? Last night, at the bull pen. Or was that . . . a joke for you?"

My stomach dips, and I feel my entire body warming. "I . . . I'm not sure." It's a lie, and we both know it.

"Bea."

"Rocco."

"Didn't we say we were going to be honest with one another during this little trip through time of ours?"

"Fine." I pinch my eyes shut, as if it will somehow make this admission easier. "Yes."

His whole body stiffens alongside mine. "Why?"

"Why did I almost kiss you, or why did I stop myself?"

He lifts his hand to my cheek, gently tilts my head until I open my eyes. Face him straight on. "Both. And don't just blame it on the Zima. Those are barely alcoholic."

I weigh my options, truth vs. various white lies. He's right, though—we did promise to be honest. I owe him that much, don't I? And maybe I owe it to myself even more.

"Because . . ." I start, forcing myself to keep meeting his eyes, even though they're making me sweat a not insignificant puddle into the sheets. "Against all odds, we were having such a refreshing night, open and honest and real. And for whatever reason, I feel so . . . comfortable with you, even now. Here. Whatever, whyever this is." I flap a hand aimlessly at the motel room, and he reaches out for it. Holds on tight. "Like I can let you see me. Judgement free. Show you all the messy bits I usually hide from everyone, even myself. Last night, watching you so willingly make a complete ass of yourself on that bull . . . you made me laugh, and I forgot about all the reasons I can't do it. A momentary slip."

"Why, though? Why can't you?"

I yank my hand out of his. "Because, Rocco! I'm terrified. And I refuse to be Trixie again. She's naive, and she's stubborn, and she hurts people—herself included."

He opens his mouth and then pauses, seeming to consider his words. What promises he can or can't keep.

Before he has a chance to speak, I ask the question that suddenly seems to matter most: "Do you want to kiss me for the Trixie I was then or the Beatrix I am now?"

"Neither," he says, not missing a beat. "I want to kiss Bea."

It's *Bea*, it's the way those cool-blue eyes seem to take in everything I'm saying and everything I'm not. The way his full lips part slightly as his breath hitches, the lock of dark hair that tumbles down across his forehead.

The air around us almost seems to crackle and snap with electricity.

I nod then, and he edges in closer, until there's barely an inch left between our lips, the last boundary to cross, and he's leaving it for me.

I close the gap, of course.

My lips crash into his like nothing in the world could stop this, us, whatever we're doing. And maybe nothing could. Maybe the universe always had its plans.

His mouth is hot and sweet against mine. I give his bottom lip a few nips and he moans, and then my tongue slips through, meeting his. He palms the side of my face, his thumb tracing along my jawline, up to my earlobe, tucking away a loose strand of hair. I hear myself moan this time and reach up to tangle my fingers around that stray lock and tug. He nips now; I give another nip back.

Rocco slips his arm out from under me in one breath, and is on top of me the next, his hands braced against the headboard. He slept in nothing but skintight boxer briefs, which are doing nothing to hide his copious amount of enthusiasm. He's grinning, so wide I can see the wrinkles around his eyes, his lips, proof of life these last seventeen years apart.

He's never been more irresistible.

Though I should, right? Resist. There were reasons, good ones, loads of them. . . .

Fuck it. When in '99, right? Within reason.

"Only kisses," I say, gasping.

"Only kisses," he repeats solemnly.

"Though I am a little stuffy in here, aren't you?"

He laughs as I tug him down, his lips melding into mine, Aero Girl shirt disappearing between us, skin on skin on skin, and I let myself fall freely into the whirlpool of time.

"So, the day before New Year's Eve, '99," Rocco says, studying me from his side of our shared pillow, head propped in his hand. "What were you and I doing, and should we try to go there tonight? Do some more covert spying? Try to . . . intervene in some way? To crack the code of the mystery world we're living in?"

I chug the last dregs of my cooling coffee. Bless Rocco, who had finally pulled on his clothes—before promptly removing most of them again—to make a run to a 7-Eleven down the block for some necessary sustenance. Gritty coffee, pizza Combos, shriveled hot dogs, and green apple Warheads, mostly for the novelty appeal (my tongue had immediate regrets; not all '90s research is as pleasurable as others)—plus a few shiny foil packets that made me blush like a Catholic schoolgirl all the way to my toes when I spotted them at the bottom of the plastic bag.

Funny, seeing as what we've already done this morning feels just as intimate.

While we had . . . mutually determined rather quickly that kisses weren't enough to satisfy us, we stopped short of allowing it to go all the way. There'd been no lack of entertaining foreplay options, both of us eager to show off the highly pleasant talents honed over the last seventeen years. Rocco had certainly learned many excellent things.

But sex, full on, Rocco inside me—had still felt like too momentous of a boundary to cross this morning. Too transformative. This newfound bond is already so tenuous.

And maybe, if I'm being honest with myself, it feels like the last card I can hold—the last thing standing between me and the immediate unraveling of everything I've worked so hard on all these years.

I hate that he thinks those foil packets might become necessary.

But I might love it even more.

It's a thought I don't want to examine too closely. Especially with more pressing things to think on, such as:

How the hell do we get back to the right time?

Is there something to be said or done—or unsaid or undone— to reverse the course of how everything played out the first time for me and Rocco?

And if so, do we have to do it before the stroke of Y2K midnight?

"It would make sense," I say slowly, pulling the duvet further up my bare chest, feeling suddenly extra naked, "that our time here revolves around New Year's Eve, that frenetic Y2K energy, no? As much as anything about this situation could make sense, that is. Like we've said, if we're here together, this time, this place, it feels like there's a reason. And tomorrow night was the last time we saw one another, before the movie forced us back together. So . . . maybe there's a piece we're missing still? And seeing ourselves, following our footsteps, will help us to figure it out? I don't know. How could we possibly know?" I throw my hands up in frustration. The blanket starts to fall, and I immediately yank it back in place. Nothing was exposed—and I've already exposed myself to him, very willingly—but I feel myself blush anyway.

Rocco doesn't break eye contact, though a small grin on his lips tells me he notices my flush. "Maybe it's worth a shot then? It feels like we should make some kind of effort to right the ship." The grin disappears. "Do you think the universe . . . wants us to stay together? For me to not mess it all up with Piper?"

I've thought about this exact question. Last night, this morning, spare moments when I wasn't sleeping or distracted by Rocco's . . . anatomy. How could I not? "It would be an enormous revision, wouldn't it? One with so many potential life-altering consequences in our futures. My short-lived marriage, for one." As much as I'd like to undo that particular decision. "Your relationship with your brother, and his with Piper." Her name on my lips elicits an ugly flare of jealousy. Especially remembering what he'd said last night; she'd been his *dream* come true. "Let's . . . take it in steps? Do some light stalking first? Immerse ourselves in what we were experiencing then. As amazing as it was watching you tumble off a bull in half a second, that probably wasn't a huge help in puzzling through our mystery."

"Maybe not, but we've been busy this morning immersing ourselves in other ways." His lips twist up again, and it takes all my willpower to not lift a finger to trace them. "But yes. Good plan. Now we just have to remember exactly what we were doing in '99."

"Let's see," I say, willing the heavy dose of caffeine to unlock still untapped potential in the cobwebbed recesses of my mind. Things and places and people I haven't let myself dwell on in years.

Really, Rocco isn't wrong. The research we've been *very* busily working on today does feel rather prudent of us; it's been one steady stream of memories since he'd left me alone for his 7-Eleven run. Maybe one of those memories will lead us to the answer we need now. Though it's hard to say how the clear-as-day mental picture of him wearing nothing but a Santa hat while prancing around his house to "Run Rudolph Run" after losing a particularly spicy game of strip poker could save us. I'd always been terrible at card games, but he'd graciously let me win.

We did have plenty of memories that didn't involve nudity. Obviously. They just . . . don't seem to be my mind's priority at the moment.

"It was a good day," I say, because I know without a doubt it had been. I'd woken up New Year's Eve morning feeling as content and as hopeful as ever. Which, of course, only made the events to come that evening more devastating. I put my empty coffee cup on the nightstand and close my eyes. Focus. No easy feat with Rocco's icy-blue eyes pinned on me. Though they seem . . . less icy now, more summer sky blue. It must be a trick of the morning light. "We were hungover New Year's Eve morning. I remember you serving me in bed: coffee and a chocolate chip banana muffin from the place around the corner we loved."

"You remember what kind of muffin you ate that morning?" I can hear the surprise in his voice, and I feel instantly embarrassed. Like I gave too much away—the care and emphasis I placed on what must be such a throwaway gesture for him. But it had been the opposite of throwaway to me; it was one more item on a carefully logged list of evidence of real affection. Or what I'd thought had been real at the time.

I shrug. "It was my favorite. Still is. So when you'd make a run for me, that's what you'd get. It's not there anymore, the café. I checked a few years back, in a moment of weakness, when I had an intense craving. Some magical juice elixir place now."

"Of course it is," he says, and I can hear his smile even though my eyes are still closed. "But I remember that, too, now that you said it. You *did* love those muffins." He chuckles, his elbow gently brushing against mine. "Got me hooked on them, too. They reminded me of you every time I went . . . after the fact. Because I did think about you. Even if I was a massive jackass who went about everything the absolute wrong way. Like I said last night, I'd been so laser focused on Piper for so long. Maybe the dream had changed, maybe *you* were changing it, but I was . . . too young and too stupid to put the pieces together."

I nod because I'm afraid if I say anything more about it, I'll cry. And there's more important things to do right now than to cry about dusty history. Especially if we might have the chance to rewrite some of it. "Right," I say, clearing my throat. "So let's see, we were mildly hungover. It was the holiday season, so you were fielding party requests right and left. Being, you know, *you*. I remember joking about how it was time for you to hire an assistant to track your social needs. You turned down almost every invite, except . . ."

Except.

I can see it now, the glitzy, fabulous party in Hollywood Hills. The sprawling white-columned mansion of a *Cutie Central* castmate, a nepotism baby whose road in Hollywood was neatly paved, however briefly, by her hotshot entertainment-lawyer daddy. We'd gone for the novelty; anyone who was anyone would be there. We were young dreamers, desperate enough for that to be alluring. Plus, she'd promised a champagne fountain the size of a small swimming pool in the backyard. I had to see it in person to believe anyone could be that gaudy. (Spoiler: yes, in fact, they could.)

My eyes snap open. "Let's go get glam. Because we have a party tonight."

My arms are in an inverted backward pretzel, trying and failing to tug up the zipper on my much snugger than anticipated new red sequin minidress, when a series of loud knocks come from the door.

"My god, I have *white hair*, Beatrix," Rocco calls out. "WHITE HAIR. I always envisioned myself as a silver fox, don't get me wrong. But I was hoping for another good decade or two first. If—*when*—we make it back, Lanie will be so mega pissed at me."

I laugh, dropping my arms in surrender as I make my way to the door. I'll need Rocco's help to finish the job. Plus perhaps another Y2K miracle. "It can't be that bad. The box clearly said 'Frosty Blonde.' It may have been my first bleach job, sure, but how hard can it be to—" I unlock the door and tug it open. "Oh."

A white fox then. Very white. Also very surprisingly foxy. An utter shock to my system, because I've never before this moment been so aroused by white hair.

Rocco is looking similarly stunned. His eyes widen as they drink me in, from the intentionally messy updo à la a youthful Alicia Silverstone I perfected back in the day—and was pretty damn excited to pull out of the vault for tonight, no matter how ridiculous it may look on a thirtysomething adult woman—to the tiny sequins that accentuate every curve and dip of my chest and waistline, a few feet of exposed leg, and chunky silver platforms that may very well test the whole "can we die while time traveling?" question many times over before the night ends.

"Wow. You look . . ." He shakes his head. "Like a total '90s dream girl. Well, woman. Dream woman."

"Yeah?"

"Yeah."

"You look nice, too. For a '90s boy. *Man*." And he does, in a way that only Rocco could manage to pull off—fresh white hair and all—in baggy wide-leg black jeans and a funky neon color-blocked button-up shirt. Thick silver chain peeking out from his neckline, a fake mini hoop on his left ear. Large wraparound shades clipped to his shirt pocket for added disguise if needed. Today's thrift shop—all goods we actually paid for this time, thanks to Rocco's funds—proved to be a treasure trove.

The look is much flashier than anything Rocco would have gone for back in the day. He wore tracksuits or sweatsuits roughly ninety percent of the time; designer suits for five; birthday suit to round out one hundred. A suit guy through and through. But for tonight's purposes, the more flash, the better.

"Remind me again, though, why you didn't have to bleach your hair?"

I shrug. "Perk of having a face no one but past me would care enough to recognize, what can I say? Now get in here and help zip me up."

He steps inside, grinning as he shuts the door behind us. "You sure you got your directions straight? You wouldn't prefer I maneuver it further *down*?"

Shit, yes. That does sound appealing. But it seems unlikely we'll somehow tunnel our way back to the proper year through our twisted motel-room sheets. "Clever. But we have a party to stalk."

He sighs, laying a warm palm against the exposed skin on my back, lingering for a few seconds, almost long enough for me to change my mind, before tugging the zipper to the top.

I make myself step away to gather my other newly thrifted gems: a long lapeled jacket, easily double the length of this dress—shiny black pleather, the edges and cuffs lined in faux fur—and a sparkly red clutch, label long gone, probably from the Deb.

"Do you think . . . the next twenty-four hours are meant to be our redo?" he asks, suddenly right behind me. Not touching, though close enough I can feel his warmth. The golden Rocco glow that absorbed me so wholly the first time around. A comfort, an invite, a torment, somehow all in one.

Our redo. Past or present, I'm not sure which he means. I'm not sure that it matters, the difference between the two. What the universe is not-so-subtly encouraging us to reconsider or redirect.

I think again about my dad, still alive in Tucson—assuming

there's a whole wide world beyond us, all exactly as it was. That this version of LA isn't just a rogue glitch, a one-off anomaly.

Even still, the universe put me here. With Rocco. Surely if there's a solution, a way out, it begins and ends with us?

But how would we change something about our relationship—one small thing, even—without possibly changing everything to come after?

Or is that the point, to change everything? Upend all we hold dear in our normal lives, one massive do-over stretching from here to then, a glittering thread in the cosmos—séventeen years rewritten in the stars, a remaking that transforms everything we know?

Or what if leaving this time, this place, isn't the end goal? If there's nothing to correct, alter, shift. Just some tiny tear in the fabric of time, a chance snag we somehow drove through head-on down Sunset Boulevard? Or maybe it's Delilah. Maybe she's the bridge between times.

I shrug. Walk toward the door without glancing back at Rocco.

I need fresh evening air. Some space and time—of which there's not nearly enough, so few minutes separating Rocco and me from the new millennium.

And I need some really fucking expensive champagne.

"Why did we come here?" Rocco asks, his arm looping through mine as we make our way up the massive circular drive. We'd parked Delilah right inside the front gate, not wanting to bring any valet's attention to the fact that a 2000 model could look so . . . lovingly aged. "Back then, I mean. It doesn't seem like our usual jam. Too highbrow. Less Del Taco, more Moonshadows."

"You forget, you were still a fledgling baby star back then." I clutch Rocco's arm tightly, laser focused on the cobblestoned drive and staying upright in these platforms. "You might have had pride—and simple tastes—but you weren't above a little elbow rubbing for a good cause. Besides, I think you'd heard Steven Spielberg would be here. You never got over losing that part in *Jurassic Park* and were so determined to make it onto his radar."

"You had to remind me," he mutters. "The role that got away."

I laugh. It stops short, however, as we step off the drive onto the lantern-lit walkway to the house, a walkway that ends with two dapperly dressed Hulk-like security guards overseeing the door.

I pull Rocco to a stop. "Why is it just now occurring to me that there's a list? And we aren't on it? Or we are, but, you know, the '99 version of ourselves, who are either here or expecting to be let in shortly."

"Please, Bea. Who do you think I am?" He turns to me, his grin so disarming I'm unable to do anything but nod and follow as he tugs me forward.

"Good evening," the elder of the two guards says, a pristinely mustached Black man who's roughly Rocco's height and perhaps double his width.

"May I ask your name?" the second chimes in smoothly before we can answer, like these are their assigned lines for the evening. Bodyguard#1 and #2, all speaking bits split fifty-fifty. What #2, a white man who looks fresh out of school, lacks in height he makes up for with thickness, and his beady eyes say less "Happy holidays to you and yours!" and more "I'll serve your innards for Christmas dinner if you mess with this family."

I smile too widely—not fooling anyone, I'm sure—and turn to Rocco.

"Good evening, I'm Tom Richards, and this is my wife. Debbie." He pulls me in even closer, my parakeet heart nearly beating a hole through my chest.

Bodyguard #2 pulls a list folded like a handkerchief from his breast pocket. Unfolds it, too slowly, and reads through, even more slowly still. I watch as his eyes skim, nearing the bottom, until he gives the tiniest of tight-lipped smiles. "Welcome," he says, at which point #1 steps to the door, pulling it open with one arm, grandly gesturing us inside with the other.

"Who the fuck are Tom and Debbie Richards?" I whisper as we step into the glistening marble foyer, surrounded on all sides by organized chaos. Servers in tuxedos and little black dresses shuffling around with silver trays heavy with bubbling flutes, a woman on a harp stringing a New Age version of Jingle Bells, and other newly arrived guests, all staring up at the three-story staircase spiraling like a vortex above our heads.

"My old manager," he laughs, pulling me further away from the door and into the crowd. "My current manager, too."

"Right. I remember seeing him on set. But was that a good idea?"

"I think so? If I recall correctly—and I'd say I'm ninety percent certain about this—he didn't show that night. He was planning on it, mostly because he's the one who put the bug about Spielberg in my ear. But he got too shitfaced at the other rounds of holiday parties and never showed. It was a rough time for him. He sobered up soon after. 'New millennium, new man,' he'd say."

"Okay." My nerves loosen, at least marginally. "That might work then. If you're sure he won't show up and get disgruntled when they turn him away."

"Nah. And old Tommy is harmless. He'd probably just smile and walk off, secretly piss on their bushes on the way out."

He sweeps me through the room then, parting the crowds like he was born to do this—which, really, I suppose he was—until we're stepping back outside through wide glass doors opened to what feels like an endless patio covered in twinkling trellises on all sides, a canopy of lights strung above us as far as my eyes can see. It's pure magic and also deeply bizarre, the immediate sensation that I've been here before, done exactly this. I'm reliving a moment over again in a way that should absolutely be impossible.

There are familiar faces in the crowd, but not ones I knew personally, aside from a few acquaintances from *Cutie Central*. B- and C-list mostly, with a few up-and-coming As. One corner of the patio is especially rowdy, swallowed up by a small mob of Nickelodeon elite, cast members of *All That*. The redhead boy from the show—Danny something?—appears to be enjoying a massive ice luge. Upside down, ankles held high up in the air. He can't be a day over eighteen, but who am I to judge? I was practically a kid, too.

My eyes continue their scan, and I see it then, the towering fountain, four ornate tiers spraying golden bubbles into the large circular pool at the base. A server on each side dips flutes in, hands them out to guests, most of whom seem to be double fisting. Pure class.

We'd had too much fun mocking the fountain that night, Rocco and I. And by mocking, I mean we couldn't resist sampling one glass after another, valiantly doing our best to help drain the supply. We likely consumed thousands of dollars' worth between the two of us. It's why I'd been so hungover the next morning, Rocco resuscitating me with my favorite muffin and coffee.

So it shouldn't shock me as much as it does, what I see next:

Rocco and I, sneaking over on exaggerated tiptoes—my feet bare, heels abandoned (and then lost altogether, I remember now, a fresh pair of patent leather Steve Maddens)—to the edge of the fountain behind the servers' backs, dipping our flutes in for a refill before running off, flushed and giggling, disappearing back into the crowd.

I follow them.

It's not a conscious decision; I just need to see them again. Need to see me. Because I'm so wildly, out-of-my-mind desperate for some scrap of a clue, any kind of sign, about why now, why us, why any of this bizarre fucking traipse back to 1999.

"Be careful," Rocco says quietly, following close behind. "Don't let them—"

It's too late, though, because she, me, *Trixie*, she's looked back over her shoulder.

And she's staring straight at me.

Chapter 12

Rocco

Thursday, December 30, 1999

"Oh my god, she saw me. I mean, I saw me?" Bea shakes her head; her whole body is shaking. I put my hands on her shoulders to help steady her, guiding her to the edges of the crowd for more privacy. "We made eye contact."

"I think you're good," I say, even if there's no way either of us could be sure. This whole holiday party venture might be our best idea yet, or just as easily the worst. "They're already heading back inside. See?" I tilt my head toward our youthful counterparts, just beyond the glass doors now. Walking into a gymnasium-sized living room. "Holding hands, smiling, giggling. It's hard to look away from them, isn't it? Their energy together. It reminds me of last night. This morning, too. The way you looked at me in the hotel room, the way she's looking at him tonight."

Dammit, mouth. Too much. I'm wise enough to shut my lips, but still, my brain won't stop whirring—is that how I look at Bea now, too? Like I've managed to find the most magical woman in the room? Against all foreseeable odds?

Bea stiffens beneath my hands and takes a step to the side,

shrugging my arms off. "Well, Rocco, I'm glad you've had that flash of hindsight. Because it's not easy for me to see them, so giddy like that. Considering the next day is New Year's Eve."

Ah yes, the icy chill returns. Understandably, after my word vomit. But at least I helped to distract from her anxieties about being spotted. A semi-win.

"I'm sorry, that would have worked better as an inner monologue. It slipped out. Because it's just . . . so strange and unsettling to see us in the flesh, I'm not sure how to properly organize my thoughts. The first time was such a shock, I couldn't take it all the way in. Tonight, though, feels so crystal clear. Showing me just how good it felt at the time. You . . . you really did make me happy."

Before Bea can dish up additional feedback, we hear a *SNAP!* from somewhere near the perimeter of the backyard, partitioned off by a bunch of arborvitaes and other dense shrubbery. Quicky followed by another snap, louder than the first. Maybe hanging out in the backyard was a bad idea.

"This is the hills!" Bea whisper-screams. "That could be a mountain lion stalking us!"

"Let's think rationally," I say, hopefully sounding calmer than I feel, for her sake. Both our sakes, really, because we don't want to cause a scene. "That is a giant fortress of thick, wild bush."

"Ugh, you said *bush*," she says, straight lipped, obviously fighting to not crack a grin.

Bea needs to pick a mood and stick with it; I need some fountain champagne to help cope with these emotional spins. She no longer seems scared, at least, but more inquisitive, squinting into the foliage. There's another round then, louder still and closer: snaps, crinkling leaves, scratches. Bea reverts back to scared mode, latching tightly onto my shoulders from behind.

Another burst of rustling leaves, and the sounds take on a new twist: some good old-fashioned expletives.

So—not a mountain lion.

"Fucking bullshit, you think you can keep me out of this damn party? Ha! Ow. You old dirty bush, piece of shit spiky branches . . ."

That voice.

So familiar.

He lets out another string of profanity, and the pieces click.

Tom Richards. My manager.

Which means: We've got to bounce.

Immediately.

"Look at this man," Bea says, cackling now. "Coming through that towering wall of bush. Probably easier than getting into the Playboy mansion." She's really letting the pervy jokes fly, maybe a stress decompression—though, now that I think about it, she did have a healthy appetite for *Beavis and Butt-Head* back in the day. She's probably the only woman I've ever dated who would watch with me.

But it's also easy for her to joke because she has no idea we're about to commit the gravest sin of time travel: talking directly to our past—who also still happens to be in our present. He's been my manager since I was ten years old.

He's going to know. How could he not?

I lean back to whisper in her ear and that smell of hers catches me. I allow myself one quick breath, then collect myself. "That's Tom," I hiss. "*Tom Richards.*"

We see snippets of him then—tan skin and dark curls, gold cufflinks beaming against a white-and-black–checkered suit. He'd be hard to miss with that look.

Without a word, Bea grabs my hand and pulls me in close—for a kiss.

Just like that, and we're full-on making out in the backyard of this Hollywood Hills mansion. Her thigh hitching up to my waist, my fingers pressing firmly down into her warm skin, Bea kissing me like I'm the most delicious treat at the party.

Every inch of me is on fire; this might be a drill, but someone's got to tell that to my body. My brain can't find the shut-down switch, and hell if I care.

There's no slowdown as Tom emerges fully from the bushes. Bea's determined to play the good old-fashioned "leave us alone, we're making out" game, and I'm all too happy to play along for as much time as necessary. The whole night if need be.

"Can you believe those guys at the door?" Tom says, laughing. He's standing right next to us now. Trying to have a conversation, like Bea's tongue isn't currently doing a slow glide against mine. We press ahead, ignoring him, but, like a fly, he's both unabashed and unconcerned with the concept of personal space. He also reeks of booze.

Drunk Tom? Boston Tom, as he used to say, here in the flesh? Tom was a prolific drinker in the '90s, our early days of working together. He almost got divorced over it—almost lost Debbie, his kids, half his millions, everything—before he sobered up and redeemed himself over time. This must have been one of his last blowout nights, if I'm doing the math right.

"They have no idea who I am and what backyard knowledge I got. Just a couple quick lefts, ha, and a few rights. If you think I look bad, you should see the back of those hedges." He laughs, coughs, wipes his face with his mostly untattered sport coat. I say mostly because his back has a large rip down the center, making mid-back coattails. Adam Ant would have been proud. And knowing Tom's tastes, this suit was big money.

Bea cannot hold it together anymore, the kiss losing momentum—his persistent chatter has got the best of her. She releases slowly, her tongue doing one light farewell run over my bottom lip before she pulls back. *Goddamn.* I want to taste her again, return the favor, but she's already out of range. Busy side-eying Tom.

Tom seems to be in full brownout drunk mode, though, so I'm not sure he's noticed any of Bea's performance.

Me though? I noticed everything.

I can't stop noticing.

"You can't imagine the trouble I've had getting here," he continues, unfazed. "And I don't even want to be; I just have to get out of the house, you know? Me and my wife aren't all cozied up like you two lovebirds, not these days, anyway. Plus, I left my wallet in the cab that brought me here. Stupid pockets of this stupid jacket are too shallow!" His firewater breath lingers in the December air. It's amazing he's even conjuring sentences at this point, to be honest, given that smell. I'd be impressed if it weren't so sad. I'm glad Boston Tom was about to make his exit.

"I don't even wanna be here, you know? Did I say that already? Blah blah. You two seem like you could care less. Lip smacking and grabbing ass out here. My wife and I used to be like that, if you can believe it."

"Shit, Tom, have some manners," Bea says, coolly. And then her eyes go wide, the realization hitting that she just said his name out loud. A name we shouldn't know, given we're total strangers.

We both hold our breath, waiting for the fallout.

But no. No fallout. "Yeah, I hear that a lot these days. Sorry 'bout that. Really." He's quiet for a beat, and then I watch him fully check out. A quick fade from brown to blackout mode in the blink of his hollowed eyes. The lights are still on, dimly, but nobody's home.

"We appreciate the apology." I try to subtly steer him toward a nearby garden bench because he's starting to sway. A slow semi-rhythmic lilt from side to side.

"I mean," he says, blinking back for a moment, "I've snuck into my fair share of backyards, mostly for affair stuff. Never these days. Just during marriage number one." He chuckles. "Numero uno." More laughter. "I used to love that game. Uno. So fun. My kids love it, too." He starts mumbling more incoherently, something about Pizzeria Uno.

I'm uncertain about this interaction in terms of overall

risk—the potential for it to change the great order of our lives. First for my old delivery pal, and now my manager? The former seems fairly innocuous. Hopefully. The latter, though, is pushing it too close to my true timeline. Oh right, and there's my friendly future neighbor. Can't forget him.

Regardless of the risk, I have to help. I couldn't forgive myself if this back-party entrance took him too far off the rails.

What if this was *the* night that he stopped drinking? I can only imagine what a mess he would've caused inside the actual party. Maybe there's a reason I never knew he made it here, not just because I was caught up on Trixie.

We've got to get him home.

Bea clears her throat, gives a pointed nod in Tom's direction. She seems to be on the same page, no words needed, as she takes an arm and starts slowly escorting Tom back toward the house. I mean, he's clearly very drunk, with an exceptional case of the wobbles. You don't have to know him to recognize how far gone he is. But still, it's empathetic of her, and I'm gladder than ever that we're in this together. Whatever *this* turns out to be.

I latch on to his other arm so we're flanking him.

"Hey there hey," he sings out. "Woo-hoo-hoo! Am I floating?"

He is kind of floating I suppose, since we're mostly carrying him at this point. He's trying to use his legs, but to very little avail.

"I appreciate this, but if I'm not out for another ninety minutes or so, my wife will be awake still, and I won't be able to go inside. We're, eh, keeping a bit of distance. Mutual. Kind of. Not really. I miss her. So much. Anyway! Just leave me. I'll sit here. Safe as a pea in its pod." With that, Tom goes limp and plops straight down. Right where the grass meets the backyard pavers, a prime foot-traffic zone. Making a scene, or at least very nearly so.

"No, nope. C'mon, Tommy boy," Bea says, grabbing for his arms and tugging him upright again. "There are better places to sit, like the back seat of my Jetta."

"The back seat of a car sounds nice. But no, thank you. I don't do that to Debbie. Not ever. No offense, you're a perfectly love—"

"Alright there," I say, cutting him off as I take over one arm from Bea, propping it on my shoulder. "Into the car of your new *platonic* friend we go. Though we commend your morals, we do."

Just as I say this, I see me: Rocco of '99. Looking out from inside, on the other side of the window, the glow of the party. Staring at his massively inebriated manager. Then . . . at us. First me. Then Bea.

I—he—looks embarrassed. Concerned. Uncertain. It's subtle maybe, but I could pick up any trace of emotion at any distance; it's my own face, after all. And I've spent my whole life studying it on screens.

I don't remember this happening that night, though. No recollection of Tom at the party whatsoever. I'm pretty sure he even talked about it after the fact—how he missed his shot to schmooze with Spielberg on my behalf. Maybe he never made it past the lobby and was too blitzed to remember where his night ended. Hell, I was pretty blitzed, too, thanks to those fountain bubbles. My memory might be unreliable.

Whatever happened, though, it doesn't matter now because on this timeline, Tom is here. And so is '99 Rocco. And me, the vintage model.

'99 Rocco looks at me again. Eyes lingering this time.

I use my hand not holding up Tom to brush other Rocco off, hopefully a universal "we got this" wave, and then pretend I'm guzzling a bottle. Tongue hanging out for emphasis, tilting my head toward Tom. '99 Rocco seems reassured enough by our involvement—makes his night easier, anyway—as he waves and disappears back into the swell of the party.

Damn.

Was that another potential ripple?

How many dominoes are we knocking over tonight?

Even one could be too many.

"I shrugged the old me off," I say quietly to Bea.

"I saw. At least you wouldn't have recognized yourself. Not in this lighting and with that platinum blonde, right?" Her voice swings up at the end.

"Right," I say, because it's the only answer that will keep us both forging ahead.

"Can we get to that platonic back seat? My legs feel . . . a little funny." Tom has reached the faulty voice modulation portion of his drunkenness, as he's suddenly yelling loudly enough for other outdoor guests to hear.

Too many faces turn our way.

"You got it, Tom, let's get you into the chariot."

I nod to Bea to push forward. She takes a few steps, eyes fixed on the pavers, and starts picking up speed as we make our way back to the patio doors. I have to hustle to keep up. She must still do yoga because her core works like a beast. I remember that now—she was obsessed with yoga in the '90s. My mom had been, too—still is—and I'd accidentally mentioned Bea to her once in passing. I didn't do that usually, didn't let those two sides of my life ever collide. Not until Piper, and well—after that epic collision, I went straight back to impenetrable boundaries.

We speed walk through the house, literally rubbing elbows, shoulders, hips with the crush of guests packed inside its walls, not stopping for a breath until we're back outside. The guys working the door are busy talking to what looks like a posse of runway models and don't even bat an eye in our direction. Home free. We maneuver Tom down the long driveway, toward the old Jetta that sits behind the rest of the pack.

Finally—we're there, the end of the line. Standing next to our silver time machine.

Bea yanks open the back door and pushes Tom inside. "Seat belt, please," she says, still hovering over him. "We want to get you home in one piece. Even if its bourbon-aged and beer-battered." She laughs at her own joke, a shriller sound than usual.

I watch over her shoulder as Tom tries to click the seat belt together, missing the hole each time.

Bea takes a step back, bumping up against me. I put my hand on her waist to steady her, a reflex. "Sorry, I didn't know you were so damn close."

"Nothing to be sorry about."

She swats gently at my hand, but she's smiling when she turns to face me. "Would you like to help Tom? I'm not going anywhere near his crotch."

"Sure, not a problem." I lean in and reach over him, taking the straps from his hands with no resistance. I would predict that, like a baby, he'll be out cold within the next few minutes, rocked to sleep by the moving car.

"I hope he doesn't puke in Delilah," Bea says, loudly enough for Tom to partly reanimate.

"I never puke! Just don't . . . just don't take me home 'til midnight. Please." His motor skills are slowing down, but the pain in his voice is still clear as glass, broken shards of it. It hurts to hear it. He goes silent then. Eyes drooping, head lolling against the seat. He didn't give us his address, but I know where he lives; I've been there a hundred times. He's hopefully too drunk to realize that omission, though.

I turn back to Bea. "Could I please drive Delilah again? I know where we're going, and it will certainly be before midnight."

She squints at me for a beat, then hands me the keys. "You be careful with my girl."

"Always." I give a solemn nod and open the driver's side door. "You hungry? There's an In-N-Out burger close to here. The wait in the drive-thru should burn some time."

She settles into the passenger seat and deliberates for a moment. "Fine, yes. It's not like we got to enjoy any fancy hors d'oeuvres. Or any fountain champagne. What a waste of such an excessive party."

"Excellent. Tom, you hungry?"

No response. Sound asleep before we even start the car. I'll take that as a maybe? A little late-night sober-up food could be good for him.

I turn the key and head out. Good riddance to this failed party experiment. Where any of it leaves us? Impossible to say. But if anything could help right now, it's a delicious burger that transcends any and all timelines.

The short drive to In-N-Out is silent. I keep glancing at Bea, and her furrowed brow that tells me she's busily analyzing every potential misstep of the evening. I wish I could reassure her, but anything I say would be a lie.

When we arrive, the car line is long as predicted, and Tom's still out. It's—I glance at the clock on the dash—barely eleven.

"Combo number one?" I turn to Bea, who's frowning up at the menu.

"Full disclosure, I'm a Jack in the Box girl. Never really liked In-N-Out. Unpopular opinion, I know. But their fries just . . . don't do it for me?"

"C'mon! The burger might be the star, but the fries are also perfection! They're so fresh!" Too heavy on the evangelizing, maybe, but I'm desperate to turn this night into more of a positive. For myself, but even more so for her.

And really, the fries are pretty damn fresh. Way better than Jack in the Box.

"Okay, okay. I'm hungry, so I'll eat. Even the fries, alright? No need to get all worked up. You would think you're a paid sponsor or something."

"I'd happily be their poster boy."

"Not surprising. Weren't you in WWF wrestling doll commercials as a tween? You clearly have no shame."

I grin. "Damn, that burns."

Twenty minutes later, two of the three combo number ones—the Double-Double combo—have been consumed in the parking lot. Washed down with icy-cold fountain Cokes. All era Roccos would approve of this meal. I might do those Michelin-starred restaurant reviews on my social media, but that doesn't mean I can't appreciate a humbler meal. No matter how much loot is in my bank account, I know who I am at heart. And that's a man who loves a good In-N-Out burger. Bea didn't say much as we ate, but she finished her meal—fries included—and I take her lack of criticism as high praise. A necessary victory, considering the rest of the night feels like straight-up failure.

"I think we should drop Tom off and let him eat his In-N-Out in the driveway," Bea says, climbing back into her seat after disposing of our trash. "All this time with him is making me more anxious."

"Yeah, we can do that. He's got a nice garden bench out front." As I go to pull out of the parking lot, I forget about the speedbump, and Delilah takes a solid bounce up and down. Enough of a jolt to both illicit a stern look from Bea and to wake up Tom. He stirs in the back, mumbling something I can't make out.

"Welcome back," I say, handing over his food. He fumbles the bag, some stray fries dropping onto the floor behind the console.

Bea visibly grits her teeth. "Tom, could you please pick those up? I don't normally eat in my car. I try to keep her immaculate."

"Sure, and by 'immaculate,' you mean littering ripped magazine pages on the floor?"

I turn back to watch as Tom picks up a scrap of paper with his free hand. A glossy page, my thirtysomething face grinning out from the top.

The vandalized tabloid page.

Fuck.

Mega fuck.

Tom stares down at it, squinting, looking slightly cross-eyed. He's silent for a beat, and I hope he's too drunk to string letters together. *Please, dear god, Boston Tom.*

But then: "Hey, I represent Rocco! Who drew all over him? And speaking of Rocco . . ." He squints at me in the rearview mirror.

Bea and I exchange panicked glances. In a moment of clear impulse, she reaches back to grab the page, but instead knocks against the food bag in his other hand. The remaining fries scatter everywhere. An explosion of greasy potato sticks.

Tom lets out a loud belly laugh. "Ooh, I'm so sorry you dirtied your car even more! Good thing I'm more of a Jack in the Box guy. I really don't like these fries anyway." Bea and Tom—maybe they could have bonded over that, under very different circumstances.

He takes the burger out of the bag, unwrapping it and taking a massive bite, and then begins picking up stray fries from the seat. Shoveling some into his mouth, despite his proclamation. I glance back as often as I can without getting us into another crash—I certainly don't want to flip ahead again in time with old Tom in the back seat—trying to track the page. I finally catch sight of it on the seat next to him, no longer seeming to be of interest. For now, at least. He's too busy being a wiseass, making a show of picking up each fry one by one, counting as he goes—skipping every few numbers. God, I do not miss Boston Tom. He would have been long since fired by now if he hadn't gotten it together.

I catch Bea looking back at the page, too, trying to be subtle. Not wanting to do anything to put it back on his radar. We nod at one another in understanding.

By the time he's finished counting fries, mostly inaccurately, we're pulling up to his absurdly giant house, a three-story Tudor. Porch lights on, the rest of the place dark. Tom could hang out and finish his food, piss in the bushes, and basically camp outside for the night before anyone would find him. No one seems to be waiting up.

"Seventy-three. There, all cleaned up. Immaculate! And I'm not too proud to take this garbage with me. To eat. You were sweet enough to drive a slightly tipsy stranger home." The slur on those s's is a mockery of the words "slightly tipsy."

"I know you said midnight, but you can hang outside until you're ready to go into your own home. Sober up, make your wife happy." I reach back and pat his shoulder.

"Fair enough. Thanks again for the ride, and sorry if I've been a bit of an ass. I'm gonna work on it, okay?" He pushes the door open and steps out of Delilah, hands clutching his remaining bounty of food, torn jacket tails flapping.

"Hope my back seat was lux enough for you!" Bea calls out as he nudges the door shut with his backside. He hobbles forward about ten feet, then drops down to sit right in the middle of his massive circular driveway. I back out the way we came in.

We're quiet for a little while. It's hard to find the right words. Probably because there aren't any.

"Holy shit, what was this night?" I finally ask, letting out the deep breath I've been holding for what feels like hours.

"If we get back to the future, I'm positive we did something regrettable. Granted he was sloppy drunk and distracted by mediocre fries, but still. I'm trying to remember everything the article said—just how bizarrely prophetic it would seem to him. I need to read it again."

Bea turns to grab the page from the back seat, but . . .

It's not there.

My view is limited through the mirror, but it's definitely not where he last left it.

"Where the hell is it?" She unbuckles herself and crawls into the back seat—despite our rapidly moving vehicle—scrounging around on the floor.

A moment passes, the road in front of me a blur, before Bea is next to me again.

"It's gone," she says quietly. "He must have taken it."

I make a U-turn without needing to question it; drive straight back to Tom's, neither of us saying a word.

But when we pull up the drive, he's gone. The outside lights are off.

Ringing the doorbell would only make a scene. Ensure that this whole night becomes much more memorable, for Debbie, too, and anyone else who's around. More sober people with properly functioning brain cells.

My chest constricts; it's impossible to breathe. As I pull back out of the drive, I roll my window down for fresh air. It doesn't help. "Maybe he tossed it into his In-N-Out bag without meaning to?" I grab at anything, desperate. "And he'll throw it out after he eats, forget he ever met us? Forget all about tonight? He was as drunk as I've ever seen him, and I saw him drunk a lot in those days. He once peed in the fountain at the Paramount lot. On a dare. But he dared himself, so."

"Yeah. Maybe," Bea says, but she doesn't sound convinced.

I'm not convinced either. This night together has been pretty damn unforgettable.

Our timeline might be well and truly screwed up.

Forever.

Chapter 13

Beatrix

Friday, December 31, 1999

I open my eyes to check the nightstand clock for what feels like the hundredth time.

Three on the dot.

There's no hope for sleep—not after this night, Tom, the tabloid page, everything we might have done, or undone, with that one split second of time. I should have tried harder to get the page back sooner. He was so far gone, no matter the means, the details would have been hazy for him in the morning.

But now he'll have concrete evidence.

Rocco and I were real. And so was that article.

I slip my legs out from under the covers, try to sit up without making the bed creak. Rocco is there, just a few inches away. Sleeping, I'm sure. He always did fall asleep straight away— I'd always joked it was just one more superpower of his, that he could remove his mind so completely from everything and everyone else in his day. Like it didn't matter, at least for those eight precious hours. We hadn't even kissed tonight when we got back. Like we both knew that was too much, or maybe too little, after this night. But I'd asked him to stay with me again anyway, because I didn't want to be alone. Not in this strange '90s world that feels so like our past but also so impossibly different.

I miss my apartment and my age-appropriate clothing, my favorite coffee shop latte, long chats with Sylvie, and life on set, the knowledge that I was finally achieving, creating, existing with a purpose. I don't miss the way I resented Rocco, the way I toyed with his emotions for my own satisfaction. But everything else, I miss.

"You can't sleep either?"

I startle, turning to look down at Rocco. "I thought you were asleep. You could *always* sleep."

He turns his body toward mine, props his head up on the pillow as he studies me. "I guess even I have my limits. And this night? Exceeded that limit."

I ease back down against the pillow, level with Rocco's gaze. "Do you think . . . did we blow up everything? When—if—we make it back, will it be different because of tonight?"

Rocco frowns. "Honestly?"

I nod.

"I don't have a clue."

"Me neither. I just keep wondering: What was on the other side of the page? What other information about the future does he have? How much more could we possibly ruin?" It's the thought that's been clawing at me every time I shut my eyes.

He rubs a hand over his thickening dark stubble. "Huh. Hadn't even thought about that. One more fear to pile on the load. Thanks for that. I may never sleep again."

"At least we'll be awake together. I could use the company."

"Yeah?" He gives me a weary smile. "Though I guess I shouldn't feel too special. I know I'm your only choice right now."

"No. I'm glad. That it's you. If I could choose anyone right now, the person I'd want to share this fever dream world with—

it would still be you." The words are out before I can analyze and then overanalyze; they're true, though. I'm exhausted and terrified and vulnerable to the point of extreme and unavoidable honesty.

Rocco's staring at me, his eyes like bottomless pools in the darkness. I want to lose myself in them, jump into the water and drown. "I would choose you, too."

It's no longer a decision to consciously make, the line in the sand gone now, washed away in the passing of hours, minutes, seconds in this impossible sliver of time. Rocco—his eyes, his laugh, his voice, his touch—he's the only thing keeping me grounded in this place, in this body that transcends every known rule of the universe.

We reach for one another in the same heartbeat, my palms pressing into the rough stubble along his jawline, his warm fingers skimming up the sides of my waist. I arc my back up to lift my T-shirt over my head, toss it unceremoniously to the floor, and then dive back in—my lips pressing into his, and my fingertips circling the elastic band of his boxer briefs, slowly, teasing, before I start to tug them down. I pull up to my knees to slip the boxers the rest of the way off, sliding past his knees, his ankles, until he is laid out underneath me, completely bare on the sheets, gazing up with an expression that looks disarmingly like reverence. I've seen him naked before, of course I have—in the real '99, in this version, too. All golden tan skin and taut muscles, long, strong limbs, everything about him long and strong. Pleasantly thick.

But somehow he's never appeared quite like this before now, like he's been exposed from the inside out. Arms, eyes, mind wide open.

It's like he's accepted that he is, in fact, breakable, and he's inviting me to give it my very best shot.

"Bea," he moans, and I've never loved the cadence of my nickname more. I've never been more relieved to have shed

Trixie and now Beatrix, too. I'm still both but I'm also neither, and neither—with him—is exactly who I most want to be. "You're sure?"

"It's the only thing in this world I'm sure about right now," I say, and am struck once again by the sharp edge of my own honesty. My own need.

"I have never wanted anyone more."

His words are like a spell, completely undoing me. My body is all hot racing blood and sparking synapses, feeling without thought. In this moment, I don't care where we are or why we're here, what comes next—if we'll go back to our future, if we have any future at all, together or apart, after everything that's happened tonight. None of it matters, not now. Just him, this, our bodies coming together, unified and whole for this precious, glittery scrap of time the universe has inexplicably dealt us.

I wrap my thighs around his waist, sliding myself up and down the length of him. He moans again, a deep rumble, reaching his hands up to tug my hair from its bun, running his fingers through the loose ends, then down along my neck. He pulls me in closer, sitting up to meet me in the middle, his lips following his fingers, first pressing against my neck, then making their way down to my collarbones, my chest, his hands moving to gently cup my breasts. I rock against him, and he shudders, gasping, and then flips me onto my back, moving himself to hover above me.

"Your turn," he says, and then sits back as his fingers skim the edge of my lacey black thong—a spontaneous purchase at Victoria's Secret on our shopping trip, a *just in case*, a choice I couldn't quite explain to myself as I handed over Rocco's bills to the cashier. "Though these barely count as underwear, they're so flimsy. I remember you despising these back in the day, no? Said you'd rather go with nothing at all than overpriced floss. Which I recall being thoroughly okay with." He smiles as his fingers trail along the lace and then down my inner thigh, slow hot circles that encompass everywhere with one exception, making me ache for him even more.

I gasp, my hips arching up on instinct, his thumb grazing against me. An electric surge. "You remembered?" It's a silly memory, really—my preference in undergarments. And I *had* adamantly bucked the thong trend with very few wardrobe exceptions. But something about it now, this intimate anecdote that has transcended so many years, so many other women with their own preferences for lacy underthings, or no underthings at all, makes my body burn even hotter.

"Rip them off," I say. "Get them off me."

He stops what he's doing, eyes widening as he seems to drink me in. "You sure?"

I nod, and he grins as he threads his fingers in the lace, ripping through each side with one strong pull.

"That was *incredibly* satisfying," he says. "And surprising. You never cease to surprise, you know that?"

I can barely pull myself together enough to nod.

He gives one last sturdy tug to each side, and they're gone, blessedly gone. Nothing left between us as he gently spreads my legs farther apart, palms burning against the tops of my thighs. He lingers there for a few minutes, his fingers teasing, exploring, rubbing, until I am frantic with need for all of him. I motion wordlessly in the direction of those foil packets, relieved Rocco had such amazing foresight. No '99 slipups for us.

He jumps up and readies himself as I watch with great interest, and then he's back on top of me, and I am more than ready, too. I tilt my hips up and he pushes inside, one swift thrust that leaves me calling out for more. I hear myself cry out his name then, and he whispers "my Bea" as he leans in to hold me in his arms. He rocks into me again and again, and I wrap my arms and legs around his back as we go, bind him in as close as possible.

The days, the years, they all break apart, strands of time free and untethered.

I let go of the strings, let go of everything but Rocco. We float away, together.

I know that he's gone, even with my eyes still closed.

It's too cold.

I'm an unpaired baby spoon.

No warm arms curled around my shoulders, no chest pressed up tight against my back, no second heartbeat thumping close to mine. I stretch my hand out over to where he should be, and the sheet feels cool.

He's been gone for a little while then.

I open my eyes to take in the room, still dim in the early morning, just a soft splinter of light playing between two thick drapes. The top sheet is twisted around my legs, the duvet half off the bed. My clothes from the party are draped carelessly on the lone chair in the room, my jacket and purse on the floor, alongside last night's T-shirt.

None of his things seem to be here. His party shirt, pants, underwear gone.

He panicked and left, clearly. To his room, to anywhere else that isn't here, with me.

I shouldn't be surprised—we're here, literally watching history repeat itself.

But I still am.

Because even without any promises, no reassurances or grand proclamations made, I now had expectations, didn't I? Expectations that had snuck up on me. Let themselves in, entirely of their own volition.

I feel the tears before I'm consciously aware of the fact that I'm crying. Thick and fast, streaming down over my cheeks. I realize now, too, just how naked I am, and tug the sheet over my shoulders, curling up inside it like it's my cocoon. The sheet smells like Rocco, like us, sweat and sex with an undercurrent of cheap motel detergent and White Tea and Ginger.

Just as I'm about to really lean into my pity party, swiftly passing through the stages of sadness and disappointment to claim my well-deserved rage, the door swings open.

I scream.

"Bea?" Rocco says, stepping into the room, a cup of coffee in each hand, along with a brown paper bag. "Shit, I'm sorry I scared you. I wanted to slip back in before you woke up."

"You weren't leaving me," I say, and the shudder of relief that passes through me is nearly as euphoric as my climax during our early morning foray. Nearly. I'm not sure anything could ever quite compare.

"Leaving?" He walks over and puts the cups and bag down on the nightstand next to me, then sits on the edge of the bed. "You thought I, what? Just walked out on you?" He's studying me with a deep frown.

"No. Well, yes. I don't know? I didn't know what to think, honestly. This morning was . . . unexpected. Everything about what's happening here is. We haven't talked about any of it, and I guess the weight of that hit when I woke up and you weren't here."

"The weight of what exactly?"

"What we're doing? Or not doing, I suppose. What we are and aren't saying. We had sex, but I'm also a fully grown adult woman, and the rational part of my brain accepts that sex is sometimes just that. Sex. We have a history, yes, but a dusty one. And it didn't exactly wrap with a happy ending, so . . ." I shrug. The sheet slips, an unintentional nip flash, and I tug it back up, tucking it securely beneath my arms. "I suppose what I'm trying to express, and doing quite poorly at, is that I realized you might have left. And that I have no clue what you're thinking or feeling about any of this. Or at least about me. Because the rest of this—" I wave my hands around the room, this place, the *fucking '90s*, and my sheet, of course, slips again. "Damn disobedient sheet," I mutter, yanking it back up. "As I was saying, the rest of this, it's beyond our control, isn't it? But you and me, the way we feel about one another—or the way we *don't* feel—that's maybe the only real thing we have. The only piece we have any power over."

"Bea," Rocco says calmly. A sort of calmness that feels utterly incomprehensible to me—in this time and place, but also on any timeline, in any location, naked in the sheets next to Rocco Riziero.

"Yes?"

"Let me say this clearly, because I don't want us to have one of those classic rom-com miscommunication moments. God, I hate those kinds of movies. You feel one thing and say another, and I feel the same thing you're feeling, but also say the exact opposite. We get mad, we go our separate ways, and then, if we're lucky, we both come full circle and realize we were a bunch of dipshits who should have just been honest in the first place."

"Rocco?"

"Yeah?"

"Please get to the point. This is brutal."

"Right. Yes." He pulls his legs up on the bed, leaning against the headboard so we're side by side, shoulders touching. "So, in plain terms to start: I don't regret any of what happened between us, not in the slightest. I'm actually pretty damn delighted it happened. And I hope it happens again. A lot." The room is suddenly twenty degrees too hot; I am a swirl of sweat and steam beneath my sheet. "Because I like you, Bea. I really, really like you. I like your incredibly pointy wit and your unfailing arsenal of smirks. I like how much you fight for yourself and for your dreams. I like that you have more layers to peel away than any onion I've ever come up against in my kitchen—and yes, before you say it, I do like to cook, and no, I do not have a live-in chef."

I laugh because he's exactly right. I was very tempted to make a crack. He knows me uncannily well.

"I like the way you laugh, exactly like that, and only when you really mean it. I like everything about you, really, on this timeline, and I suspect on every other possible timeline, too. And I'm pretty certain, looking back at us now, seeing how you made me feel firsthand . . . I was a total ass, to not put two and two together sooner. I should never have done what I did, Bea. And not just because it was a selfish thing to do to any woman. That, too, yes. But specifically to do it to you, because I think we could have been something special if I hadn't imploded everything. Or we already *were* something special, but I was too thickheaded to wrap my head around it. And maybe we're here, caught up in some impossible snag in the universe, because . . . we still can have that. It's not too late for us. Or maybe it's random that we're here, but this is our silver lining. Either way, it's the same for me. I want this. I want you."

It's arguably the most perfect monologue, in content and execution, I've ever witnessed, in real life or on the screen. Ten out of ten, no notes.

I'm thinking so many things, feeling so many things. Most of them good. Tinged with anxieties, of course, because what is romance, especially in the early phases, without anxieties? But of all the options, what comes out of my mouth is: "If those were your plain terms, I'm desperately curious to hear the fancy explanation."

He laughs. Hoots, really. "That is the most Bea Noel response possible. Part of your appeal, obviously. But you still don't get to avoid the real talk. Remember what I said? No rom-com miscommunication for us. There's a reason I don't do those movies, and it's not just because there's an inordinate number of shirtless scenes. It's all just so painfully avoidable. Pure torture, really."

"I like you, too," I whisper.

"Say that again? Couldn't quite hear it from all the way over here, a good six inches from your lips."

I lift my hands up to cup both sides of his face, look him dead on. "I like you very much. And I also have no regrets. Well, I may regret the events of the party, the car ride . . ." I shake my head, dismissing the thought of Tom, the article, worries for another moment. "But with you and me? None. This time with you here has been the most outrageously bizarre gift of my life. I don't understand what's happening to us or why, but I do believe that you're real. *This* is real. The only real thing we have. And sure, I'm mildly terrified because I'm not in the mood to have my heart broken, now or ever again. Because of what happened with us in the past, yes, but also because after my divorce, it's harder to be . . . optimistic about the long-term for any romantic connection. But right now? I feel hopeful. I feel strongly enough about you to try. I'm not sure this is what the universe intended for us to realize, but I do know it's the takeaway I choose."

Rocco leans in, closing those six inches, and presses his lips to mine. So gently. It's as much a whisper as it is a kiss. We stay like that for a moment, eyes locked, neither of us moving. Not pushing further. Because in the moment, this kiss is more than enough. It's everything I need.

"Do you think," Rocco says, his sweet coffee-laced breath hot on my lips, "we're here to make us work the first time around? So we don't waste all the years in between?"

This time when he asks, the answer feels clear. I shake my head, my lips brushing soft lines against his. "No. I don't."

He nods.

I lean across his lap to grab one of the coffees. "Your breath smelled so good, I had to have some of my own." I take a long swig. Delicious creamy latte.

"I got some banana chocolate chip muffins, too. Had to walk a few blocks and try a few cafes, but I was on a mission."

I smile into my cup. "Thank you." I take another few sips, close my eyes as the caffeine soaks into my veins. "I don't think we should change anything about our relationship then," I start again. "For one, we've talked about how dangerous that could be, how much of our lives it could rewrite. You wouldn't fall out with your brother, a good thing on the surface, sure. But then who knows how that would have changed both of your lives? He could still be with Piper, or back in Hollywood, or married to someone he's not with on our original timeline. Or maybe we broke up later on, and you found someone new. I found someone new, not my actual ex. You could have kids. *I* could have kids. Maybe my career path would have changed, and I wouldn't have written the script, wouldn't be making *Murder in the Books*."

I shake my head. Take another sip. Rocco watches me, waiting for more.

"And besides," I continue, "say we did somehow keep ourselves together back then, which magically sends us back to our real time again . . . we would miss our whole love story, wouldn't we? Or maybe we would have lived it in some parallel-universe kind of way, and some alternate version of ourselves would hold those memories. But if we're going to make this work, I want the real deal. Present and future. Even if that means we both made bad choices along the way, lost time together. We learned. Made our paths. All the shitty side hustles I worked, the disappointing ex-boyfriends—the disappointing ex-husband—that's all part of it. Maybe we wouldn't work together now, not without those things."

"You're right," he says. He picks up the brown bag and pulls out an oversized muffin, just as much top as bottom. "About all of it. I can feel it. I just . . . don't know what that means for us here. What we're supposed to do; if there's anything *to* do. If we're not trying for a do-over, how do we reset the clock?" He takes a large bite of muffin, top of course, and sighs. Passes it over to me. "Not quite as good as your old favorite, but darn close. I almost thought about driving all the way over to the one by my old house, but *A*, I didn't want to be away even longer, and *B*, didn't want to have another run-in with my past self. Though I suspect I was still sleeping off the champs fountain."

I take a bite of the top, too. Swallow. It is pretty good, even if it's not an exact replica. I pass it back to him, and we finish it that way, bite by bite, top to bottom, not talking.

"While we're being honest," Rocco says, brushing the last crumbs off my chin, "there is something I keep coming back to. About our past. Something I don't quite understand."

"Yeah?" I take his hand from my chin, wrap my fingers around his. He gives a soft squeeze.

"Why didn't you tell me about your dad? At the time, I mean. If you felt so strongly about me. What stopped you from opening up? Did you not . . . trust me? To be supportive enough of what you were going through, or to take it seriously enough, or . . . what? Because I'm trying to make sense of that."

"No." I shake my head. "I don't know. I did trust you. But it was hard for me to talk about it to anyone, and mostly I just wanted a new life for myself. A place where no one saw me as William Noel's daughter. Not the bestselling author, not the suspected murderer. I did want to tell you—it almost slipped out a few times. But the longer I went without mentioning it, the harder it felt to casually drop it in. And then when things ended between us, I'd felt justified in keeping myself closed off."

"But it's that exactly," he says, his voice extra gentle. "Because maybe if I'd known, things would have been different. Maybe you wouldn't have ended up at the Roxy party. And maybe I still would have gone, and I'd have made the same bad decision. Or . . . maybe I wouldn't have. Maybe telling me, opening up like that, would have made things different between us. Stronger. We'll never know. It was just such a big piece of your life at the time, and you . . . said nothing about it. I was thinking about that last night, when I couldn't sleep, trying to remember anything about your family at the time. I drew a total blank."

The weight of it hits, what Rocco is saying—because I'd never thought about that side of it before. I only thought about the consequences of opening myself up, the risks instead of the benefits. Maybe I did hold him at arm's length. Maybe telling the truth could have been enough to change everything.

"I'm sorry," I say, looking down at the crumpled bed sheets. "I should have tried to be more open. It wasn't anything you said or did, not at the time. You made me feel good. And I needed that. Simple, easy good. But that's not what a real relationship is."

"Hey." Rocco nudges my chin up with our interlocked hands. Looks me in the eye. "Don't apologize. Like you said— maybe we needed all the mistakes to get to this place. You and me, in actual working order together. I was just thinking . . ." He trails off, though his eyes only become more focused as whatever thought he's having takes form.

"What?"

"Maybe if there's something that could or should be different, it's . . . about your dad after all."

Every one of my senses sharpens; the room spins, everything around me suddenly in hyper focus. "How? What do you mean?"

"I'm not totally sure, to be honest. It's a new thought. Half-baked. And I'm not saying it will change our circumstances, jet us back to the future or anything. I don't know that it's any kind of solution or ticket out. Like we said when it first came up—LA, our paths here, that feels most likely to be the fix, if there is one. But maybe that . . . doesn't matter now? Or it doesn't matter as much as this. Because if we're here, and we're not trying to mess with things at the Y2K party tonight . . . you should take the chance, Bea. See your dad again. Before . . ."

Before he dies.

On the first day of the new millennium.

I check the clock, do the mental calculations: eight hours of driving to get to Tucson, best case, plus some time for bathroom and food breaks. We should be there well before midnight—and whatever will or won't happen for us when the clock strikes twelve and a new year begins.

Like Rocco said, seeing my dad probably won't get us out of here.

But at this point? With no other better ideas about how to redo the night?

I don't really give a damn.

Dad.

I'm jumping out of the bed then, tearing through my piles of clothes until I find the sweater and jeans I arrived in; it gives some comfort, this reminder of the woman I've become. I scrounge around for my underwear from last night, remember it's in scraps, littered like black-lace confetti around the room.

"So, we're doing it then," Rocco says, handing me the last clean pair of new underwear from my stash on the bureau.

"We're doing it," I say, giving him a quick peck on the lips as I grab the underwear from his hands. "We're going to Tucson."

Chapter 14

Rocco

Friday, December 31, 1999

Eight hours to Tucson sounds faster than I would've thought, but Bea swears by it.

Truth be told, I haven't taken the 10 freeway anywhere past Joshua Tree. Mildly embarrassing to admit, my trips there . . . but that place, it's magical. Lots of deep reflection, aided by a smidge of hallucinogens.

Basically, I know where I'm going. Roughly. No smartphone, so memory will have to do, at least until I snag an actual *paper* map somewhere along the way.

"You want to drive first, or you want to take a load off?" I ask, watching as Bea stuffs her recently acquired wardrobe into a large Aero bag. "I like driving Delilah, to be honest. I suspect it's mutual. We have a bit of a rapport."

"Let's not go too far—she *tolerates* you. But sure, happy to split it up. You drive to Arizona, then I'll take over. Sound like a fine compromise, Mr. I-got-the-hots-for-Delilah? Truly, who knew you could fall for such a plebian car?" She smiles at me, then stops what she's doing to kiss me. Lingering, despite the urgency buzzing through the room.

Kissing Bea feels remarkably . . . normal. A good kind of normal—fucking great, really. Like it's just how it should be. Should have always been, maybe, if I hadn't blown it all up.

But I did, and that's over, and it's not what we were brought here to change.

Hopefully, anyway.

With her, it's got to be about the future now.

We just have to get back there first.

"Alright," I say, grinning when she pulls away, because no matter how anxious I might be, I can't help but smile. "First stop is Frank's for grub, right on our way out of town. Fair warning, the food is mediocre at best, gross at worst, but if it's the last time we're here, I insist. I need to have one more slab of blackened toast with too much butter and slimy eggs on a semi-clean plate thrown at me by an ornery waitress. For nostalgia purposes." Rudy and I used to eat there sometimes after particularly long days on set at our Burbank studio. Just one of our things, no matter how shitty the food.

"Wow, Rocco, are you even an actor? Because you just did the most atrocious job of selling that place."

"I promise, it's worth it for the vibes. Quick breakfast, then we're off. We need more than these muffins in our bellies for fuel."

Bea gives one of her patented scowls, but it's soft around the edges. "Fine. But only because I like you so much."

My grin grows even wider, and that scowl of hers slips away altogether.

Frank's is exactly what I'd hoped it would be.

The food isn't even as bad as it was in my memories. The awful service, though—still very real.

"I can't believe that waitress grumbled over me not drinking my coffee fast enough," Bea says, rubbing her stomach as we settle back into Delilah for the long ride. "As if I wanted to be there any longer than necessary. Also, that sausage left a funny aftertaste. I'm feeling a little . . . intestinally bubbly, let's say. I hope you're pleased."

I chuckle. "I've never heard such an eloquent way of referencing gas." She gently whacks me on the arm. "Sorry, sorry. I take full responsibility. But we had to eat, didn't we, or we'd pass out on the ride. Once we're past Indio, it's slim pickings. I remember well, since I was at the first-ever Coachella. October '99. No big deal or anything." Saying that brings back so many amazing memories. Rudy had just started college on the East Coast, but he'd flown back out for the festival. He'd been the one to make me go—he was a huge Tool and Rage Against the Machine fan. I was sold, mostly because I'd missed the hell out of him, and also because of Beck.

That trip was probably the last solid brotherly time I had with Rudy before . . . everything imploded. Before New Year's Eve and Piper and a decade and a half of being too stubborn—too ashamed—to make things right.

If only we could rewrite time without consequences. If only it could be that simple. Because I would choose family, Rudy, every time.

I'd pick Trixie, too.

Bea.

I can't imagine this journey with anyone else. I care about her, and not because of *Murder in the Books*—not out of misplaced guilt or empathy or obligation. It's everything she is and isn't. I'm grateful the universe gave us this reboot, but I'm terrified, too.

Terrified to screw it up a second time.

Bea sits silently as I drive along the 10 freeway, probably doing her own mental cycling. Staring out the window at the Inland Empire. We've officially moved out of LA, heading toward the end of civilization as we know it.

"You want to talk about anything, Bea?" I ask gently. "I

know this felt like a good idea in theory, while securely in the confines of a Los Angeles hotel room, but I want to make sure you're still okay." I put my hand on her shoulder and squeeze.

"I'm just . . . replaying everything. My escape to LA, tuning out all the ugly noise. With Sylvie and the movie. With you. Even after he got released from jail. As he lay in a hospital bed *dying*." Her voice cracks on that last part, and I turn to see tears streaming down her face. My hand moves from her shoulder to her cheek, wiping gently. "I'm scared to upset him, showing up like this. Scared to say the wrong thing. I just want to give him some comfort, you know? Peace. I want him to feel loved in the end." She pulls my hand from her cheek and holds on tight.

"I can't imagine, Bea. What you're working through. I've had my moments with my family, Rudy especially, but none of it compares. So while I might not have anything especially eloquent to say, just know I'm here. I care. I want you to have this closure, for both of you. And I'm so damn sorry I took it from you the first time around."

"No." She shakes her head, firmly. "We've covered this. It's on me. I could have gone. But I chose you." She squeezes my hand even more tightly. "I might be quiet for a while. I hope you don't mind. Feel free to put on some tapes—in the center console." She reaches over to open it with her free hand, and I glance down at the stash.

"No worries, I can sit in silence, too . . . though, hold up, is that *You'd Prefer an Astronaut* I see in there? Man, I love that album. Come to think of it, I remember listening to that one together. And wait, you liked Hum, too? Whoa, and the Toadies' *Rubberneck*? Who are you, my little brother?!"

Bea laughs. An earnest one, despite everything. "And *Tragic Kingdom*, which rounds out the tape collection I bought once I realized Delilah had no CD player because I didn't pay the premium. Classics, *no doubt*. Get it?"

It's a relief, hearing her make a bad pun. "Oh, I get it. And I'll be as quiet as I can be. No promises on some big chorus sing-alongs, but I'll try my darndest."

She gives a small smile, then looks off, out the window, her face going slack. I put in the Hum cassette to distract myself. Let Bea have her time. She rightly deserves it.

She deserves everything I can give her, and so much more.

"Is it okay if we take a quick detour?" My words break her silence rule. Bea looks slightly confused, dazed. "We'll still be in Tucson well before midnight."

She nods. "I need to stretch my legs. Walk off that god awful breakfast you forced me to consume."

"Ha. Perfect, because this detour is a mini hike. A dip into Joshua Tree. I'm hoping it'll give us some clarity and calm. At the very least, a short walk to get the blood flowing. It's so beautiful here. Have you ever been?"

I pull off the highway, turning into the south entrance of the park.

"No way. Too hipster for me. Besides, I was never that into Jim Morrison." She winks at that last bit, her lips giving a light, smirky twitch.

"Hey, I'm no hipster either! And even without any *enhancements*, legal or otherwise, it really is ridiculously beautiful, and this trail is short but nice. Good desert views. No heavy hiking, just a breezy walk. The quick leg stretch you're looking for."

I glance over as her expression changes again. A somber glaze slides over her face.

"My dad, he was a big Doors guy. That's how I knew Jim Morrison was a fan. Drove his '67 Shelby through the desert, didn't he, manifesting his poems and connecting with the Mojave? My dad always said he wanted to bring me here someday, when I was older. I haven't thought about that in years."

I pull into a spot and shut Delilah off. Her fan continues to whir. Even a time-traveling beast of a car needs a break, especially when cruising through the desert at high speed.

We climb out and set off together in silence. The walk is just as I'd remembered. Tan. Lots of tan. Tiny spots of green, yellow, purple littering the dry, dusty soil. The overall effect is stunning in its austere simplicity. And the air, it just hits different here, so cool and fresh, at least this time of year.

"Keep an ear out for rattlesnakes," I say, my first words since we left the car. "I've seen them on this trail before."

Bea grabs a stray stick from the ground and waves it near my face. "As an Arizona girl, I assure you I'm highly tuned into that particular sound. We used to find them in the garage all the time." She pokes the stick into my chest, relatively gently at least, and smiles. "This is gorgeous, Rocco. A-plus detour. Glorious place to stretch my legs."

I wrap my arm around her as we continue this half-mile loop showcasing the *desert flora*. I read that on a sign—there are a lot of them peppering the trail. But this place really does reconnect me to the world at large. The sharp colors, the wide sky, and the scorched earth that somehow still has enough nutrients to sustain life for others? Magic.

Enough of the vision quest, Rocco. That was last October . . . seventeen years removed.

Mostly I just hope it's doing the same thing for Bea. The calm before the storm of everything coming for her.

We're silent again for the rest of the walk, taking in the views, occasionally stealing glances at one another. That feeling of magic is doing something funky to me, because there's a word that drifts into my mind out here on the trail.

Love.

It's too soon.

I haven't dropped that word on any romantic partner since Piper. Too loaded. Too intense. Too much, period.

It's this air, this place, this time that shouldn't be possible but somehow is.

Whatever this feeling is or isn't, I shove it down.

Because today is about Bea. Adding anything else to the already complex hot pot on her stove would be too much. We'll have plenty of time to figure us out another day—maybe in another decade—hopefully.

We wind our way back to the parking lot and I open the passenger door, helping Bea settle into Delilah. And then I lean in and kiss her on the lips. She's caught by surprise, letting out a low gasp. But then her warm palms are pressed against the back of my neck, tugging me in closer.

When I finally pull away, there's a grin on those soft, pouty lips of hers. She moves the seat back and gets cozy, sighing contentedly. Her eyes close as I settle into the driver's seat, but she reaches over to grab my thigh. Squeezes.

Against all odds, we are here, now, for one another. This connection—it's real.

And despite the bizarre circumstances, it's somehow the most real I've ever felt.

I watch the digital clock on the dashboard tick ahead.

Counting us down to midnight, to Y2K. To William's death tomorrow.

We're close to the Colorado River now, the state line. Delilah's doing admirably well, though she does require sustenance. The Exxon station I land on is extremely Route 66. Kitschy placards of all sizes adorn the front, complete with an "E-Z Stop Food Mart" sign. A bold lie; there's nothing easy about gas station food bubble gut. But Frank's was hours ago now, so I might take my chances. As soon as I turn the car off, Bea wakes up. She stretches and blinks her doe eyes in this sweet, dreamy way, like all is right in her world. It takes a minute for that wave of calm to leave her face, replaced by the hour at hand.

"How long have I been out?" she asks through a yawn.

"Well, I've listened to all your cassettes twice. I forgot how good *Tragic Kingdom* is. Really hit the spot once we got going through the desert."

"Good thing you liked it so much, because a third listen once I get behind the wheel is nonnegotiable."

I laugh. "Fine by me. Now should we just grab some snacks to hold us over until we get closer to Phoenix, then find a real restaurant? Or do we power through on whatever E-Z meals they have?"

"Rocco, please." She lifts her brows, serving up some side-eye. "I might be an anxious mess, but I still require proper fuel, especially now that the breakfast grease has evaporated. Nothing would pain me more than eating a premade gas station sandwich when there's some of the best Mexican food in the country just a short drive away. So go grab some Doritos and a Gatorade to tide yourself over."

"Yes, m'lady. As you wish." I get out, snack up—with Taco Bell *and* Pizza Hut Doritos, a real score—and map up, too, and fill Delilah with gas.

Back on the road.

So close now.

"My god, Bea," I moan. "These tamales are out of control. Best decision in the world to make this pit stop. Though I do wish I'd grabbed the bigger bag of chips."

"And right off the highway! El Norteno was always a stopping point if we were heading west. My road trip chilaquiles and tamales of choice. My dad's, too, which made this feel especially appropriate. It's still here in the present time, but . . . I don't get back much. You had Frank's, I had this. My '90s core food memory beats the heck out of yours, I gotta say." She smiles, then pops the last bit of tamale in her mouth.

"I'll give you a win on the food, but I do enjoy a curmudgeonly waitstaff every now and again. Everyone here was a smidge *too* nice. Like, in a vaguely creepy way. The makings of serial killers, if you ask me."

Bea tosses a crumpled paper napkin at my head, then stands up from our small roadside table, lit from above by a strand of white twinkly lights hung along the storefront. I get up, too, gathering my trash.

It's getting dark now. Time to go.

"I can assure you," she says, "there are no serial killers here. Yet. I don't think. But c'mon, let's get going. The hospital probably doesn't allow visitors in too late. We're about two hours and change away." She takes a second to consider, and then a look of painful realization sets in. "*Shit.*"

"What's up?"

"Mountain time. We crossed into Arizona, and I miscalculated. We lost an hour."

Damn. "We still got this. I'll keep the Gatorade bottle in the car for emergencies. No more stops."

"Emergency for who? You think I can pee into that tiny hole while I'm driving?"

"Er. Right. Valid point. Just looking for time-savers."

"It was hard enough to watch you get bright-red Dorito crumbs on her seats and floor, but I'll be damned if anyone attempts a piss in Delilah. She's a lady chariot!"

I'm not going to argue with her; I wouldn't ordinarily choose to, and I especially wouldn't now. This drive, inching closer to the hospital, her dad, this goodbye that shouldn't even be possible. It's heavy and hard, and being silly right now feels both outrageous and necessary at the same time.

As we approach Delilah, I wrap the bottle in my arms like a baby. "I'm sorry, tiny toilet, but we must let you go. I know you could've been helpful, but it's about respect. Our fine-ass lady chariot is *not* a bathroom. Even for emergencies."

Bea claps effusively, a smile on her face. I'd make all the potty jokes in the world to help add a little levity to Bea's hard moments. Or I'd be dead silent if that's what she needed more. I'd do anything, for her. "Now you're getting it. A time-traveling, fine-ass lady chariot! A true wonder of a vehicle. Next stop, Tucson."

We settle into the car, Bea at the helm, and, like it's old habit, we lean across the console and kiss. She grabs for my hand, and we cruise back onto the highway.

It's 10:05 mountain time when we pull into the hospital lot.

And according to the large sign posted by the parking garage entrance, visiting hours were over at 9:00 sharp.

We should never have stopped at Joshua Tree. Though even without it, we likely would've missed our window. The clock was against us, no matter what.

Bea quietly climbs out of the car. Stands on the curb, hugging herself as she stares out at the sprawling hospital. I follow behind, stand close without touching. Giving all the space she needs.

"I'm so sorry, Bea. I should have driven straight through. Maybe disregarded the speed limit more. Delilah's a four-cylinder engine, though. I didn't want to push it. Or risk a cop pulling us over and seeing our plates, checking our futuristic licenses. But still. Would have been worth the consequences if it meant you seeing your dad."

"I was born here," she says, eyes still fixed on the building ahead. "Haven't been back since. Anyway. I'm not worried about visiting hours being over. It's New Year's Eve. People are probably too bitter about working tonight to care about rules. Or too busy worrying the whole system will implode at the stroke of midnight. Y2K fear was no joke."

Her optimism is almost alarming. Is she starting to crack?

"Besides, I have you, Rocco. You're a sweet talker. The king of sweet talking, really. I know you'll get someone to let us up. Give them a good holiday sob story."

Damn, she's right.

I am a legendary sweet talker, aren't I? I knew I was here for a reason. "I'm always down for a challenge. Plus, I'm here for you—I would do anything you needed." She shivers in the brisk night air, and I wrap my arms around her shoulders.

She swivels around, slowly, and kisses me. A kiss that's both sweet and full of electricity at the same time. It slow burns its way through my veins.

"That means so much," she whispers, lips brushing against my neck, sending a trail of shivers down my spine.

It's hard to pull away, but I do—mind on the time, the heavy task at hand. "I'll go see what I can do."

"Thank you." She leans back in, gives me another kiss, a quick one this time. "I'll wait out here while you go work those charms of yours. I need a minute to compose myself."

I salute her and start off for the main entrance.

There are three people stationed at the lobby desk when I step inside. Two of them staring at monitors, one of them staring me down. Christina Diaz, according to her nametag. Can't be more than early twenties.

"Hey, Ms. Diaz! Happy New Year's Eve!"

"Christina's fine. And hold on one freaking minute! Do you know how much you look like Rocco Riziero? But like if he was a dad, all white-haired and whatnot. Andrea! Your hall pass's father is here!"

Oh shit. A hall pass is an honor. Not many celebrity accolades do much for me, at least not after this many years in the biz, but a hall pass? That's commitment. Even if it's partly just a joke and not a true "pause the relationship for a night" kind of deal, it certainly does wonders for my confidence. Even if I am relegated to "hall pass's father" in this go-around of '99. There are worse fates.

But before I can decide on an appropriate risk-free response, Andrea herself cuts in, now studying me instead of her computer screen. "Yup, definitely not our Rocco, but I can see the resemblance! I'm gonna have to keep this precious hall pass of mine for the real Rocco. Though he'd be lucky to look like you in twenty years." She gives me another once over, then turns back to her work.

Christina examines me further, eyes narrowed, then shakes her head. "Ha. Nice try, handsome. I bet you get away with that a lot. Not here, though."

"To be fair, I never claimed any Rocco connection. I just wasn't necessarily going to deny it either. I'm not below pretending I'm his foxy father, at least for the right cause." I flash what I happen to know is definitively my most charming grin. "Look, I'm just trying to get my friend in to see her fa . . ." I cough. "Uncle." Wouldn't do to have Bea's mom hear her wayward daughter visited overnight. Let her be confused about a niece. "I know visiting hours are over, but we drove a long way to be here. If playing the Rocco card would've given me a better chance at getting in, how could I have resisted?"

Christina chuckles. "You got me good for a second. Your face, plus something about the way you said hello . . . you could definitely be a Riziero." She shakes her head at me. Stares up at the ceiling. Sighs. "Listen. It's well after visiting hours and I'm *really* not supposed to let you in. But since you would've been willing to use such a sad little bar trick for this 'friend' of yours, you must really care about her. I respect the gesture, so . . ." She puts a finger to her lips and winks, then slips two visiting passes onto the counter.

"Thank you," I whisper, fighting the urge to jump the desk and kiss her on the cheek.

"Hey, it's a holiday. Plus, I did always think Rocco was pretty darn cute. At least until I developed a thing for redheads. Now if you only had a much younger friend who looked like Rudy, my god . . . I'd let him rock my world at the stroke of midnight."

Wow. Quite a departing line.

"Ha-ha, great idea, maybe I should do a casting call, 'Looking for wingman, must be a twentysomething with flaming red hair!' Anyway, er . . ." Move it the hell along, Rocco. "Could you tell me where William Noel's room is?"

She eyes her screen, clicks a few times. "Third floor. Room 312. If anyone hassles you, tell them to give Christina a ring. And let me know if you find him. The redhead, not your friend's uncle." She giggles again, then turns back to her computer.

We're in.

This is happening.

I walk to the nearest window and flash the passes for Bea, who's made her way up the sidewalk, closer to the entrance.

"Alright then," I mutter, bolstering myself. "Let's go rewrite history."

Chapter 15

Beatrix

Saturday, January 1, 2000

The door marked 312 looks like every other door in the hallway.

A dull beige, scuffed along the bottom from passing feet over the years, clipboard holding a thin stack of papers pinned in the middle, just below a small window.

It's completely unfathomable to me now—standing here, with my own two feet planted in a hospital hallway that looks, smells, sounds too real for any dream—that my dad could exist on the other side of that door. Flesh and blood. All the things about him that no camcorder at the time could have captured, and we'd never really been the kind of family who was good at documenting life's big or small moments on film. His warm, gravelly baritone that could have gotten him a voiceover career, if his books hadn't taken off as they did; that trademark rumbling chuckle, building in speed as it rolled out, instantly cutting through any bad day at school, like a ray of sunshine or sip of warm soup in laughter form. The bright glint of his gray eyes, the fusion of mint and cedar that followed him wherever he went—a fervent devotion to both Old Spice and Doublemint. He could chew through a pack a day when he was working through a particularly thorny plot point.

Though he'll surely smell like hospital through and through now, the glint most likely rubbed down flat, from jail, from sickness. From me.

"You ready for this?" Rocco asks, quietly, as he leans in from behind.

I let myself fall into him, steadying my back against his firm chest. "I don't think I could ever possibly be ready for this."

"Right. Yes. Relatively speaking, I suppose. More like ready enough."

Sweat prickles down the back of my neck. My stomach swirls; I regret every car snack from the day. Everything I ate, except for the tamales. "You peek in the window first, okay? To be sure we're alone. I know my mom's always regretted that she went home. That she didn't make a special request to stay over, and he was alone for midnight on New Year's Eve. Alone for his last midnight, period. She knew he wouldn't have long— the cancer had spread everywhere by the time he was getting proper care. But the cardiac arrest . . . she blinked, and he was gone."

That thought, this night, the brutal finality of it all, sends a fresh wave of anxiety coursing through me. I close my eyes. Take a deep breath. Swallow.

"Of course, Bea." Rocco cups his hands on top of my shoulders, leaning in for a quick peck on my neck from behind. I will the warmth he radiates to seep into me. "But you got this. You've spent the last seventeen years thinking about everything you wish you could have said or done. You wrote a whole script to help you to process. So right now? Let it all out. Because I have a feeling this really is your last chance. Unless the universe has more tricks up her sleeve, and I kind of hope she doesn't. This trick's enough for me."

"God, imagine that?" I laugh, grateful for the fleeting distraction. "Living this whole week over and over, until we adequately unlock the puzzle. Hm. That's actually helpful. If I tell myself that's a possibility, it takes pressure off tonight. Maybe it's the first of many goodbyes."

"Let's assume the best," Rocco says, his hands moving from my shoulders down the length of my arms. His fingers find mine, latch on. "As grateful as I am for this last week with you, I'm also looking forward to my obnoxiously expensive but very worth it memory foam California king bed, in the home on the property I actually own, whilst living in the appropriate decade. Though hopefully that bed will have you in it now, too."

"I would like that. Being in your decade-appropriate bed. With you."

"Good."

He gives me a smile so soft and sweet, I feel an actual ache when we let go of one another.

Rocco edges in front of me and leans toward the door, peering into the window. A long moment passes, and then he looks back at me, shaking his head. "All clear," he says. "You got this."

I nod, and take the first step closer.

"I'll be here if you need me."

"Thank you," I whisper, and I feel that gratitude deep in my bones. I'm not sure I could do this alone, without the knowledge that Rocco's right here with me.

My hand is on the door handle then, pushing it open. My feet somehow move forward, carrying me into the room.

I pry my eyes off the tiled floor to look up, and gasp.

Because it's him.

It's my dad, and he's alive, and he's staring straight at me.

"Daddy," I say, the word falling apart on my lips.

A pause, those gray eyes wide, confused, but still alert, and then, "Bea?"

I rush over to his bed, not bothering to swipe away the tears that are already spilling down my cheeks. "You recognize me?"

"Of course I do, I'd recognize you anywhere, but . . ." His eyes go even wider as he takes me in up close. I take him in, too, so precisely as I remember him, but also not at all. He's at least forty pounds lighter, maybe more; grays peppering his thinning hair; skin pale and fragile-looking under the too-bright fluorescent ceiling lights. I want to swallow him up in my arms—too easy to do now, his shoulders are so narrow—and tell pretty lies, promise that everything is going to be alright. "You've aged more than seems, ah, reasonable since I last saw you. Maybe I'm . . . hallucinating? The exceptionally kind nurses have been rather generous with painkillers these past few days."

"You're not hallucinating." I hadn't adequately planned this part out. But . . . why not tell him about this past week? He'll keep my secret. He has less than a day left on this Earth; it's probably safe to say he'll take it to the grave. The thought makes my throat squeeze; I let out a mangled sob-laugh. "This is going to sound ridiculous. Full-on bonkers. The kind of fiction you usually avoided, far too absurdist for you. Because 'there are enough fascinating truths in our real world—' "

"To exclusively write and read realistic stories, for all of time," he finishes, smiling. It's what he'd always said; magic, fantasy, sci-fi, all fine creative endeavors, but for other people. Never for him. No, he'd prefer to lose himself in crimes that could very conceivably happen. Which, of course, proved to be too true.

It was the sheer believability of his books that undid him in the end.

"Yes, you'd ordinarily despise this story," I say, smiling, too, because we're here, together, talking. "But I'm hoping you quite like this one."

He leans back against his pillow, and there it is—that glimmer in his eye I knew and loved so well. It wasn't lost for good after all, despite everything.

I sit down on the edge of his bed, taking his hand between both of mine. I wrap all ten of my fingers securely around his, like if I hold him tightly enough, we'll never have to come apart. "Well, it started a few days ago, on a seemingly inauspicious late December day in LA, in the year of 2016, with a highly flawed yet surprisingly endearing A-list actor and a trusty old silver German steed. . . ." And from there I tell him everything—about my film, the accident, our week as time travelers—succinctly enough for him to easily follow, but with enough colorful details to pull him in entirely. After all, he's William Noel. I can't disappoint him in his final hours with the last story he'll ever hear from me.

Thank goodness he taught me so well.

When I finish, leaving off at our arrival here and Rocco charming his way past the front desk, he's silent. His eyes have been closed for the last few minutes, but I can tell he's very much awake, his attention tuned to every word I say. The thoughtful furrow of his brow, the soft flutter of his lids, and the gentle curl of his smile that tips up higher as I go.

Another moment passes, and then he opens his eyes. "That was quite a story."

"Thank you. I have no idea how it ends for me and Rocco, but when we were trying to decide how best to spend tonight, the only idea that made sense was this. Driving here to see you."

"You know how this ends for me, don't you? Or more specifically . . . when."

He doesn't look altogether sad as he says it. Tired. Resigned. But also curious, like it's just any other fact of life—another detail in a long and twisting story.

I nod.

"Soon?"

I nod again.

"Huh. Well, alright then. That's about what I expected, I suppose. I can feel it, you know. Sense something's shifting. I feel . . . different? Partly from the meds. But it's more than that." He shrugs, and I can see his collarbones poke through his thin hospital gown. "I won't lie and say I don't wish I had more time. We've missed too much as it is. The last year has been . . . less than ideal." He chuckles, that throaty rumble I've missed with every cell of my body. I wish I had a smartphone, something, anything to record it. "But you're here now. And you just told me what I suspect will go down as the very best story I've ever heard in my life. Maybe I should have read more magic-y things all along. I've been missing out."

"No. You only like this particular magical story because it's also real."

"You are real then, aren't you? This is actually happening? It's not the meds?"

I nod, and the tears are back then. My body shakes, the weight of the sadness threatening to crash down on top of me.

"Come here," he says, his arms open wide. I let go of his hand and fall against him, as gently as I can, given his state. "My sweet, sweet girl," he says, his warm palms smoothing over the back of my head.

"Why don't you hate me?" I ask, the words muffled against his chest.

"How could I ever hate you?"

"Because I didn't believe you." The words sound so impossibly ugly out loud. *How?* How did I ever think my own father was capable of something so evil? "I should never have doubted you."

"Eh, well. I should never have lied to you about my calls with Marjorie. That's on me. But I was too scared to be honest. And there was quite a lot of other evidence that wasn't necessarily in my favor. Circumstantial, but still. Compelling enough to do the trick."

"It doesn't matter. One lie shouldn't have derailed a lifetime of truths. And they could have found the scissors in your hand, at the crime scene, with a full confession from you, and I still should have known it could never be possible. That there was another story hiding beneath the surface."

"I guess if I should be disappointed in anything, it's that you assumed the most obvious suspect was the correct one. The neighbor who just so happened to be at the library, too, while his family was conveniently out of town. An eccentric writer obsessed with true crime, who was a perfect match with every known detail of her mystery lover. And who was of course writing a secret new manuscript with a plot that mirrored the crime itself." He lets out a long-suffering sigh. "Just . . . so easy, all of it. I thought I taught you better than that."

I can hear his smile without having to tilt my face up to see for myself. "How are you smiling at a time like this?"

"How do you know I'm smiling?"

"Because I still remember everything about you. You'll be pleased to know you've proven very difficult to forget, even for five minutes at a time."

"I'm not pleased—not if it means you've been holding on for so long you can't appreciate your own life in the present."

"How could I let go? After I was so horrible to you. Even when your name was cleared, when everyone else was tripping over themselves to apologize to you—the media, the publishing world, our neighbors—I didn't come home."

He's quiet for a moment. I count the soft thumping beats of his heart against my cheek; it's both a glorious miracle to hear it at all—my dad's heart, still beating—and completely devastating, to know that hours from now, it will shudder and stop. Forever.

"Why didn't you?" he asks then, quietly. "Come home? I've been wondering if I'd get to see you again. I was planning to write you a letter, tomorrow maybe. But I guess you never got that letter? Which means . . ."

He died before he could write it.

Or . . .

A flashing thought sears through every synapse of my brain. My breath hitches. I'm seeing stars, even with my eyes still open.

"Beatrix?"

"Sorry—I didn't come home because I was too ashamed. But I just realized something. Maybe. I don't know, because none of these rules make any actual sense."

"Oh, another twist to the story!" He hugs me even tighter. "Tell me."

"Maybe you didn't write the letter before you . . ." Died, I can't say, silly as that is because it's the obvious, inevitable truth. "Maybe you didn't write it because you didn't need to. Because you saw me first."

"Meaning . . ."

"There was never a version of time in which you didn't see me. I just . . . didn't know it yet. Not until today. But if I'm here now, maybe I was always here. We always had this time together. You never left before I had the chance to tell you I was sorry. And that I loved you more than anyone on this planet. Always have, always will."

I'll probably never know for sure—never know if it was always this way, that there was no parallel December 31, 1999, with a different outcome. But I want to believe this. Need to. And even if I'm wrong, if I wasn't here the first time around, it's hopefully a cosmic clean slate, at least for my dad. This, right here, is the only version he'll take with him.

"Ah." I hear the joy in his voice. The wonder and delight. "That's a fun theory."

True or false, it's the surprise twist in his final hour that he never saw coming.

My father, the consummate creator of the literary world's most shocking plot twists, could have received no greater gift on his deathbed.

"If I had written you that letter," he says, "your path might have been very different. On one hand, it might have saved you some of the grief, the guilt you've let consume you all these years. But on the other . . ."

"It might have been too risky—might have changed too many things. That guilt was the fire that got me to where I am now. For better and for worse. *Murder in the Books* . . . it's the only apology that felt remotely adequate. If I couldn't say sorry before you left, I could say sorry to the world with my movie about you."

"And now you can do both."

I've barely been holding it together as it is, but these words split me down the middle—the beauty and the sadness twining together into something wholly new and incomprehensibly heartbreaking.

I tilt my face up to see him, and he's looking down at me, his eyes as bright as I've ever seen them. Where will that light go in a few hours? How can something so luminous cease to exist, just like that?

"I love you," he says.

"I love you better."

"I love you best."

"I love you most best."

"Unacceptable. Best is the most. My superlative wins."

It was how we'd always said it. I wonder now, for the first time, if my mom had sometimes felt left out. She'd never said anything if she did. But then again, my mom and I had never been the best at communicating.

"How is she, your mother?"

"How did you know that's who I was thinking about?"

"Because I know you."

"She's . . . okay, I guess. We haven't exactly been close since we lost you. She . . . resented me for not coming home to see you. For everything, really. As if I didn't resent myself enough."

"I'm sorry. I wish I could help to change that."

"You can't. Because she can't know—that I was here. That would change too much."

He nods. "I promise I won't tell her. But you've got to promise me something, too."

When I don't immediately respond, he stares me down.

"Fine, I promise. Even though I suspect I won't like it."

"Make things right with your mom. When you get back. Because you will get back. I refuse to die thinking your story ends here, in the wrong time. I may not know all the twists to come, but you're far from the end."

"Okay," I say, because there's no other choice, is there? It's the least I can do to redeem myself. Maybe I'll even tell her, someday, about what happened; maybe she'll believe me. Maybe she won't. But I need to try.

"Now bring him in here," he says, grinning at me.

"Who?"

"Rocco! Your time-traveling companion. More than that, I suspect." The grin grows wider.

I lean in and kiss his cheek. I kiss it a few more times. I breathe him in as much as my lungs will allow.

"Okay." I slowly pull away, reluctant to lose even a second of this time together.

Rocco is right where I left him, standing in the hallway with a look of such deep concern on his face when he sees me, my heart swells. My heart is filled with so many things—too many, more than I knew it could possibly withstand all in the same moment. "Come in," I say, and he nods and follows.

My dad and Rocco exchange hellos like old friends. Rocco hugs him with great care, like he would do anything to keep my dad whole for as long as the universe would allow. He perches on one side of the bed then, and I settle in on the other.

"It's been the honor of my life, playing you in Bea's movie," Rocco says. "The greatest challenge—in part because your daughter didn't go particularly easy on me." He catches my eye, smiling. "Not that I would have wanted it any other way. And it's also been the greatest reward, because the role is so complex and rich. Your daughter, she wrote a true masterpiece. I'm incredibly sorry that any of you had to experience what you did. But your daughter made an exceptionally special kind of lemonade out of some very nasty lemons."

The laugh that erupts from my father feels impossibly large for such a fragile-looking man, and it's the most beautiful sound I've ever heard in my life. It's a sound I'll replay in my mind for the rest of my time on Earth, this moment here with Dad. With Rocco.

My dad is okay. He's dying, but he's okay.

We all are, or at least we're going to be.

I tell him about how I spend my New Year's Eves now, each one after this night; I found a drive-in theater in Glendale that plays Alfred Hitchcock marathons every December 31, his old tradition. *Our* old tradition, before everything fell apart. Nothing and no one topped Hitchcock for him. I was more neutral, but it delighted him when I joined, so I did. So that's what I do now, every year—tucked inside Delilah, comfort eating my way through a buffet of snacks, sobbing my eyes out to Hitchcock flicks.

"You couldn't have found a better way to honor me," he says, smiling so big, it looks like it might crack his sunken cheekbones down the middle.

We tell him more about 2016 then—dazzling him with stories about smart cars and smartphones and i-everything—and I've lost all track of time until Rocco says, "It's midnight. Happy 2000."

I take a deep breath. We all do. Waiting.

Is this our Cinderella moment?

Did we break the magic spell?

The clock on the wall above my dad's bed continues to tick. 12:00 becomes 12:01 becomes 12:02.

We'd known, of course, coming here, that this likely wasn't

the solution, if there even is one. But even now, stuck here on the other side of the millennium, it was still the right choice. For me, at least.

Rocco . . . he put our return on the line to gift me this moment right here.

It's the most selfless thing anyone's ever done for me.

"We're still here," Rocco says, staring at the clock. Looking dazed but not surprised.

"For now," my dad says, extending a hand to each of us. "But have some faith."

We talk for a little while longer, about nothing, really, all of us distracted with everything that has and hasn't happened tonight. When I notice my dad's eyelids growing heavy, blinking shut during lapses in conversation, I look at Rocco. He nods back.

As much as I don't want to admit it, I know.

It's time to go.

"I love you, Daddy." I kiss him again, keeping my lips against his cheek for a moment, trying to absorb any of his warmth that I can to take with me. "I'm sorry, and I love you, and I'll carry you with me forever."

"It's been a pleasure," Rocco says, his voice as somber as I've ever heard it. "I'll help Bea do the carrying, I promise."

My dad is sleeping now, looking deeply peaceful. A small smile playing on his lips.

Rocco stands first, coming around the side of the bed to help me up. My eyes stay pinned on my father as my feet move toward the door, an invisible tether connecting us even after the door has closed.

We walk down the hallway and out of the hospital.

Back to Delilah.

We don't discuss it, but I settle into the passenger seat this time.

I'm not sure where we're going now. Back to LA? Somewhere else, anywhere else, because maybe nothing we do matters? But I do know I'm not in driving condition.

I'm so overwhelmingly grateful for everything that just happened. The proper goodbye I never knew I'd have. I got to apologize to my father. I got to see him, hear him, hold his hand. I got to introduce him to Rocco—something I couldn't have comprehended the importance of before today. I'm relieved, comforted, hopeful.

But above all, I'm devastated.

Because I've lost him all over again.

"I'm sorry," Rocco says, reaching for me from the driver's seat. The car is still off. He doesn't know where we're going either.

I lean against him, letting my head fall against his shoulder. "It's awful, reliving it all again. But I'm glad we did this. Thank *you* for supporting it. Because there's nowhere else I would've rather been at midnight. Even if . . ."

"Even if we're still here," he finishes for me. "And nothing's changed."

I nod. "Even then."

"I'm glad, too."

It's as simple as that. Even if that leaves us with no answers, no ideas, no way out.

He's silent for a beat, and then: "Do you want to go back to LA?"

"Yes? Maybe? I don't know. I'm not sure how to make sense of anything right now." Whatever adventurous rush there was from the first few days, the adrenaline of the shock, the novelty of it all . . . it's gone now.

I want to go home.

I want to call my mom, say hello, ask her how she's doing. Talk about something real with her. Try to be something more than what we are now.

I want to be back on set.

I want to spend more time with Rocco, relearning him on our own terms.

"I'm so glad you were here with me," I say, because that's the strongest truth I can put words to right now. There's more there, I'm certain there is; I can feel it, something new—or maybe something very old—taking shape along the edges of my mind, filling in the tiny spaces that haven't yet been overtaken by grief.

But for now, all I can say is, "You decide where to go. I trust you." I really do. I trust him as much as I've ever trusted anyone.

He nods, his chin grazing against my forehead. I tilt my head back and press my lips against his, kissing him as deeply as I ever have, and I hope it says all the other words I'm not ready to put out into the world. Especially this world, the one that feels like it's no longer meant to be ours. If it ever was, this second time around.

We pull away and put our seat belts on, and Rocco starts the car.

"Let's go back to LA," he says. "I don't know how or when we're going to sort this out, but my gut tells me we belong where it all started. Then and now. It should be a smooth ride, driving through the night."

"That sounds good." Or as good as anything could at this point. The least wrong.

He rests his right hand on my thigh, and I turn to look up at the row of windows on the third floor as we drive out of the parking lot. Counting, trying to pinpoint which window is Dad's—squinting as if I can see his sleeping shape from behind the drawn blinds—until the hospital disappears from view.

The drive home—or not *home*, but the closest thing we have to it right now—is as efficient as any ride from Tucson to LA could be.

I sleep for most of it, minus one bathroom stop at a grimy roadside gas station that feels like a crime scene in the making. Rocco orders a twenty-four-ounce coffee that tastes like "charred ass sweat and sawdust"—his words—that he drinks anyway, playing my tapes on loop to keep himself alert.

When I open my eyes next, sunlight is streaming through Delilah's windows, and we're in LA. Driving along Sunset.

"We're back," I say, turning to Rocco.

He glances over, giving me a sleepy smile. "We are back. To 1999 LA, that is. Or no . . . Welcome to 2000." He tilts his head toward the window, and I look out as we cruise past Tower Records. Still there. Still operational.

I let that sink in for a moment. The shock of it hitting all over again, even if I didn't rationally expect anything to be different. "Where should we go?" I ask. The idea of going back to our motel makes my stomach knot. Not that I don't have plenty of . . . *pleasant* . . . memories there, but it felt like a temporary way station, on the way to something better. Not this, us still here, more confused than ever.

"Maybe we grab food and then drive to the beach or something? I've always loved Zuma. I could do with a little ocean gazing to set me straight."

"Yeah, that sounds—"

Before I can finish, I feel Rocco's arm press firmly across my chest. I hear the loud squeal of brakes on pavement, metal on metal, like a rumbling peal of thunder, and then everything goes dark.

Chapter 16

Rocco

Tuesday, December 27, 2016

My eyes blink open, the bright California late-morning light making me wish I could immediately close them again. But I can't.

I'm in the middle of Sunset Boulevard.

What the hell happened? Did I fall asleep at the wheel? I can't believe I made it to Tucson and back in a day only to crash at the bitter end.

Bea. My stomach twists.

I turn, and she seems okay, thank god, looking alert in the passenger seat. No blood, no injuries I can see.

"What the hell—"

Loud knuckle thumps on the driver-side window interrupt me.

"Mierda! You two okay?"

A fellow morning motorist on Sunset has pulled over to check on us, a big hulking man in a sporty tracksuit who'd be well-suited for a WWF ring. He makes me look delicate. "What a flaming asshole! Hit and runs are the worst. I couldn't make out the plate, but it was a taco truck. Needle in a haystack in this town. Either of you hurt?"

I glance back over at Bea. Her expression is hard to read, but she shakes her head.

The man keeps going: "That prick sheared your bumper clear off. I took it off the road for you on my way over here. No biggie. You can probably get it reattached. Could have been way worse than some cosmetic damage, though. That taco truck blew the light completely. If you'd been another five feet ahead, I might not be talking to you right now. Still got a little end-of-the-year luck!" He gives a thumbs up, then leans in closer. He's squinting at me, brows wrinkled, a look I know too well. His brain is working hard. "That white hair was throwing me, but I know you. Rocco, right?"

Busted. But . . . there's no quick retort about my age.

And wait—he said *end*-of-year luck.

Not beginning.

Are we . . . back?

That tracksuit of his transcends time. He's blocking most of my view, and I'm afraid to look out Bea's window.

Afraid to get my hopes up if I'm wrong.

"It is indeed." One thing at a time. Deep breath. I turn the car on, and thankfully, Delilah roars to life. "Thank you for stopping to check on us—we really appreciate it. Car's still running okay, too. You're right, we really lucked out."

I glance back over at Bea, who's staring off into space. Maybe it's the lighting, but her skin looks paler than usual.

"Maybe you two wanna drive to a hospital? Get yourselves checked out? Just to be safe." The motorist has eyes on Bea, too, and is looking concerned.

"You're right, we'll do that," I lie, ready to move along. Find the answers I need. "Thanks again, really. Happy holidays!" I wave him off with a big grin, and then watch as he crosses the lane and climbs up into his large Chevy Tahoe.

A sleek, rounded, non-boxy Tahoe.

I had a Tahoe in my early twenties, and they didn't make them like this one.

Which means . . .

We're back.

We must be.

Before I can shout the news to Bea, she's already out of the car, picking up the bumper from where the friendly motorist left it by the side of the road. She leaves the Styrofoam, takes just the silver bumper and carefully places it in the back. Then she returns to the passenger seat. We stare at one another for a moment, and I can see it in her eyes.

She knows, too.

"Do you see where we are?" She says finally, pointing out her window, and of fucking course—The Roxy. Where else would we be? "We did it, Rocco. We made it back!"

She leans in and kisses me. A kiss that feels just as powerful as her words.

Did that happen?

Did we really just time travel?

We must have. Because if that was all a weird fever dream, why the hell would Bea be making out with me right now? In pre-accident 2016, we'd been hotly—and not the good kind of hot—arguing over why she'd been acting so cold to me on set. Nothing that would ignite a kiss, let alone one as deep as this.

We pull back, eyes wide open, watching one another up close. "Can two people share the same dream in a moment of trauma?" I ask.

She hits me with a classic Bea smirk that gives me all the same sensations I've been feeling during our week gallivanting around in the past.

It was very real. No question.

"Let's see if Delilah can make it to my place. I need to see it to believe we're back. Plus I need some rest after that road trip. Or maybe just a strong Irish coffee. Double whiskey, double espresso." I put Delilah in drive and push the gas pedal. She moves, albeit with a slight rattle in the front, and we start cruising down Sunset.

Bea nods along, but she's looking dazed again, her eyes focused outside the window. At our world, our time.

"I was going to suggest you stay at my place, but I know you need to get your bearings straight, too. How about you hang out as long as you'd like, go home when you need your own space. And then we can take Delilah to my body shop later this week and get her back in shape. My treat."

More nodding. A few silent minutes pass. And then, "I guess we had to be back in LA after all for the . . . magic to happen. I can't believe you only stopped once to fuel up. Very impressive."

"I've always loved a good road trip. I don't have much time or reason for it these days, so I was glad to do this. You missed an epic sunrise through the desert. I only got it from the rearview mirror, but it was beautiful. You looked too peaceful to wake, though."

She cozies up to my arm as we drive the rest of the way to my place without speaking. *Tragic Kingdom* is still in the tape deck, playing at low volume. There don't seem to be any words right enough for this moment.

I'm relieved. Stunned. Happy. Confused. Worried that whatever this was, whatever we were, will fit differently in these modern times.

Pulling up to my house—it's *here*, it's actually fucking here!—my mind goes straight to The Surveyor. The initials I'd scratched onto the side of it, low down, where I'd never checked before now. More potential evidence that what happened wasn't a dream.

That we really did go back in time.

Together.

"Can we go look at something? I left an inscription when we came here, over on that rock." I'm eager, my whole body buzzing with the need to know. Bea nods, but she's still not all here with me. It's like she woke up to a seventeen-year reprogramming on her dad. I can't even begin to imagine what her mind, her heart, are going through right now. I'm certainly not going to push. Not about him. Not about us.

Bea gets out of the car and follows me to my trusty overlook.

"Would you like to do the honors?" I ask when we get to the edge, stopping right in front of the rock. "Tell me if you see *TS* on the side over here, along the bottom."

She starts toward it and then stops, turns back to me. "Let's do it together, okay?" She leans in and gives me a fluttery kiss on my cheek, then pulls me toward my rock.

We both squat down, looking.

Looking more.

More still.

Nothing.

The disappointment is crushing. What the hell is going on? Are we stuck in some kind of twisted loop? Am I alone in this—in my head? It's just been a long, elaborate dream this whole time after all?

Bea smiles at me, puts her hand out, and spits into it.

My mouth drops. "What the heck was that? Do I need to take you to the hospital? Maybe that crash really did bump your head."

"No, silly. You're just not looking closely enough." She swipes her hand along the bottom of the rock, nearly at the ground. Scrubbing her fingers around in circles.

Gradually, the T and S start to appear.

"I thought I saw it but had to be sure before I got too excited. So . . . is this proof enough then? What do you say?" Before I can respond, she wipes her dirty hand along the front of my shirt. Grinning. "Sorry. I'm just so giddy."

Glancing down, I realize the T-shirt I'm wearing—dirt smeared, thanks to Bea—is one I'd nabbed from my old place, vintage Fila. Bea's in her original outfit, the tight jeans and loose black sweater she'd worn the morning everything started. No rhyme or reason, nothing we'd tried to plan for, at least not consciously; I'd grabbed the first thing I saw before heading out for the hospital. But the Fila shirt, it traveled through time with me.

I stare at the T-shirt, the rock, Bea. Nothing makes sense, or maybe all of it does. It's too much: the evidence, the questions. I claw a hand through my mangy curls—*white curls*, I realize. Shoot. I'll have to deal with that. Immediately. "This is stratospherically bizarre. I know we were operating as if we were time traveling, but seeing the actual evidence is . . . blowing my mind."

Bea continues grinning at me, that haze of hers long gone now.

Because this proof confirms what matters most for her.

She'd made amends with her dad.

That really happened.

I can't know if these letters were here before today—if this future would always have been our future, that past always our past. Just like we can't know for sure if she was there with William in the hospital the first time around, or if we rewrote things, had a proper redo.

But it also doesn't matter, does it? Because the end result is the same now.

We were there with him. Last night. Seventeen years ago.

Just like we'd been here a few days before that.

"We weren't imagining it," she says simply, that grin growing even wider. She does a happy little twirl, then turns and starts walking back to a beat-up Delilah.

I don't want her to go.

It's an instant, visceral, full-body reaction.

"You're leaving already?" I ask, following behind her like an overeager teenager who doesn't know the right thing to say, is incapable of playing it cool. He just wants. So badly. I'm not used to that, wanting this much.

But I've spent almost every waking hour with her these past few days.

The idea of being without her, even back here, now, feels desperately lonely.

Bea turns, takes a breath before leveling me with those wide gray eyes. Her dad's eyes, I realize. "I think it's best I get home, really sit with my thoughts, you know? After . . . everything. A whole lot of everything. It'll be good for you, too. We've had the most incredible adventure, Rocco. The best of my life. But let's just reacclimate, reconvene in the morning. There's no rush, right? We're back. We did it. We have all the time in our world now to figure this out." She takes me by the arm and pulls me in, wraps herself around me. "This is just a 'see you soon.'"

I go in for a kiss. My hands against the back of her neck, her arms snug around my waist. She sighs into me, and I breathe it in deep. The magic is still there. Very much so. No time stamp could change that. Not for me. Not now.

I'm too far gone.

I pull away first, even though I don't want her to go. But it's what she needs. "You're right, although I'm going to miss the hell out of you, even for a night. And call me when you get home, please, so I know you didn't go time traveling again."

She tilts her gaze up at me, a little smile on her lips. Those lips that only knew how to frown at me a week ago; earlier this morning, really, at least in this time. I don't ever want to go back. "Will do. And I'll see you tomorrow? Lanie's big holiday bash, if I'm doing the math on my days right."

Shit, Lanie's party. The real world in high-def, and so soon. I'd forgotten about it entirely. I nod.

"And then," she continues, "we'll need to get Delilah fixed, like you said. I wasn't that out of it! You're a good man, Rocco. Delilah thanks you. I do, too. We're both happy to ride with you anytime."

With that, she hops into the driver's seat, turns on the car, and takes Delilah down the driveway and out of sight.

Well, shit.

How am I going to function for the rest of the day? How does one reacclimate post, you know, fucking *time travel.*

I walk back to the rock, plop myself down. My fingers mindlessly rub along the initials as I stare out over the ocean below. I'm relieved this view is mine again. Glad that much hasn't changed.

I hope nothing else has either—aside from these letters and our goodbye in Tucson. I hope we kept everything else exactly as it's always been.

Please, dear god. Universe. Whatever powers that be.

I hear a clanking sound, and turn to see Tony on his back porch, wielding a big metal watering pot. Tending to his giant succulent garden. He probably has over a hundred of them. The biggest succulent devotee I've ever encountered.

I'm frozen for a moment, watching him, deliberating.

Should I say anything? Go fishing? It was seventeen years ago, during his more experimental days . . .

Only one way to find out.

"Hey, Tony! Need any help?" I call out as I'm already walking over. We haven't seen one another much lately, not with all the time I've devoted to *Murder in the Books.* Lots of smiling and waving as we pass by one another, with an occasional stop and chat out here in our driveways.

"Nice to see you, brother!" He puts his pot down, comes in for a hug. "Always happy to have another set of hands."

He starts off toward the garden then, and I follow his lead, contemplating how the heck to connect this endeavor to what transpired in '99.

"Just adding a couple of new aloe plants today," he says when we reach his neatly edged plot, pointing to a freshly dug corner. "Some nice new friends."

"Great! Were there . . . aloe plants here originally? During the wilder heyday of this hill—before my house came along?" Smooth, I hope. A subtle transition to the old days.

"Nah, this place was a bare, dusty old hilltop. Just me and the Airstream for a long while—over on your side of the hill, actually. Before I sold off some of the land so I could finally afford to build my pad. Back then it was just me and the views, food over the fire, sweet tunes, and a revolving door of adult beverages and brain fuel." He jabs me with his elbow and gives an emphatic wink. Yes, Tony, I know there was a copious amount of drug intake here on these grounds.

Time to go in for the real fishing expedition: Does he remember meeting two trespassing hooligans, perhaps in the last days of the old millennium . . . ? "It's a shame," I start, clearing my throat, "it took me so many years in LA before I discovered this place. What was it like . . . in the late nineties? What was I missing?"

"Late nineties? Eh. Much quieter by then. The scene had moved on. We got old. I pretty much just hung out and got some producing gigs here and there when I could. The seventies and eighties were the golden era up here. You know Christopher Cross?"

Yes, of course I do, and I also know this story about their magical studio time together—one of his favorites. The first anecdote I heard the day I moved in, as a matter of fact. But I continue to nod and smile like it's the first time I've heard it.

"I'd been riding like the wind on the tails of that 'Yacht Rock,' as the kids are calling it now, you know, but nobody really cared by the time the nineties rolled around."

"Right. But . . . did you ever have people poking around up here then, because they'd heard the old stories? Music buffs and the like?"

He squints out toward the ocean, quiet for a beat. Somber thinking face on, the gears slowly churning. "Hm." Another pause. "That's funny. I do remember one particular couple that found my place. Big fans of that whole Laurel Canyon scene. I let them stay for a night or two. They seemed a bit . . . lost. So, we broke bread, had some drinks by the fire, but that's really it. Nothing momentous. I'm sure there are many more folks interested in you and your location. Speaking of, happy to go in on a bigger gate if you're feeling like it."

He remembers us then. I shouldn't be surprised, not after finding the letters on the rock, but I am. I don't think anything about this could ever not be shocking.

I smile at him. "Nah, I think I'm far enough off the Hollywood grid up here. And I love that the fence at the bottom of the road makes it feel like you might be heading up to a serial killer's old mansion." Tony gives a hearty laugh. "But thank you, for the offer."

"It's all about optics, you're right on. Who needs a fancy castle gate if the overgrown earth is intimidating enough? We're wild and strange up here. Best way to be, my brother."

We continue to chat for a while as we plant, about everything and nothing. It's nice to have this time to decompress. A brief reprieve between the past and the future.

Once the plants are in, Tony murmurs a blessing to them, and we part ways.

Back to the house.

Back to reality.

First order of business once I'm home is my phone.

Dead still, even though I know I'd left the coffee shop with a decent charge. But of course, I left the coffee shop days ago. Or I did, but I also didn't.

Time-travel math is impossibly hard.

I thought I'd be more relieved, being back inside these walls. But the house feels so . . . empty. What was once my precious fortress of solitude now feels entirely too quiet. I miss Bea. Her voice. Her laugh. That dirty, perfect smirk.

Damnit, Rocco, it's only been an hour. Get yourself together!

I refocus, find a charger in the living room, and plug my phone in. The instant string of dings and alerts that follows is astounding. Even for me, on a busy day. You would think I was an actual influencer! Other than my restaurant reviews, I'm mostly off social media, much to my team's chagrin. Tom's, especially. Drives him nuts. Call me old-fashioned, but it's just not my thing. Never has been. And, as I like to remind them all, it hasn't exactly held me back from landing the big gigs.

Tom, though . . . shit. How's that going to unfold?

Too much to process right now.

I scroll through my messages. There are seven texts from an unknown 323 number in the last few days.

So . . . yeah. Can't believe that happened last night.

I was more than a little tipsy, but . . . it was fun.

How are you feeling about it?

Rocco? Hello?

You have nothing to say about it?

Not sure why you're not responding. It's, uh, not like you can ghost me, lol

Alright then. Left you a VM. Guess I'll . . . wait to hear from you?

Uh. Shit.

There's a lot to unpack here.

Clearly a woman.

Most certainly somebody I hooked up with.

But . . . who? And how?

There was no one in the picture. There hasn't been, not for a few months. I've been too in this role. Tuned the rest of the world out, stayed in my cave with the exception of seeing Rudy and Lucy. So how did she pop up?

The timeline . . .

Oh god.

What did we possibly screw up? Is this the beginning of the ripples?

It seems impossible, though, that anything we did could have landed me a random hook-up seventeen years in the future. Bea was right to worry as much as she did. Damn. Who knew screenwriters were so on point with time traveling?

I search for the number in my call log, and—bingo!—a voice-mail. More definitive evidence. I hesitate for just a beat, then jab my finger at the play button.

Hey, Rocco, maybe you lost your phone, or maybe it broke, but I would really, really love to talk about what happened. I know it was spontaneous, and probably the last thing either of us was expecting to come of this. But it was . . . nice? And it made me think. About us, and the past. Where to go from here. So. Yeah. Either way, I'm just glad we're back on speaking terms. The kiss was a topper, I suppose. So . . . yeah. I just want to talk. Clearly. Make sure we're on the same page. Sorry for the long message. Bye.

That voice.
I'd know it anywhere.
Piper.

Chapter 17
Beatrix

Wednesday, December 28, 2016

I squint at myself in the mirror—my mirror, in the apartment I rent, as a grown adult woman in the year 2016—and wish my makeup bag had more than some middling mascara and blush and a bronzer I've still never figured out how to use. Sleep was impossible last night, which was . . . to be expected. Playing through every detail of the last week on loop, wondering how and why and what next.

Am I the same person I was before the trip, the same version of myself—the same collection of cells, carrying the same memories and thoughts? Did my body come apart on a molecular level to traverse through years and universes, then get remade, twice over?

Is this the same home it was six days ago? Yesterday morning? If anything had changed, would I even know?

I'm here, but am I? Rocco's here, too, back in this old, new LA with me, but is he?

And if we're here, are we here together?

All of it's real, or none of it, and I look like proper crusty shit. Just in time for Lanie's blow-out cast and crew holiday party in a few hours.

Wonderful.

The idea of calling out sick is tempting. But a larger piece of me needs to go, needs to bask in the familiar, to reassure myself that everything really might be okay.

Nothing lost, nothing altered.

Nothing aside from one new memory gained with my father, a perfectly contained moment in time that shouldn't spill over into anything to come after. At least not for anyone but me. And Rocco. We'll have a better movie for it. And I'll have a better life.

I pick up my phone, scroll through my recent calls list, my finger hovering over Sylvie's name. She's missing the festivities tonight; she and Eden have had reservations at Nobu for ages, and Lanie's party doesn't top that. But she would whip me into far better than average shape in twenty minutes flat, make a masterpiece of me—maybe not an original work of art, but at least a reasonably high-quality knockoff.

She would ask questions, though. And I'm not ready to give answers.

There are no adequate words to explain our experience to anyone. If I even wanted to, and I'm not sure I do. At least not yet.

The longer I hold it in, keep it for just myself and Rocco, the safer it feels. It's ours and it's confusing and stunning and precious, and I'm not ready to share it with the world. Not even Sylvie. Partly, too, because she was there the first time around; she helped me pick up the many jagged pieces after Rocco, after my dad.

She knows exactly how hard my heart broke then, and she sure as hell wouldn't want to give him an opportunity to do it again.

I close out of my calls, planning to scroll mindlessly through social media to ignore the problem at hand—the problem being my massive under-eye bags that all the fresh cucumbers in LA wouldn't be able to contain—when a text comes in.

Rocco.

A frizzle of excitement flares through my veins, and I click to read.

Rocco: Wow, you owe me big time for the bleaching. ☺ **The very expensive and hopefully very discreet hair stylist has been here for hours undoing your damage.**

I laugh. I'll miss my white fox. Before I can respond, another text lands.

Rocco: Anyway. I miss you. I'm excited to see you tonight. Less excited to schmooze at the party . . . too much too soon, I think only half my brain made it back to this decade. Honestly, if you weren't going, I wouldn't either.

He misses me.

That flare of excitement burns hotter, a buzzy warmth filling my chest. I miss him, too, even though it's barely been twenty-four hours since I last saw him, and I managed to exist perfectly fine without him for the last seventeen years. But after these past few days, I'm not sure I want to anymore.

Dots pop up as he types, and I wait.

Rocco: So I got some weird messages on my phone that I don't really understand. I need to tell you about them. After the party. Sleepover at my place?

Weird messages. The warmth disappears, a sinking dread taking its place.

Beatrix: Everything okay?

Rocco: Yes! Yes.

Beatrix: You sure? The double yes has me worried.

Rocco: Promise, it's nothing you and I can't figure out. By the way. Check your door. I think something just got dropped off.

Genius of him—distracting me at a time like this. I put my phone down and start toward the door. I don't realize until I'm already there that I'm wearing nothing but my dad's ragged old XL Arizona State T-shirt, the only pajamas that had felt right last night.

Sure enough, there's a young woman at the door holding a tall garment bag. "Bea Noel?"

I nod, and she hands the bag over, smiling at me in a bemused kind of way before heading back toward the main stairs.

I carry the bag to my bed and then slowly unzip it to find a red sequined dress—not quite as mini as the one I wore on our adventure, but with a hemline still a good three inches shorter than anything else I've attempted in the last five years. Maybe ten. It's stunning, though, and surely ten times the price of the one I thrifted, the red sequins stitched in tightly against intricate clear beads that amplify the shine. I set the dress down on my duvet, gently, scared of tugging a single sequin out of place, and go back to my phone.

Beatrix: You didn't have to do that. But it's perfect.

Rocco: Yeah? You like it?

Beatrix: I love it.

Rocco: I'm glad. I know it's a strange day, and I wanted you to feel special. So that sleepover . . . ?

Beatrix: Resounding yes. For the record, would have been a yes even without the dress.

Rocco: Pick you up at 6. ☺ And don't worry, I called a nice doc for Delilah. We can take her in tomorrow. She'll be her old self in no time.

I grin at the screen. Maybe everything *will* be okay, this new normal. Better than okay even.

But . . . shit.

A dress like this one deserves proper hair and makeup, doesn't it? The blush in my makeup bag that's always been two shades too peachy for my complexion would be a total affront to this gift.

I let out a long sigh. Sylvie it is.

Beatrix: Hair and make-up SOS!!!

Her reply is immediate—a voice note because she's always doing too many things at once to allow for anything as menial as typing:

Be there in an hour, bitch. What would you do without me?

Hopefully a few little white lies and the cheap champagne from the back of my fridge will help get us through.

I'll tell her everything. Probably.

But not today.

It's a good thing Rocco had a driver escort us, because I wouldn't trust him on the road.

He can't take his eyes off me.

We don't say much on the ride to Brentwood, but we don't

need to. It's more important just to see one another, a reminder that this is now, we are here, solid and whole and together.

If it weren't for his driver seated just a few feet in front of us, someone on his payroll, not a stranger we'd never have to see again, I don't think I'd be able to resist kissing him. But a kiss, once we started, wouldn't be nearly enough. There might be no stopping us.

For now, we hold hands.

We stare into one another's eyes, our hot palms pressed tightly together, clasped against his thigh, his thumb rubbing slow circles against mine, and . . .

Goddamn.

Why are we going to this party again? What time is it socially acceptable to leave?

We pull up to Lanie's house—if one can call it a house, given that it's sized more like an airport—and slowly make our way up the cobbled path lit from above with a canopy of twinkly lights.

It's not until we're at the door, arm in arm, that the fog of our car ride lifts and realization sets in—anyone here would positively lose their mind in bewilderment to see us stroll in together. My surly set behavior toward him was surely not that subtle.

"Rocco," I start, "should we perhaps not—"

But before I can finish, the door is thrown open. Lanie's there, luminous in a floor-length second skin of a golden gown that leaves absolutely nothing to the imagination. "Welcome, welcome," she proclaims, loudly, reaching out to usher Rocco inside. Our arms come apart, quickly enough that I'm sure no one noticed, not even Lanie, who is too busy parading her star through the gilded two-tier foyer as I fall in step behind.

We're winding our way through crowds of crew members, all huddled around servers with their flute-and-tumbler-filled trays, Lanie clearly on the hunt for someone or something in particular. It's no easy feat to stay on them.

"Ah!" she says finally, pulling Rocco to a halt. I stop, too, nearly catching myself on the heel of her six-inch stiletto. "There she is! Our dear Catherine Noel."

Catherine Noel?

My *mother*? I must have heard her wrong. My mother has never once visited LA.

I step to the side for a better view, and no. It's not my mother. It's Piper Bell.

Radiant, of course—even more radiant than in the glossy magazines, which should quite frankly be impossible—in an emerald-green corseted bodice that's as flattering and as tempting as any corset in the world has likely ever been, paired with a frothy pistachio green tulle skirt that flares out just above her knees. Her golden hair is done in simple waves, dangling above her perfect cleavage, and her tanned skin seems to glow. Her makeup is simple, but in the deceptive way that surely took hours to perfect. Or maybe not. Maybe she's just this stunning with little to no effort.

Why the fuck are you here, I ask, in my head.

Or so I think.

But the way Lanie and Rocco and Piper stare at me, it would seem it slipped out aloud. Whoops.

"Sorry," I say, hoping that Sylvie's generous application of various cremes and powders is masking my blush. "I was just surprised, that's all."

Lanie's expression, already aghast, turns even sharper. "Why on earth would you be surprised to see one of our stars here? She's going to be racking up the award noms for this, mark my words. The way she fights, a veritable lioness, to keep the family together when you . . ." She shakes her head, giving me another pointed look before focusing back on Piper. "Anyway. It's exquisite, Piper, really remarkable, the work you've been doing. The work you've both been doing," she says, tightening her grip on Rocco and angling him so that the three of them are in a tight triangle formation. "Top-tier stuff. You're taking this project to the next level, and we are *all* so grateful."

I feel dizzy and disoriented. Frantic.

Frantic to understand what the hell is happening. Why Piper is in my movie. Playing my mother. Where is Darla? This is Darla's role. She was perfect for it. Equal parts fierce and tender, switching between the two in a blink, just as my mother did. Darla is pretty but not flashily so, more "prettiest mom in the PTA" than "prettiest star on the red carpet."

Piper—she's all wrong for this.

And even if she weren't, there's no way I would have agreed to watch her and Rocco together—*playing my parents,* a fact that cannot be overstated—day in and day out on set. Rocco had been enough of an unpleasant reminder. Rocco *and* Piper, a package deal, would have been an unthinkable new form of torture. I would have found another route to that green light.

"Rocco, can I have a word?" I ask, reaching out to tug at the arm unclaimed by Lanie. "It's, er . . . exceptionally urgent."

He turns then, the first time I've seen his face since we came upon Piper, and his eyes are showing me so many things at once. Shock and confusion, of course. But it's more than that. Panic, maybe.

Or . . . guilt?

But what could he have to feel guilty about? He couldn't have orchestrated this himself. Not on our disjointed timeline.

"Wait, wait," Lanie says, tugging him back. "I was looking for Piper because I have a sneak peek of some footage, and I wanted you both to see. It took my breath away, really. I was going to ask our screenwriter and muse to watch as well, but she seems to have arrived at the party missing half of her mind, so . . ." She shrugs, and I feel hot anger rising up from the pit of my stomach. Why did I ever think partnering with Lanie was the right idea? She was flashy, sure. Hard-assed and intimidating enough to push things through, not only get the movie made, but get it made well. Right now, though, I have regrets. Many of them.

Lanie snaps her fingers, and one of her three on-rotation personal assistants appears out of nowhere from the side of the room, tablet in hand.

"Right, here we go. The scene when the police have come to escort William away, and Catherine vows to do everything she can to clear his name. . . ." She pauses, releases a loud, overdone sniffle. "See! I get choked up just thinking about this scene."

I burrow myself further into the group, between Rocco and Piper, the triangle now a wobbly square. I need to witness this for myself. Piper, in footage I've never seen. Even though I must have been there. Rocco, too. We were there, but we weren't. I clutch Rocco's arm more tightly, the only thing keeping me upright.

Lanie hits play with a long, red-tipped nail, and the scene unfolds—a scene that is both very similar to one I witnessed the other week, and also very different, because it's Piper instead of Darla, and her presence is so magnetic it's like she's the only one on the screen. Which is nearly impossible when Rocco is present, too, but somehow she's doing it. She's sobbing and screaming, and she is both so desperately sad and so viciously angry all at once, professing her love for William while railing against the police with each alternating line. Seamlessly.

It's her conviction, though, that is a razor to my heart. The absolute faith that William is innocent; no matter what the evidence may suggest, no matter what any witnesses might say, she knows the truth, the only truth.

She's done it perfectly. In this moment, she is my mother.

She is my mother, and I am my horrible, guilty self, reminded yet again of all the mistakes I made, the person I should have been.

That should have been my conviction, too. The end result would have been the same—my father arrested, held in jail for those long months awaiting the trial. He still would have been exonerated and released, still would have been too sick already by that point, too far gone for freedom. Still would have died. But he would have done all those things knowing I believed in him. And my mom and I, we would have been in it together. We still would be today.

I watch, numb, as Piper throws herself at Rocco on-screen, even though I really should look away because I know what's coming next.

They kiss.

Just as he did with Darla. But this—this kiss is entirely different. With Darla, it had been passable, wracked with a bittersweet desperation. But this kiss now with Piper, it's fire and ice, the raw need of it clawing at me from the tablet screen. It's a scalpel skimming the skin off all my old wounds.

The scene ends and I'm barely able to stay upright, but Rocco's arm is suddenly the last lifeline I want.

How could he have done that?

How could he have kissed her like that?

"I need to go," I say quietly, not that anyone seems to be listening.

Lanie is in raptures again, talking about how that scene alone might be enough to bump Piper from supporting to lead when awards season rolls around. Rocco is a statue, the tight mask on his face entirely unreadable. Piper's gaze is flicking between Lanie and Rocco, questions in her eyes that I don't want answered.

I spin around, with no idea where to go, but needing to be anywhere but here. With them. Him.

It's a blur around me, sparkling glasses, twinkling lights, beautiful people and their loud laughter, soft string music filtering in from some corner of the maze-like first floor. Everywhere I go has too many people, which should be impossible in a place of this size: a billiard's room where Lanie's husband

Dylan is holding court, a small glassed-in conservatory where a group of people are smoking beside an open window, another living room that is somehow both fancier and more jammed with bodies than the first.

Of course it only seems right when the first empty room I stumble into is a library-like office. Much grander than my dad's had been, but far more sterile. The books look untouched, spines in perfect condition, arranged in tidy rows, no wobbling towers or triple stacks.

I take in a long gulp of air, my first full breath since seeing her.

"You weren't easy to chase."

I startle and turn, and he's there, Rocco, red-faced and huffing.

"I would have expected you to be in better shape," I snap back, which is easily the most unimportant and absurd thing to say in this moment. But I'm at a loss for anything better. My mind is more maze-like than this house.

A brief smile tips up his lips before they retighten. "I took a few wrong turns. Had to double back." He steps further in then, shuts the door behind him. "I'm really sorry. About . . . all of that. I hope you know this is just as surprising and confusing for me."

"You didn't remember that kiss?"

"Of course not." He rakes his fingers through his perfectly tangly hair—as dark as it always was, a perfect replica of his natural color. "I remember Darla. I have no idea why . . . *she* . . . is here now."

"Okay." Of course it's not, though.

"How are you feeling?"

I laugh. "How am I feeling? Pretty damn terrible, as a matter of fact. Having you play my dad was punishment enough—before now, that is—but having her involved, too? As my mom? Doing a bang-up job of it, clearly, based on that nice sneak peek we just got? It's way too much. This movie—it was supposed to be my safe space, my nightmare turned dream come true, the most important project of my life. And now . . ." Tears spill down my cheeks; I've lost all of my usual capacity to hold them in. One more change this week has forced on me. I swipe at the tears, not caring how messy my made-up face might look. "It's ruined. For me, anyway. I'm sure it'll be an amazing movie, a critic's darling, the awards will rain down on you all, etc. But every minute of the experience will be pure torture for me. I guess that's what I deserve, isn't it? For taking so long to get it right."

"Bea," Rocco says gently, edging closer until he's pressed against me, his arms wrapping around my shoulders. It feels so natural, leaning into him like this, letting him take me in. Too natural. "We'll get through this. Together. I don't remember that kiss, but it doesn't mean anything. Not to me—the me now, the one standing here with you. I promise. You're the only person I want to be kissing." He stops then, and I tilt my face up toward his. His eyes are clouded; there's more to it. More that he's not saying.

"What is it?" I ask. Because whatever this is, whatever we are, we have to trust one another. That trust is the only thing that feels real.

His brows pull together. "You're not going to like this. But I don't want to keep any secrets."

"Okay."

"I had . . . texts on my phone when I powered it back on. A voicemail. From Piper."

"Okay."

"It seems we . . . kissed? Aside from the one we saw on set. Not for the cameras."

My whole body goes stiff in his arms.

"I don't know the details. Don't know anything about it. It wasn't me! Or it was, but it wasn't this me, and I don't know,

Bea. I am so fucking confused about all of this, but I'm not confused about you. About us. And I need you to—"

"I need to go home," I say, lifting his arms from around my shoulders. "This night has been too much. Nothing makes sense."

"I know it's a lot. But it's a lot for me, too. This isn't my life either, Bea."

I know that, I do. Deep down. It's not what he chose. It's nothing this Rocco that I know and quite possibly love—do I, is that what this is?—did or didn't do.

But it also is, isn't it?

Because even if the memory isn't imprinted in this Rocco, here and now, it was still essentially him who went down this path. Who kissed Piper, not just as a job, but for more than that. For pleasure.

He picked her last time, and how could I believe he won't pick her again? She's here, in all her beautiful, brilliant glory, the obvious choice. Anyone's obvious choice.

Laughter drifts in from the hall, and the door opens, Dylan poking his head in. "Ah, sorry! Didn't know anyone was in here. I was just popping in to grab my old yearbook to show Tom here, apparently we were the same year, fancy that, but neither—"

"*Tom*," Rocco says. "Tom."

"Tom?" I repeat. "What about—"

"Yeah, what about me, Rocco?"

He's in the office now, Tom Richards, standing next to Dylan. Seventeen years older than I last saw him, hair far more salt than pepper now, lines more pronounced, but looking much more put together than his previous incarnation. "What are you kids getting up to in here?" His eyebrow is raised for effect, though he looks more amused than curious.

"I'm glad you found us, because you're just the man we need to talk to," Rocco says, his voice sounding unnaturally upbeat. "It's important. And, er . . . a rather sensitive topic."

"Color me intrigued then."

"I'll leave you to it," Dylan says, stepping back. "I'll grab that yearbook later."

"Could you explain," Rocco starts when the door is shut again, "why Piper Bell is my costar in this movie?"

Tom smiles expectantly, like this is a joke and he's waiting for the punchline.

"I'm serious, Tom."

"How could you possibly be serious, Rocco? As if you and I didn't endlessly dissect the pros and cons—all pros, from my perspective, not a con in sight—before we got her on board, too. It was a no-brainer."

"Why would costarring with the ex who ruined my family life for a decade and a half be a 'no-brainer'?"

Tom isn't smiling now. He's staring wide-eyed at Rocco in bewilderment. Maybe frustration. "What is this all about? Are you having second thoughts? Is this about"—his eyes flick to me—"another woman? Old Rudy issues dredging up? Talk to me straight."

"Take me to the beginning," Rocco says, "back to when the idea first came up. When, who, how."

"Well sure, that was all me. You know that. The jacket, the one I last wore at some holiday party in '99, some shitshow I don't remember. Except it somehow left me with that magazine piece from the future! Well, not the future anymore. But it was."

The tabloid. It was the tabloid.

We knew, didn't we? That it could be our undoing.

I've never wanted to be less right.

"Fuck," I say, eloquently. Rocco looks too shocked and horrified to speak. "When did you find that?"

Tom turns from Rocco to me, back to Rocco. To me. Squinting, like he's trying to puzzle through our line of questioning. "Surely Rocco has told you this story. Or maybe not, since you two have . . . whatever you have. Anyway, I was moving last year, organizing my disaster of a closet, and I found a ripped jacket in the back. Out of style, dirty, useless to me, but still worth a small fortune, so I was going to toss it in the thrift store pile, a nice little treasure for someone else. But I heard a crinkle in the pocket, reached in, and . . ." He laughs, shaking his head. "It's hard to explain this, but there was a ripped and scribbled on magazine page. A piece about Rocco and Piper being a power nostalgia couple, how great it would be to see them together again, on or off screen. Anyway, it was the date that caught my eye. December 2016. But, you see, the day I found it, it was only *October of 2015*."

A pause, for dramatic effect.

I suppose he expects me to be stunned. And I am, but not because he found an article from the future. More that it managed to stay hidden for nearly sixteen long years—only to be found just in the nick of time to turn my life into a waking nightmare.

"Anyway," he continues, unruffled despite the lack of a satisfying reaction, "I thought it must have been a joke. I mean, of course. Why would I have a magazine page from a year ahead? I'd been wasted to oblivion the last time I wore that coat, but surely I'd remember if I'd lived through *Back to the damn Future*! But. On the other side of the page, there was a year in review piece. One by one, at the beginning of 2016, things kept . . . happening. Like a checklist. The most impossible, improbable checklist in the world. So I figured, 'hello, this is your grand sign, Tommy.' Nostalgia's more hot ticket than ever, and Rocco and Piper? The hottest ticket there is. The stars all aligned for this reunion: Rocco wanted indie tearjerker, Piper was looking for the right mom role to help her be taken more seriously in Hollywood, bombshell that she is, so . . . here we are. Rocco got on board. Piper hopped right on, too, needed very little convincing. You grumbled, but ultimately saw the light. The bright *green* light. In the end, even you couldn't deny the atomic power of the casting—especially once you watched the chemistry read. And there we have it, so the story ends. Ta-da."

"Ta-da," Rocco repeats woodenly, still looking blank-faced.

"Yes. Ta-freaking-da." Tom claps his hands together hard in front of Rocco's face. "You there, kid? You're starting to scare me."

Rocco nods. "Yeah. Just . . . processing. That story. It's uh. Bizarre, isn't it?"

"*Fate* is what it was. The golden ticket to take you to the next level. Matted and framed in my office now. Anyway. I'll leave you two to process, reprocess, whatever you need. I'm gonna go grab a seltzer. Seventeen years off the hootch this January, you believe it?" He laughs, pats Rocco on the shoulder, and walks out.

"We did this," I say quietly.

He nods. "We did."

Of all the risks, of all the mistakes, of course our meddling in time would lead to this:

Piper and Rocco, together again.

Chapter 18

Rocco

Thursday, December 29–Friday, December 30, 2016

Our ultimate punishment for screwing around in the past: *Piper.*

Here.

At Lanie's party.

Acting in this movie with me. Bea's passion project, her life's work. Her apology and her ode. And Piper and I, we're playing her *goddamn parents.* Kissing on screen—and off?

I could vomit right now.

And Tom, just casually tossing this mystical listicle idea around, like he's talking about finding a lucky twenty-dollar bill. Completely cavalier, so nonchalant about the whole thing. His hawk eyes solely on the golden nostalgia cash cow.

It's all confusing as hell. Honestly, I'd hop in Delilah and go straight back to '99 if I could. Stay put this time. That seems far easier and more desirable than this.

Why? Why didn't I stop this from happening before it ever started?

I should have taken the article from him. Should have made sure it was still in the car when he got out, whatever it took.

Knocked on Tom's door the next morning, camped out on his porch until it was safely back in our possession.

But I didn't. And now . . . here we are.

Bea backs out of Dylan's office, her shoulders shaking. She takes off down the hall without a backward glance. Lost, seemingly, in the labyrinth of Lanie's palace, because she's heading in the wrong direction—back to the center of the party when the only place we should be headed for is the front door.

I'm not ready to see Piper again; to stand near her as everyone else eagerly looks on, watching. I had felt it, their beady eyes, the palpable buzz while we'd watched the footage with Lanie. And why wouldn't they buzz? It's dream PR. Good for everyone involved. Just like Tom had hoped.

I don't want any of that, though.

I just want Bea.

I pick up my pace and follow her, a smile tight on my lips— probably more rigor mortis than party fabulous—as I weave through the crowd, nodding and waving to vaguely familiar faces from set.

She spots the throngs ahead in the main room, hugs tight to the wall. We're nearly out of the room, the shimmering foyer mirage-like, so close, when she appears. Straight ahead. Piper. An impassable hurdle. Bea stops in her tracks, lightly panting. I close in a few seconds after, step up beside her. Close, but not too close.

"Ah, at last we meet again," Piper says, eyes on me, taking a step closer. "I've been looking everywhere. For you, that is." She reaches out a hand, lightly rubs my lower back.

I want to flinch away, but I keep my composure. To be honest, it sort of does still feel inherently natural—like an old mitt you spent countless hours sleeping on, holding a baseball for maximum breaking in. No matter what shiny new glove you may get as you grow older, that previous one always still fits like . . . well . . . a glove. Yours.

"Can we chat for a minute?" Piper asks, edging in closer. I can smell spearmint on her breath, just as I remember. She'd been a relentless gum chewer. Minty fresh every hour of the day.

I can't dissect any of this, not tonight. Not with Bea by my side. I can feel her staring at me with straight displeasure and confusion, rightfully so. She deserves to leave this hellscape that's somehow our new reality.

And I want to leave with her. If she'll have me.

"Let's . . . catch up tomorrow? I'm sort of feeling a little, uh, bubbly gut. You know how it is. Too many mini crabcakes, I think. Afraid I might get the runs." *Jesus, Rocco!* Major TMI, even for a lie. Surely I could have thought of a less off-putting excuse?

"Yikes," Piper says, grimacing. "Sorry to hear it. Tomorrow's perfectly fine. Coffee at Pat and Lorraine's? I haven't been there in years. That was such a favorite of ours."

"Sounds good, yeah." Anything to wrap this up. "I'll, uh, text you in the morning."

Piper leans in all the way and . . . kisses me on the cheek. Slow but firm, with a little light suction at the end to cap it off. My skin tingles as she pulls away.

"Get home safe. You sticking around, Beatrix?" She asks in a benign way, looking over at Bea for the first time since we nearly ran into her. So casually that maybe she really is just trying to be polite—no jealousy radar pinging.

"No, heading out. I have an early day tomorrow, lots of exciting housework to do, you know how it goes." There's a sarcastic lilt to her voice; Piper obviously does not know how that goes. I doubt she's ever scrubbed a toilet in her life.

Bea grabs for my arm then, a clear dominance move. Piper doesn't seem to notice, already flitting off to another circle. She'd always been like that at parties, talking to everyone and no one at the same time. The goal was to be seen, with very few exceptions.

I turn toward the front door, steering Bea with me. "For the love of everything, let's please get out of here. You still want to come back with me, I hope?"

Bea doesn't respond, but she keeps her arm tucked against mine as we walk out through the door and down the front path to where my car sits in the circular driveway. Our driver for the night is posted up against the trunk, smoking a cigarette as he chats with another driver two cars down the line. Not expecting us to dip this early.

"I'll make it right tomorrow," I say, coming to a stop a few feet away from the car. I turn to face her, taking both of her hands in mine. Desperate for something, anything from her. Desperate to know she understands. I didn't ask for this. This wasn't *me*. At least not the me I am here and now. "I need to know what happened. And once I've got my head around it, I'll explain it was a mistake—spillover emotions from set. It happens."

Bea refuses to make eye contact. She takes a long inhale. Even longer exhale.

And then: "I think I just need to go home. This night's been . . . overwhelming. I know that what we saw on the screen, it's technically not you, or at least the you that's standing here with me. But . . . it also still is you, isn't it? Your life. Your feelings. Your choice." She shakes her head, still looking away from me. "It's too much to think about right now. Okay?"

"Okay." I'm not sure what else to say. No words feel right enough. I give her hands a squeeze.

She still gets in the car with me, though we ride in silence to her apartment. A kiss on the cheek, and then she leaves me alone again.

I can't be upset, though, can I? I literally made this happen.

Past and present Rocco, every version of me on every timeline, always screwing up.

* * *

There's ordinarily a lot to love about Pat and Lorraine's.

It has the best drip coffee going, plus a chorizo breakfast burrito that easily destroys all competition. Home fries stuffed inside the burrito, no need for sides. Complete game changer. It also happens to be the location where they shot the opening scene in *Reservoir Dogs*—discussing their hypothesis on the true meaning of Madonna's "Like a Virgin." Never gets old, that cinematic factoid.

Today, though, I'd rather be anywhere else.

I can't even stomach the idea of the magical burrito. Because this may get ugly. Or at the very least, downright uncomfortable. Canceling a redux so special, it took a cosmic time traveling event to bring us to this point.

I post up in a booth, my hoodie up high, head down low, plowing my way through one-and-a-half drip coffees before Piper walks in, roughly twenty minutes late. As she proved last night, fluttering around at Lanie's party, some things never change. She charges toward me, then goes in for a European two-sided kiss before I even realize it's happening. I tilt my cheek too abruptly, eager for our little greeting to end, and her lips graze alarmingly close to my mouth. I overcorrect, our noses doing a quick nuzzle before she pulls away.

"Interesting take on *la bise*. Anyway, sorry I'm late," she says, settling into the seat across from me. Our knees bump, linger for too long of a beat. I readjust, determined to stay contact free. She's dressed to be low key, too, in a baggy hooded gray sweatshirt and gray yoga pants, her long blond hair swept up in a messy bun. No makeup, so she doesn't necessarily look like the Piper Bell people know from screens, but she looks remarkably like the Piper I knew. The behind-the-scenes Piper I liked best. "The 110 was a mess. And last night went super late. You know Lanie. I could use several oversized mugs of coffee right about now."

The waitress comes over, fortunately, providing more time

before we're forced to engage in real conversation, and I order some food. A short stack of pancakes. More coffee. Piper orders coffee, too, and some wheat toast, dry. When the waitress moves away, she forages through her purse and pulls out some fancy looking jam packets.

"It's all good," I say, picking things up, probably after too long of a pause. "Gave me some time to lap you in a cup of coffee. It's the only way I can keep up, talking to you."

She laughs. As if it's a joke, but it's most certainly not. Piper is a fast talker and if I'm not careful, I'm liable to agree to a whole bunch of shit I might not have actually heard. Focus is key today—there's a crucial task at hand.

"Well," she says, "I'm glad you're feeling better. You seemed like you'd, I don't know, seen a ghost or something last night."

I laugh now. Nervously. "What? Nope, nothing weird going on. All good. Nothing some sleep couldn't cure, anyway." I laugh again. Try for a casual smile. God, I'm a terrible actor in my real life. I guess that's a good thing? Except it sort of sucks here and now.

"Right, so here's the thing, Rocco. I really do think this movie could catapult us both into the stratosphere, and this angle . . ."

Angle. My hackles go up. But it's not surprising coming from Piper. She's never shied away from owning her ambition. It's part of what I'd loved about her. Whether there are genuine feelings now or not, this is certainly part of her motivation. That *catapult*, as she says. Not that we both weren't fairly catapulted already, before taking on *Murder in the Books*. But there's always higher, isn't there? Always more. Money. Fame. Awards.

But this movie . . . it's about so much more than any of that outward success. This is Bea's life. That matters, at least to me. It's mattered since the beginning, even if I wasn't so great at articulating that to myself, or to Bea.

"About that," I cut in, before I have to hear more about the pros of our romantic reunion buzz. "After more time to pro-cess, I suspect that . . . it was likely emotions from the project that fueled our, er, extracurriculars. On-set spillover. That, and maybe some vodka." A solid guess since I'm not privy to the specifics. High-end vodka had always been her drug of choice, at least back in the day.

"Oh yes, the vodka." She laughs, but then her face settles into something more real. Piper isn't all smoke and mirrors; she never was. There's always been more, at least for the chosen ones she lets in. Who she chooses, when she chooses. First my brother. Then me. A long line of others since, I'm sure. I haven't been closely following. "And yes, there was maybe some spill-over, as you say. There usually is if you're doing it right. But being on set with you, it triggered those old feelings, too. How could it not? The fiery history we have. My god. Our kiss the other night . . . I didn't feel like I was kissing William. It was you, Rocco. I was kissing *you*." She takes a sip of coffee. Sighs. "I don't know. It's confusing, isn't it?"

Yep. So damn confusing.

More confusing than I'd like, by a long shot. A groveling ex I'd once thought was the one—enough so to turn my back on family for her, my own little brother—and a new relationship that's so shiny and perfect and all-consuming. Or technically, no. Bea's from my past, too, isn't she? Either way, a real-life second chance rom-com.

Like I'd told Bea, there's a reason I never sign on for rom-coms. Too mentally and emotionally draining, even when it's just pretend. And this? It's too real for anyone's good. Espe-cially my own.

"Anyway," she continues, "Tom had said you were into this whole idea. He was rather convincing on that front. And I've been looking for a role like this—a way to age up gracefully, you know, no easy feat. I signed on for the nostalgia, too. Peo-ple just won't let go of us, will they?"

"What idea exactly did Tom say I was into?" I focus on that

to start. The least intimate piece to process. "That pairing up again would be dynamite for this movie—for our careers?"

Piper nods. "Something like that, yes. And that it was destined to be. A tad prophetic and vague, but strangely sincere, too. He really believed in what he was saying. I can see why you've kept him around all these years without upgrading to a newer model. He's a good manager." She laughs again, low and throaty. Piper laughs have historically been heavily intoxicating. I'm a sucker for them, always have been.

"He's good," I say, trying to focus. "Always has my best interests in mind. But I'm . . . not really into a PR stunt to sell tickets and generate buzz. That's not my bag. More honest ways to get attention with our work, right?"

Piper looks confused; there's a soft wrinkle to her brow, and I'm pleasantly surprised she hasn't loaded herself up with Botox. "What do you mean, 'stunt'? I kissed you because I wanted to kiss you, and it seemed pretty damn obvious you wanted to kiss me, too. Tom wasn't trying to set us up, not outside our roles. That kiss? That was on us. It was *honest*, at least on my end. And to be candid, it felt . . . nice. Much nicer than I would've anticipated. You've grown up, Rocco. We both have."

I'm taken aback. It feels good to hear her say that, after everything we've been through. And all scripts aside, I can attest to the chemistry we've always had. Way back to the early days, when we were just kids on the set of *Black Hole Sons*. Not that I don't regret imploding my relationship with Rudy over her, but there was a reason for it. It sounds like a cop-out, but at the time, it had felt like chemical forces outside my control, pushing me toward her. She was it for me then. Had been since our first casting read through.

"It . . . wasn't a stunt for me either." It couldn't have been, even if I don't remember the details. If I kissed her, then I wanted to. Simple—or as complicated—as that. "The chemistry's still there, clearly. The dailies don't lie. You and I even breaking bread like this would have seemed impossible to me not so long ago. I like this—that we've moved forward. We've got too much history to be strangers in this town."

Piper agrees with her eyes. She knows how big this is, too. A vindictive, highly publicized and heartbreaking dismissal doesn't typically scream, "let's be friends." It's hard to even say at this point who officially ended things for good; there'd been so many rounds in the end, stops and starts, messier and more volatile with each new temporary reunion.

But, miraculously, here we are now.

"I'm glad we've finally talked about it. It felt like you were perhaps . . . avoiding me for a little bit there? You can't ghost your on-set wife, you know." She cocks an eyebrow, but her pursed lips look more playful than angry. "I'm okay to take things slow, see how it goes. I don't want to push you into any-thing. I don't want to push *myself* into anything either. I just wanted to be forthright with you. Start there." She sighs. "My life's changed in so many ways, and so have I. This is part of that change—trying to be as straightforward as possible. I've ruined a lot of relationships because of my . . . inability to com-municate. Present company included. We both had a knack for that, I suppose."

The waitress returns with our food, and we eat in silence. Piper swipes a few bites of my pancake. That's familiar, too. It feels like we've done all this before. But now that we're older, maybe we'd finally be able to do it right, at least under dif-ferent circumstances. Some things never change—but maybe others do.

That's what I'm trying to prove to Bea, right?

Fuck. My head hurts. It's somehow been two days and a week and half of my lifetime, all at once.

"Let's take it day by day," I say, putting down my empty mug, three refills deep. Probably not the right thing to say; or no, more like definitely not. It's too loose, too promising, too slippery, and I promised Bea I'd make things right today, but I'm not sure how this kind of breakup etiquette should go. Everything feels fragile and tenuous and strange. Surreal. We're exes, we're costars—everyone's counting on us to carry this project smoothly to the stars. "Thanks for being honest and upfront. I hope that's been working well for you. I've got to run—I'm supposed to meet up with Rudy soon. I, uh, won't tell him you say hello?" I'd texted him this morning, a brotherly SOS. He's both the best and worst person I could talk to about any of this. The only one, really, either way.

"Hm yes, probably a wise choice." She frowns, those brow lines returning as she balls up her napkin. It's strange, seeing your girlfriend from your early twenties like this, so much more mature, inside and out. "I know how much I hurt him. Some old relationships don't get a do-over. But I've heard his new show here is hilarious. I can't help but check his socials sometimes—don't tell him that either. I'm glad, though. Happy for him. He was always too good for both of us, wasn't he?"

I nod. "He sure was."

She's quiet for a beat, looking at me without really seeming to see me, and then her eyes clear again. "I'll see you Saturday, right?"

"Saturday?"

"My New Year's Eve party, silly!" She laughs, reaching out to pat my wrist. "Everyone from set will be there. Well, except for *Beatrix*—you know how she is." I do now, yes. But I didn't—wouldn't have—on this remixed timeline. "I was surprised to see you two so chatty last night." A raised eyebrow, like she's tempted to ask more, but then it lowers, her face perfectly symmetrical again, and she rolls right along. "Lanie's coming, of course. Loads of other good people, too. Kevin Smith is even a maybe, and I know you always went totally moony-eyed over him. Anyway, come around nine. It'll be fun."

She stands then—always keen to be the first to exit any situation, her terms—and leans in for a quick peck on the cheek to say bye. Leaves me alone with the remains of my short stack and my thoughts. As I take another bite, "Like a Virgin" comes on the radio. Appropriate, being here.

And it reminds me of more than just that scene in *Reservoir Dogs*. There are Piper memories, too. We'd loved dancing around to Madonna during set breaks, she and Rudy and I. Goofing off. We'd even snuck into a VIP show once, without any parents finding out.

That's the thing about Piper; she's ingrained in a million old memories.

But there were never supposed to be new ones.

The Redwood Bar is a favorite haunt of Rudy's.

It sits at the bottom of the tunnel on Second Street, where they filmed parts of *Blade Runner*. Very divey, nautically themed. But they have surprisingly delicious burgers and live music some nights, so another quintessential Rudy spot.

Rudy's already perched at the bar when I walk in, watching what looks like an encore presentation of the LA Kings game from last night. I clap him on the shoulder, and he turns to me, grinning. "You can always count on the encore view when there's nothing else happening at . . . two thirty in the afternoon," he says. "I figured you wouldn't mind getting a late lunch here. A nice frosty beverage, too."

He stands and gives me a bear hug. It's been so nice, having a friend who's also a brother nearby. Not being the only Riziero on this coast. Maybe I should look for a gig in New York, too? Run away from all of this for a good long while?

"You know me too well," I say.

"Of course I do." Rudy steps back, smiling, then flags the bartender. "Two PBR tall boys, please. And two cheeseburgers, medium rare. Double steak fries." Perfect order. I suppose our taste has always been similar; too much so, in some cases. "So," he says, turning back to me, "what's going on? What can I help with today?"

Rudy's plugged in like that. Not that we couldn't enjoy a weekday beer lunch just because, but we both know when it's about the hang and when it's about working through some serious shit. It's an innate brotherly connection, still intact after too much time apart.

I wait for the beers to arrive to launch in. This story needs some suds to be believed. We each take a few sips first, no small talk.

And then I tell him—the essentials, anyway.

Starting with the coffee date gone wrong . . . or maybe gone right. Ending with our second crash after the hospital. Waking up on Sunset like only seconds had passed. But with white hair, a T-shirt recovered from '99, *proof.*

"To be clear," he says afterward, crumpling his quickly drained can, "you're saying that a 2000 Volkswagen Jetta is a time-traveling car. Not just you and Beatrix defying laws of the universe? It's a trio?"

"I guess so, yeah. Who knows? But it started and ended in Delilah, after all. Delilah—that's the car's name."

"Right. *Delilah.* I suppose I'm in a state of disbelief, but . . . who am I to judge? Wait, no. I'm your brother. I'm judging so hard right now. Come on, Rocco! You weren't fed some unidentified chocolate or anything like that? There's nothing psychedelic going on? I know your neighbor is a trippy hippie, you sure he didn't accidently spike your drinking water?"

I laugh a little at that. Because of course it sounds utterly ridiculous when you spell it out for someone. It sounds ridiculous to me, too, and I lived it.

"Well," I say, clearing my throat. We've reached what may be the most improbable part yet. "It, uh, gets weirder. Apparently in this new timeline, Piper is in Bea's movie with me. Playing my . . . wife."

He looks at me, brows raised. "Um. Yeah? I know. We talked about that before you both signed on. I gave you my brotherly okay. We've moved on."

Shit. That makes sense, I guess, hard as it is for me to fathom. For this Rudy, it's always been this way. There was never Darla Dee. Only Piper, from the beginning.

"Right, well. That's not how it was before, that was Tom's doing after . . ." I wave my hand, flustered. So many side stories, so much to explain. "Anyway, apparently I kissed Piper recently, off set. Which I don't remember at all, because the universe is playing cruel and unusual tricks with us, and that was . . . me but also not me? And now she's interested in the potential to date again. Or something like that. I don't know. I don't know anything. I'm supposed to be at a New Year's Eve party at her house on Saturday. With other people from the movie, but still."

Rudy's silence in response is telling. The scowl on his face further reinforces his displeasure.

My tallboy, it's not nearly tall enough.

"Listen," he says finally, after I've visibly squirmed enough to satisfy him, "as far as Piper goes, I'm good. No jealousy. She's way back window. But c'mon, bro! Beatrix!"

"I know. But it wasn't *me*. This"—I point to myself emphatically, waving both hands—"me right here. Like I said, Piper was never even supposed to be in this film, not originally. Bea and I, we had a run-in with Tom at a party in '99, accidentally put some prophetic ideas in his head. Let him snag a magazine page from the future that got him thinking about what a nostalgic dynamo coupling Piper and I would be. I never would've agreed to the pairing as me in this moment. It's all so damn confusing."

I cover my face with my hands, feeling guilty on so many levels: For telling my brother that I've possibly rekindled the relationship that threw us apart for so long, even if he's so clearly moved on. And framing that poor decision in the context of some absurd experience that's too impossible to believe. How could anyone who hasn't lived it buy in? Even a brother? Or maybe especially a brother, at least in my case, with our history.

"I have to say, I was surprised when you first asked me about the two of you being together on screen again. You were good about that, flew into Brooklyn to ask—promised you wouldn't agree if I wasn't okay with it. And for what it's worth, you didn't seem to really want it either; it was Tom pushing. But I wasn't expecting a ripple in your timeline to be the cause." Rudy pauses, a contemplative look on his face. "How does this somehow feel so . . . normal? I'm sure the bartender thinks we're both on LSD right now." He starts slowly waving his hand in front of his face, like he's marveling at the movement.

"Whoa, man. Those trails are so colorful." I laugh, swiping his hand down. Joke it off, even though I'm genuinely in awe of how easily he's taking this news.

I'm loving this new Rudy. His own unconventional love story has really worked wonders on him.

The bartender drops our food plates, and Rudy motions for another round of beers.

"My take is this," he continues. "Everything happens for a reason, right? Maybe Piper needed to be here for you now. A final test. What happened with you and Bea in the past, that seems like the important stuff here. Piper being in her movie, while shitty in the moment, sure, will blow the film up. Let's be real. Who doesn't want that?"

I nod, feeling a little sheepish. Tom is a good manager. Annoyingly so. "I cannot stress enough how good she is in this role. I saw dailies last night that were . . . mind boggling, honestly. Like nothing she's done before. She's going to get an Oscar for this. Piper is proving something, that's for sure."

Rudy nods, picking up his fresh beer. "Then you prove

something, too. To Bea. To yourself. Keep things reasonable with Piper; use me as an excuse if you'd like. Whatever it takes. In another timeline, I'm sure I'd be going bonkers over what's happening here. But I'm an engaged man. Lucy's the only one for me. Everyone else was just . . . training wheels for the real race. You're the one who helped me to see that last year when I came here to LA, all lost and confused about life and work and Lucy. And I see it in your eyes now, bro, that you're without a compass. So let me be your sherpa. I want to return the favor."

"You're pretty smart for a baby brother, you know that?"

"Oh, I know. It's a wonder you made it so many years without me."

I throw a steak fry at his head.

The bartender gives a finger wag of disappointment. "Another move like that and I'm gonna rat you out to TMZ, you hear me?"

"Sorry, so sorry," I say, hands raised in surrender, and then I turn back to Rudy. "Thanks. Really. I appreciate your ear. I was coming to the same conclusions, but it feels good to hear it from someone else. Especially from someone who shares my DNA. You know this life, too. You get me in a way no one else possibly could."

Rudy slaps me on the back. Hard. Cheering for . . . the goal that happened eighteen hours earlier. "Go, Kings, Go! I'm right there with you, Rocco! Time traveling back to rewatch a defenseman by the name of Drew Doughty top shelf a one-timer!"

Classic Rudy.

We return to our beers and burgers. In all this chaos, it's nice to know a good old fashioned family chat can still be so grounding.

Nice to know that, even after all the things I've done wrong, Rudy is still here next to me.

Chapter 19
Beatrix

Friday, December 30, 2016

My phone pings, the latest in a string of texts from Rocco. A steady stream since Lanie's party two nights ago.

> **Rocco: Can we talk today?**
> **Rocco: I miss you.**

Ellipses appear. Disappear. Reappear.

> **Rocco: Also . . . don't go online today. Please. Don't. Okay?**
> **Rocco: I'm so sorry.**
> **Rocco: For all of this.**
> **Rocco: Ok. I'll stop.**
> **Rocco: For now.**
> **Rocco: But know I'm thinking about you. Let's talk soon?**

I wait a few minutes, just to be sure. No more ellipses.

And then I open a browser tab and type in *Rocco Riziero*. It becomes immediately and abundantly clear why he told me to stay offline.

He—*they*—are splashed across every celebrity media outlet. Every news outlet, really, known to humankind. It's a slow news week, clearly, these long days between Christmas and New Year's, and Rocco and Piper are helping them score much needed hits.

I click on the first article, scrolling until I come to a series of photos from yesterday's breakfast at Pat and Lorraine's.

They look happy, Rocco and Piper. Comfortable, relaxed. They probably wouldn't have been had they known someone was snapping these pictures. Or maybe they wouldn't have cared—shrugged it off in the name of good press for the movie, whatever will be will be. In the first one, Piper's leaning in, presumably to say hello, eyes closed, lips pouty, nuzzled up to his cheek. Then across from one another at a small table, camera angled low to show their knees visibly touching. And lastly, my least favorite of the batch, Piper is mid-laugh, her amusement at whatever Rocco had just said radiating from the screen. And Rocco, he's got a tiny smile on his face, but it's his eyes that skewer straight through my heart. Looking at her like he can't believe he got this lucky twice.

My eyes snag on a quote from "a source close to Piper": "Her private life is exactly that, private, so I cannot confirm or deny that she and Rocco are back together, but I'll say it's been clear to everyone on set that the heat is still there. On camera . . . and off. I haven't seen her this happy in years." And then from the Rocco side, another "cannot confirm or deny," which, quite frankly, reads like a confirm, otherwise why not deny?

And Piper, she's apparently reposted that photo of herself laughing on social media. No caption. But she doesn't need one, does she?

That photo more than speaks for itself.

I close out of the article and throw my phone across my bed.

Rocco was right. I shouldn't have looked.

Because that Rocco in the photo, looking at Piper like she's the most delicious treat in the world, is somehow the same Rocco who drove me to the hospital in Tucson. The same Rocco who held me so close, kissed me so deeply.

Cannot confirm or deny.

What we'd had back there had felt so real. The most real part of our otherwise completely surreal trip. Maybe that's all it ever was, a trick of the light and the unusual circumstances. And it never would've held up, not when we came back here, and everything else made sense again. Everything but me and him.

I sit up, throw the blankets back. I've barely left my bed since getting home from Lanie's, and the need for both a shower and real food has reached critical levels.

A shower first. Long and hot, and though I lose track of shampoos, I'm confident it's at least three rounds. When my mind has a will of its own and wanders back to Rocco's old house and that glass shower, I instantly shut it down.

Some fresh clothes, a cup of coffee, a bowl of scrambled eggs and old French fries—the only edible things in my fridge—and I'm feeling semi-repaired.

Except I have no plans, nowhere to go. I think about how good it'll feel to be back on set next week, back to work, busy and distracted, and then—*shit*. Of course that won't feel good. Rocco and Piper, together on set, the three of us in the same not nearly large enough studio space while I'm forced to stuff it all down and act at least reasonably professional.

I check the clock. Not quite noon. Too early for whiskey, and I have neither vodka nor bubbles nor orange juice to concoct something that could pass as reasonably suitable for the morning. Popping that bottle with Sylvie the other night had been a mistake.

Sylvie. I could call her now. Spill it out, purge all the messy, unbelievable truths of the last week. Ask her what she's witnessed on set, given she'll have seen it all play out firsthand.

In hindsight, I'm surprised she didn't mention Piper when she fixed me up for the party. Though we've probably already dissected it all endlessly. There's nothing more to say.

I'm not ready for that deep dive, though. Not yet.

And besides, there's someone else I suddenly want to call even more.

Need to.

I go back for my phone where I left it on the bed, ignore three more new texts from Rocco, and find her in my contacts before I lose my nerve.

She picks up after two rings.

"Beatrix? Did you leave something here?"

"Hey, Mom. And no. Not that I know of, anyway."

"Oh."

"I was just calling to say hello."

A pause, and then again, "Oh."

She's not wrong to be surprised. Off the top of my head, I can't recall ever calling her just to say hello before. It's not something we do. Not something we've ever done.

"It's been hard, you know. Working on this movie. Thinking about Dad every day. Thinking about you. Watching it all play out again on set."

"Well," she starts. Pauses, like she's probably trying to think of the least offensive way of saying whatever's to come next. "This is what you wanted, isn't it? You asked for the daily reminder. You've worked yourself to the bone for *years* to keep reminding yourself of it. To get to this place now. That was a choice. I . . . I don't know how you do it. The why—that I think I understand."

My breath hitches. This, the territory we're closing in on. My guilt, her anger, that ugly, messy line between us that's kept us at arm's length since I was a teenager. It's a shock to be this close to it. To talk about something other than the weather or groceries or relatives I mostly never see anymore.

"I'm sorry, Mom," I say, more of a whisper as my throat seems to constrict around the words. I take a deep breath and push on before the moment passes, before it's out of our reach and we never find our way back to it again. "I've spent almost half my life feeling sorry. For Dad, for you. For myself. I never needed you to punish me for the choice I made. Because I've punished myself every day since we lost him."

"I know. And I'm sorry, too."

The phone nearly slips from my hands. I clench my fingers around it more tightly, not wanting to miss a word.

"I was so busy being a wife, that . . ." She sighs. "I think I lost sight of being a mother."

I'm nodding then, not that she can see me, hot tears spilling down my cheeks.

She continues talking, which is good, because I'm nowhere near capable of forming words. "I didn't agree with you, of course. I didn't need the police to tell me that he wasn't guilty. He would never have done it. Never. But still. I should have realized you needed to come about it your own way, in your own time. You were young. And it was so deafening, what everyone outside our house was telling you. I should've given you more grace while you sorted things through. Processed. Before your father passed, and even more so after. By the time I realized that . . . ? Well, I guess it felt too little, too late to apologize. But here we are. And I am. Sorrier than you could ever understand."

I take a deep breath and close my eyes. Letting this moment sink all the way in, so that when we hang up the phone and I go about my day, I won't wonder if this conversation actually happened. "Thank you. For that. I needed to know you felt that way."

"And I needed to tell you. It was just . . . easier to not."

"He would hate this, you know—the fact that we barely know one another now. It'd be torture for him. A prison sentence would have been a breeze, comparatively."

She laughs. But there's a hitch to it, like she's crying at the same time. "He would absolutely be out of his mind furious at us."

"So . . . what do we do about it?" It feels so bold and scary, this question. But this call, it isn't nearly enough. Not for me.

"Maybe more calls just to say hello?"

"I can do that."

"And maybe we could plan a time for you to come back here? We don't have to wait for a holiday. We'll make it our own special celebration. Or anti-celebration. Whatever you want to call it."

"I'd like that. Maybe you can visit me here sometime, too."

She laughs. "Let's not go wild here. I've still never been on a plane, you know."

"I'll pick you up. Delilah would love to make the trip."

"That car of yours, I can't believe it's still running. A long drive in that thing terrifies me more than a plane ride."

"She's a good car, Mom. And not a *thing*. She's so much more than that. A best friend really." And, you know, *a time traveler*. Best to leave that bit out, though.

"That's rather alarming. Best friend? You need to get out more. Interact with real humans. Are you in sweatpants right now?"

I look down to confirm. I'd gotten dressed in a daze. "Yep."

"I knew it. Put on something cute. Nothing too wrinkly. I bet you don't even have an iron, do you?" She steamrolls on without waiting for an answer. "Anyway, dress up a little and go to a coffee shop or something, have yourself a nice meet cute, whatever the fancy city folk are always doing in the Hallmark movies."

I laugh. "No one meets like that anymore, Mom. Hate to break it to you."

"Well, whatever means necessary, I just don't want you to be alone. I worry about you, you know."

"Really?"

"I guess that's another thing I haven't said enough."

"You know what else we should say more?"

"What's that?"

"I love you."

"I love you, too, Beatrix."

It's not the meet cute my mother would've had in mind, but I do change into a mostly unwrinkled black jumpsuit and make plans to see another human being.

I can't ignore Rocco forever.

Let's be honest, I can't even ignore him past this weekend, since we'll be back on set bright and early Monday morning.

Rocco suggests we meet at the beach where we sipped our nips of whiskey, the ocean view that helped us start to process—or at least temporarily numb—the reality of our surreal circumstances. I drive Delilah, still bruised and battered; the last few days have distracted me from making sure she got the promised TLC she needs. I get there a half hour early to stare at the waves—preparing myself for everything I don't want to say but have to anyway.

Because there's only one choice here, and it's not a good one. I've played it out over and over in my mind, and there's just not a happy ending in sight. It's one big mess, no matter how you slice it. So, I'll take the fastest cleanup route. The most efficient.

"Hey there," Rocco says, startling me as he drops a picnic basket in the sand by my side. I look up, shielding my eyes from the sun as I take him in. He looks handsome, as he always does, and in such an effortless, comfortable kind of way, black joggers and a plain gray sweatshirt, a few days of scruff on his sharp cheekbones. He's so beautiful it makes me ache, an empty pit in my chest that I'm not sure I'll ever be able to fill again.

He has a smile on his face, a small, hopeful-looking one, but I don't smile back. If Rocco notices, he pretends otherwise, settling in next to me and opening the basket. "I brought some

Maker's, of course, ethically sourced this time. I had this grand plan of baking you banana chocolate chip muffins myself, but that, er, didn't work out, so I stopped by the café from our perilous meeting last week, picked up some there. A few different kinds of cheeses because I realized I don't adequately know your taste in milk curds these days, some grapes, salami, nothing too spicy because I remember that back in the day you—"

"Rocco," I say, pushing his name from my lips to stop him now, before I lose the will altogether. Before I throw back some whiskey and cheese and forget what I had every intention of doing today. I remind myself: Those photos. Piper's post. *Cannot confirm or deny.* "We have to talk."

He nods, flipping down the lid of the basket. "I was so glad you finally texted me back, I maybe got . . . a little ahead of myself with the charcuterie basket. Overly optimistic."

"Rocco . . ." I flail my hands uselessly in the air, grabbing at everything, nothing. I've never felt quite so undone. "I can't do this."

"Can't do what?" He looks genuinely confused, which only makes this more excruciating.

"This. You. Us. Any of it. Outside the movie, that is, which can't be helped." His face crumbles—the expression has never felt so apt or so absolutely devastating. Those lips that have pressed hot against every bit of me this last week, a few days and a lifetime ago, twisting down. "I've played this game once before with you, didn't I, and I lost. I'm just not willing to play another round, regardless of how strongly I may feel about you right now. I won't put myself through that again."

He might be headed for a romantic do-over, but it won't be ours. It can't be.

If our trip together taught me anything at all, it's to not make the same mistake twice. I won't hurt anyone else this time. Including—*especially*—myself.

He rakes his hands through his hair, and I resist the urge to twine my own fingers through those thick, dark waves. "Whatever happened with Piper and me, it means nothing. Whatsoever. You've got to understand, Bea. That wasn't me, and it's not going to be me."

"How could I possibly understand? I saw the pictures, Rocco. The whole world did. Her post, too. And what source exactly said they couldn't 'confirm or deny' a romance between the two of you? Did you okay that?"

"I told you not to—"

"*Of course* I was going to look! And I would have seen them no matter what because the story's not going away, and you're our stars. It's literally my job to know what's being said about the two of you."

"But you know how tabloids smear things. It's not real, none of it's real. I don't manage Piper's social media—I'm sure she pays someone for that—and I have no clue who the sources were, but of course I didn't okay any of it." He looks pained as he says this, disappointed that I'd even suggest he might be complicit. "Piper and I just had a friendly conversation. Mostly small talk while I tried to wrap my head around what happened between us. Because it's unnerving, you know, having someone else remember something about you that you don't or can't. And then she asked about tomorrow night—some New Year's Eve party at her house that apparently everyone from the movie is going to, that I'm supposed to be at, too. Of course, I didn't remember that either. Because I don't remember anything about this life with her in it."

"Right. So, you ended things? Told her it was all a hilarious, mind-bending mistake, and you'd absolutely never entertain the thought of kissing her off set ever again? And you certainly wouldn't be showing up at her place to ring in another new year together?"

"Well, no, not exactly, in so many words, but . . ."

Heat rushes through me, and not at all the pleasant sort of

heat Rocco's stirred up more recently. The old righteous heat. "Tell me then, what words did you use? *Exactly?*"

He sighs, shaking his head. "I have to be delicate about it, Bea. I couldn't just go stomping in there, telling her . . . what, exactly? That you and I went from on-set enemies to lovers overnight? That I wasn't in my right mind when I kissed her—I wasn't in my own damn mind at all? None of it would make sense to her! It barely makes sense to me!"

Something about his exasperation only makes me more confident. More committed. "Oh come on, I think it makes perfect sense."

"What? How?"

"She's Piper Bell, Rocco. Your first love. Hell, your only real love, probably. The only one that mattered." I pause for a beat, baiting him. He doesn't say anything, but his face reddens. I suspected as much, and this is just confirmation: It was always, only, Piper. "She's ridiculously attractive, I get it. More attractive than any human has a right to be, if you ask me. Just as talented. Not totally dim. And seemingly very interested in you again, despite the epic dumpster fire of your first breakup, at least based on what I managed to glean from the tabloids I pretended not to obsessively track. Honestly, seems like a no-brainer. Ride that meteoric rise from pairing up again in our little old film together and seize that future I'm sure you never fully stopped dreaming of."

He's silent for a moment, his eyes fixed on the strip of sand between our legs. He's silent for so long I wonder if that's it, we're done here. Not a word left. Maybe it's best that way. Nothing either of us says will change the inevitable.

But then, "That's really unfair."

"How?"

"Because I have no romantic interest in Piper. I want you. That's it. Just you. I'm asking you to please believe that. To trust me."

"But don't you get it? Even if you can't remember it, that was still you who kissed her. If that other version of you could drum up the desire for her these past few weeks, this you could do it again now, too. If I wasn't here, you'd fall right into it. I know you would."

"You *are* here, though."

"We had one great week, you and me. I got to say bye to my dad because of you. And you got to meet him. It was win-win for both of us. Let's leave it at that."

"I don't understand. I did nothing wrong yesterday. But you're still punishing me."

"That doesn't mean you did it right. You didn't end things, didn't set her straight. Gave the media some juicy gossip to blast around the world."

"I didn't cut it off all the way because I didn't know how to. I needed to let it sink in first. Plan a way to do it more sensitively, knowing all the facts. And for the record, it's not my fault the tabloids caught us—I can't control that, unless I never step foot outside my house. Even then, they'd find a story somehow! That's part of my life, Bea. The burden to go along with the blessings. Anyone who chooses to be with me has to accept that, and to trust my word over whatever horseshit the glossies are spoon-feeding the masses."

"I would just have to *accept* that everyone would believe lies about you? About us?"

He throws up his hands. "Yes! *Yes*, Bea. Because you and I, we would know what's real. That's trust. And it's the only way this would ever work. To be honest, it's probably why I've been trash at relationships for most of my adult life. That's why Piper and I worked, at least for a while. She got that part. She's in this life, too. I didn't have to explain myself to her, ever."

"See?" My throat tightens around the one-word question, the most I can manage.

"See what?"

"It came back to Piper. Again."

"Jesus, Bea . . . that's your whole takeaway from everything I said?"

No. Yes. But does it matter? The other details?

"When we were together on our trip," I say, "the things we did and said, the way we thought we felt . . . you didn't know then that Piper could still be in the picture, that a life with her was a real possibility. I don't hold it against you. I can't." I mean that. Mostly. Even if I despise the reality of it. "And maybe we were meant to change the facts, to rewrite the path between then and now so that she's here, in this movie with you. Playing *my mother*, for the love of god." I laugh, because how can I not? The universe has been equal parts absurdly kind and absurdly cruel in this last week, and the whiplash of it all is too much.

I saw my father again. Something that should have been an absolute physical impossibility. Kissed his cheeks, held his hand. Breathed him in. I don't need anything more. I shouldn't. That would be greedy.

And maybe Rocco is right, the media, the rumors—none of that is his fault. But just because that's his lot in life doesn't mean it has to be mine. The media ruined my dad's life. Why would I let them ruin mine?

Rocco isn't laughing along with me. The opposite; he's looking dangerously on the verge of tears, and I can't let it happen, can't let him cry—those tears might dissolve too much of my resolve. "I'm so sorry I hurt you," he says, "back when we were first together. I'd apologize every day for the rest of my life if that's what it took for this to work with you. But I was still a kid. I made a terrible and selfish choice, and I own that. But I'm asking you to believe that I'm not that person anymore. I don't want the same things—the same people. I want you. Only you. And I would never hurt you like that again. I promise you can trust me."

"I believe that you believe that."

"Because it's the truth." His voice has more edge now. Good—that's a positive—anger feels so much easier than sadness. Anger is fuel. I should know, after all the years I let it drive me forward. And it worked, didn't it?

"Maybe it is. Or maybe more time with Piper would change your mind. Once I'm removed from the equation."

He closes his eyes, taking in a deep breath. As if the cool sea air could be enough to calm either of us down. "Please," he says, much more quietly. His voice is barely audible above the crash of an especially large wave, the water creeping closer to where we sit.

"No. I . . ." The word hovers there, on the tip of my tongue, and I swallow it back down. "*Like* you so much." More than that, maybe. Probably. Yes. But there's no room for that level of honesty. Not with him. Not with myself. "But we've had our time in the past, twice over now. And both times, just as I was letting you in . . . Piper came along. Don't you think that's a sign from the universe?"

"Why can't you believe that the *sign*, if there was one, was the universe making all of it happen in the first place? Putting you and me together, in that shitty old Jetta, crashing and—what? Flying back through seventeen years in a blink? Why us? Why then?"

I shake my head, push everything away, any lingering thoughts of us together, the how and the why. Then laugh again because it's that or sob. "Delilah is not shitty, thank you. Or she wouldn't be, at least, if you'd followed through and had her fixed like you promised. But . . . you've been rather busy these past few days, haven't you?"

"That's . . ." he sputters, pushing himself up from the sand to stand, angrier now—as angry as I've ever seen him. His cheeks are flushing again, bright-red heat coursing just below the surface. "That's your takeaway from what I just said? Okay then. Back to the old Beatrix, I see. Where anything that comes out of my mouth is subject to resentment. Or mockery. Or, on a lucky day for me, both."

I stand, too. Lower than him by half a foot, but still closer to eye level. More equal footing. "It's not my fault you make it so easy."

His mouth hangs open, frozen for a moment. Then, "What the hell, Bea? Are we suddenly kids again now, stuck in 2016? Did I blink, and the reverse happened?"

"Nah, I don't think so," I say, giving an exaggerated squint. "You didn't have those deep crow's feet back then, so." I shrug. I'm being a complete and utter shrew, I know it, but it's so much easier to slide back into these dynamics. This back and forth with Rocco, it's safe. Effortless. My comfort zone.

"Wow, got it. Thank you for making it so clear to me exactly how over we are. The clarity, it's super helpful. So sensitive of you. Thank you for that."

"We need that clarity to be professional, don't we? Back on set next week."

"Yes, professional. That's right. You were so great at that before. Maybe you could try to shame me just a touch less? Let me do my job. Now that I've—" He stops himself, frowning, a twinge of apology mixed with the bitterness.

"Now that you met my dad and are such an expert?"

"That's not what I was going to say. I'm grateful I was there. Partly, yes, so that I can play him even more accurately. Your movie deserves my best. But mostly because I wanted to be there for you. Not that it matters now. Or that you'd believe me."

"So let's leave it at that then," I say, bending over to pick up my purse and the booties I'd kicked off in the sand.

"Have a nice New Year's with Delilah," Rocco says, staring at the waves, far away from me. "Enjoy that drive-in feature together."

"We certainly will. And you"—I blink my eyes shut, will

back a pool of tears I refuse to cry—"enjoy Piper's party. You really should go. Good for appearances and all that."

"Yep. Will do. And Bea?"

"What?"

"Maybe think about how not trusting someone worked out the last time."

I walk away. Refuse to look back. I channel my rage and keep adding distance between us, one step after another, until I'm sitting inside Delilah.

I press the gas pedal down and move forward, and only forward, a straight line between me and the only possible future.

A future, a new year, without Rocco.

Or at least after the movie's wrapped—after the press and the premiere.

No more rewinding.

Never again.

Chapter 20

Rocco

Saturday, December 31, 2016

I flop down on the patio chair, stare out over the ocean below.

I'm cold in just a T-shirt and boxers, but too drained to grab a blanket from inside. My sunrise espresso, a frigid swim, and the double espresso shot I just sucked down have all failed to give any boost today.

Probably because I slept maybe three hours all in last night. The last few days replaying in my head while I lay in bed awake, and then in my dreams, too. Inescapable.

Why Delilah, why me and Bea, why any of it?

I refuse to believe that Piper being in the movie was the greater purpose. And as important as it was for Bea to see her dad, it felt like it was about more than that, too.

Or selfishly, at least, I wanted it to be.

Everything I told Bea yesterday was true—though I probably should have skipped my closing jab about trust. The not-so-subtle reference to William. I was too angry to think straight because there's nothing to worry about between Piper and me. But I guess it's hard to be clear on the dividing lines around emotions when another Rocco, this age, this timeline, *did* want to kiss Piper, just a few days ago. Bea's right to be skeptical, isn't she? And she has the right to end things.

I should have been more up front with Piper. At least about Bea. But the way Piper had mentioned her during breakfast—that cool, detached Beatrix I'd known before our life-altering adventure . . . how to explain when and why I'd come to see her in a whole new light? Piper probably wasn't wrong to assume the worst in her; Bea had done her no favors, I'm sure. I hadn't lived through our time on-set together in this timeline, but based on my own experiences, I've got no doubt things have been frosty. And Piper would have no idea why. She'd need a long ride in Delilah to understand the true cause of Bea's simmering wrath.

It's hard right now—impossible, really—to drum up genuine enthusiasm about ringing in a new year in a few hours.

But I can't stay here alone, in this state, playing video games all night. Or go out to a bar, flying solo. Both options are equally dismal and would involve way too much self-pity and therefore way too much self-indulgence. I've got friends, sure, and more acquaintances than I know what to do with, but most of them are work relationships—great for a happy hour drink to talk shop, but not necessarily holiday wingman material. Rudy and Lucy are on a romantic excursion in Palm Springs to ring in the New Year, otherwise I'd hitch a sad third wheel onto their ride.

Going to Piper's party feels like the easiest option.

My morale will still be low, but the cast and crew will be there, and maybe the Kevin Smith factor will pay off for me, finally. I'll take whatever spark of hope I can get. Bea's made it clear we won't be celebrating together, tonight or ever again, and I'm not the type to push another person to feel a certain way. I put my heart out there. I tried. I really, really did. Our trip gave us all the hindsight we could've ever asked for in this life, but still—it wasn't enough for Bea.

Or maybe, in the end, it was too much hindsight.

Too much clarity, at least about me.

Murder in the Books will blow up, we'll rake in awards, and Bea's family story, the unfiltered truth—or mostly unfiltered, with one notable exception—will be everywhere. It seems as perfect as any contract with the devil could be, all of us winners. There were no souls bought and sold in our case, just a wild tangle in the timeline. And Tom and his greed that usually feels more boon than burden. Our human egos getting in the way.

' I force myself to get up and go inside. I need food to soak up that espresso. I need a nap and a shower.

I need to move forward, even if I'd much rather go back.

I'm an actor; I can convince myself of anything.

Party suit on, hair artfully mussed, one beer down.

That stiff upper actor lip of mine is holding strong. For now. I feel the hot swarm of feelings simmering beneath my skin, but luckily I've got a nice and durable outer layer of machismo to contain the mess—an accessory I'm used to pulling on day in and out for roles.

But I need to get to the party fast, adequately distract myself before I lose control and all emotional hell breaks loose. Because this is the hardest I've ever had to act. The most challenging role of my life.

I get into the car, my Maserati once again up and kicking. First step achieved. The rest will be a breeze, I assure myself, pulling down the driveway. I turn the XM radio station Lithium on, as one thirtysomething might do. "Stars" by Hum is coming to an end. And I'm back there, just like that: Bea. Road tripping through the past.

Damnit. Must keep focused on the things I can control. Bea? No one ever could or should control her.

A few deep breaths. In. Out. I'll be okay.

But then "Possum Kingdom" by the Toadies starts up next.

What the hell?

The universe, more of her cruel jokes. I switch off the radio. "Why?!" I yell out.

The Maserati doesn't respond. Not altogether surprising, though I have this strange feeling Delilah would give me some sympathetic vibes. Or no, maybe pissed off ones in this case. For hurting her owner's heart, two times over now.

I shake it off; I will not resort to talking through my sad problems with automobiles.

Back to what I can control—making the movie a hit. The only real way for me to help Bea now is to act my ass off, and to play the PR game—sans faux romance with Piper. Make sure I tout it everywhere, at every opportunity. I can't right past wrongs or change present feelings, but I can make sure I'm bringing her up, not down, from here on out.

I continue to the party in silence for a few minutes. But then my addled brain and twitchy fingers get the best of me, and I turn on the radio again.

No Doubt is raging. Not "Don't Speak," but "Spiderwebs."

Leave a message, and I'll call you back.

Seriously? What kind of awful cosmic fuckery is going on right now?

Don't have the courage inside me
To tell you please let me be

The lyrics ring so true and so deep, my protective outer layer of bullshit starts to dissolve. Not so durable after all, huh? Those sour feelings, they're fully at the surface now. And wow, do they sting.

But these feelings, brutal as they are—they're mine. They're real.

My feelings for Bea, they're the most real of all.

My . . . I can't deny or push it down any longer. . . .

Love.

Because that's what it is. Pure and simple—or maybe more un-simple, in this case. But love, nonetheless.

I can't let her down again.

I can't make myself believe I tried everything I could when, in fact, there was more I should have done and said.

Damn you, Gwen Stefani. Your truth, it hurts so hard. But I needed it. Needed that right hook to the gut.

Because suddenly, without a doubt, I know what I have to do.

I pick up my cell and ring Piper. Hoping, of course, that she's too busy with party duties and I can just leave a message. Who picks up the phone these days, anyway?

"Rocco!"

Shit. Piper does, apparently. A telltale signature of an elder millennial.

"You on your way over?" She rolls right along before I can work up the courage to say hello. "We're still at a maybe for Kevin Smith—that's LA to a T, isn't it?"

A pause.

"Rocco? You there?"

C'mon, dude. Be the Rocco that Bea needs.

"Ah yes, very LA indeed." I clear my throat. Forge ahead. "Listen, Piper, the more I've been thinking about what happened between us, the more certain I am it was . . . a mistake. A fun one, don't get me wrong. But more of a nostalgic misadventure. We need to keep it platonic going forward."

I did it; it's out. *Nostalgic misadventure.* Surprisingly eloquent of me.

She lets out a loud sigh, and I stiffen as I sit at a red light, waiting for a potentially messy storm of shit to land on me. A storm I'd likely deserve, even if the memory of our kiss is beyond me. "If we're being totally honest here, and it seems like we are, I've been giving it a lot of thought, too, and I . . . feel the same way. It was nice to go back in time for a little, even if it brought up some bad memories alongside the good. And I suppose I figured since we were both single and making magic on screen that, I don't know . . . it was just an obvious move to get back together?" She laughs, and my whole body feels infinitely looser, lighter. "It sounds ridiculous, doesn't it, hearing it out loud? Like we should live our personal lives to appease our professional and public ones. I'm sorry about the silly repost by the way; it only added a tanker's worth of fuel to the fire. That was my assistant, and she's been . . . *corrected* on that particular PR choice. But we both deserve to treat ourselves better than that, to live our truths. To find the right people for *us*, not for them."

"Thank you for that. And also," I say, feeling emboldened by our confessions, "now that you mention it. . . . There is someone else."

A pause, but only for a blink. "Oh?"

"Long story short, I lost her once, and I was just finding my way back when you and I had our brief rekindling. I'd be a fool to let her get away a second time." I pause. Consider my words carefully. "You and I . . . what we had mattered to me. So much. But it feels like our story was meant to end back then, at least the romance part. And I like knowing we can be friends and colleagues now, no hard feelings. Plus it'll be nice to not have to hide from you every awards season."

"God, so nice!" She laughs. "Seems like we've both grown up a lot, huh? You're a better man for it. Maybe another reason why it was so enticing to me, why *you* were so enticing. The idea of you, anyway. But I get it. Who is she? Anyone I know?" I hear a high-pitched yelp, the sound of plates shattering in the background. "Shit! I just lost half the appetizers! I've got to go.

Will I still see you tonight? Purely platonically?" A loud alarm blares from her end of the line.

"I can't, I'm sorry. I've got to make things right. But happy New Year, Piper."

"This is the last time I try to do it all myself in the name of pride," she mutters, and I'm not sure she's still listening at this point. I'm about to end the call, but then: "Yeah, okay, Rocco, happy New Year to you, too. Go get that person of yours. Grab your love story sequel, okay? I'll tell Kevin you should do lunch sometime. Buh-bye."

More relief surges. *Closure.* I'm enjoying mid-late thirties emotional handling. Much less yelling, more rational thinking.

Speaking of rational thoughts—what now?

New Year's Eve. So Bea will be . . .

At the drive-in theater, sobbing her way through an Alfred Hitchcock marathon. Glendale, did she say? A quick search on my phone gives me everything I need to know. My plan is flimsy, but straight from the heart: 1) find Bea, 2) convince her I'm all in. Because deep down—or not so deep down anymore, screaming at the surface, impossible to ignore—I know this all meant something. A once-in-a-lifetime chance to change the past. For both of us.

As I reprogram my GPS to Glendale, I'm buzzing with a wave of excitement.

This feels right. Now I've just got to hope, by some stroke of New Year's Eve midnight magic, Bea will agree.

My GPS is freaking out.

This drive-in is apparently impossible to locate. Maybe it shuttered and Bea and the internet both didn't know? Because I'm idling in front of the address clearly marked on my map screen—an office building with an attached tiered parking lot. Not a screen in sight.

I start scanning the FM dial and, sure enough, on 88.1 FM

I hear what sounds like Jimmy Stewart speaking. Either *Rear Window*, *Vertigo*, or *The Man Who Knew Too Much*. I'm a big Jimmy fan, could pick his voice out anywhere. But now where the hell is the screen?

As I stick my head out the car window, I hear an echo of what's coming out of my speakers. What the hell? Looking up, I finally see it—the romantic black-and-white glow. On the roof! Pretty cool, I have to say; I'd definitely come back here, ideally under less fraught circumstances. It's been too long since I really enjoyed going to a movie theater, outside of premieres—and our *Sixth Sense* foray. Too much attention, no one can enjoy the movie. Especially not me. But this? Tucked away in my car, free to eat whatever I choose with whoever I choose, an invisible member of the audience and not the main event? Dream scenario.

I start cruising through the parking garage, making my way up. I consider calling Bea, but odds are low she'd pick up. Better to surprise her. I hope? Anyway, it's all I got. No turning back now.

There are easily a hundred vehicles on the top tier. I abandon my car in the back and make my way through the rest of the lot on foot. Searching. Feeling all the frantic butterflies in my stomach as I go. I'm nervous, excited, and absolutely flying by the seat of my pants.

She won't just tell me to get lost, right?

Except . . . this is Bea. Of course she might say exactly that.

But I still have to try. I won't be able to live with myself if I don't.

I continue down the aisles, enjoying snippets of *The Man Who Knew Too Much* as I go. Total classic, and a pleasant distraction from my worries. The audience seems mostly riveted, aside from what looks like some steamy back seats and a duo of pickup tailgaters engaged in rowdy face-sucking, spilling drinks with their haphazardly wandering limbs.

Eight rows deep, still no sign of Delilah.

Maybe I should just call her . . . after I check the last two rows.

A few more minutes in, no aisle unturned, and still no Bea. Which makes no sense. She'd been so passionate telling William about this event, her New Year's Eve standing engagement in his honor.

It's time to be a grown adult and call her. I start back toward my car, mumble a little prayer to the universe, and press her name.

It goes right to voicemail.

I try again. Just in case. The second call goes through, and I catch a few rings before I hear her. A gasp.

Bea.

"Please come get me." She sounds rushed, flustered. "I'm walking up to Piper's front door."

"What the hell are you doing at Piper's? Wait . . ." Could we actually be on the same page here? "Were you coming to find me?"

"Um. Yes? I didn't see your car, but I assume because you're filthy rich you probably have at least a dozen of them, or maybe a driver dropped you off."

"Three, Bea. I only have three. But no, I didn't go. I called Piper earlier, told her everything had been a mistake and we should just be friends. Make the best movie we can but leave the romance where it belongs: In the past. And I said . . . there was someone else."

Her breathing starts to get heavier. Like she's huffing on a treadmill.

"Bea? You okay?"

"Yes, fine. Just running back to Delilah. I've got to get the hell out of here before anyone sees me." There's a loud rustling sound then, like she's clutching me against her chest. "I'm sorry, Rocco. I couldn't stop playing back over everything we

said to one another yesterday. Even if it meant doing the unthinkable and showing up at Piper's party to find you, I had
to do it. Had to apologize to your face. Because I should have
trusted you, Rocco, when you said you weren't interested in
her. You were right, what you said. About how not trusting in
someone has burned me before. I just got so caught off guard
by everything, and then the media blitz—it dredged up all the
ugliest parts of the past for me. I know the tabloid rumors
aren't your fault, but it was so cloudy in my brain, and I needed
a day to decompress. Reevaluate. I went out for a long drive
this morning, and suddenly there you were, staring down at
me from a *Space Blasters IV* billboard, wearing the ridiculous
flaming jetpack that makes you look like Buzz freaking Light-
year, and I started laughing so hard, and then, just like that,
I was crying so hard I had to pull over at an In-N-Out of all
places, and who can sit in an In-N-Out parking lot and not
get those mediocre fries you adore? You can smell them from a
mile away! So I cried and ate fries and thought about you and
everything we've been through, and . . . well, here I am. Almost made it inside, too, where it would have been so tremen-
dously awkward without you. Which—" She takes a breath,
maybe the first once since she started her apology. "Where the
hell are you, by the way?"

"At the drive-in! I needed to apologize to you, too, because
I regret everything I said. I was just so hurt that you couldn't
take my word for it, but how could you? It happened once,
why couldn't there be a repeat performance? Especially when it
was already happening in this timeline. And you shouldn't just
have to 'accept' the media garbage. It's the real shit end of the
Rocco Riziero stick, but I could've been more understanding.
I'm sorry for dismissing your feelings." Deep breath, a quick
internal debate about whether I can hold it in until we're together, but . . . nope, it's here and it's coming out hot:

"I love you, Bea."

It feels so good to say it, here and now. The right year, the right woman. Like every path would always have brought us here.

A few seconds pass. Long seconds. If it weren't for her breaths, slowing now, I'd think we'd lost our connection.

And then: "I love you, too, Rocco."

"You do?"

"Of course I do! Why else would I be *here*? God, I hope nobody saw that sprint. I'm a horrible runner, a stiff upper back, arms flapping like duck wings. Not a good look. And we'll see all these people back on set this week."

I laugh—it's hard to stop laughing, I feel so giddy. I'm back at my car now, and I lean against the hood to steady myself. "You deserve so much better than how we left us. Which is why I'm on the roof of this parking garage, watching a giant blow-up screen, Jimmy Stewart escaping from bad guys through a bell tower. Great movie."

"I'm sad I'm missing it. Though I'm sure my dad would approve of my reasons. I just wish we'd made different choices so we could've been there together right now."

We're both quiet for a moment. It feels so crucial, whatever we say and do next. How we choose to end this year, ring in the next.

Bea starts us off: "So ding-dong, since we've both now tried and failed to find one another, how do we make it right?" Ah, there she is—the old wiseass Bea I know and very much love.

Suddenly, I know. Of course. "Let's meet where it all went wrong. Well, the first time around. This last time, it's where things went right. The beginning of our second chance."

"What the hell kind of riddle is that?"

"The Roxy."

"Oh." I can feel her smile through the phone. Her smirk-smile, the most perfect smile there is.

"I'm sure there's some big show tonight, but we can meet

outside and figure out the rest. Another new year, another fresh start."

"Let's do it. To be honest, I've held a real grudge against that place. Missed out on quite a few killer concerts because I refused to go near it. You know, because of you. And my stinginess when it comes to money for shows. Mostly you, though."

She snickers into the phone, and my heart skips a beat. Oh, how I've missed getting gently ribbed these past few days.

"It's a date," I say, already back in the car, starting up the engine.

"It's a date. Safe travels, Rocco. No crashes through time, okay?"

She hangs up before I can respond—of course she does, it's Bea—and I drive out of the parking garage, get back on the road. Sunset can't come soon enough. A quick search on my phone says the band X is playing The Roxy tonight, one of Rudy's top five. No way we will be getting inside, but that's okay. The location itself is the main event.

The ride from Glendale is relatively quick to start, but as soon as I get to Sunset, I'm on a path with thousands of other last-minute party revelers, or just cruisers who want to be seen on this road. The slowdown gives me time to think, though, about everything. The past, so vibrant in my mind . . . like it just happened yesterday—or at least a few days ago, *because it did*—allows for so much clarity in the present. What a wild gift from the universe, the hindsight and the foresight I'd likely have been incapable of otherwise.

We'll never understand all the whys and hows of our cosmic road trip, but that's okay—as long as we have one another.

Proof. Enough for a lifetime.

As predicted, The Roxy is packed out when I drive by, so I park a few blocks away. I double back on foot quickly, wading through the crowds, and post up on the sidewalk to watch for Bea. Delilah shouldn't be hard to miss, especially with her busted front end. To be fair, though, a 2000 model anything sort of sticks out here, driving down Sunset these last few minutes of 2016. Most people have traded in, traded up in the last decade and a half.

But not Bea. And I love that about her. Besides, who knows, maybe with a different car, none of this would have happened?

Delilah's got a spot in my heart—and my oversized garage—forever.

I see her then, that bumperless but still shiny silver chariot. Ten cars or so back. I start jumping up and waving, onlookers be damned, and Bea flashes her lights as she cruises closer and then double parks in front of me.

"There are no open spots," she calls out, rolling down her window. "The Roxy is too popular tonight."

"I know, but it doesn't matter." I step off the sidewalk, make my way to the driver side. "We've got a clear view of the place where we first broke apart. And then, somehow, got put back together. In the most bizarre, irrational way possible."

Bea glances up at The Roxy sign, a thoughtful look on her face. "It's strange, being back at this place by choice. And it doesn't hurt this time."

"I'm glad to hear that."

"But seriously, where do I park?"

I laugh. "Right here looks good to me. Put on those hazards. Who knows, this could be the scene of our next hit-and-run. Another taco truck, maybe. Or a film RV this time."

Bea raises an eyebrow at me, her lips scrunching into an adorable pout.

"Another dose of magic from Delilah? No? You don't want to time hop again?"

"Hell no," she says, but her hazards are on and she's climbing out of the car. "I'm perfectly content to stay put, thank you."

We're right next to one another, as close as we can be without touching.

"I love you, Rocco," she says, eyes locked on mine. As good as it felt to hear those words earlier on the phone, it's a million times better in person. As real as it gets.

"I love you, too, Bea. And I'm sorry I hurt you all those years ago. Though it sure made for a wild trip back, so maybe we're lucky I was a screwup?"

"Hm, let's not go that far. But I forgive you. And I see the value of how we got here, the silver linings. I mean, how would I have rekindled my love of White Tea and Ginger otherwise?" She lifts her wrist to her nose, sniffs despondently a few times. Sighs. "I miss it already."

"You brought some back, right? Did you check our bags?" Her eyes go Disney-princess wide. Without a word, she runs to the trunk.

"Rocco, you genius! It's all here! Our clothes, and the Bath and Body Works stash!" She squirts some lotion into her palm, takes a deep, reverent breath. Shudders with joy.

"Really enjoying this moment, I see?"

"Sure as hell am."

I move in closer and wrap my arms around her shoulders. Breathe in even more deeply than she is. "So addictive, that smell. Not the only reason I need to be this close to you, though. Just a bonus." My gaze catches on a piece of paper sticking out from pants tossed in the trunk, and I reach out to grab it. That *Notting Hill* note from Bea, Trixie, that I'd slipped from my old room, just because. My fingers graze her hair as I tuck it behind her ear. "I'd like to cash this in, but we've got to find a VHS copy, keep with the original spirit of the date. I know a few places."

Bea snatches the paper away, opens it. Grins. "Of course, Rocco. My coupons last forever, at least with the right person. I'd most certainly deny one Francis McLean of the eighth-grade Spring Fling dance if he tried to cash in a movie date to watch *Sister Act*." She laughs. It's the best laugh of all the laughs.

Bea, she's my person. It's stunning, really, how obvious that is.

"How was I so dumb?" I ask. Knowing I'm likely setting myself up for a fierce ribbing, but asking all the same, because it's genuinely that bewildering. "You were there, and I knew how good I had it, I did—but I still somehow screwed up so royally." I tilt my head skyward, close my eyes. "Thank you, universe, for granting me this second chance to find her. For our batshit yet brilliant as hell road trip rewind."

"I've let go of my regrets from that night in '99, the first time around, and you need to, too. Because it brought us here. Today. Together. And it let me see my dad again."

Her voice catches, and I pull her in closer, both of my arms gripping snugly around her waist. I lean in and kiss her. I kiss her like I've never kissed anyone before; not Trixie, not Piper, certainly not any of the more transient partners who've crossed paths with me in between. And she kisses me back with just as much steam. It's a kiss that marks so much more than just my lips. It burns through all of me, every last inch, torching what needs to go, lighting up the rest of me, the rest of us, the best parts.

A few horns sound off as they drive by. A happy accident? Nah, just a couple of lovers settling old scores and starting new ones.

Bea laughs into my mouth, and I laugh back. A magical echo chamber.

She pulls away, just a bit, our lips still grazing. "What should we do now? I think we may be overstaying our welcome on this double-parked Sunset spot."

"How about I hop in Delilah, and we head to The Surveyor? Ring in the new year looking out over the Pacific. The Santa Monica Pier fireworks are spectacular."

"That sounds perfect." She kisses me one more time and then heads to the driver side door. I climb in the passenger seat, and off we go down Sunset. A few stray fireworks shoot off in the rearview as we head west, like glittering white stars scattering behind us.

Another universe intervention? Perhaps.

Whatever it is, it's a nice touch.

I wouldn't want to end this year any other way.

Epilogue

Beatrix

October 2017

"Mom, get over here!" I call out from the end of the red carpet, my gold high heels still squarely planted on the sidewalk. I won't take my first step on it, not without her. I've never been one for superstitions, but tonight I want to appease the universe at every turn, do all things possible to make this a perfect premiere. And that means sharing every moment of it with my mom. We've missed so many moments, I refuse to miss any of these.

It's what he would have wanted, too.

Her widening eyes flick from me to the carpet, the cameras, the crowds. *Murder in the Books* in big letters on the glowing marquee. She takes a step, carefully, because she's not used to high heels either—she's more of a practical pumps woman, but practical pumps are not fit for Hollywood premieres—then turns like she might barrel roll herself back into our car if the driver wasn't already pulling away from the curb. "Oh no, you don't need me in these photos. I'll just make my way in more . . . discreetly. Surely there's a back entrance?"

"Nonsense, Catherine," Rocco says, stepping up next to

her in all his black-tuxedoed glory, taking her by the arm. "This night is just as much about you." He's looking as dapper and delicious as I've ever seen him, every inch the grandly polished Hollywood superstar. So different from the man in old T-shirts and sweats I'm privy to most days, his hair in a permanently windswept state, dark stubble on his cheeks. But it's still him, at least in the twinkle of those blue eyes as he looks down at my mom. It's hard to comprehend now how I ever thought those eyes were ice cold; they're a sunny Pacific blue, summer all year long. At least for me and for the people I love most.

The crowds are in a frenzy now; you would think Rocco had ripped his shirt open by the buttons based on the volume of feral screams coming in from all directions.

For a second I wonder if she'll resist him, too, bat away his hand, but no—she's fully taken in by his charm, as she's been ever since we picked her up from the airport two days ago. She'd been so worn from the many firsts of her travel day—first airport, first security line, first flight, first time out of Arizona since my father died—I'd seen the frazzled look on her face when she'd stepped out of LAX, frowning up at the California skyline, and wondered if this had all been one terrible idea, a big step backward after all the forward momentum of the last year. But just a few short minutes of cruising next to Rocco in the Maserati and she was entirely in his thrall. His calming effect was more potent than a generous pour of Chardonnay paired with a warm brownie. She's been that way ever since, even while meeting Rocco's family last night—his parents and Rudy and Lucy, all of them flying in of course, too, for our big day. It felt nice, everyone together like that.

"You're sure I look okay for this?" Her face is an endearing mix of nerves and pride, because, even without my validation, she knows she's wearing the hell out of the snugly fitting floor-length emerald dress we picked out yesterday on our girl's trip to Rodeo Drive. Green had been my dad's favorite color; he wore green in every author photo he ever took. My dress is green, too, a few shades brighter and flaring out above my knees, with a plunging neckline that made my mother *tsk* at first glance when I pulled it off the rack. But when I came out of the dressing room to show her, she cried, said "that's the one," and it felt like I was choosing my wedding dress. And really, this very well might be the most important dress of my life, so many eyes on me, our nearest and dearest gathered around.

Damon and I had gotten married in a courthouse, thrown a little cocktail party with friends afterward at a bougie rooftop bar; I'd picked out a white summer dress off the sales rack of Urban Outfitters the day before. I love Rocco dearly and can see myself walking down an aisle to him someday—a small wedding, wearing a simple dress, with my mother in attendance this time.

This night, though—it's about me and everything I've worked for all these years, channeling all the grief and the rage and the regret, wringing every drop of it out of me to tell this story.

This night is for me and for my dad. And thankfully, it's now for my mom, too.

"You look beautiful, Mom. You're glowing."

I swipe at a stray tear as she does, too, and then she grabs for me with her free hand. "Don't you dare make me cry, not after forcing me to endure hours in the makeup chair with Sylvie!"

We're laughing then, all three of us, as we make our way down the red carpet. It's a wild blur of lights, smiling, posing, answering questions. Other people join in for group photos, Lanie and Maisy and, of course, Piper, a vision in daffodil-yellow tulle; Sylvie joins us with Eden, Rudy's there then, too—the Riziero brothers reunited on the red carpet, with

Lucy and their parents, one big happy family; I hold on to my mom for dear life through every iteration of poses. She holds just as tightly back.

I've seen *Murder in the Books* before, of course, but never like this—in a theater filled with people, soaking in their responses, their tension and tears. It feels like I'm both reliving my past and a stranger watching it play out for the first time. It's mine, but it's also not at all, because it's everyone's now. And it's better than I ever dreamed it could be.

We do a Q&A up front at the end, Rocco and Piper and Maisy with Lanie and I. There are more photos, more interviews, and then we're shuttled off to a restaurant terrace for champagne and fancy finger foods and so many people, questions, congratulations.

A few hours in, the celebration still in full swing, I plunk down beside my mom on a plush white couch tucked away at the edges of the party, sipping at the dregs of an old fashioned. Just the two of us for the first time tonight. It's been lovely— beyond lovely—celebrating with old and new faces, but the comfortable silence is like a cozy blanket. I contemplate closing my eyes, just for a moment, a brief refresher, when my mother leans in and presses her cheek against mine. I freeze, imprinting the moment; it's maybe the most intimate physical connection we've had in my life, aside from when I was too tiny to remember the details.

"It was phenomenal," she says, and I can hear it, the pride. I didn't realize before just how much I needed it from her. But I do, and I drink it in. "Painful to watch, to remember, but . . . restorative, too. I feel lighter than I've felt since it happened. So, thank you. For bringing his story to life. And for making sure I was here to see it with you."

I'm incapable of words, so I nod, squish my face even tighter against hers.

She reaches into the pocket of her dress—because of course

she's exceptionally wise and practical like that, factoring pockets into her decision. I've been toting lipstick in my bra all night. "I have something for you."

There's a small envelope clutched in her hand. *Bea* written in a messy scrawl on the outside.

I'd recognize that scrawl anywhere. His messy letters. Carefully messy, in his own particular way.

I slip the card from her fingers, slowly peel the flap open to avoid any tears.

> Bea,
> Thank you for giving me the single most unusual and most enchanting last night of life anyone could ever hope for. It was real, wasn't it? You were real. I know that's true, without a doubt. You were here, and you were as brilliant in your grown years as I knew you would be.
> Our story was one for the books, wasn't it? So good to start; too perfect, I suppose, because no great story worth its salt is happy all the time, or even most of it. The hard, messy bits in the middle, so much to untangle, resolve. And just when the clock was ticking down and readers might have worried there was no neat ending in sight, there you were—with the twist no one could have ever anticipated. The twist of a lifetime. Certainly mine, at least.
> In case it needs to be reiterated one more time: I forgive you. I love you. 1999 you, 2016 you, all the yous, always.
> I suspect that movie star of yours, he loves you, too. And obviously you love him. You know I always hated the preachy stories, but I have to say, the theme of yours, ours, is forgiveness. So make sure you do: forgive. Trust, too. Fully and absolutely.

So yes, this was a story for the books. And
perhaps . . . one for the movies, too?
Love you mostest. (I've caved in my final hour, what
can I say? I demand the final word.)
Dad

I read it again. Three, four times.

My mom is silent, keeping enough distance that I know she's not peeking.

I neatly fold the letter, smooth it against my palm. Unsure what to say, what to ask.

She starts for me, thankfully. "He handed me that, the morning before he left us. He made me promise on all that's good and holy in the world that I wouldn't read it and that I wouldn't tell you about it. He was very specific about that. Had precise instructions for me."

"What did he say to you?"

She laughs. "Honestly, at the time, I just thought it was the painkillers talking. I didn't overthink it. He'd told me to give you the letter when you were much older—when I came to your *big premiere*. 'What premiere?' I'd asked. 'How will I know?' And he said: 'Trust me, you'll know.' That was that. I didn't push. A few hours later he was gone, and you and I . . . well . . . you and I didn't exchange many words after that. I put it in a drawer in my room, out of mind. I was curious, but not enough to break my word, and then the years passed. It faded in my mind. Never gone, though. I wouldn't forget a minute of our last day. And then there was this, the movie, and when you started talking about your premiere . . ." She pulls back, enough so to really stare deep into my eyes. "Do you understand, Bea? How he knew?"

I consider lying. Not because I don't want her to know. But because I haven't plotted out the words yet, crafted the most logical way to explain a completely illogical story.

But it's my mother, and I can't lie. Won't. Not in this fragile new peaceful era of ours.

"I do understand," I say, slowly. "But it's a long, strange story."

She lifts an eyebrow. "Well then. You know I appreciate a good story. There's a reason I loved your father so dearly, after all."

I nod, lifting a hand in the air to wave over a nearby server. "Two espressos, please."

And then I tell her everything.

I can't remember the last time I stayed up until the sun rose. Years. A decade, at least.

But I was too buzzed from everything—the premiere itself, the drinks that magically refilled in my hand throughout the evening, the round of espressos. But most of all, I'm lit up from my dad's note, the conversation with my mom; telling her our story, seeing the wonder in her eyes, the absolute faith she held in me. No uncertainty, no skepticism. She was all in. Because it was far better to believe, sure, that Dad and I had really had that moment, made our proper peace. To know he wasn't alone for his last night—far from it. But it was so much more than that, too—she believed because she's my mother and I'm her daughter, and it's as pure and as simple as that. It's never been so simple between us.

My mom's been asleep upstairs for hours. Rocco's parents, too, sleeping in two of the many extra rooms he'd never fixed up as actual guest rooms—or any kind of room for that matter, just four white walls and dust bunnies—before now. Before me and the last six months of intensive revamping since I'd moved in here; his too sterile, too empty mountain lair is now a proper home, with personality and spirit—or at least it's well on the way.

Rocco is still up with me, just as buzzed from these last twenty-four hours. We've taken our party of two to a comfy sofa on our bedroom's north-side balcony, mugs of steaming minty tea in hand as we watch the sun rise above the line of mountains to the east.

"How did it feel?" Rocco asks, eyes hazy as he looks out, still absorbing the fact that my mother knows. He's told Rudy, who of course told Lucy. And Sylvie has gotten bits and pieces, the only way she could fathom my giving Rocco a second go. But the rest of our families and friends—we've still been reflecting on the right way, the right time and the right words. And it's felt important, keeping it to ourselves, our secret. At least for a little while.

"Pretty damn great." I tilt my head up to smile at him. He leans down, brushes a light kiss against my forehead. "It made it feel more real, telling her, sharing it with someone else who believes. Even if she hadn't given me the note. And the note— that just put it over the edge. And it had already been a perfect night."

"It was perfect, wasn't it?"

I nod. Too perfect for words.

"It's set too high a bar for all other projects, you know," Rocco says. "The film itself, of course, but also sharing it with you. I got so used to being on set with you. Doing publicity tours with you. All of it, together."

With Piper, too, of course, but we got through it. More than got through it; we *enjoyed* it. Piper was surprisingly pleasant once I let the past stay where it belonged, squarely back in 1999.

"Well . . . what if we do another project together?" I ask, before I've given it a single second of thought. It just rose up and out, all on its own. Because it's the right question. The best and only next move.

"Another project?"

"Yep."

"You got something in mind?" His brow furrows, confused, but he's smiling. Game for anything.

"You read my dad's note." He'd read and then reread it multiple times since our car ride home, handling it as gently as I've ever seen him with anything. Like he was even afraid to breathe on it, for fear of ruining it.

"Of course."

I see it then, the light that flashes on behind his eyes. The understanding.

My dad's words:

Perhaps . . . one for the movies, too?

"You mean . . ." he starts, stops. Eyes wide. Wider.

"Yes. Let's do it. Let's tell our story."

He shakes his head. Ruffles his already very ruffly hair. "People won't believe it."

"Who cares? They don't have to. It's a good story even if it's fiction."

"A great fucking story, if I do say so myself."

"So . . . does that mean you're in?"

He lets out a loud whoop; it bounces across the hills, a volley of Rocco's delight. I feel each echo burrow deeper into my bones. "I couldn't possibly be more in."

"Yeah?"

He nods, looking suddenly very solemn. "Let me put it as clearly as I can: I'm in with everything for you, Bea Noel. Absolutely everything. For all the time we have on this planet. Beyond then, too, if it's up to me."

"Good. Because I feel the same way. You can't shake me, Rocco Riziero. The universe wouldn't stand for it."

"No, it most certainly wouldn't. Not after initiating that little joy ride of ours."

He kisses me long and deep, hands warm against my neck, and then we stay tangled up in one another, silent, watching. The sun climbs further up the sky, spilling like droplets of molten gold over the waves to our west.

Right now, this view of the coastline, it could be any year,

1999 or 2017, before, between, after. And it wouldn't matter. Wouldn't make a bit of difference.

Because no matter the year, I'm in the exact right place. With the exact right person.

My road trip companion through every decade.

Acknowledgments

Writing one book together was a dream come true. Writing a second book? That was such a wild idea, we didn't even know to dream about it in the first place. But it happened and it's real (!), and we are grateful and ecstatic beyond words. *The First Date Prophecy* was so much of ourselves, our story. But this—*The Road Trip Rewind*—is wholly new and different, a surprising ride (even for us!) from beginning to end. From: *What if we wrote a Back to the Future-style book that transports us back to the '90s? What if it's Rocco's story?! What if an old 2000 silver Jetta was their DeLorean?!?!* To this, here and now: writing acknowledgements, one of the hardest parts of the process, because there's no easy way to put all the big feelings into neat words. But we try anyway!

A big thank you to our agent Jill Grinberg for believing in this zany idea from the beginning, for helping to make it a reality, and for your wise notes and guidance along the way. Thank you to Denise Page for all the hard work behind the scenes to help make this book happen, and to make it the best it could be. Endlessly happy and grateful to be a part of the JGLM family.

Thank you to our editor Elizabeth Trout for opening your heart to Rocco and Bea, and for your thoughtful notes that helped it to be a hopefully worthy follow-up to TFDP. Thank you for the wisdom, the understanding, the insights on how many F bombs is too many F bombs, etc.; we're so glad to have you in our corner. And a huge thank you to the whole team at Kensington, for all the work you've done to launch these books into the world: Jane Nutter, Lauren Jernigan, Barbara Brown, Alexandra Nicolajsen, Jackie Dinas, Lynn Cully, Steve Zacharius, and Adam Zacharius.

Thank you to Sam Farkas for championing our books on the audio side, and to HighBridge for believing in these stories—and Danny as a narrator, helping to bring Rudy and now Rocco to life.

To Heidi Vanderlee and Audrey Black at Positive Jam PR, so appreciative of all you do to spread the good word about our book babies.

So many thanks to our readers! To those of you who have found *The First Date Prophecy* and now *The Road Trip Rewind*, and who might see bits of yourselves on these pages; the weirdos, the dreamers, the forever '90s kids at heart. You are our people, and we're so grateful for your support.

To our families, the Detweilers and the Tamberellis, no simple "thank you" could ever do the job, but we'll say it anyway, over and over again. Thank you for making all things possible, from the beginning of our timelines until now. We're so glad the universe put us exactly as it did, all of us in the same orbit. It's how it was always meant to be.

And to Alfred and Penelope, thank you for inspiring us every day with your humor and creativity and good old soul wisdom. It's not always easy having two author parents on the same deadlines, but you let us do our thing, with so much love and patience. We adore you beyond measure.

Lastly, to Rocco and Bea, Rudy and Lucy—thank you for

filling our hearts and our souls for these last few years. You've made us love and respect one another even more, from co-parents to co-authors, and infused so much joy and hope into our lives. You belong to the world now!

Visit our website at
KensingtonBooks.com
to sign up for our newsletters, read
more from your favorite authors, see
books by series, view reading group
guides, and more!

Become a Part of Our
Between the Chapters Book Club
Community and Join the Conversation